BROKEN SHELVES BOOK 3

RESISTING THE *temptation*

DAISY WREN

Developmental editing, Copy/Line editing, and Proofread by Brittany Uller and Jen Bernacki at The Author Experience

Cover design by Brittany Uller at The Author Experience

Formatting by Brittany Uller at The Author Experience

For rights and permissions, please contact:

daisywren.author@gmail.com

Paperback ISBN: 9798991718929

The Broken Shelves Series

Loving the Sinner
Living for Truth
Resisting the Temptation

This one's for me.
For the girl who felt like she didn't deserve love, but dreamed of happily ever after anyway.
For the girl who felt like she was too much, but not enough at the same time.
To younger Daisy: You are just the right amount.

Author's Note

Dear Reader,

This book is near and dear to my heart. Emma's story closely reflects my own, and I poured a lot of myself into her.

Emma's family dynamic mirrors my own, and the things they say to her have been said to me.

It was very cathartic to have someone stick up to the versions of my siblings I've written, and I hope if you have a terrible relationship with your family, you can find some comfort in knowing it's okay to take space and step back from them.

You need to protect your peace, and you deserve to have supportive people in your corner.

Xoxo,
Daisy Wren

CONTENT WARNINGS

This book contains topics that may be triggering for some readers such as:

- Fat shaming/fatphobia

- Mention of self-harm tendencies

- Mention of death

- Mention of suicide

- Mention of rape—non descriptive

- Emotional abuse towards the FMC

- Religious trauma (Mormonism specifically)

- Victim blaming

- Racist comments made toward/about the MMC

- Shitty family

*This book contains explicit content that is **not suitable for anyone under the age of eighteen**, such as:*

- Impact play (hands and paddles)

- Restraints

- Anal

- Use of honey in a sexual way

- D/s dynamics

- Exhibition

- Voyeurism

*Please note that this is **NOT** a guide for BDSM practices, and should not be used as one.*

Reader discretion is advised.

"DICK"TIONARY

If you would like to skip some of the spicy scenes, here's where they are:

RESISTING THE *temptation*
PLAYLIST

"Love Bites-Remastered 2017" by Def Leppard

"I Think I Like You" by The Band CAMINO

"When Emma Falls in Love (Taylor's Version) (From The Vault)" by Taylor Swift

"Kick" by Def Leppard

"Why Can't This Be Love" by Van Halen

"Think I'm In Love" by Eddie Money

"Slow Hands" by Niall Horan

"I Can See You (Taylor's Version) (From The Vault)" by Taylor Swift

"Matilda" by Harry Styles

"Treacherous (Taylor's Version)" by Taylor Swift

"How to Be a Heartbreaker" by MARINA

"Break My Heart" by Dua Lipa

"Accidentally In Love" by Counting Crows

"Brokenhearted" by Karmin

"Read your Mind" by Sabrina Carpenter

Glossary

Beniamino: Benjamin (Italian)

Vieni a sederti, figlio mio: Come sit, my son (Italian)

Ciao, Papà: Hello, Father (Italian)

Dulzura: Sweetness (Spanish)

Deliciosa: Delicious (Spanish)

Ricitos: Ringlets or curls, a pet name for a loved one (Spanish)

Congratulazioni, mi cara: Congratulations, my dear. (Italian)

Ciao, figliolo: Hello, son. (Italian)

Mamá: Mom (Spanish)

Amor senza baruffa, fa la muffa: Love without a quarrel, it makes mold. (Italian)

Non sono innamorato di lei: I'm not in love with her. (Italian)

C'è una linea sottile tra amore e odio, figliolo: There's a fine line between love and hate, son. (Italian)

Idiota: Idiot (Italian)

Pazzo: Crazy (Italian)

Loco: Crazy (Spanish)

Vita mia: My life (Italian)

Mi hijo: My son (Spanish)

Hola, Señora Rossi: Hello, Mrs. Rossi (Spanish)
Bella: Pretty (Term of endearment, Spanish and Italian)
Mierda: Slang for "shit" or "crap" (Spanish)
Ciao, bella: Hello, beautiful (Italian)
¿Por qué no?: Why not? (Spanish)
Lo siento, Mamà: I'm sorry, Mom. (Spanish)
Está bien, hijo mío: It's okay, my son. (Spanish)
Grazie, Papà: Thank you, Father. (Italian)
Prego, figliolo: You're welcome, son. (Italian)
Che cazzo?: What the fuck? (Italian)
MEP (Mechanical, Electrical, and Plumbing) Plan: Plans that provide a comprehensive overview of the building's systems, including pipe layouts.
Shop Drawing: Detailed drawings that show the fabrication and installation details of specific components like pipe spools or fittings for MEP systems.
CAT 825 Soil Compacter: A large machine used to maximize soil spreading and compacting.
Sei impazzito: You're crazy (Italian)
Sono innamorato di lei: I'm in love with her. (Italian)
Lei si sente allo stesso modo?: She feels the same way? (Italian)
Santa cielio: Holy shit (Italian)
Ti amo: I love you (Italian)
Sono così orgoglioso di te, figlio mio: I'm so proud of you, my son. (Italian)
Farai grandi cose: You're going to do great things (Italian)

PROLOGUE

Emma

Four years ago...

I gulp down half of the wine in my glass, wincing as the bitter alcohol burns my throat. I don't really like wine, but I had a box of it leftover from a slumber party, so why the hell not? I've got nowhere to be tomorrow.

This is my third—fourth?—glass in a little less than an hour, and my head is feeling swimmy while the stab of my girlfriend's—*ex*-girlfriend's—break up monologue slowly fades into a sting.

I was shocked she called things off. I thought we were going to get married. We were going to have a house and a dog, maybe some cats.

No, wait. I'm allergic to cats. Boo.

Then, when we felt ready, we were going to talk about having a baby. Something I wasn't sure I'd be ready for anytime soon, but it's what Trinity wanted, and I would have given it to her.

But apparently, Trinity didn't want that future. At least not with me.

She said the same things I've heard my whole life from other people who were supposed to love me, but it doesn't hurt any less to hear them.

You're too needy.

You're too emotional.

You're too much.

I can't help the fact I cry a lot, and believe me, I've tried everything. No matter what I do, the tears come.

I haven't been diagnosed because the testing is hella expensive, but a few years ago, my therapist suggested I'm probably autistic on top of my previous diagnoses of depression, anxiety, and PTSD. The online tests I took seemed to agree.

Fucking brain chemicals. Why couldn't I have gotten the neurodivergent type of brain that means you're super smart and good at math? Instead, I got the kind that latches on to anyone who shows me an ounce of attention, cries at any minor inconvenience, only wants to eat sesame chicken, and cringes at the feeling of velvet.

The fabric of the devil.

My best friend, roommate, and support system in times of crisis, Jordan, is currently in Japan with their parents and won't be home for five more days. We made a few friends at the Pride parade in June, but they're not sob-over-girls-and-get-drunk-with status yet.

One would think having nine siblings would mean I'd be able to call one of them and find comfort, but I don't talk to my siblings often due a whole encyclopedia of reasons, and my parents would use this as an excuse to tell me it's because I'm "living in sin" and "not following God's plan."

Blech. I did the time in therapy and mostly got over the religious guilt I felt over being bisexual and leaving the church. Doesn't mean my parents don't try their hardest to make me feel it again.

I briefly think of my cousins, Elli and Hannah, and wish we were close like we had been as kids. They're still in the church, though, so there's no telling how they'd feel about my sapphic troubles.

With no other options and no better ideas, I chug the rest of my wine and change my "depressed" playlist to my "bad bitch" playlist. It's time to make some rule changes so I don't go through this again.

Jordan has had to console me more times than I can count after getting my heart broken *again* over a person I got too attached to too quickly. I can't burden them anymore with my issues. I don't want them to get overwhelmed with me, too.

I clean the kitchen while I try to figure out what I can change so I don't get my heart broken again, and halfway through washing our reusable straws, it hits me.

No more serious relationships.

If I don't have a serious romantic partner, I can't be broken up with.

Mentally high-fiving myself for that *brilliant* idea, I devise a plan.

I like sex. But sex doesn't equal love. I know if I hook up with the same person more than once, I'll start getting attached.

Hookups only. No repeats.

No repeats, no serious relationships.

No serious relationships, no heartbreak.

No heartbreak, no burdening Jordan.

No burdening Jordan, no worrying they'll get overwhelmed by my neediness and want to end our friendship.

Yes, this plan will work.

It has to.

Chapter I

Emma

I finish inputting the invoice I'm working on and stamp it with the date, then look up from the computer for the first time in over an hour. My vision's gone fuzzy, and I blink rapidly to clear the haze.

The calendar notification pops up at the same time, reminding me of the meeting Josh wants to have with me. When I asked him about it, he shrugged and told me he needed to talk to me.

Normally, someone saying they want to talk to me without telling me what it's about would send me into an anxiety spiral, but Josh's "somethings" usually mean he wants to pick my brain about a new building idea or a way to make the office more functional.

"Ready for our meeting?" Josh pokes his head out of his office.

"Sure. As long as it isn't too long. I need to print checks before the end of the day."

Josh shakes his head and chuckles. "You've worked here for four years, Em, you don't have to try and impress me. You work too hard."

I roll my eyes. "Oh, hush, Joshua. You know this place couldn't run without me."

Daniel, Josh's brother and business partner, walks past and pats Josh on the shoulder. "She's right, Joshy. We wouldn't be where we are without her help. Be nice."

I've worked at Kirkham Creatives for the last four years. Originally, it was just supposed to be a temporary job to get their office organized efficiently, but somehow I turned into an executive assistant/accounts payable person. I file, input invoices, write checks, and help them keep their calendar running smoothly.

I can't complain too much since they're flexible with my schedule, and the pay is great. Watching them go from a three-person team to one with almost fifteen and still growing has been amazing to be a part of.

Josh punches Daniel in the arm. "I wasn't being mean, dickhead. I'm just teasing her. Want to join us? I'm going to order lunch and tell Emma what we talked about."

A beat of anxiety pulses in my stomach, so I try to cover it with humor. "I already turned down your offer for a threesome, gentlemen, you won't be changing my mind."

Daniel groans, and Josh snickers. It's a running joke with us that I won't have a threesome with them. A year into working for them, we were at lunch, and the waitress asked us if we were a throuple. I jokingly told her I was giving them the duration of the lunch to convince me to be with them. When we finished eating, she asked if I was convinced, and I shook my head and turned them down.

Nothing romantic has ever happened with either Kirkham brother, and nothing ever will. Josh and Daniel are relationship types, and I don't do serious. Besides, they're more like brothers to me than my real brothers are.

Daniel sighs. "Of course I'll join you." He points at both of us. "No more threesome jokes."

"Fair enough. What are we feeling for lunch? Jun's?" Josh directs the question at me.

"Ooo. I could go for some japchae right now. Jun's sounds good. Do you need me to call?"

"Nah, I figured you'd be on board, so I already placed an order. It should be here any minute." Josh checks his watch, and sure enough, the bell above the door rings, and the delivery person brings in bags of food. The smell makes my stomach grumble. I didn't realize how hungry I was.

I follow them to Josh's office, and we set the food on the coffee table between the two couches, unpacking and dishing up pork mandu, japchae, beef bulgogi, tteokbokki, and rice while Josh and Daniel talk about a project they're working on. I'm not a huge tteokbokki fan, but it's Josh's favorite, so we get it every time.

Looking at the two brothers, I can acknowledge they're attractive, but I've never felt a sexual pull towards either of them, thank goodness. The last thing I need is to be attracted to a coworker, much less my superior. Daniel is thirty-five, and Josh is thirty-two. Both brothers are fit and muscular with suntanned skin. I don't know shit about height because I'm five-foot-one on a good day, but they're probably close to six feet, maybe taller. They both have dark chestnut brown hair, but Josh's is slightly curly and always styled whereas Dan's is usually shaved close to his head. Josh's eyes are a darker blue than Daniel's, but they're both kind and warm.

"So, how does it feel to finally have graduated college?" Josh asks.

I chuckle. At twenty-seven, I finally earned my bachelor's degree. It only took me six years to figure out what I wanted to do with my life, on top of just not being good at school. My neurodivergent brain has a hard time focusing on things, especially when I'm not interested in the subject. I jumped from Criminal Justice to English to Communications before finally landing on Construction Management.

It was kind of an epiphany moment for me. Josh's best friend's dad owns a construction company, and they helped build one of Josh and Daniel's designs from the ground up. I was in total awe seeing Josh and Daniel's design come to life.

I thought I wanted to go into architecture design at first but then realized I don't want to come up with the idea and hand it to someone else, I want to execute the project. Plus, I'm shit at drawing. Daniel suggested I look into construction management, and everything clicked into place.

There's also not a lot of women in the construction world, and I want to change that.

"It's *so* nice. I find I have a lot more free time now, though it's weird not having to account for homework time in my weekly schedule."

Daniel nods. "I remember not knowing what to do with my free time when I didn't have homework to do anymore."

Josh nods too. "And are you still looking for jobs in the construction field?"

"Yes, I've applied to a few jobs, but no one's responded. I think they see a woman's name and automatically assume I don't know what I'm doing. Which, to be frank, I *don't*. Not really, but I can't learn unless I'm taught, you know?"

I dip the crispy mandu in the tangy dipping sauce while Josh and Daniel share a look. I hate not being privy to their fraternal mental conversions sometimes.

"Well," Daniel starts, "as much as we don't want to lose you, we know you'd make an amazing PM."

"So," Josh continues, "I talked to Enzo Rossi, Ben's dad. They're expanding and looking to add another project manager to the team. I told him about you.."

From what I've gathered, Ben is Josh's friend from high school. They were both on the tennis team and—knowing Josh—he forced Ben into being his friend. Josh talks about their friendship fondly, like Ben's another brother to him, even if Josh also describes him as a grumpy asshole. Even though I've worked here for four years and have been invited to parties where Ben might be present, I've never met him.

Anticipation skitters down my spine as I wait for Josh to continue, but he doesn't, always one for dramatics.

Finally, after what feels like hours, Josh starts talking again. "I ranted and raved about you, Em. I told Enzo what a hard worker you are, how quickly you learn new things, and how passionate you are about the projects we've had you work on."

"Joshua Allen Kirkham if you don't get to the point I'm going to take all the tteokbokki for myself," I threaten, pointing my chopsticks at him.

Josh gasps. "You wouldn't *dare*. You don't even like tteokbokki!"

"Don't underestimate me. I've done a lot of things out of spite."

Josh laughs, unaffected by my threats. "Enzo Rossi would be more than happy to have you on his team."

I gape at him. "Are you serious? He doesn't want to interview me first?"

Josh shakes his head. "Nah, not a formal one. He'll give you a call when we're done with lunch to go over the position, though. Enzo likes to go with his gut. Me vouching for you, and the fact you have a degree and passion for the job is enough for him. Everything else you need to know can be learned. "

"I—" Emotion clogs my throat, and I push down the urge to start sobbing. "I can't express how grateful I am, Josh. Truly. Thank you so much." I get up and round the table, wrapping my arms around him in a tight hug.

As I sit back down, Daniel gives me a sad smile. "We're going to miss you a lot, Em. But we're excited to watch you succeed."

"Thanks, Daniel." I just hope I don't let them down.

CHAPTER 2

Ben

"**I**s there *anything* else I can get for you, *Ben*?" the barista at the coffee shop asks, practically purring my name. She's been batting her lashes at me this whole time, but instead of looking flirtatious, she looks like there's something in her eye.

"Just the coffee," I grunt.

Her shoulders slump a little bit. "Your total is three-fifty."

I hand over a ten-dollar bill. "Keep the change." I pull out my phone and move away from the counter while I check emails.

My dad's company—and my place of employment—Rossi Construction, is looking for a new project manager so we can take on more jobs, but so far, my dad hasn't approved of anyone we've interviewed.

It's not like the candidates weren't qualified or experienced, some of them even had my dad laughing in the interviews, but he didn't want to hire any of them.

He was hoping my brother Mateo would want to come work for us, but he's happy with his accounting firm.

"Ben!" someone calls from the counter, signaling my coffee is ready. I walk to the counter, pick up the cup with my name, and notice the string of numbers scribbled below it.

While I admire the boldness, it still makes me want to roll my eyes.

I'm sure the barista at the register is watching for my reaction, but luckily for me, I've learned to school my emotions. I make sure my face gives no indication I've seen her number, and I don't glance back when I walk out of the coffee shop and get into my truck.

A truck in San Diego isn't the most economically conscious, but when you have to drive out to unpaved job sites or haul equipment, a hybrid isn't going to cut it.

I drive the few miles to the office and park at the back of the building but take a minute to prepare myself for the meeting with my dad before I get out.

I love my dad, and I love that he's still a big part of this business he created, but he's known for making spur of the moment decisions sometimes. If he's calling me in for a one-on-one meeting on a Wednesday morning, it means something big is happening, and he wants me to be warned.

I take the concrete stairs two at a time to the second floor, passing by empty offices, which will soon be filled with our employees.

Every office—except my dad's—is made of glass that can be switched from clear to opaque, so I knock on his door frame before entering.

"Ah, Beniamino, vieni a sederti, figlio mio." Come sit, *my son.*

"Ciao, Papà. What did you want to talk to me about?"

Lorenzo Rossi is a third generation Italian American, all dark hair, tan skin, and thick eyebrows. Even though he grew up in America, he still prefers to speak Italian and has the faintest accent. Mamá is from Puerto Rico, so I learned Spanish as well as Italian and English growing up.

As I look at Papà, I realize he's getting older. His skin has more wrinkles, and there's more gray sprinkled in his black hair. He's worked hard to build this company from the ground up, and I'm trying to get him to train me to take over so he can retire in the next few years. He deserves to rest. "As you know, we are starting to take on more projects, and it means we need to hire another project manager," he says slowly, switching to English like he does when it's business related.

"Yes, that's why we've been conducting interviews. Should I call the Jackson guy back? He was a good candidate."

Dad waves me off. "No, no, no. No need to worry about calling him. I already hired someone."

My jaw tenses as frustration bubbles in my stomach. I hate when he makes big decisions without asking me. No, it's not *my* company, but it affects me. I'm about to ask for details, but he beats me to the punch.

"Joshua called and said his assistant, Emma, has just finished her degree in Construction Management and is a very hard worker. I had a lovely phone call with her yesterday. She's enthusiastic about the job and eager to get into project management. She starts two weeks from

Monday. I want you to take her under your wing, *Beniamino*. Show her the ropes, teach her what she doesn't know."

"Josh called *you?* Why wouldn't he ask me?" I ask through gritted teeth. Josh and I have been best friends for years. It stings a little that he would go over my head with this.

My dad arches one bushy eyebrow and scoffs, "He knew you would say no without even hearing him out."

Well, he's not wrong. Emma clearly has no experience in the role she's been hired for, and while she might be a great assistant at Kirkham Creative, I don't know how her current job would translate to this one. Sometimes it feels like I'm the only rational thinker in my family. Papà has business sense, yes, but he likes to lead with his heart.

"I don't like that I've never met the person you've hired, *Papà*. You should have consulted me before hiring an inexperienced, freshly graduated candidate."

"Well, *Beniamino*, I'm still the CEO of this company. I don't have to run this by you when I think it's the best decision. Give the girl one month. If you still don't feel like she's the best fit for the role, then we will let her go. But you have to promise me you'll give her a fair chance." He cocks his head to the side. "She's worked for Joshua for four years, and you've never met her?"

"No. I've only ever been to Josh's office after business hours, and she hasn't attended any events where we might have run into each other. Have *you* met her?"

Papà hums, ignoring my question. A phone call doesn't count as a meeting, in my opinion. "Promise me you will give her a chance."

"I'll give her a chance." Begrudgingly, and I have low hopes, but I'll give her a chance anyway.

We talk about regular business for the next half hour, then I leave his office while he takes a call with one of our wood suppliers.

As soon as I'm in my own office, I close the door and dial Josh's number.

"Benny! How the hell are you, man?" Josh says happily.

"What the fuck, Kirkham?"

Josh lets out a long, defeated sigh. "I'm guessing Enzo told you about Emma coming to work for Rossi? I'm sorry I didn't talk to you, but I know you, man. I knew you'd say no before I could even get my spiel out."

"Why are you trying to get rid of Emma? I thought she was the 'best assistant.'"

"She *is*. Daniel and I are extremely sad to see her go, but she can't grow here. She worked her ass off in school and deserves the opportunity to grow in a career she *actually* wants. Emma is hella smart, dude. Quick learner, super friendly. She'll be an asset to Rossi, just like she's been an asset at KC."

I scrub a hand over my neatly trimmed beard. "If she worked her ass off in school, why did it take her so long to graduate? Most people graduate with their bachelors at twenty-two, twenty-four at the latest. You said she's twenty-seven. That's a long time to be in school." Now I'm just grasping at straws to find *something* to stop this nonsense.

Josh is silent for a minute, which is odd. He's usually extremely eager to share information. A total gossip.

Something I usually hate, but now that I want information, he chooses to stay quiet.

He clears his throat from the other end of the line. "It took her a while to figure out what she wanted to do, so she just kept switching majors until she found one that clicked." There's definitely more to the story, but I'm not one to pry information not willingly given, so I let it go.

"What makes you think she won't change her mind about this?" If she couldn't even pick a fucking major, how do I know she's not going to get bored with project managing and leave us in the lurch when she realizes how boring it can be?

"Emma doubled down on classes when she figured out she wanted to get into construction management. Before she decided, she was only taking two classes a semester, but in the last few years she's taken four or more. As soon as she graduated, she started applying for jobs, but you've seen how people treat women in the industry. Especially when they don't look the way they think someone in this field should look. She's all pinks and flowers and girly. No one wanted to give her a chance."

I hate to sound like a misogynistic asshole, but that's another hangup I have with Emma working here. Not necessarily the fact she's a woman, but from what Josh and Daniel have told me, she's a sunshiny girly girl. I don't need some frilly woman working here and distracting the other PMs or our crews when we're on job sites.

I don't need someone trying to worm their way into my life and trying to be my friend. I come here to *work* not to make friends. If I want Papà to trust me to take over the company in a few years, I need to keep my mind focused on quality projects—not "friendship."

"*Papà* made me promise to give her a month."

I swear I can *hear* Josh's smile. "You won't be let down, Ben. I promise. I wouldn't have gone to your dad if I didn't know for a fact Emma would thrive there. This is going to be a good thing for everyone involved."

Doubtful. "I hope you're right."

We agree to have dinner soon and catch up, then hang up so we can both get some work done.

I roll my shoulders trying to ease some of the tension in them. I've been under so much stress lately and haven't had a chance to blow off steam. Maybe it's time for me to make a visit to the club.

Chapter 3

Emma

They say everyone you know is battling something you can't see, so you should always be kind.

If that's the case, then this douchebag is battling a severe case of fatphobia with an added diagnosis of dominant-dysphoric-disorder.

About a year ago, I stumbled upon a romance book that was kinky as hell. It did things to my brain—and my body—and I started researching BDSM, wondering if it's something I would enjoy. At first, my purity culture upbringing got the best of me and made me feel dirty for wondering what it'd be like to be tied up or handcuffed. To be spanked, spit on, and used like a toy.

It took me about a week of research and internal pep talks to get over the feeling of being dirty, just like it took me a while to not feel dirty about the fact that I *love* sex. A lot.

After the initial hang ups, I spent the better part of last year learning as much as I could before I finally got the courage to sign up for a BDSM dating app last week—despite my anxieties surrounding dating apps in general—and agreed to drinks with Carl, who says he's an experienced Dom.

I'm pretty certain he lied.

He started off by telling me I was only to refer to him as "Master" for the duration of our date, then proceeded to go into detail about the workout and diet plan he would put me on as his submissive. He tried to order me a drink, and when I refused, he told me there would be consequences for not following the rules.

Hard fucking pass.

He's in the middle of telling me all about his preferences, but he hasn't asked me a single question or let me speak.

There are Dominants, and then there are the men who think they're "alphas" or whatever, but they're actually man-babies who think the world owes them everything. Carl is the latter.

I swallow the rest of my mojito and put up a hand to halt his spiel of why he only fucks a woman if she's tied up.

"Listen, Carl, it sounds like you're about one wrong move away from being arrested. I don't think this is going to work out between us, so I'm going to go. Best of luck in your search for a human blowup doll."

Carl rears back as if I've slapped him. "*Bitch.* You're not going to make a very good sub if you talk back like that. Good luck finding someone who will want to train your fat ass."

I push out my bottom lip in an exaggerated pout. "If your dick couldn't fit past my ass, just say that. I can be *so good* for the right person, you just aren't them. Goodbye, Carl."

I walk out of the bar, leaving the douche to pay for my drink. It's the least he can do after the pain he put me through—and not even the fun kind.

I'm about to order an Uber when Jordan's name flashes on my screen.

"Jordyyyy. Tell me you have something fun to do to take my mind off of one of the worst interactions I've had."

Jordan chuckles. "Was it that bad?"

"The worst. He wanted me to call him 'Master.' In *public*."

"Ew. Well, luckily for you, Kiera, Moss, Jaime, and I are all on our way to McGrath's. Care to join us?"

"Hell yeah. I'm two blocks away, so I'll meet you there."

"See you soon."

I turn in the opposite direction of where I was headed and make my way to McGrath's, our favorite LGBTQ+ bar. A night out with friends is exactly what I need after the last few days. I haven't even had a chance to tell anyone but Jordan about my new job, and that's only because I live with them.

From the outside, McGrath's looks like any other dive bar, even though it's on a busy street in San Diego. The brick facade is worn, and the windows are framed with wood that's seen better days. The "c" and the "r" are going out on the red neon McGrath's sign, but the Pride flag is pristine, like they just switched it out for a new one.

Inside, the floors are a dark oak, matching the long bar top. The neon signs on the wall reflect off of the glass bottles of liquor behind the bar, giving an atmospheric glow to the place. Tim is bartending tonight, and he gives me a chin nod as I walk past.

I find my friends at our regular booth, the worn vinyl sticking to my bare thighs as I slide in next to Kiera.

"Ooo, you look like a total *snack*, babe. Who's the lucky person who got to see you in this dress?" Kiera coos, running a finger over the spaghetti strap of my hot pink mini dress.

"A douchebag named Carl. I met him on that BDSM dating app I told you about. He said he was an experienced Dom, but I think he just wants to control women. I will *not* be using that app again."

Kiera works at The Temptation Lounge—a members-only BDSM club—as a client relations manager. She helps submissives find Dominants and vice versa, making sure their preferences match up and they're compatible kink-wise. She also makes sure everyone is up to date on their STD testing and consent forms.

I can't afford the membership fee right now, but even if I could, the club has a months-long vetting process, and the waitlist is astronomical.

Kiera was my go-to person when I started researching the kinky side of sex, and she's been so helpful with answering my billions of questions. She even had me fill out the club's kink negotiation/interest form so I could get a better idea of what it is I like. It's been nice to have someone to talk to about it without feeling ashamed or "dirty."

Kiera frowns. "I'm sorry, babe." Then she smirks. "I'll dominate you anytime, though."

Kiera is stunning. Tall and willowy, with dark brown skin, which contrasts beautifully with her buzzed pink hair. She's probably a good six inches taller than me. In another lifetime, I'd have jumped on the chance to spend a sweaty night with her, but I don't mix friendships and pleasure.

That's how hearts get broken.

I roll my eyes at her shameless flirting. "Babe, you don't even like ordering your own drinks. I don't think you could dominate me in the bedroom."

Jaime, our Latino gay bestie, barks out a laugh. "I agree with Emma, Kiki. I can't picture you ordering our spicy friend around in the bedroom. You'd be the one on your knees."

Jordan and Moss nod their agreements, and Kiera shakes her head. "I want to say you're wrong, but you're not." She sighs like she's defeated. "I might be able to help, though. My boss has implemented a new perk of my job to help people learn more about the club. Each employee can bring one friend a month to the club to get the word out. You'd have to do the STD panel and give proof of birth control if you want to forego condoms and, obviously, sign the NDA. If one of our guests fucks around and breaks the rules, we're responsible and will therefore be fired, so bear that in mind before you agree."

"You know I'm a stickler for rules. I'd never do any-thing to jeopardize your job, either. Are you sure you want *me* to be the guest, though?"

Kiera lifts a dainty shoulder. "Unless Moss wants to get in on the action at the club, you're the only person I know right now who would be interested."

Moss shakes their head, their mop of shaggy red curls bouncing at the movement. "No, thanks. I'm good with vanilla."

"Shocker," Kiera deadpans. "I'll email you all the forms you need to fill out, and as long as you don't have any STDs, we can get you in next Saturday." She taps her chin. "I have just the guy for you, but I haven't seen him come in for a while. I'll email him and see if he's interested in meeting you."

"Thanks, babe. I owe you big time." I wrap my arms around her as best I can and squeeze her in a tight hug.

I don't know why it feels like a weight has been lifted off of my shoulders, but it does. If I can get into the club next Saturday, it means I can hopefully start my new job relaxed and satisfied, which will help to calm my nerves.

We spend the rest of the night updating each other on the goings-on in our lives. When I tell them about my new job, Kiera orders us celebratory shots.

Jordan and I Uber home together, and I go to sleep feeling more hopeful about my future than I have in a long time.

STRUCTION // UNDER CONSTRUCTION // UNDER CON

On Wednesday the following week, Kiera texts me to let me know I've been cleared to come to the club, and the man she mentioned has agreed to meet me. She sent me his list of kink negotiations, and other than one or two things I'm not sure about, it seems our preferences align pretty well.

I don't know his name, just his first initial—*B*.

Kiera says she'll walk me through what to do when I get to the club.

These are my last three days at Kirkham Creatives, and it's so bittersweet to be leaving a job that was a lifeline for me, but I'm excited to start this new adventure.

I hope Saturday ends up being something to help calm my nerves because I'll be an anxious mess the rest of the week.

CHAPTER 4

Ben

When I got an email from Kiera at The Temptation Lounge, I was surprised. I haven't been to the club in almost six months for various reasons, and even though I thought about attending this weekend to blow off steam, the last thing I wanted was to meet an inexperienced submissive.

Why would I want to teach someone new when I can just play with someone who already has experience and I know I have chemistry with?

Then, I clicked on *E's* kink negotiations and reading through them made my cock stir with interest.

She's unsure about a few of my preferences, which is understandable if she's new to the lifestyle, but those aren't deal-breakers for me.

It's like she was made for me and my desires. Even though I'm not a rash man, I emailed Kiera back with my approval, and we worked out a plan for her to introduce me to my potential new submissive this weekend.

BDSM was something I've always been interested in, but my ex was never keen on trying anything outside of some light spanking. When we broke up, I decided to explore that side of myself instead of traditional dating. I tried to have the happily-ever-after with someone, and it didn't work out. I didn't want to try again so soon after such a long relationship.

Enter: The Temptation Lounge.

A place I could go where no one tries to make small talk or expect me to make nice with their friends or family. A place where the expectations are clear and relationships don't extend beyond the scene. I don't have to worry about it bleeding into my work life or having my attention taken away from more important things like it would in a serious relationship.

Exactly what I need before *Emma* starts on Monday.

Simply thinking her name makes my blood pressure rise.

I've spent the last week helping my dad clear out the office we were using as storage for Emma. The other two project managers, Drew and Alex, are wary of a woman joining our group, but my father quickly set them straight. We don't discriminate based on gender.

There's been high tension at the office with the anticipation of Emma starting, especially after we were denied a bid with the biggest developer in San Diego—again. We've been schmoozing the pants off Derek Allridge, but he's denied us three times, saying he just doesn't think it's the right job for us, even though our work speaks for itself.

Tonight will be a much needed release of all this tension and a good way to make sure I don't snap at Emma simply for existing.

I scan my pass to the underground lot for the club and park, slowly making my way inside.

I'm in an all-black ensemble tonight. My dress shirt is unbuttoned to show off my chest and the gold chain around my neck. My suit jacket is tailored to perfection to fit my broad shoulders.

I haven't dressed like this in what feels like years, but putting on my "Dom" clothes made it easier to get into the headspace I need to be in for tonight's activities.

As soon as I walk through the doors of The Temptation Lounge, I'm no longer Ben Rossi, heir to the Rossi Construction legacy. I'm just *B*. Experienced Dom, equal parts gentle and rough. One who likes to bring pleasure to the point of exhaustion. The worries of my everyday life lift away as sensual music washes over me, and I make my way to the coat check to hand over my phone and my keys.

Daisy, the coat check attendant, smiles as she sees me. "Welcome back, Mr. B."

"Thank you, Daisy."

"Are you here for Kiera's friend?" I give a brief nod, and Daisy's smile widens. "She's so lovely. I hope you enjoy your night."

I appreciate that Daisy doesn't try to pry any more information from me, but a twinge of irritation tenses my jaw at Daisy knowing who I'm here to meet.

She must sense my irritation because she quickly says, "Kiera asked me to let her know when you arrived so she can adequately prepare her friend, that's all, I promise. No gossip has been spread about you or Kiera's guest."

I let out a breath to relax myself. "I'm sorry if it felt like I was frustrated with you. I assure you I'm not. Thank you for elaborating."

"Of course."

I give her a final nod and stride to the bar in the main room. The space looks like it could be any other bar, with a wood bar top and industrial stools covered in black leather. Abstract art hangs on the walls, and the lighting is sensual and low. There are private booths around the edges where people mingle and meet to see if they mesh. Everyone gathers here before either breaking away into private rooms down one hall or to the voyeur/exhibition areas down another.

The club is busy since it's Saturday, but I've already booked a private room, so I meander to the bar and order two fingers of Macallan on the rocks. I don't indulge in alcohol often, but I need something to calm the nerves I'm pretending don't exist.

I can't pinpoint why I'm nervous, which irks me to no end because I can't find a way to fix it. I've never felt this much anticipation over meeting a new sub, even when I was just starting out as a Dom.

Something about *E* makes my nerves spike, despite having never met her. Maybe it's her kinks and our compatibility, or maybe it's the gut feeling my dad is always talking about. I've always thought he was talking crazy. He constantly tells me to trust my intuition, but I go based on logic and numbers. I've never felt a tug in my stomach like I do now.

I spin around on my bar stool and survey the room. My eyes land on a few women I've had pleasurable nights with who are looking at me like I'm a piece of ripe fruit, ready to be plucked.

They're going to be disappointed. My attention isn't on them for more than a brief glance before I move to the next person. My interest in them is non-existent, my mind is focused on finding the woman I'll be teaching all about pleasure tonight.

I scan the faces of the women I'm unfamiliar with, but my intuition tells me none of them are *E*.

It's not until my eyes slide to the opposite side of the room that I see *her*. And God, I hope this is *E*. My gut—the one I'm learning to listen to—tells me it is, but it could just be wishful thinking. She's like a dream come true.

The woman standing with Kiera barely reaches her chin, her blonde hair is in soft waves, hitting just above her peach shaped ass. The short, blush pink satin dress she's wearing hugs her ample tits deliciously and emphasizes her sultry curves. Her calves look strong in gold heels, and her thighs... *Goddamn* I want to take a bite out of them.

Her left arm is covered in black and white tattoos that look like stickers with little pops of color scattered throughout. Her right arm has a full black and white sleeve with what looks like florals and something else I can't make out in the low lighting. Above her right knee is a colorful butterfly, and her button nose glints with a gold piercing in her left nostril.

The black ink on her arms is in juxtaposition to the lightness of her dress and the brightness in her smile, drawing my dark cloud to her sunshine.

I'm on my feet before I realize what I'm doing, tossing the plan I had out the window. All thoughts of being aloof and uninterested until I got her alone are nowhere in sight.

Kiera sees me approaching first and straightens, her eyes going wide. Whatever look flashed across her face is gone, replaced with the professionalism I'm used to.

"Hello, Mr. B. This is E. The woman I was emailing you about."

E gives me a quick once over before looking down at her shoes, but I catch the faint blush on her cheeks as she averts her gaze.

"Hello, Kiera. Hello, E."

E looks up hesitantly. "Permission to speak?"

I can't help the slight upward tilt of my lips. She's too sweet. "We haven't set any rules yet, so you don't need to ask permission."

She nods, rolling her plush pink lip between her teeth before gifting me with a shy smile. "Hello, Mr. B. It's lovely to meet you."

"It's lovely to meet you, too. If it's not too presumptuous, I'd love to take you to one of the private rooms so we can chat a bit more without distraction."

E looks at Kiera who gives her a hesitant nod, then switches once again to professionalism. "I'll leave you to it. Let me know if there's anything else I can do for you."

"Thanks, K," E says at the same time I say, "Thank you, Kiera."

E takes a deep breath before turning to face me, and I'm nearly bowled over by the intensity of her blue eyes. They're an azure blue with specks of lighter shades smattered throughout the irises. They remind me of the ocean when the sun's reflecting off the waves, sparkling and pure. They're accentuated by a thick, precise wing of dark eyeliner and framed by long eyelashes coated in black mascara.

Fuck, I want to see them filled with tears as she gags on my cock. I want her makeup smeared because she's overwhelmed by the sheer number of orgasms I wring from her curvy body.

Slow down, Ben. She's new to this. Don't go overboard with her the first time.

I swallow down the rest of my drink and set the tumbler on a nearby table, then lead her down the hallway to a red door marked with a number four.

There's a keypad on the door, so I input my unique code and open the door for E, motioning for her to go first. She steps in, and I once again admire the way her satiny dress flows over her hips and the swell of her ass. She spins in a slow circle, taking in the room.

It's not overly fancy, but it has a four-poster bed with black sheets, two pillows, and a soft black comforter. The walls are painted a dark gray, and there's a set of cabinets full of condoms, wipes, and extra sheets. Along the other side of the wall is a gray leather armchair and a matching chaise lounge.

There are less than two-hundred members at the club—last I heard—and only twenty private rooms. They have to be booked in advance, but they have flex rooms for last minute needs on a first-come-first-served basis. Each member has a locked box of their own toys to keep at the club, so if their preferred room is booked, one of the staff can move the toys to a different one without compromising the sanitization.

I haven't been here in a while, but I know where everything is. I usually only use the club for one-night stands. If I want to continue a relationship with a sub, we meet at my house where I have a room very similar to this one, filled with more toys and tools to play with.

I can picture E there, kneeling on the floor as she waits for me to come in and give her instructions.

Goddammit, Ben. Slow the fuck down.

I clear my throat, and E turns to me with wide, expectant eyes. "Can you tell me a little about what got you interested in kink?"

E swallows. "I read a romance novel—well, several—where kink is a prominent part of the storyline. I got a little fixated on it and started reading articles and blogs regarding the topic, and I... I really liked the things I read about. It fascinated me, and I started thinking about things I would like. The idea of letting someone make decisions for me, of giving them total control over my pleasure..." She trails off and bites her lip, her chest flushing before she shakes her head. "It turned me on more than anything else."

"That's the appeal for a lot of submissives. I'm glad you've done your research. Some people walk into this not knowing anything, and their expectations are different from reality. Kiera sent me a list of your preferences, but is there anything you'd like to discuss or elaborate on?"

"There wasn't a place on the sheet for it, but I don't want there to be any kissing."

"I see. Kissing anywhere? Or just on the lips?"

"Kissing anywhere above my shoulders."

I bite back my sigh of disappointment. I'd really, *really* like to taste that sensuous mouth. To mark her pretty neck. But I want to taste other parts of her more. A limit exists for a reason, and I'll respect it. "Would you mind me asking why that's a hard no for you?"

"Not at all," she chirps. "It's a rule I have in place with everyone I hook up with. Kissing in those places leads to deeper feelings that lead to heartbreak when our time ends. I'd rather walk away from this experience knowing there will be no future, rather than risking attachment."

I ignore the stab to my gut at her mention of *other people*. I just met this woman, and she's clearly comfortable in her sexuality, so it's only logical she's had... *relations* with other people. I wonder who hurt her so astronomically she refuses to do even a simple thing like touching her lips to another person's.

But I don't need that information because it's not important for what we're doing here.

"Understood. No kissing from the shoulders up. Anything else?"

"I have some questions."

I motion for her to sit on the chaise lounge as I sit in the armchair, propping my right foot on my left knee. My eyes roam her body, getting a better look at the sleeve on her arm. A mix of different flowers, a hummingbird, a dragonfly, and what look like little stars filling in the empty spaces.

Her eyes take in the way my tailored pants hug my thighs, and I smirk as she presses her own thighs together. Sweet little E is turned on.

"Ask away."

"How will I know we're in a scene?"

"Tonight, the scene will start once you give me consent to touch you. If we continue to meet up, our scenes will start as soon as we're both in the club."

"That makes sense. Do I need a safe word?"

"I think since this is your first experience with kink, we will use the traffic light system. Are you familiar with it?"

"Green means good to go; yellow means slow down, I need a minute; red means stop immediately."

"Good girl." E preens at my praise—something I know she's interested in from her list. Her eyelids flutter, and her thighs clench again. The blush she's meticulously brushed on her cheeks is no match for the color of desire underneath the makeup. I also know she's interested in some light degradation. If she reacts so beautifully to my praise, I can't wait to see how she reacts to being called my good little slut.

"Any other questions?" I ask, eager as fuck to get this scene started.

"Can I ask you something kind of personal that has to do with kink?"

"Go ahead."

"Have you ever collared a sub?"

The question takes me by surprise, but I remain cool. I don't get the feeling she's asking because she wants to be collared. "I have not. I assume you know how serious and... sacred a collar is in a Dom/sub relationship?" She nods. "Good. Some subs expect their Doms to collar them after a certain period of time, but it's a very serious commitment and should not be taken lightly. I've had to end a few partnerships because we weren't on the same page."

"Oh, that's unfortunate. Well, no need to worry about that with me. I am under no illusion this... *relationship* will get that far."

The way she says "relationship" sounds like she's tasted something unpleasant. I hope whatever asshole broke her heart realizes what a fucking mistake he made.

"I like a reasonable partner. If there are no more questions, I'd like to talk honorifics. We can keep calling each other 'E' and 'B,' but I'd prefer if we used something else."

"I'm okay with that. I would prefer not to be called 'baby girl' or 'babe,' but anything else is fine."

"Noted. In scenes you will address me as 'Sir.' Does that work for you?"

"Yes, Sir."

My already half-mast cock stands at attention. "What a quick learner you are," I croon. "Do you have any preferences on nicknames?" She shakes her head. "Alright. Are you ready to begin the scene now, honey?"

"Please, Sir."

"Then be a good girl and take off your pretty dress. I want to see what's mine for tonight."

CHAPTER 5

Emma

I stand and pull my dress over my head and gently lay it over the arm of the chaise. *Sir's* eyes greedily roam over every inch of exposed flesh—which is pretty much all of it. All I have on underneath is a matching pink thong, which is now wet and sticking to the lips of my pussy.

He stares for so long I start feeling self-conscious. I'm not a small girl. I'm a size twenty on a good day, with a round belly, thick thighs, and big, saggy breasts. I will say, my ass is popping though. I've done a lot of work to get over the internalized fat phobia ingrained into me by my family and society, so I appreciate my body for what it is.

Even though I've done the work, sometimes I still get insecure. Especially when the people looking at every stretch mark and imperfection look like B does. *Holy moly.*

Even in my four-inch heels, I barely reach his chin. He's got jet black, curly hair that's been perfectly styled without a strand out of place. My hands itch to mess it up. His dark beard is perfectly trimmed over his sharp jaw. Olive skin, brown eyes, and muscles for days.

Huh, he kind of looks like that one FBI agent from that crime show. The one in the newer seasons.

Maybe we can role play sometime; he can be the FBI agent, and I'll play the technical analyst.

Finally, he ends his perusal at my eyes and licks his thick, dusky pink lips. "I can't wait to take a bite out of you, *Dulzura.*"

God, I don't know what that means, but it sounds so good coming from his mouth. I think I like it more than "honey."

"Sit on the chaise, spread your legs, and pull your pretty little thong to the side. Let me see what you're hiding under there."

I do as he says, spreading my legs and pulling my panties to the side to reveal my bare pussy. His chest rumbles with an appreciative groan sending a pulse of arousal straight to my already throbbing clit.

"Such an eager little slut for me." My pussy pulses at the degrading praise. "What's your color, honey?"

"Green, Sir." God, I'm so fucking needy right now. He hasn't even touched me, and I'm ready to combust.

"What would your color be if I got on my knees and put my face in your pussy?"

"Green," I sigh. B arches an eyebrow at me, and I realize my mistake. "Green, *Sir.*"

He hums, standing from the chair, revealing the tent in his perfectly tailored slacks. My mouth waters as I imagine what his cock might look like, feel like against my tongue.

"Since this is your first time, I'll let the mistake slide, but if you forget to address me properly again, you'll receive a punishment. Do you understand, *Dulzura*?"

"Yes, Sir."

"Good girl. Pull your panties off, I don't want to be restricted while I ravish you."

I ungracefully shuck my panties and lay them with my dress, then resume the position I was in. B takes off his suit jacket and lays it on the arm of the chair, then rolls his black dress shirt sleeves up to his elbows, revealing muscled forearms that have me salivating.

He kneels before me and takes off my shoes, then runs his hands up my legs slowly, a trail of goosebumps following their path. His hands are rough and calloused, a stark contrast to the soft, dimpled skin of my thighs. He runs his thumbs over the matching garter belt tattoos on each thigh. They look like delicate black lace around my thick thighs, tied together with a bow that looks like it's made of satin. They were done in more than a few sessions because of how detailed they are and because of how thick my thighs are, but they're one of my favorite pieces.

"These are gorgeous, *Dulzura*."

"Thank you, Sir."

"I almost wish they were real so I could pull them off with my teeth."

I wasn't asked a direct question or given a direct order, so I don't say anything as he leans in and inhales deeply, just a hair's breadth away from my pussy.

A low, satisfied grumble works its way up his throat, and my pussy clenches at the sound. "You smell absolutely *deliciosa, Dulzura*. I bet you taste even better."

B looks up at me from between my thighs as he leans in the rest of the way and licks me slowly between the lips of my pussy. I gasp at the sensation.

It's not like I've never been eaten out before, but for some reason, everything is heightened right now. Maybe it's because I haven't had sex in a few weeks, or maybe it's because this dynamic with B is different from past hookups.

Whatever it is, I don't want it to stop.

Of their own accord, my hands move, intending to grab onto his mass of curly hair. Before I can get my hands on him, B's large hands wrap around my wrists and stop them.

His espresso-colored eyes meet mine as he pulls away. "Did I give you permission to touch me?"

I shake my head. "No, Sir. I'm sorry."

B tsks. "I believe that's grounds for punishment, don't you think? Good girls ask for permission before touching."

I suppress a needy whine. "Yes, Sir. I want to be your good girl."

B stands, then sits back down in the armchair he vacated just moments ago. "Come lie across my lap."

I stand but hesitate. Obviously, he's strong, but I'm not a small girl. "I..."

He wings a dark eyebrow. "Tell me why you're hesitating."

"I'm not a small girl, Sir. I don't want to hurt you."

"You think you're too heavy?"

"Yes, Sir."

B stands and crowds my body, using his pointer finger and thumb to tip my chin up so I'm forced to look into his eyes.

"I will not tolerate you body-shaming yourself, *Dulzura*. If I ask you to do something, trust I know whether or not I can handle it. Understood?"

"Understood, Sir."

B's eyes dart down to my lips, and his tongue pokes out to wet his own. I'm cursing myself for enacting my "no kissing" rule with him right now. I *want* to kiss him. I bet his kisses are commanding and intense, just like him. But my limits exist for a reason, and I have to keep that in mind.

He releases my chin and steps back to sit down again, then pats his lap in a silent command. I obey this time, draping myself over his strong thighs. His hard erection prods my side, but he makes no move to adjust it.

"I'm going to spank you five times as your first punishment for not asking permission to touch me and five times for not following my instructions and body-shaming yourself for a total of ten strikes. You will count them out loud. What's your color?"

"Green, Sir."

"Excellent."

With no warning or warm up, he brings his palm down harshly on my left ass cheek.

"One," I gasp.

Smack.

"Two."

Smack.

"Three," I moan. The initial shock of pain is morphing into an aching pleasure, and I fear I'm going to soak through his nice pants.

Four and five come in rapid succession, then he rubs his palm gently over the sore spots he's smacked.

"Color, honey?"

"Green, green, green. Sir." I squirm on his lap, desperately needing *something* to give me friction on my clit.

"This is supposed to be a punishment, *Dulzura*. Is your cunt getting wet from me reddening this perfect ass?"

My cheeks grow hot at his blatant teasing, but when I don't answer fast enough, he smacks me again.

"I asked you a question."

"Yes, Sir. My pussy is wet from you spanking my ass."

"Seems I might have a little pain slut on my hands. I can't wait to explore that more. Count the last four for me."

I'm almost embarrassed by how hot being called a slut makes me. It's the second time he's done it, and the fire in my lower belly grows hotter each time.

He spanks me four more times, and I count them out. My pussy is leaking by the time B is done with my punishment. He rubs my sore ass gently, then traces a single finger over the swell and down towards my dripping sex. He doesn't touch me where I need him most, but I'm so worked up from the spankings I almost come right then.

"You took your punishment so well, *Dulzura*. Your ass looks so pretty in this color, with my handprints marking it. Would you like to come now?"

"Yes, please, Sir." He traces his fingers over my lower lips, still avoiding my clit, then dips just the tip of his finger inside to gather the wetness.

He leans down so his hot breath fans against my ear. "Beg for it."

"Please, Sir. I need to come. Please let me come. I'll do anything. *Please.*"

He drags his wet fingertip up to my swollen bud and rubs in slow, teasing circles making me sigh in relief. It's not enough, I need more, but I don't want to be too greedy.

"Do you need more, *Dulzura?*"

"Yes, please, Sir."

He pulls his fingers back from my clit, and I whine at the loss. "Go spread yourself out on the chaise again. You interrupted me last time, and I'd like to finish."

Chapter 6

Ben

E follows my commands beautifully. She took her punishment like a champ. I was worried I'd gone too hard with her for her first time, but it seems she's thoroughly enjoying everything we've done so far.

Watching the way her ass rippled as I spanked her and seeing my handprints on her body has me feral. Possessive.

I haven't felt this sort of possession over someone except maybe my ex-fiancée, and it was never the primal level I feel for my *Dulzura. Sweetness.*

And she is *so fucking sweet.*

I could have gotten her off with my fingers while she was on my lap, but I *need* to taste her. I *need* to feel her come on my tongue—to feel her pulse and drip in my mouth.

E spreads her beautiful body out on the chaise, and I kneel between her spread thighs. I place gentle kisses on her inner thighs as I make my way up to her dripping pussy.

Before I dive in, I pull back. "Grab the back of the chaise with both of your hands, honey. I don't want them to move."

"Yes, Sir." She reaches up and grabs the cushion, which pushes her tits forward, tempting me.

I refrain from lavishing her breasts the way I want, she's already begged so sweetly for me to let her come, and I'm a man of my word. "Good girl. You may come as many times as you can while I'm down here enjoying myself."

"Thank you, Sir."

Not wanting to wait any longer, I lean in and lick the arousal from between her lips and groan as her sweet, tangy flavor dances across my tastebuds. She's got such a unique, earthy taste, and I'm ravenous for more.

My tongue circles her hard clit, and she bucks her hips up at the sensation. I use one of my arms to pin down her pelvis so I can continue my feast, sucking on the little nub while she moans and writhes beneath me.

"Oh, Sir. *Fuck.*"

I pop off of her to say, "Such a dirty word to come out of such a pretty mouth." Then take two fingers and slowly insert them, crooking them to find that rough spot that will surely push her over the edge.

"Oh my God!" she moans, trying to buck her hips again, but they're still trapped under my arm.

"Not God, *Dulzura,* just me."

I thrust my fingers against that spot inside her and flick her clit rapidly with my tongue. Within seconds, her pussy clamps my fingers in a vice grip, and she screams as she comes. I don't stop my assault, I want to see if she'll squirt for me, so I continue my ministrations.

"Sir, I can't—"

"You *can*. Give me more, *Dulzura*."

"Sir, I *can't*."

"You know the word to make this stop. Say it, and I'll stop."

I wait, still slowly pumping inside her. She doesn't say "red" or "yellow," so I pick up my pace and lap at her clit again.

I could stay down here for hours and hours if I thought her sweet body could handle it. One day, I'll overstimulate her to the point of exhaustion, but I have to remind myself she's still new to this.

I pump my fingers faster, then take her swollen nub between my teeth and bite it gently, which does the trick. She comes with a scream, and I'm rewarded with a rush of wetness hitting my chest, face, and arm.

I take my mouth off her so I can pepper her with praises while I slow the speed of my fingers, working her through her orgasm.

When she finally stops pulsing around my fingers, I pull them out and make eye contact with her, then put them in front of her face. "Taste how sweet you are, *Dulzura*."

She wraps those plump lips around my middle and ring finger, swirling her tongue, sucking off her own arousal while keeping eye contact with me. It's enough to almost make me come in my pants.

When I retract my hand, she licks around her lips to gather the last remnants off them.

I notice then she still has her hands behind her head on the chaise, gripping the leather like a lifeline.

"You did such a good job, honey. You listened so well and came beautifully," I coo, scooping her up.

She opens her mouth—probably to protest—but quickly shuts it again, then whispers, "Thank you, Sir."

I lay her on the soft sheets of the bed while I find wipes to clean her up, then grab a bottle of water for her. After I've gently cleaned the dampness from her thighs and she's downed half the bottle, I lie down next to her and pull her back against my front.

I'm still hard as stone—fully clothed while she's naked—and my cock prods her ass as she scoots back. She gasps, but I ignore it. I can take care of myself later—and I definitely will, over and over again as I replay tonight.

After about ten minutes of cuddling, her breathing turns steady, so I tuck a strand of hair behind her ear and lean in, taking in her smell. Whatever perfume or lotion she's got on smells like summer. Fruity and sweet with a woodsy undertone.

It's intoxicating and seductive, just like the woman in my arms.

"Are you feeling up for talking about tonight?" I whisper in her ear.

She rolls over and faces me. "A-are we done with the scene?"

"Yes. This is the aftercare part. Even though our scene wasn't as intense as it could have been, I still need to take care of you after. Help you come down gently."

"But you didn't..." She looks pointedly at my still tented slacks.

I run my hand over her right arm, tracing the delicate ink. "Tonight was all about you. Don't worry about me."

"Okay," she sighs. "I really enjoyed everything we did. I was a little... wary about spankings because of how I was raised, but it was actually really hot."

"Did you feel safe? With me?"

Those ocean blues shine bright, even in the dim lighting of the room. "I felt more safe with you than I have with anyone else in a long time. I felt... in control, even if I wasn't."

"You're always in control. You tell me 'red,' and everything will stop immediately. I may be the Dom, but you hold all the power."

"It was nice not having to overthink my every move. I like that your expectations were clear and direct."

"That is a big appeal to a lot of people." Is it too forward to ask her to continue this? To invite her over to my house to play? Kiera has my address, so it's not like no one would know where she'd be. Still, I could see her feeling a little nervous to take such a big step with a virtual stranger.

Sometimes the risk is worth the reward, though.

"Is this... *arrangement* something you'd like to continue?"

E sighs, "I would. But I can't afford the club fees right now. It's a miracle Kiera got me in."

Right, I remember there being an email about staff being able to bring a friend once a month to generate more buzz for the club. I was dreading it at first, but the situation brought this lovely woman into my orbit, so I can't be too upset.

I clear my throat. "If it's not too forward... I have a room at my house similar to this one. If you'd feel comfortable coming to my place, I'd love to continue helping you explore."

E takes her plush bottom lip between her teeth, and I resist the urge to pull it free with my thumb.

Finally, she responds, "As long as you're okay with me sharing my location with my friends, I think I'd really like to continue this as well."

I'm not someone who cheers or fist pumps, but I find myself fighting against both of those reactions. "Absolutely. Your safety is my number one priority."

"I guess we better share our names with each other, then?"

"Hmmm. Let's keep the mystery alive just a little while longer. We can share names when you come over next Saturday night?"

"I'm looking forward to it."

"As am I. Are you ready to get up and get dressed? Are you feeling okay?"

"I feel great. I should probably get home, anyway. I have a lot to do tomorrow."

"Of course." I help her off the bed and over to her discarded clothes and shoes.

I help her step into her discarded panties, then pull her dress over her head and fix her hair so none of it is stuck in the delicate satin. She sits on the chaise to put her shoes back on, but I kneel before her and slip them on her small, dainty feet.

"Thank you," she breathes when I help her stand.

"My pleasure." I want to kiss her. Just a small, delicate peck on her lips. Just to know what they feel like against mine.

But I'd never cross a line she's set in stone, so I step back and offer her my arm.

She takes it, and together, we walk out of the room and into the main club area, where I offer to walk her to her car. She declines, saying she's ordering a rideshare since she didn't know if she'd be drinking.

After collecting our respective personal items, we head out to the curb to wait for her rideshare. I put my number in her phone and send myself a text so I have hers, then we stand side by side, not touching, until the car pulls up a few minutes later.

"Text me so I know you made it home safely," I command before she gets in the car.

She nods, then waves as she gets in the backseat.

I drive myself home, and as soon as I walk in the door, I get a text.

E: Home safe and sound! Thank you again for tonight. I'm looking forward to next weekend. :)

B: Thank you for letting me know. I'm looking forward to it as well. Get some rest. Goodnight, E.

E: Goodnight, B. :)

I take off my clothes, my cock still hard as fuck since I've been replaying the events of tonight over and over again on my way home, imagining all the different ways I can play with my new sub. As soon as I'm under the stream of warm water, I wrap my hand around my length.

Embarrassingly, within ten pumps I'm coming on the shower floor, feeling nowhere near sated.

Waiting a whole week to taste my *Dulzura* again is going to be pure torture.

But I'm a patient man, and the torture will be worth the wait.

CHAPTER 7

Emma

I turn to the side in the big gold mirror across from my bed, assessing the twentieth outfit I've tried on this morning.

At Kirkham Creatives, Daniel and Josh didn't care much about what I wore. I always made sure to look professional, but some days called for a hot pink pleather mini skirt and off-shoulder, balloon sleeve top, while other days called for a pair of jeans and an old band shirt.

I don't have a set style, I just wear whatever I like, and sometimes it can make for quite the eclectic outfit. Jordy calls it "dopamine dressing." I call it "freedom after trauma since I was raised in a family where my dad had to approve every outfit."

I want to make a good impression on my first day at Rossi Construction, so I opt for a pair of professional, light blue wide-leg pants made of a flowy material, and a white mock neck shirt. I clasp a simple gold chain around my neck, slip a pair of gold hoops in my ears, and don my usual rings on my fingers before heading out of my room.

I could probably stand to wear something more conservative to hide my tattoos, but I promised myself a long time ago I would stop hiding myself to make others feel comfortable. If someone doesn't think I'm qualified because of my tattoos or piercings, tough shit.

The smell of coffee and cinnamon rolls assaults my senses as I open my bedroom door, and I see Jordan at the counter meticulously frosting the fluffy cinnamon goodness.

"Good luck cinnamon rolls for your first day at your dream job!" They beam, rounding the counter and wrapping me in a hug. "I'm so proud of you, Mimi," they whisper against my head.

"Thank you, Jojo. I'm nervous but excited. I just hope they like me, and I don't mess things up."

They scoff. "They're going to *love* you. And you're going to build so many cool buildings and make so many connections. You've got this in the bag."

"I sure hope you're right," I sigh. "I've got to get going soon to fill out the HR paperwork, so let's dig in."

Jordan slides a plate with a cinnamon roll the size of my head over to me, as well as a travel coffee tumbler. "I made your latte with a protein shake because I know you get sleepy without protein in the mornings."

"Thanks, babe. You're the best house spouse." I give them an overdramatic wink, and they roll their eyes at me. Jordy works from home as a therapist, so they take care of a lot of the domestic tasks like grocery shopping, while I make sure the bills get paid on time. We trade off cooking dinner and have a cleaning schedule that helps us keep our place tidy with our busy schedules.

Jordy and I have been best friends since kindergarten, and even though we had a few fights in our teen years, we always made our way back to each other. We've been roommates since we graduated high school, but we've lived here for seven years.

Once I'm done with my breakfast, I take my coffee and drive over to my new place of employment. The building is a classic industrial structure you'd expect of a construction company. The outside is gray with the Rossi logo, big windows, and glass doors.

The floors inside are sleek, dark gray concrete, and the walls are white. There's a wall of tiles across from the reception desk that depict some of the projects Rossi has worked on. I'm greeted by the receptionist, who shows me to the HR office, where I fill out all of the necessary new hire paperwork. I didn't even think to ask about the salary when I accepted this job, and my eyes bulge at the amount I'll be paid. It's almost double what I was making at Kirkham Creatives.

"Is this number correct?" I ask Katrina, the Director of HR.

She chuckles. "Yes. The number is correct.

"That's a lot of money. I feel like I'm dreaming."

"I want to make sure my employees are well compensated for their efforts," a familiar deep voice says from the doorway.

I turn in my chair to see a man with olive skin and dark hair streaked with gray leaning against the doorframe in a black polo with the Rossi logo on it. He looks vaguely familiar, but I can't quite figure out why. The only interaction we've had was over the phone.

"Hi, Mr. Rossi." I stand quickly and extend a hand to the man. "It's so nice to meet you in person. Thank you *so* much for this opportunity. I'm excited to learn from one of the best."

Mr. Rossi grins, grasping my hand with both of his. "*Ciao*, Emma. It's a pleasure to have you with us. Joshua and Daniel have nothing but good things to say about you."

My cheeks heat under his praise. "Thank you, sir."

He waves his hand in front of him. "No need to address me so formally, Emma. You can call me Enzo."

"Thank you, Enzo."

Enzo turns to Katrina, "If Emma is finished with her paperwork, I'd like to introduce her to the guys upstairs and show her her office."

Katrina nods and takes the paperwork from me. I follow Mr. Rossi—*Enzo*—up a set of concrete stairs. At the top, I notice a long hallway of offices all encased in glass, and I hear laughter from a few different people coming from the office at the very end of the hall.

"This is my office right here, my door is always open should you need anything." Enzo motions to an office that's separate from all the rest, on the opposite side of the stairwell. "Across from it are the restrooms for this floor. There are restrooms downstairs as well."

He leads me down the hall, telling me who occupies each space as we pass. Dave, the operations manager, then Alex and Drew, who are the other project managers.

"The last office is my son Ben's. Your office is directly across from his. He'll be in charge of training you and showing you the ropes," Enzo says as we reach the end of the hall. "Oh great, they're all here."

"Hey, Enzo, this the new girl?" a man with blonde hair asks from the doorway to Ben's office. I can't see past him into the office as he greets me with a warm smile.

"Emma, this is Alex," Enzo introduces us.

"Nice to meet you." I give him my best confident smile, hoping my hands aren't sweating.

Alex steps out of the way, and a man with cropped brown hair and black framed glasses steps forward. "I'm Drew."

"Emma."

When Drew steps out of the way to make room for the last man, my stomach flips, and my heart rate speeds up. Now I know why Enzo looked so familiar. Standing right next to each other, the resemblance is obvious.

"This is my son, Ben," Enzo says, nudging Ben as if to push him forward, but he doesn't budge. He stands there, scowling at me with his arms folded across his wide chest. His eyes, which were so full of heat and desire on Saturday, are now cold and stony.

His dad isn't wrong. Ben *was* training me. We just never got to the ropes.

Mustering as much confidence as I can, I plaster on a smile and extend my hand to him. "Hello, Ben. Pleasure to meet you, I'm Emma."

CHAPTER 8

Ben

Pleasure *to meet you, I'm Emma.*

Emma.

E.

This cannot be fucking happening.

I *never* mix business and pleasure. Did she know who I was when we met at the club? Did she just want to fuck with my head, knowing we'd have to work in close proximity to each other?

"She can't work here," I snap, and Emma startles, pulling her hand back to her side.

"*Beniamino.* Don't be rude to our new coworker. Why would you say that?" my father admonishes, totally unaware I had my tongue in the pussy of our *new coworker* less than forty-eight hours ago. A pussy I've jacked off to three times since. A pussy I planned on fucking this weekend.

Obviously, that won't be happening now.

"I'm curious as to why you would say that, as well. Why can't I work here?" Emma challenges, folding her arms over her ample tits. She holds herself confidently even though I've insulted her. There's a wildfire of rage in her ocean eyes. Such a contrast from the submissive, demure woman at the club who was nervous to even look at me.

I hate that I *don't* hate it.

I feel the confused gazes of Alex and Drew on me. I've always been a grumpy, keep-to-myself asshole, but I've never been *impolite.*

"She'll be a distraction." Not just to me but to the crews. To Alex and Drew. The salesmen. The vendors.

Emma straightens her spine and addresses my dad, "I assure you, Enzo, I will do my best to stay out of everyone's way and not make things difficult. I promise not to be a *distraction.* I'm here to learn, not to cause issues."

"Of course you won't be a distraction, Emma. I wouldn't have hired you if I didn't think you were the right fit for the job. I don't know what my son is talking about," my dad says pointedly in my direction.

I scowl instead of answering.

Alex and Drew make excuses about heading to job sites or filling out paperwork, and Emma gives them warm smiles and the promise to get to know them over lunch this week.

My dad leans in while they're distracted. "I raised you better than this, *Beniamino.* You will not treat her any differently just because she's a woman. If you're not up for the task of training her, I'll ask Alex or Drew to do it. Either way, she stays unless she proves to be a problem."

"I can do it," I grit out. Papà tasked me with this job, and I'll be damned if I disappoint him.

"I'm so sorry about my son, Emma. If he isn't treating you well, please let me know, and I'll have Alex or Drew train you. I'm *very* happy to have you here." Papà gives Emma an affectionate squeeze on the arm.

"Thank you, Enzo, but I'm sure there'll be no problems." Emma gives him a reassuring smile.

Papà gives me another pointed look then leaves the office, and I'm left alone with the woman I haven't stopped thinking about all weekend.

Despite my anger and confusion, my cock's been half hard since I recognized her, so I sit down in my chair to hide the bulge and grunt, "Sit down," motioning to the chairs across my desk.

She sits, folding her hands primly across her lap, then shocks me by speaking first. "I'd like to know why you're so against me working here."

I ignore her and say, "Did you know who I was on Saturday?"

Emma rolls her eyes. "No, *Ben.* I did not. If I did, I wouldn't have gone through with it because my livelihood is more important than a hookup."

I don't know why it bothers me that she's reduced us to a simple "hookup." My frown deepens at the cavalier way she says it. Did our time together not mean that much to her?

"I don't mix business and pleasure. If you're going to get all clingy and expect more from me, that's unacceptable. And obviously what we did can't happen again. I think it's best if we move on and forget it ever happened."

"Oh my God, get *over* yourself. It was one night of—admittedly—good oral, but you're not some anomaly. I'm not expecting you to hold my hand and be my boyfriend. I don't do relationships. If you can forget it happened, I can forget it happened."

Usually, "good oral" would be a compliment. From Emma, it almost sounds like an insult.

"Obviously we can't have our scheduled... *session* on Saturday. It would be unprofessional. If you show up at my house—"

Emma holds up a hand, effectively cutting me off. "I guarantee you that won't happen. I'm not going to beg for attention or risk this job. I can keep things professional if you can."

I don't know if I believe her. She's different than she was at the club, like she's wearing a mask. She sounds confident she can keep things professional, I guess I just have to take her word for it.

"Fine. Let's get started with your training then."

Emma leans over her bag and pulls out a hot pink notebook with five pens hooked on the front.

"What's that?" I ask.

"A notebook so I can take notes?" She gives me a "duh" look.

"I know it's a notebook. What's with the different colored pens? Why do you need to take notes?"

Emma straightens her spine defensively. "Sometimes, too much new information at once can overwhelm my brain. If I write it down, I can keep track of it better or go back and look at it later and not worry about having to ask questions over and over. The pens help me organize the information: black is general information, pink is personal things for me to remember, red is vital information, green is for programs, software, and passcodes, and orange is just an extra color in case something doesn't fall into those categories."

I don't understand why someone would need more than one color of pen. I don't understand why someone would need such elaborate notes for a job like this. Alex and Drew certainly never took notes when I was training them, but they also knew more of the basics than she does. "If this will be too much—"

"I'll be just fine, thank you. If you'd prefer I didn't take notes just say so," Emma says firmly.

It's really not a big deal for her to take notes, especially if it will help her retain the information better, I don't know why I'm so hung up on it.

"It's fine. As long as it doesn't slow us down."

Emma nods but doesn't say anything else. Before I move on, I blurt out something I've been thinking since she walked in, "Your hair."

"What about it?"

"It's... different."

"There's this miraculous thing called a curling iron," she deadpans. "My hair on Saturday was a special occasion thing, this is how I wear it the rest of the time. Is that a problem for you?"

No. Other than the fact I want to feel the curly strands in my grip.

"No," I grunt. "Enough chit chat. This is the software we use to track our bids." I pull up ProConnect and log in, talking rapidly while she takes notes.

I hope she can keep her word and keep things professional.

Chapter 9

Emma

S *he'll be a distraction.*
Ugh. That asshole.

I will admit, I like that I ruffled his feathers just a little. The stoic, in control man showed just a sliver of vulnerability.

For all his talk of *me* keeping things professional, I don't think he realized how obvious he was while checking me out during our training today. More than once, I noticed his eyes on my chest while he was going over the basic programs the PMs use, and more than once, I noticed him shift in his seat.

My nipples have been hard all day from being surrounded by his scent and his domineering presence, so I'm not one to talk.

Any other situation, with any other person, I would have flirted and teased him about being hot and bothered, but I didn't want to give him any more reason to hate me.

I also really want this job to work out, so showing Mr. Grumpy I *can* be professional even though he's had his tongue in my pussy is my top priority.

During one of my bathroom breaks, I sent a text to the besties group chat requesting an emergency dinner debrief. I especially need to talk to Kiera because she's the only other person who knows Ben.

Once we settle into our usual back booth of Jordan's parents' restaurant, River's End, I don't wait until we have our drink orders in before diving into the whole mess.

Since Kiera and Jordan are the only ones who know about my night at The Temptation Lounge, I briefly tell Moss and Jaime I went to the club and had a session without giving them any explicit details.

Moss turns as red as a tomato at just the mention of the club, so telling them how *B* devoured my pussy like he was the champion title holder would probably make them explode with embarrassment.

"We agreed to meet at his house this weekend and exchange names then—"

"*Ricitos,* why would you agree to go to a stranger's house?" Jaime interrupts with a look of horror on his face.

I roll my eyes. "Kiera knows him, and he promised I could share my location with her and Jordy." I point a finger at him. "If you saw what he looks like and felt the way his tongue moves, you would agree too."

Jaime holds up his hands in surrender. "Fair enough, continue."

"So, I get to work today, and the owner, Enzo, is introducing me to my coworkers. We get to the last office and guess who's sitting at the desk."

A collective gasp echoes around the table.

"Yeah. Imagine my surprise when the man who gave me the most intense night of my life is not only working at the same company as me but is also the one *training* me."

Jaime mumbles something in Spanish under his breath, shaking his head.

Kiera groans. "Emma I swear I had no idea when I set you up with him. It didn't even occur to me that he might be related to Rossi Construction. It clicked when I saw him at the club, but it was too late to tell you, and by the time I got home, I forgot. I'm so sorry! I'm such a bad friend. If I had just thought about it for one second—"

I reach across the booth to squeeze her hand. "I don't blame you at all, K."

"But your job—"

"Is safe. He doesn't want me there, but his dad does, and his dad makes the rules. As long as things stay professional and I do my job well, everything will be fine."

Kiera bites her lip but nods.

"One good thing to come from today is I found out my salary is double what I was making at Kirkham. Sooooo, I was *hoping* you might be able to pull some strings and get me a membership to the lounge? I can finally afford the fee."

Kiera narrows her hazel eyes at me. "Is joining the club a good idea? What if you run into him?"

I shrug. "I obviously won't be fucking him, so I might as well fuck someone else. I really liked the Dom/sub dynamic and would feel safer exploring it at the club where everyone is vetted. I'm sure there are other people I would be compatible with."

Kiera nods. "Alright, girl. I'll see what I can do. Congrats on getting such a pay raise, too! That's amazing."

"So, I take it dinner is on you tonight, *Ricitos*?" Jaime teases.

"Please, you know Mom and Dad would never let us pay," Jordan chides.

"Ah, I love your parents. I wish mine were as cool as yours." Jaime sighs, and everyone but Jordan holds up their cup and mumbles, "Same."

That's one thing about our friend group I both love and hate. Other than Jordan, we all have shitty or non-existent relationships with our families, so we've formed our own little family. We've been lucky enough to have Jordan's mom and dad take us all under their wing and become the parents we needed.

We spend the rest of dinner chatting about random things, gossiping about the drama at our respective workplaces, and by the time Jordan and I walk through the door of our townhome, the mask I put on to be little miss sunshine is slipping. I'm ready to crawl into bed and cry for a while over today's events.

As much as I let everyone think the interaction with Ben doesn't bother me, it does. I *hate* that my heart was already starting to get attached to the idea of him after one night, but I was really looking forward to seeing him again. Now, I *will* see him again. Five days a week.

I'll have to pretend I'm not still wildly attracted to him. I'll have to pretend our night meant absolutely nothing when that's not even remotely true.

This is why I always stick to one-night stands with strangers. The less time spent with someone, the less chance my heart gets attached. I've done really well at not getting attached to people I have sex with, mostly because I never see them again.

I just hope my heart can stay unattached and resist the grumpy asshole because this job is my dream job, and I refuse to throw it away over fucking *feelings*.

CHAPTER 10

Ben

As it turns out, Emma *can* keep things professional. She's been here almost a month, and other than one conversation on her second day where she brought up *that night*, she's remained professional and cordial.

I remember feeling smug about the fact she brought up our one night, but the conversation didn't go the way I anticipated. This woman keeps surprising me, and I hate it.

We're sitting in Emma's office, logging her into all the software, when she turns to me and says, "I know I said I'd forget it happened, but I have a question."

Here we fucking go, I groan internally but motion for her to continue.

"Your last name is Italian, right? And your dad speaks Italian?"

I nod, wondering where she's going with this.

"At the club, the nickname, was it also Italian?"

"No. It was Spanish."

"Trilingual, nice. I took German in junior high, but I don't remember anything useful. I tried to learn Spanish but kept getting it mixed up with German, so I stopped. I should probably try learning it again considering the field I work in."

"German and Spanish aren't even that similar." I don't even know what we're talking about right now. I've never just... offered up information about myself like that. Does she do this often?

Emma shrugs. "Maybe not, but my brain doesn't understand that."

Then we continued on as normal, no more conversation about the languages I speak, and she hasn't mentioned the club or the nickname again. I thought for sure she'd at least ask me what it means or allude to the night to get a rise out of me, but she hasn't. She barely talks to me unless it's work related. It's like she's truly forgotten about it, and even though I'm mostly relieved, a small part of me is upset I have no valid reason to be irritated with her sunshiney presence.

If she kept bringing it up or vying for my attention, I'd have a reason to be on edge when I hear the *click clack* of her heels on the floor as she comes into the office. I'd have a reason to dread being stuck in the truck for hours while we make our rounds to job sites. But I don't have a good reason because she's being *professional* just like I wanted.

Everyone else in the office adores her, and she's so goddamn friendly with everyone when we're out in the field. Even our most misogynistic superintendent, Ralph, isn't immune to her charm. I've been working with Ralph for almost ten years and have barely seen him crack a smile, but he always has one at the ready for the bubbly blonde. He hasn't even said anything negative about her working for us.

Most Barbie-esque women would be intimidated by the men on our crews—burly, sweaty, and some heavily tattooed—but not Emma. She treats everyone as if they're important and tries her best to make everyone feel welcome.

Even though a majority of our crews speak primarily Spanish, and she doesn't understand most of what they're saying, she's always polite and tries to communicate as best she can.

If I'm not translating for her and the crew, she's asking me about all of their backstories and their families, but I don't know them that well. I'm not their friend, I'm their boss.

Through her interactions with other people, I've reluctantly learned a lot of information about her. Turns out, she *does* just offer information about herself to people. Something I still don't understand.

I know she's originally from Utah, she loves pink and purple—that one was obvious—and she likes to read. I know she loves the beach but not when the sand gets stuck to her body or between her toes. She's never broken a bone, but she did have her gallbladder removed. She hates the feeling of the microfiber cloths we use to clean our computers, and she prefers fruity gummy candies to chocolate. Her comfort meal is sesame chicken, but she has a difficult time with reheated meat.

I hate that I remember these things. It's taking up space in my brain I should be using for other, more important things.

We've seen an influx of salesmen from different vendors in the last three weeks which grates on my nerves. Apparently, word got around about our new PM, and now the reps are intent on introducing themselves to Emma.

Currently, she's talking to two reps from a waterworks supply company who brought her donuts as a "welcome gift." It doesn't sound like they're talking much business though, if her repeated giggling is any indication.

I *should* close my office door so I can get the rest of these invoices approved, but I can't seem to make myself do it. I want to make sure they aren't selling her some bullshit just because she's new and a woman they think they can manipulate.

She's already proven to be more than a pretty face, though. With her knowledge of the computer systems and her organization tactics and ideas, she's demonstrated herself as an asset already. She's quick to pick up on what's needed at which job sites and knows what vendors have the cheapest options available. She's quick with her paperwork and is firm in what she wants. She's easily picked up on the software we use and has already placed a bid for a city recreation center.

She's memorized the names of the salesmen and vendors, and I've seen her jot down little tidbits of information about them, as well as some of the contractors and developers we work with.

It vexes me that she's so good with people.

Today, much to my annoyance, we're meeting with Derek Allridge to attempt to win a bid for another job. I don't know why my dad insists on schmoozing the asshole, but he's adamant. Instead of sending Alex or

Drew, he's sending me and Emma. *Papà* thinks it will be good for her to talk to him, give Derek a fresh face to work with.

I think it's going to be a train wreck.

Small talk and ass kissing—not the fun kind—make me itchy. I don't fucking care about the weather or what sports team is in the playoffs. I just want to talk about business and be done. I don't get why we have to make a big deal of it.

"Well, gentlemen, it's been a pleasure chatting with you, but Ben and I have a lunch date with a developer, so we have to cut this meeting short." Emma's saccharine voice floats into my office.

"Of course, it was *so* good to meet you, Emma. I hope to see more of you from here on out," Salesman One practically purrs.

"Let us know if there's *anything* we can do for you. Day or night. We'll give you our personal cells in case you need us." Salesman Two pulls his card from his pocket, scribbles something on it, and hands it to Emma.

I *almost* roll my eyes at the pathetic attempt at flirting.

"Thank you, I'll be sure to let you know if there's anything I need."

The salesmen leave, and I watch Emma tape their cards into her notebook, scribbling something down next to them, then she closes the book, puts it in her purse, and knocks on the open door of my office. She's wearing a pink checker print mini skirt with a white shirt under a matching pink checker print blazer and white heeled booties. Her curly hair is held back by a light pink headband. Her lips are shiny with some type of gloss—not that I've wondered what it is.

If Mattel had a project manager Barbie, she would look like Emma.

"I'm ready to go when you are. I'll be waiting down in the lobby," she says before I hear the *click clack* of her heels disappear down the hall and down the stairs.

I really, really don't want to go to this godforsaken lunch, but I refuse to give my dad any reason to think I can't handle it, and I won't let Emma meet with Derek alone.

When I finally make my way down to the lobby, Emma is chatting with our receptionist, Gia, but they stop when they see me coming.

"Emma and I will be gone for a few hours."

"Of course, Ben. Enjoy your lunch." Gia smiles and bats her eyelashes at me.

I nod once in response and head out to my truck, assuming Emma is following me.

Once we're both in the truck and pull out of the parking lot, Emma turns to me. "Tell me about Mr. Allridge."

"He's the owner of Allridge Developments, the biggest developer in San Diego. We've bid with him three times, and he's rejected us every time."

"Okay... did he say why?"

"Just that we weren't a good fit."

"Okay, tell me more about him."

I glance over at her, and she has her pen poised to take notes in her notebook. "What am I supposed to know about him?"

I swear she rolls her eyes, but I can't be sure because I'm looking at the road. "Is he married? Does he have kids? Grandkids? What are his hobbies? Why did he want to go into development? What's his story?"

"Why the fuck would I know those things?"

"Because, *Ben*, that's what you do when you're trying to make connections with someone. But I suppose you wouldn't know much about that. You don't even know anything about your own crew members." She takes her headband off and rubs her temples.

"Why would I need to know personal things about them? They're employees, not my friends."

We're stopped at a red light, so I *do* catch her eye roll this time. God, it makes me want to bend her over my knee and spank her—

Nope. Not professional.

"Any good employer gets to know their employees."

"Technically, my dad is their employer."

"But you're going to be taking over the company eventually, right? Enzo is great at connecting with people. You'll need to be able to do that to keep the connections he's made."

I'm pretty sure this is the most we've spoken since she started.

I don't like it.

I especially don't like that she has a point. No one else has ever been so bold as to tell me to my face I need to work on my people skills. Everyone else lets me be a broody asshole.

"I like to think our work speaks for itself, so the people we do repeat jobs for will continue to hire us, even after I take over the company."

The sigh she lets out makes my skin prickle with irritation. "Whatever. I guess I'll just have to make my own connections with him."

"Yeah, good luck with that."

Emma doesn't grace me with a retort, thankfully, so we spend the rest of the short drive in complete silence. I notice she doesn't put her headband back on until we're pulling into the restaurant, and I wonder if it hurts her head.

I curse myself for giving a fuck.

River's End was Emma's suggestion. I've been here once with my family and enjoyed the atmosphere and the food, so I agreed, but I'm not sure it will impress Mr. Allridge.

Emma walks right up to the hostess stand and tells the girl her name for our reservation, and they chat like they've met a million times before.

How and why *is she so friendly?*

Mr. Allridge walks in, and Emma immediately turns to greet him with a professional handshake and beaming smile. "Mr. Allridge, I'm Emma Price, the new PM at Rossi Construction. It's a pleasure to make your acquaintance."

How did she know it was him?

Mr. Allridge seems taken aback by her forwardness but shakes her hand anyway, giving her a quick once over. "Hello, Emma. The pleasure is mine. Please, call me Derek."

"Of course. You already know Ben."

Derek gives me a handshake in greeting. Before anyone else can say anything, the hostess lets us know our table is ready and leads us to a quiet booth situated in the back of the restaurant.

I slide in on one side, and Derek slides in on the other while Emma worries her bottom lip as her eyes bounce back and forth before she slides into the booth on my side.

Logically, it makes sense we're both facing Derek, but my body freezes up at the close proximity to the blonde.

It's going to be a long lunch.

Chapter 11

Emma

I hadn't considered I'd have to sit so close to Ben when I asked the hostess for this booth.

Of course, the other option would be to sit next to Derek, and that would be awkward as hell, especially if I'm trying to talk business.

Ugh. I hate this.

Ben has barely said a word other than to comment on how well things are going with the business when Derek asks, so I've been the one carrying the conversation with the developer.

If Enzo has only ever sent Ben to smooth talk Derek, no wonder we haven't been able to land him as a client yet. Getting Ben to make conversation is like trying to make a fish walk.

It's a good thing small talk and getting to know people quickly are specialties of mine, otherwise this whole lunch would be a fucking bust. I clock the silver wedding band as soon as he shakes my hand and make a mental note to ask about his partner. It's easy enough to see Derek Allridge, like most powerful men, likes to have his ego stroked a little, so that's what I do.

I gush about the layout of a townhome complex in La Jolla he finished last year and lament that I can't afford the luxury apartments right on the Windansea Beach because they're so beautiful.

His chest puffs with pride the more I praise his work, and by the time our food has arrived, he's laughing and telling me stories like I'm part of the good ol' boys' club.

Derek asks me about my work experience and how I'm liking working at Rossi. I answer honestly, telling him while I'm new to this, I'm loving the work, and Enzo is a great boss.

He asks me about what kind of projects I'm most excited to work on, and I tell him I'm not particular. Working on something large-scale like a hospital or an airport would be incredible, but I'm just as happy working on retail spaces or apartments.

When I glance at Ben, he looks irritated—which is his normal look—but also a little surprised. Is he surprised at how easy I'm getting Derek to interact? Or is he surprised by my answers?

"So, Emma, I don't see a ring on your finger. Are you seeing anyone?"

The question takes me by surprise, but it's not a *completely* abnormal thing to ask. "Not at the moment."

Derek's bushy brown eyebrows raise to his hairline. "Now, why not? Pretty thing like you must have men tripping over themselves."

Fuck's sake. Why can't a woman just want to be single?

I demurely raise a shoulder as I stab a piece of grilled chicken with my fork. "I'm keeping my options open at the moment. Waiting for the right person to come along, focusing on my career. You know, all the cliché reasons."

"Always good to keep your options open. Wouldn't want to miss out on something special. My wife and I took a long while to find each other, but it's the best thing that ever happened to me."

I perk up at the mention of his wife. This is my in to make a personal connection. "I love that. How did you two meet?"

Derek gives me a wistful smile. "Before I started my own company, I was an estimator at another company, and she was the HR Manager. We didn't like each other at first. She thought I was rude and impersonal, and I didn't like how bubbly she was all the damn time."

Sounds like Ben.

I brush the thought away as Derek continues, "One day, we got on the elevator to leave at the same time, and the power went out." I gasp, and Derek chuckles. "We were stuck in there for three hours because the outage was city-wide, and the fire department couldn't get to us any sooner. She's claustrophobic, so she started having a panic attack as soon as the elevator stopped, and I had no idea what to do other than hold her and walk her through some breathing exercises. I'd never seen her so... vulnerable. The bubbly girl I knew was a mess, sobbing into my dress shirt, and my heart split right open for her.

"Once she calmed down, we spent the next few hours getting to know each other, and by the time we were rescued, we already had a date set up. I knew at the end of our first date I wanted to make her my wife. We've been married almost fifteen years now."

"That's so beautiful. I love hearing stories like that. Makes my jaded heart believe I could have a love like that someday."

I may imagine it, but I swear Derek's eyes dart to Ben before they settle back on me. "Well, don't let one bad apple spoil the whole bunch. There's someone for everyone. Sometimes they're the person you least expect—or want." Derek checks his watch. "Thank you for the lovely lunch, but I'm afraid I have to get back to the office."

"Oh, but we didn't get to talk about—"

"I'll be calling you when we have our next project finalized. I like your 'vibe,' as the kids say, and I'd love to have you working on it, Emma."

My mouth opens and closes, surely looking like a fish before a big smile takes over my face. "Thank you, Derek. I'd be honored to work with you."

We all stand and shake hands then promise to do this again soon before Derek leaves the restaurant.

Ben pays for our lunch on the company card, and we silently get back into the truck and make our way to the office.

I'm buzzing with excitement from Derek wanting to work with me, but I keep my excitement internal so I don't upset Ben, who seems broodier than usual.

When we're back, everyone crowds into the doorway of my office to ask how lunch went.

I give them a brief rundown, not that there's much to say other than, "He said he wants to work with me when their next project is finalized!"

Enzo claps me on the shoulder. "*Congratulazioni, mi cara!* That's amazing news! I'm so proud of you."

My eyes burn with happy tears at the praise from Enzo, but I blink them back so I don't embarrass myself. "Thank you, Enzo. I'm really excited for this opportunity."

Drew, Alex, and Dave offer their congratulations as well, then leave me to finish out the workday in peace.

I can't help but feel a little disappointed Ben didn't congratulate me, too. Even when he had the opportunity to do so in private on the way back to the office.

I shake my head, I don't need his approval or his praise.

Even if I want it.

CHAPTER 12

Ben

The next day, before Emma comes in to work, Alex and Drew invade my office, plopping down in the two chairs across from my desk.

"What do you two want?" I snap.

"Wow, someone put extra asshole powder in your coffee today," Alex teases, and I shoot him a withering glare.

Unfortunately, they know me well enough to not be afraid of me, which only upsets me more because I want to be left the hell alone before I spend the day surrounded by Emma's presence.

"Just tell me why you're here, please. I'd like to get this bid placed before the end of the day so I can enjoy my weekend and not worry about work."

Drew scoffs. "Please, Ben, you always worry about work."

"Anyway," Alex says before I can respond, "we're both curious about why you were an asshole to Emma yesterday after she *finally* got us a job with Allridge."

"I don't think she earned it." Not a total lie, but it's not the whole truth. "I think Allridge took one look at her and liked what he saw."

Drew's brows furrow. "I honestly don't think he'd give a big project to someone based on looks."

"Rossi Construction has a good reputation for quality work," I grunt.

"But why would he give the job to Emma and not you?" Alex asks.

"Because she's a pretty face, obviously," I scoff.

"Tell me what you really think of me, Ben," Emma says from the hallway, which makes Alex and Drew whip around in their seats, and my head snaps up to meet stormy blue eyes filled with undiluted rage.

"Emma, I—"

"Save it," she cuts me off with a raised hand, then looks at Alex and Drew. "I didn't mean to eavesdrop, but you guys aren't exactly quiet. I don't know why Derek decided to work with me and not one of you because you're all extremely good at your jobs, but I'm not going to turn this offer down to appease some male ego. All I can do is work my ass off and prove I was the right pick for the job. If you have a problem with that, you can talk to him yourself."

With that, she storms into her office, shuts the door, and turns the glass opaque. An obvious "fuck off" to us.

Alex and Drew turn back around in their chairs and glare at me.

"What the hell are you looking at me like that for?" I grouse.

"You're the one saying misogynistic shit, dude. Do you still honestly think Emma doesn't deserve her place here after almost a month?" Alex shakes his head in exasperation.

"*You* asked *me* why Derek gave her the job!"

"*I* was trying to get *you* to admit to being an asshole. To admit Emma is good at this. Derek hasn't asked any of us because, let's face it, we're not the best at getting personal with him. Drew and I are too analytical to make the personal connections, and you have the whole 'grumpy asshole who doesn't talk' vibe. Emma balances it out. She's easy to connect with. Hell, even *Ralph* likes her, and that asshole doesn't like anyone."

"Then why didn't you just say that?" I bark at him.

"Because you don't listen," Drew states.

"Look, I think you need to learn to be nicer to her or you risk running her off." Alex runs a hand through his blonde hair.

I take a deep breath and let it out with an exasperated sigh. "Fine. I'll try to be nicer."

With a nod from both of them, they leave my office.

God, this last month has been nothing but stress. I need a fucking break. I log in to my Temptation Lounge portal to reserve a room for tomorrow night, relieved to see my preferred one is open on such short notice.

Then, once I finish the bid, I walk across the hall to Emma's office and knock on the door.

"Come in," her voice clips from behind the glass.

I slowly open the door and hear the unmistakable sound of her nails clicking away on the keyboard. It always amazes me how fast she can type. I don't know how she does it with the length of her fingernails.

When she stops typing and sees I'm the one in her doorway, she lets out a loud sigh before continuing whatever she's working on. "What do you want?"

"I came to apologize."

In a truly impressive move, she rolls her eyes without even stopping her typing but doesn't respond.

I sigh and sit down in the chair across from her, waiting for her to acknowledge me or stop typing so I can apologize.

After a minute, I decide to just start talking, "I'm sorry for saying Derek only chose you because you're a pretty face. I shouldn't have reduced you to that. It was really impressive you got the job."

One minute passes. Nothing. Just the *click click click* of the keys.

"Are you going to say anything?" I keep my voice level, even though I want to bark at her for not even acknowledging me.

God, if she were my sub still, I'd have her bent over my knee—dammit. Why do I keep thinking about that? It's been almost a month. Tomorrow night can't come soon enough. I need to cleanse my palette with someone who isn't *her*.

She finally stops her typing and looks at me. "Thank you for apologizing. You can go now."

I rear back as if she's slapped me. "Excuse me?"

"I said, you can go now."

"Are you seriously still pissed off at me? Even after I apologized? And complimented you?"

"What day is today?"

What? "September fourth?"

"Ah, well, according to my calendar, my 'give-a-fucks' are on vacation until October. So, I accept your apology, but if you think that qualifies as a compliment, you're sorely mistaken."

I truly don't understand how this woman is the same sweet submissive girl I first met at the club. It makes me wonder which side of her is the real Emma because surely they can't both be.

Right?

"Fine. It was really admirable you were able to relate to him so quickly and get him to tell you the story about his wife. He's never once mentioned his wife to any of us, so it was cool you got him to open up. I'm..." I swallow harshly. "I'm *impressed* with you. You've done a really great job this last month. You're a vital part of our team, and I'm sorry for making it seem otherwise." The words burn coming out of my mouth, not because they're a lie but because they're true.

Emma blinks, her cheeks tingeing a light shade of pink before she clears her throat. "I—uh... Thank you. It means a lot coming from you. I appreciate it."

Having reached my word quota for the day, I simply nod and leave her office.

After the disaster that was this morning with Emma, I've been holed up in my office with the glass opaque, so everyone leaves me alone. I should be done with these

invoices and the plans for the next phase of the townhome complex I'm overseeing, but I can't focus.

I hate that I hurt Emma's feelings.

A lot more than I want to admit.

I'm not used to caring about the feelings of my
coworkers, but I was an asshole.

I've just about given up on getting anything produc-
tive done when there's a knock on my door, and Papà
waltzes in like he owns the place.

I guess he does.

"Ciao, figliolo." Hello, son.

"Ciao, Papà." Hello, Father.

Papà settles in the chair across from me, giving me
thorough onceover and nodding his head.

"It's been a month since Emma was added to the
team."

"Yes, it has."

"And?" He raises an eyebrow at me.

"And I'll admit, you made a good choice."

Papà grins and claps his hands together. "I told you!
I knew she would be an asset to us. And she landed a
job with Derek. That's going to put our company on the
map for other developers."

I flinch at the mention of Derek, the guilt over saying
she only got the job because of her looks bubbles in my
stomach and makes me feel ill.

"She did well," is all I say.

"Well, she has to work harder to be taken seriously.
You haven't exactly been easy on her."

"You heard?"

"Of course I heard. And you're lucky I don't tell your
Mamá about what you said. She would slap you over

the head for being so rude to a sweet woman like Emma. We raised you better.”

I groan at the subtle threat. “I know, you and *Mamà* raised us well. I don’t know why, but Emma just gets under my skin and drives me crazy.”

“Amor senza baruffa, fa la muffa.” Love without a quarrel, it makes mold.

An Italian saying meaning disagreements keep a love alive. But this isn’t *love.*

I roll my eyes. *“Non sono innamorato di lei.” I’m not in love with her.*

“C’è una linea sottile tra amore e odio, figliolo.” There’s a fine line between love and hate, son. “You never know when you’ll cross it,” he says as he stands, knocking on my desk before he leaves.

I want to shout after him, “I’m never going to cross it!” but I don’t. Clearly, he’s delusional if he thinks I’m going to fall for a coworker. Why would he want that anyway? If things went badly, he’d lose one of us.

Sure, she’s gorgeous. She’s witty, smart, and sassy as fuck. She takes no shit from me, even though she could. She’s incredible in a scene...

I scrub a hand over my face and shake away the thoughts threatening to take over my brain again. I can’t think about her in that capacity again.

We’re coworkers. Not even friends. There’s nothing more to it, and there never will be.

CHAPTER 13

Emma

Yesterday was... odd.

I figured Ben was upset with me because of what happened with Derek, but I didn't know *why*.

Hearing him say I only got it because I'm a pretty face was a blow to my self-esteem. I've been working my ass off to be a vital part of the team and prove I belong here.

Alex and Drew came to my office before Ben came to apologize and assured me they didn't agree with him. They told me they were excited for me to work with Derek and enjoy having me here, which helped ease the sting of Ben's words a little.

Although they assured me I was doing a good job and praised my work ethic, it didn't seem to hold the same weight as when Ben said the same thing.

I hate that my brain craves the morsels of praise he tossed at me.

I hate that my body still craves the attention he gave me.

I haven't been with anyone since him, and my body is in desperate need of a release that doesn't come from a battery-operated companion.

Kiera was able to expedite my membership since I was already approved as a guest, so I'm getting dolled up to head over to The Temptation Lounge tonight to get out of my head and find someone who can help distract me for the night.

The black dress I'm wearing is tight enough that I don't need a bra, contouring to my body like a second skin. I swipe on red lipstick and put on a pair of matching red chunky heels before sliding my phone, lipstick, keys, ID, credit card, and shiny new Temptation Lounge membership card in my little clutch.

Jordan is on the couch when I come out and wolf whistles when they see what I'm wearing.

"Oh stop, you're going to make me blush," I tease.

"Someone's going to make you blush tonight, but it won't be me. You look hot! You plan on coming home later?" Jordy asks.

"I'm not sure. I have my keys though, so don't feel the need to wait up for me."

"I'll be awake for a while, probably. Moss is coming over to play some Animal Crossing and chill..." They shrug.

I narrow my eyes at them. "Is there something going on between you two?"

"What? No! We're just friends. Their roommate is having a kegger, and they don't want to be there." Jordan's pale face turns redder than a ripe tomato.

I don't believe them, but I'll let it slide for now since they clearly don't want to talk about it. "Alright. If they want to crash here, you know it's fine with me."

Jordan nods. "Of course. I'll let you know in case they're on the couch when you come home."

"Sounds good. Oh, my Uber is here. Have a good night! Love you!"

"Love you, too! Be safe!"

"You know I will!"

STRUCTION // UNDER CONSTRUCTION // UNDER CON

This may have been a bad idea.

Without the assurance of Kiera introducing me to one specific person, the task of meeting someone falls to me. Kiera asked if I wanted to be set up again, and I stupidly said no because I thought I could handle it myself.

I cannot.

When I got here, the staff took everything but my membership card and stored it in a safe locker, then gave me a selection of ribbons to choose from. Only submissives and switches—people who can be both Dominant and submissive—get ribbons, so it's easier to define roles.

Much like the traffic light system, green means someone is available to all genders and looking for a partner, purple means they're available and looking but have a specific preference, and red means someone is unavailable. Switches will wear a black ribbon in addition to their color choice.

I happily tied a green ribbon around my wrist and walked into the main room, immediately overwhelmed with the options available to me.

I've been nursing a strawberry gin and tonic at the bar for ten minutes, not making eye contact with anyone because I'm worried I'll say something stupid out of nerves, they'll run away, and I'll be the weird girl at the club.

Just when I'm thinking of calling it quits and going home, a man sidles up next to me at the bar and orders a rum and coke. I don't look up, but I see his burgundy pants and shiny brown loafers.

"Hello, I'm Ri—*R*. Sorry, I'm not used to the 'first initial only' thing yet."

I turn my head to make sure he's talking to me, giving him a small smile when I see he is. "I'm E. I'm new here, too, so I understand."

The bartender gives R his drink, and he rumbles, "Thank you," before giving his attention back to me. I scan his person for a ribbon, my stomach twisting with nerves when I don't see one. This is a Dom looking for someone.

"So, E, I'll be honest, I've been watching you for the last few minutes trying to see if you were wearing a ribbon. As soon as I saw the green, I knew I had to come over."

"I assume you like what you see, then?" I take a sip of my gin and tonic, letting the bitter alcohol warm my tummy and give me a bit more courage.

R looks like a blonde Hugh Jackman with his perfectly styled hair and clean shaven face. His smile is radiant, and he scoots his bar stool just a bit closer to me.

"I absolutely do. I'm hoping our preferences align and we can take this somewhere else."

"I'll be honest, R, this is only my second time here, and I'm still exploring some of my kinks. I do know I enjoy spanking."

Do NOT think about Ben spanking you right now, Emma. Focus on the hot guy in front of you.

"What are your hard limits, E?" he purrs, setting his hand on my exposed thigh.

"No bodily fluid or knife play. Age play isn't my thing, nor is being smacked around. And no kissing."

R tilts his head to the side, considering my answer. "So, exhibitionism and bondage aren't off the table?"

I shake my head.

"Hmmm. Good. I think I'd like to take you to an exhibition room, tie you up, and see how pretty you are when you come. Are you up for that?"

That seems a little extreme for my second time at the club. Plus, I don't know this guy. Shouldn't there be more of a conversation? I don't think—

"Actually, she's not," a deep growl comes from behind me.

R and I whip our heads to the lurker, and my breath hitches even as my stomach drops.

"I'm sorry?" R asks, still keeping his hand on my thigh.

"I said *she's not up for it,*" Ben practically snarls.

"I think she can speak for herself," R states, turning back to me. "Are you up for it, baby girl?"

I cringe at the nickname, and my eyes bounce between my coworker, whose brown eyes are burning with barely contained rage, and the man with his hand on my thigh.

I don't think I am, honestly, but Ben doesn't get to waltz in here and tell me what to do.

Outraged, I whisper, "Yes."

R smiles wickedly, and I'm already regretting it. I remind myself he's been vetted by the club, and we'll be being watched by other members. He can't hurt me if we're being watched. It'll be fine.

Oh God, will Ben watch?

I shiver at the thought, and my arousal deepens. I'm more turned on by the thought of Ben watching me than being fucked by this guy.

"Like hell you are," Ben growls at me, nostrils flaring.

"Who is this guy to you, E?" R asks.

I stare into Ben's eyes as I respond, "Just a pretty face."

Chapter 14

Ben

I was feeling excited, ready to come in here and fuck someone who isn't the curvy blonde who's invaded every sexual thought I've had for the last month.

I was ready to replace the memory of how beautifully she submitted to me and came for me with the memory of someone else.

Until I walked into the main room and saw this guy's hand on her thigh.

Apparently, my body isn't done with her, even if my brain knows it's a fucking bad idea.

I came into the conversation at the perfect time. What good Dom wants to throw someone new to kink straight into not only bondage but bondage *and* exhibition? Emma's not ready for that.

You just don't want someone else's hands on her.

I ignore the voice in my head. I'm just... looking out for her. As the first person she trusted to submit to, it's automatically my responsibility to look out for her.

You're reaching a bit there, idiota.

Stormy blue eyes, so full of defiance, bore into mine. "Just a pretty face."

I see how it is.

God, I want to fix that sassy attitude.

"Then I think it's best if you leave us to it, bro. But you're more than welcome to watch when we get in there." Blonde guy throws a wink to Emma, who only gives a forced smile in return.

My gut is telling me she's only doing this to spite me, and I won't let her suffer just because she wants to be a brat.

"Em—*E*. A word, please?"

Emma straightens her spine. "I don't have anything to say to you that hasn't already been said. I'm fine. There are plenty of other submissives to choose from, go talk to one of them."

I clench my teeth so hard I'm surprised they don't crack. I'm clearly not going to get through to her, so I try a different tactic.

Looking at the blonde, I say, "Are you aware E is inexperienced with kink?"

He furrows his brows. "I know she's still exploring her kinks, and this is her second time here—"

"And you want to tie her up in the exhibition room knowing that?" This guy is a power-hungry douche. I thought maybe Emma hadn't told him she was new, which would have given him a bit of a pass.

"She's into it!" he argues.

"Part of being a good Dominant is reading body language. Look at her right now, and tell me you think she's comfortable."

We both look over to Emma who has her hands clenched into tight little fists while her lips are turned down at the corners. My gaze snags on the green ribbon—available to anyone, *interesting*—before moving on. Her spine is rigid, and her foot is bouncing anxiously against the rung of the stool.

God, those legs need to be wrapped around my—no, Ben, focus.

The guy shrugs and throws her another flirty wink. "She looks gorgeous to me."

He doesn't see the way she cringes when he looks away, but I catch it.

"Of course she's gorgeous. But her body language is screaming she's not interested. I suggest you leave her alone before this escalates and someone does something they regret."

The douche scoffs and stands. "Whatever, man, she's not worth this kind of hassle."

Wrong. She's worth every second of it and more.

Emma relaxes the tiniest bit when he walks away, but it doesn't last long. "What the hell was that?" she whisper-shouts. "How *dare* you try to—"

"Not here," I cut her off. "If you'd like to have a conversation, follow me."

I walk away, crossing my fingers she follows me. I hear a huff of annoyance that almost brings a smile to my face before I hear the sound of her footsteps following me down the hall.

I unlock the door and motion for her to go inside. She hesitates for a moment before entering.

Then she whips around and pokes me in the chest. "What the hell is the matter with you? You can't just go around telling other people they can't fuck me, Ben."

"You clearly didn't want to go through with his plan. I was trying to help you."

"I'm a big girl, I can make my own decisions."

"But you were making the wrong one!" Why is she being so goddamn difficult about this? I was *helping* her!

"Maybe I was! But again, it's *my choice.*"

"Why would you agree to something that extreme with someone you don't know?"

Emma glares at me. "I let you spank me when I didn't know you. Some people would argue that's extreme."

Good grief. Now is not the time to get hard thinking about that.

"You and I were paired together *by your best friend* for a reason. We talked about things before we even started, and set boundaries. Were you really just going to dive right off the deep end with a guy you don't know?"

Emma's shoulders slump. "Not until you started being an alpha-hole."

Alpha-hole? "I don't know what that is, but you're telling me you were going to do it out of spite?"

"Yes."

I'm shocked speechless by her honesty, so she continues.

"I don't enjoy being treated like a child who can't make her own decisions. When you barreled into our conversation to answer for me, I was feeling petty." She shrugs a delicate shoulder.

"Emma, part of kink is making safe choices. If you want to be tied up and fucked in front of an audience, you'd need to be able to trust your partner explicitly."

"Well, the last guy I trusted ended up being my coworker who thinks I'm nothing more than a pretty face. So clearly, I can't trust my own judgment," she snaps.

Her words hit me right in the chest, making me feel like an ass.

"I think I've had enough for tonight. I'm going to go. See you Monday," Emma mutters as she heads towards the door.

I should just let her go. I should let her walk out of here and go back to my place, or better yet, find someone to fuck to ease the tension I'm feeling.

But I don't want to.

"Wait," I say, and she turns back around. "Is exhibitionism something you're really interested in?"

She gives me a sure nod.

"And bondage?"

Another nod.

I'm going to regret the next words coming out of my mouth. "Let's make a deal then."

Emma's cute nose scrunches up in confusion. "What do you mean?"

"You want to explore your kinks with someone you trust. I'm an experienced Dom. Let me help you."

She's shaking her head before I've even finished. "You're the one who was adamant about not mixing business with pleasure."

"So, we don't. We only meet at the club, and we don't discuss work while we're here. In turn, we don't discuss anything about the club at work. I can keep the two separate. Can you?"

"I think this is a bad idea."

Yeah, me too. But I can't find it in myself to care right now.

I step towards her, she steps back. We continue our little dance until I have her caged in against the wall by the door. I lean in close to her ear, never touching her. "I'm sure your body remembers how good I can make you feel, *Dulzura*. I know mine does."

"I don't understand why you'd want to help me."

"Call it a mutually beneficial agreement. You get to explore your kinks and receive pleasure in a safe space, and I get the release I need."

Emma bites on her plush bottom lip, and I, once again, have to fight the urge to pull it away with my thumb. I won't touch her until she agrees, even if I'm dying to feel her soft body again.

"Can I have some time to think about it?" she whispers.

I step back and put my hands in my pockets. "Of course. Take the week to decide. If you agree, meet me back here next Saturday night at eight o'clock. I'll have them give your card access to this room. If you don't show up, I won't bring it up again."

"Okay. Um, goodnight, Ben."

"Goodnight, Emma."

Then she leaves.

I sit in the room, trying to muster an ounce of the regret I *should* feel for wanting to fuck my coworker, but all I can find is anticipation.

I want her to say yes so badly.

I just don't want to look too closely into why.

CHAPTER 15

Emma

Benjamin Rossi is giving me fucking whiplash. The *audacity* of that man.

Ugh. Infuriating asshole.

I spent all of Sunday thinking about his offer, writing a pros and cons list and how I feel about him in my journal. Then, I spent Monday and Tuesday pretending nothing happened at the club.

Again.

Every time I close my eyes, I picture him crowding me against the wall. I swear I can still feel his breath against the side of my face as he detailed his offer. My pussy clenches every time I think about it.

Even if his offer feels a lot like exclusivity, even if it's nothing more than a sexual relationship.

I don't know if I can do exclusivity after almost four years.

I don't want to risk falling for him.

I have a list of questions I need answers to before I can agree to his deal. I know he said he doesn't want to bring the club business into work, but I need to be able to have enough time before Saturday to organize my thoughts without getting caught up in the lust of being around him.

We're in his work truck headed to a job site about an hour away, and I'm trying to muster the courage to bring it up.

Clearing my throat, I say, "I know you don't want to mix business and pleasure, and I wholeheartedly agree, but in order for me to make an educated decision, I have some questions about your... offer."

Other than the tense strain of his jaw, I wouldn't be able to tell he's affected by my words. "Go ahead and ask them."

I pull out my notebook and a black pen, turning to the section where I wrote down my questions. "We would only be meeting at the club, correct?"

"Yes."

"Okay. How often would we be meeting?"

"I think every other Saturday is good. Does that work for you?"

"I can make it work. Would this be... I mean, would you..." I take a deep breath. "Would we be able to have other sexual partners?"

Ben's jaw works while he considers his answer. "No. If we're doing this, I don't want there to be any other variants. It's safer if we don't have any other sexual partners."

"Okay." My palms start sweating at his answer. I wasn't expecting that. "What happens if one of us has an *urge* and it's not one of our assigned nights?"

Ben's arms flex as he adjusts his grip on the steering wheel, and I swear I almost drool. Why are his arms so sexy?

"If we do this, there will be rules. I will own *all* of your orgasms. If you have an *urge* outside of our designated time together, then you'll have to take a cold shower."

I gape at him. There's no way he wants me to go *two weeks* at a time without an orgasm. I haven't gone that long without an orgasm since I had a mono flare up three years ago. "You won't know if I get off if you aren't there," I argue.

"That's true, but I think you like being a good girl and following directions, especially if the reward is worth it." He glances over, and I swear I see a flash of heat in his espresso eyes. "Besides, your fingers or a toy wouldn't be nearly as satisfying as what I can do to you."

I squeeze my legs together. My slutty vagina agrees. She certainly remembers what he's capable of, and she gives a wistful sigh at the memory while urging me to say yes.

"Okay, um, I think that's all of my questions." It's not, but I don't want to talk about this anymore. I shut my notebook and slide it back into my bag.

"Eight o'clock Saturday."

As if I could forget.

By Thursday morning I knew I was going to go.

I could say it's only because I'm curious about kink and want to explore that side of myself, but it's not the whole truth.

Honestly, as much as the exclusivity aspect of it scares the living shit out of me because I'm scared I'll get attached, I'm tired of having to find new people to fuck.

The routine of every other Saturday will be helpful and knowing I can trust Ben with my body gives me peace of mind.

I really hope my heart can stay the fuck out of it, especially because I'll still see him at the office.

I arrive at the club at seven forty-five so I have ample time to psych myself up for what's to come. This time, I put a red ribbon around my wrist. I don't go to the bar because I want to have my mind clear for what's about to happen.

When I get to the door of the room I've been in twice already, I take a deep breath before scanning my card. It flashes green, and I hesitantly poke my head in before stepping inside and scanning the empty room.

My heart sinks, and anxiety threatens to swallow me whole.

Ben's not here yet.

Maybe he's not coming at all. Maybe he's changed his mind and doesn't want to be stuck with me.

He said eight o'clock. He still has a few minutes.

I sit on the chaise, and memories of the last time I was sitting here assault me, and my lust flares. I squeeze my thighs together and try to relieve the arousal quickly working its way through my bloodstream, gathering at my clit, but it doesn't help.

It's been too long since I got laid.

The door *clicks* and opens. Ben's sculpted body filling the doorway kicks my arousal up by ten degrees.

He lets the door close softly behind him before he addresses me, "You came."

I stand quickly, though I don't know why. "I did."

Ben nods. "I wasn't sure if you would."

I swallow. "I wasn't either."

"What convinced you?"

Lust. Desire. The overwhelming need to please you even though I don't really understand it.

I don't say that, obviously. That would be embarrassing. "I don't want to have to find someone new to show me the ropes. So to speak."

I rarely see Ben smile at work, but the corners of his mouth tip up into a lecherous grin full of dirty promises. "I'll definitely show you the ropes. But later. It's been a while, and I think we need to go over the rules again."

I roll my eyes. "I remember the rules."

Ben raises an eyebrow at me. "Did you just roll your eyes at me?"

There's no point in lying, so I raise my chin defiantly. "Yes, Sir."

Ben prowls towards me like a panther sneaking up on its prey. "The first time we were here you were so sweet. So submissive. So eager to please. What's changed, *Dulzura?*"

God, that nickname. I want to know what it means, but I don't dare ask and ruin the mystery.

"I didn't know you as well back then," I admit, even though it's mostly a lie.

The truth of the matter is the first time, I immediately felt safe with Ben. I felt like I could give up control to him, especially since Kiera's the one who paired us. I didn't feel like I had to present myself as a confident, bubbly person. I could just... let go and let him make the rules.

Now, I feel like I'm at war with myself because outside of this room, I'm one person, and in here, I'm another. But I can't tell Ben that because what if he thinks I'm not being authentic? Both sides of my personality are true to who I am, even if sometimes I have to force the happy side.

Ben tsks. "I don't think so, Emma. Try again. The truth this time." He's right in front of me now. Every breath I take has my breasts brushing against his broad chest, and he's staring into my eyes like he's trying to solve a puzzle.

I blink and look away, the intensity of his stare too much to handle right now.

"This doesn't work without trust."

"If I promise to not sass you again, promise to just follow your directions, can we just move on from the topic? *Please*?" I beg, crossing my arms over my chest.

Ben grips my chin between his pointer finger and thumb and tilts my head, so I'm forced to look into his chocolatey brown eyes. They seem softer than they were a moment ago, but I don't trust the warmth will stay.

"I see this is hard for you, so I'll let it go."

I let out a breath of relief.

"For now."

I scowl at him, and he releases my chin with a quiet chuckle.

"Do you remember your safe words?"

"Red for stop, yellow for slow down, green for good to go," I recite. I haven't looked at stoplights the same since our first time.

"Good. Are you on birth control?"

"Yes. I have an IUD. I can give you proof with medical records if you need it."

Ben shakes his head. "I trust you."

Those three words are like a punch in the gut. I like that he trusts me, but a small part of me wonders why he trusts me here but not in the office.

This has nothing to do with work. He's your Dom right now, not your coworker.

In the next breath he commands, "Take off your dress."

Let the scene begin, I guess.

CHAPTER 16

Ben

Emma doesn't hesitate to follow my command, quickly unzipping the side zipper and shimmying her pretty black dress down her curvy body before it pools at her heeled feet, and she steps out of it.

My breath catches at the sight of the delicate emerald green lingerie that was hidden beneath her clothing. It looks stunning against her skin. The cups of the bra are almost translucent, giving me a delicious view of her perfectly peaked dusty rose nipples. Her panties are cut high on her hips, but the panel covering her pink pussy is made of a sheer fabric, giving me a teasing look.

I think green might be my new favorite color. Right after the blue of her eyes.

I circle her while she stands there, nearly groaning at the sight of the thong disappearing between her glorious ass cheeks.

I want to rip off the panties and devour her.

I trace the delicate strap of the bra over her shoulder. "This is a lovely set, *Dulzura,* did you wear it just for me?"

"Yes, Sir."

I smile at the honorific seamlessly flowing from her mouth.

"I would hate to ruin it by ripping it off of you." Her breath hitches with arousal at the threat, and I make a mental note of it for later. "So, let's remove it."

I nimbly unclasp the bra, letting the garment fall away, and Emma removes it further, holding onto one strap so it dangles in front of her. I take the bra from her, pick up her dress from the floor, fold everything neatly, and place them on one of the cabinets in the room.

When I'm standing in front of her again, I lift her chin, wanting to look in her eyes.

"Tell me, *Dulzura,* have you played with your pretty cunt since our last scene?"

"Yes, Sir." She tries to look at the ground, but I don't let her.

"Has anyone else touched you since our last session?" I know she's been tested again, as is customary for new members, but I need to know if anyone else has touched what's mine.

Mine. Every other Saturday.

"N-no, Sir."

Possessiveness mixed with pride swirls in my stomach, and my cock hardens further in my slacks. I like it way more than I should that she hasn't been with anyone since our last session. The egotistical part of me wants to believe it's because she was so satisfied with me no one else could compare.

The logical part of me knows it's more likely she hasn't had the time since she's been busy with her new job.

"Good. From now on, no one else touches *my* pussy. That includes you. I will decide when you get pleasure. I will decide when you come. Understood?"

"Understood, Sir."

"Good girl." She preens at the praise. "Take off your panties and kneel on the bed."

Emma is quick to follow my command, divesting her panties, leaving them with her other garments before climbing on the bed and kneeling with her hands in her lap.

It's a heady thing, having this beautiful woman listening to my every command.

I slowly undress myself, loving how her ocean blue eyes never stray from me. She takes in every inch of my skin like she's studying a piece of art and doesn't want to miss a single detail. Her eyes roam my chest and arms, then wander down to my legs as I take off my pants.

Her eyes hungrily lock in on my stiff length tenting my underwear, and they flash with disappointment when I don't take them off.

"Awe, does my *Dulzura* want my cock?"

Emma's eyes shoot up to meet mine, a delicious blush painting her cheeks. "Yes, Sir. I would really like to taste it."

Oh, fuck me.

I cup her cheek and gently push a lock of curly hair behind her ear. "I want that too, *Dulzura*, but I need to taste you first. I've been craving the taste of you for weeks."

I reluctantly step away from the gorgeous woman on the bed and walk to the cabinet I know holds what I need.

I remove the item from the drawer, walk back to the bed, and hold it in front of Emma. "You wanted me to show you the ropes. This isn't rope, but it is a restraint. I'm going to tie your hands above your head. What's your color?"

Emma eyes the satin ties and then the bed frame before answering with a breathy, "Green, Sir."

"Lay down, hands above your head."

She lays against the soft sheets and puts her wrists together before raising them above her head towards the headboard.

I climb on the bed and straddle her hips, loving the feel of her skin against mine. I loop the satin ties around her wrists before tying them securely to the headboard. I have her flex her hands to make sure the ties aren't cutting off her circulation. Satisfied that she's secure but not in danger, I ask her color again. When her answer is green, I descend down her body with my mouth.

I'm about to lean in and kiss her on the mouth but remember her limit when she sucks in a harsh breath. I don't want to think too much about why I hate it.

I change my course of direction and place a gentle kiss on the sensitive spot where her neck meets her shoulder, towing the line of her boundary. Her scent assaults me. I smell her perfume every day at the office, but being this close is intoxicating.

I gently bite the spot where I left a kiss, and she whimpers, so I continue the pattern. I kiss and bite and lick my way down to her ample tits. I didn't get to play with them last time, so I take my time swirling my tongue around one rosy nipple, working it into a stiff point before I move to the other one.

Emma arches her back into my touch, and when I look up from her breast, I notice her mouth clamped firmly shut. That won't do, I want to hear her pretty sounds.

"I want to hear your moans, *Dulzura*. Don't keep them from me," I say right before I bite down on her nipple, drawing a harsh breath and wanton sound from her lips.

"That's right, honey. I love hearing how much you love it."

I continue my path down her body, nipping and biting and licking. When I settle between her legs, lavishing her thighs with bites and kisses, I feel the heat from her core and swear I can smell her arousal.

I spread her legs with my shoulders, getting the first glimpse of her pussy after a month and growl with the need coursing through me. Not wanting to wait any longer, I dive right in, licking straight up her center. It draws the sweetest moan from her mouth, and her body jerks as she fights against the restraints.

I flick her hard little clit with my tongue, groaning when her thighs tense around my head.

"Are you going to come, honey?" I mumble into her wet pussy.

"Please, Sir. Can I?"

"Mmm, I love when you beg. You may come as many times as you want until I'm done with you. You don't have to ask permission."

Maybe I should be going harder on her, be more demanding and withhold her pleasure, but I can't find it in me to do that right now. The urge to taste the evidence of what I do to her is too strong to resist.

As soon as my tongue is back on her and I slip two fingers inside her tight cunt, she detonates, nearly crushing my skull with her thighs.

I work her through her orgasm but don't let up on my ministrations with my fingers, curling my fingers to find the spot that will surely make her see stars. I want to see if she'll soak my face again.

"Please, I can't take it anymore," she whimpers, writhing against the restraints, but I don't stop.

"You can, and you will. I decide when you've had enough. I want you to come all over my face, *Dulzura*."

I add a third finger, pumping rapidly inside her while bringing my thumb to her clit. Within seconds, she cries out, her pussy clamps around my fingers, and a rush of warm liquid splashes across my face, her thighs, and the bed.

"That's it, good fucking girl," I growl, slowing my fingers as she comes down.

I place a gentle kiss to her clit before I kneel on the bed watching as her chest heaves, loving the flush of arousal covering her chest and face. A sheen of sweat covers her forehead, and a few strands of hair stick to the dewy skin.

I untie the restraints and rub at her wrists to make sure the blood is flowing all while fighting the urge to kiss her.

I want her to taste herself on my lips. I want her to know how fucking good she tastes. I'm dying to know what that sassy mouth feels like when she submits to mine.

I'll just have to settle for feeling those plush lips around my cock.

I hop off the bed and quickly take off my boxer briefs, and her eyes widen as my cock juts out from my body.

That's right, honey. This is all for you.

"Are you ready to taste me, *Dulzura?*"

"*Please*, Sir."

"Come here and get on your knees."

She eagerly climbs off the bed and kneels in front of me, looking up at me through long dark lashes. I hold the base of my cock and rub the head against her pretty pink lips, marking her with the precum beaded at the tip.

"Open your mouth, honey. Tongue out."

She eagerly listens, and I tap the fat head on her tongue. Her eyes flutter at the contact, like she's been dying to taste me.

"Show me how eager you are to please me, *Dulzura.*" I let go of my cock, and Emma's small hands take the place of mine as she eagerly licks from the base to the tip before swirling her tongue around the head, collecting the small bead of precum in the slit.

I nearly fall to my knees as she takes me deep into the wet heat of her mouth and sucks. I gather her hair into a ponytail and grip the curly strands, giving an experimental thrust so my cock hits the back of her throat.

When she gags, I pull out and ask, "What's your color, honey?"

"Green, Sir."

Satisfied with her answer, and without giving her any warning, I thrust back into her mouth, hitting the back of her throat until she gags again. She quickly recovers, swallowing around me and continues to give me the best blow job of my fucking life.

After a minute, I know I'm going to blow my load, but I don't want to—not yet.

I pull out, and she pouts at the loss, causing me to chuckle.

"Such a cock hungry slut. Don't worry, honey, I just don't want to come in your mouth today. I want to come in that tight pussy. Up on the bed. All fours."

Emma scrambles up on the bed presenting me with her beautiful ass. I crawl up behind her and knead the creamy globes, admiring the way they look beneath my hands.

Unable to resist, I pull my hand back and give the right cheek a gentle spank. Emma gasps and rocks back into my hand.

God, I love how responsive she is.

"Please, Sir, fuck me. I need to feel you," she whimpers.

"So needy, *Dulzura*. But since you said please..." I notch the head of my cock at her entrance and push inside with one brutal thrust.

As her tightness envelopes me, I swear my vision blurs from the pleasure. No one has ever felt as good as she does, and I fear when this is all over, I'll be craving the feeling of her for the rest of my life.

Emma moans when I'm fully seated inside, and I nearly come from the hot vice-like grip of her squeezing my length. I'm not even moving, but I swear I'm going to bust.

"Fuck, *Dulzura*. Your pussy is pure heaven."

Your pussy feels like it was made specifically to fit my cock. I'll never get enough.

"I'm going to fuck you hard now, *Dulzura*," I say in warning before I gather her hair and wrap it around my fist. I pull all the way out and plunge back into her—deep.

Emma moans in pure pleasure as I set a brutal pace, fucking into her with such force her ass jiggles with every thrust. I feel almost out of control with lust—with *need*. The need to feel her come on my cock, the need to feel her pulse around me. The need to *claim* her.

I groan when she starts meeting me thrust for thrust, and I don't hold myself back from spanking her again as I tug her back by her hair.

Emma's pussy pulses around my cock as she screams her release, and the vice grip of her pussy forces my own orgasm out of me.

As I release ropes of cum into her tight cunt, I groan her name.

Not honey or *Dulzura*, but her actual name.

What is she doing to me?

When her orgasm subsides, I reluctantly pull out, immediately mourning the loss, and walk to the small bathroom to gather some wipes to clean her up.

When I come back and see my seed dripping out of her swollen pussy, my brain short circuits, and a primal possessive part of me wants to shove it back inside her where it belongs.

Mine.

I mentally punch those thoughts away. I've never had a breeding kink, and I won't let this woman change that. Emma is a temporary vice, a fuck buddy for a limited time. Once she's learned all she can from me, she'll move on to someone else.

That's the way it has to be.

Chapter 17

Emma

After Ben cleaned me up on Saturday, he made me drink a small bottle of water while we debriefed about the scene.

On the outside, I was—hopefully—the picture of nonchalance and a care-free attitude, but on the inside I was freaking the fuck out.

I loved every single thing we did, and I had to clamp my mouth shut to keep from begging him to do it again.

I don't know how I'm supposed to go two weeks without an orgasm, especially since every time I think about what we did, my vagina perks up and begs to be stretched by Ben's massive cock.

I could barely breathe while giving him a blow job, but my desire to pleasure him was greater than my desire for air.

Death by blow job wouldn't be the worst way to go, especially if it's Ben's cock in my mouth.

After I assured him everything was good and I wanted to do it again, we confirmed our next session, and he sent me home in an Uber.

Moss wasn't at my place when I got home, but Jordy was still awake. They peppered me with questions about my night, and I was as vague as possible while still trying to be truthful.

Today, I'm spiraling. I don't know how I'm supposed to pretend nothing happened with Ben at work, and I don't know how to keep myself from getting attached to him when we inevitably fuck again.

Dammit. This is why you only hook up with strangers and only once, I think angrily as I pull out all the clothes from my closet to reorganize them.

I'm halfway through when Jordy knocks on my door, comes in, and sits on the bed.

"Are you going to tell me what's got you in an organizing tizzy?" they ask, scanning my room.

I scoff. "I'm just switching out my summer clothes for fall clothes. I'm not in a *tizzy*."

"Mimi, you forget I've known you for twenty-three years, and we've lived together for eight of those. You're seriously going to tell me you're not stressing about something?"

Ugh. They only call me "Mimi" when they sense I'm in emotional distress or if they're proud of me. Sometimes I really hate that my lifelong best friend is also a therapist. They're too perceptive. They know too much about me and what I'm like when I'm keeping something inside for too long. Though they're always helpful, I can't rely solely on them for emotional support. I don't want them to get burnt out from my issues and then hate me for it.

"I'm just overwhelmed with work. That big developer guy said his plans for the project are almost done, and it'll be my first solo project at Rossi. I'm terrified I'm going to mess it up." It's only partially true. I *am* nervous about Derek's project, but I also haven't told anyone I'm seeing Ben. I don't want them to think less of me because I'm fucking a coworker.

Kiera probably has suspicions since she works at the club, but I don't think she'd say anything to anyone.

Jordan narrows their hazel eyes at me. "Is that all that's going on? Did something happen at the club last night you didn't tell me about?"

I stop rifling through my clothes and sigh. "I don't want you to judge me."

They crawl off the bed to join me on the floor. "When have I ever judged you? You've been so supportive and haven't judged me about anything. Let me be here for you, please."

"I'mseeingBenandwefuckattheclub," I rush out in one breath.

"One more time, but slower."

"I'm seeing Ben. We fuck at the club."

Jordy's eyebrows practically disappear into their hairline. "You're *seeing* Ben? Like, in an exclusive way?"

"No. Kind of? We're not dating, it's just sex. He's helping me explore my kinks and stuff." *And totally rocking my world, ruining me for anyone else.*

"I don't think I've seen you with the same person more than once since... well, since Trinity."

I blanch at the sound of my ex's name. I don't hold any ill will towards her, but she's not someone I actively want to think or talk about.

Jordy doesn't know the full extent of what Trinity said to me when she ended things, no one does. I don't need their pitying looks or reassurances that she's wrong. I just want to move on and never experience heartbreak again. *Easy peasy.*

"Well, I promised myself I'd stop getting attached to people after Trinity so I wouldn't get my heart broken. It's worked thus far." Kind of. There was that one girl three years ago I spent a whole night with. We talked and fucked, and by the end of it, I had to force myself to leave her hotel room while she was asleep to make a clean getaway.

Then, there was the guy I met at a party last year who didn't want to fuck until we played twenty questions. He was so freaking sweet and genuine, and it was awful to watch the hope fall from his face after we did the deed and I said I had to go. It felt like I was kicking a puppy.

"That's why you haven't had a serious relationship since her? Emma, you—"

"Please, JoJo. I can't get into it. I'm trying to get my heart on the same page with my brain so we don't get too far into this with Ben. I've never had to see the person I've hooked up with day in and day out, so this is just throwing me for a loop."

Jordan frowns, seemingly unhappy with that answer. "Okay. Just know I'm here for you."

"I know. Thank you."

They wrap me in a hug, and my stomach bubbles with guilt over not being totally honest with them.

But at the same time, how can I? I don't need to be a burden for Jordan to carry. They have enough going on. Working exclusively with LGBTQ+ youth—mostly trans kids—takes a lot out of them emotionally. They're a key-note speaker for an upcoming convention, too. They need to focus on that, not my drama.

They leave me to finish my organizing, so I put on my headphones and blast my "Bad Bitch" playlist. No love songs allowed.

Everything is going to be just fine so long as I can pretend nothing's changed between me and Ben.

CHAPTER 18

Ben

Emma's acting like nothing's changed between us, and it's driving me *insane.*

It shouldn't, really. I should be ecstatic that over the last ten days she's been bold and sunshiney and treating me the same as she did before, but I find I don't like it.

Every time she says something sassy to me, I want to bend her over my knee and spank her ass red or shove my cock in her mouth.

Every time she gives her dazzling smile to another man, I want to wrap my arms around her waist and growl she's *mine.*

Every time someone else makes her laugh, I want to grab her by the back of the neck and cover her mouth with mine so I can taste the sound.

I'm going fucking *pazzo. Loco. Crazy.*

I've never had an issue detaching myself from a sub before. Then again, I've never had to spend every day with one and pretend I haven't been balls deep in her pussy.

That's all it is. Sexual frustration from being stuck in close proximity to her.

Two weeks is too fucking long to go without her.

Especially since we spend most of our time in the truck heading from one job site to another to make sure work is getting completed on schedule. September and October are our busiest months for asphalt paving because the rain makes it more difficult between November and March. But in order for the asphalt crew to do their job, the pipe crews have to install the water lines and other utilities first. The last thing we want is for a pipe to be laid wrong or missed and have to go back and redo the asphalt. That could put us months behind.

We're headed to an apartment complex where the paving process is set to begin in a few days when Emma's phone rings.

"Hello?"

I can't hear the other side of the conversation, but the voice sounds like a man.

"Oh! Hello, Derek. Yes, it's good to hear from you." She pauses to listen. "Mmhmm. As soon as you send me the plans I can get you an estimate for the cost of the job."

My shoulders relax a little at the mention of the developer, it's just a business call.

"Oh, no, I'm not busy that Saturday. What's the occasion?"

Never mind. Not just business.

Is this fucker—who gushed about his wife—seriously asking Emma on a date? She shouldn't be dating a client, let alone a married one. But it's not my business. It better not interfere with our plans. I don't think I can go another two fucking weeks with my hand.

I wonder if Emma's been following the rules or if she's tried to play with her pretty pussy. I'd love to punish her for breaking the rules... maybe with the flogger this time.

Great, now I'm hard.

"Perfect! I'll let the rest of the Rossi team know. We're so grateful you thought to include us." There's a pause before she says, "Of course, we'll see you then, Derek. Have a good day."

Emma ends the call and puts the phone back in her purse.

"What was that about?" I ask.

"Oh, the plans for Derek's next complex will be done by the end of the week. I'm nervous to start on a solo project. I don't want to mess it up."

Something mushy pokes the hard wall around my heart. "You're going to do great, Emma. Besides, no one's just going to throw you in the deep end. If you need help, we're here for you. We're a team here."

Emma blinks and clears her throat, rubbing her palms down her thighs. "Um, thank you. He also invited the Rossi team to a party he's hosting to celebrate the ten-year anniversary of Allridge Development. It's next Saturday at The Hotel Del Coronado. Black tie. Everyone is allowed a plus one."

Well, at least it doesn't interfere with our session *this* Saturday.

"Are you planning on going?" I refuse to ask if she's bringing a plus one. I have to believe she won't.

"Of course. I'll probably bring Jordan. What about you?"

Who the fuck is Jordan?

"Black tie events aren't my thing."

"You'd look delectable in a tux." She sighs then straightens. "Sorry. That was supposed to be an inside thought."

I keep my face neutral, even though I'm practically puffing my chest. At least now I know she's not *entirely* unaffected by me.

"My dad will probably talk me into going to show a united front. I hate it though. The schmoozing is the worst part of this job." I don't know why I keep talking. I don't need to tell her this. She doesn't need to know anything more than what I like in a scene.

"I never would have guessed," she deadpans.

"What's that supposed to mean?"

"You're not exactly 'Mr. Personable.' Most of the sales guys are scared of you; that's why they usually only ask for Alex, Drew, or me. Same with the crews. You have a really good work ethic, have innovative ideas, and you're great at planning, but you don't take the time to get to know people."

"I'm here to do a job, not—"

"Be friends. I know. But what's the worst thing that could happen if you showed you were human and not a robot?"

I don't know why I find it hard to connect with people. My parents are both extremely friendly, it's what makes my dad a good businessman. My siblings have no problem charming people. They thrive off of attention and interacting with people, but I'm the opposite. An hour into a company party and I want to crawl out of my skin. Ten minutes with a salesman and I start getting irritated because I have work to do, I can't be chatting the day away. If I need their services, I'll give them a call.

I prefer to focus on the job. Maybe because I saw how hard my dad worked to build this company with my Nono, and I don't want it to fail. Schmoozing may be an important part of the job, but the work part is what keeps the business afloat. If everyone only focused on connections, then the work wouldn't get done.

Instead of answering her seriously, I break my rules and give her a suggestive smile. "You know plenty well how *not* robotic I am, honey."

Emma's jaw literally drops open, and she sputters, "You—you broke your own rule! We're at work!"

I shrug. "I'm the one who made the rule, I can break it without punishment. Besides, we're in the truck, which doesn't count."

She scoffs but remains quiet, her cheeks flushing as her thighs squeeze together.

Fantastic, now I'm thinking about pulling the truck over and making her ride me right here in the driver's seat.

Saturday can't come soon enough.

CHAPTER 19

Emma

I'm running late, and Ben's not going to be happy when I finally make it to the club.

I hope he spanks me as my punishment.

God, I'm so mad at him though. How *dare* he break his own rule by talking about our arrangement at work? I was so shocked I couldn't think of a single witty thing to say back.

The rest of the day he acted like nothing ever happened, reverting to his grumpy self. I don't understand why he's so sweet and talkative with me at the club but barely says a word at work.

I guess it's the same reason I'm bubbly and talkative at work but submit to him. Two sides of our personalities. I want to see more of the club side of him. I want to know why he's so grumpy all the time.

That's girlfriend territory, Emma. Stop it.

When I finally get to the club, I rush to our room and unlock the door with my card.

Ben is sitting in the armchair, and his head whips up towards me when I step inside.

He looks extra mad. His shoulders are tight and his jaw clenched. He stands abruptly and crosses his arms over his broad chest, showcasing the muscles I don't get to drool over daily.

"You're late," he barks.

I slowly walk towards him. "I'm sorry. Traffic was bad, and Jordan needed to—"

"I don't care what *Jordan* needs. When we set a time, I expect you to show up. Or at least let me know if you're going to be late."

"I texted you twenty minutes ago."

"I was already here, so I didn't get it."

Right.

"I'll be on time next time."

"You better, or today's punishment will seem like a piece of cake." His tone turns dark with dirty promise, and I suppress a shiver. "Take off your clothes and shoes, *Dulzura.* No more talking unless I ask you a direct question. Understood?"

"Yes, Sir," I answer as I slip off my dress, underwear, and shoes then place them neatly on the cabinet while I wait for my next instructions. The urge to keep apologizing is strong, but I already know I'm in for a punishment, so I keep my mouth shut as I stand there, unsure where to even look.

Ben circles me slowly, trailing a single finger up my right arm, across my shoulders, and down my left before tugging me back into him by my hips. He's already hard, and I feel a bit proud my naked body does this to him. *I make him hard.* With all my jiggly bits and stretch marks.

His hot breath tickles my ear as he whispers, "I've been dying to touch you for the last two weeks." He trails his hands up my sides to cup my breasts and tease my nipples with his thumbs. I lay my head back against his chest and nearly sigh with relief at having his hands on me. "Do you know how difficult it is to watch you strut around the office in your pretty little outfits and not be able to put my hands on you?"

He pinches my nipple, and I gasp. My body is on fire. I'm so pent up from the last two weeks one strong breeze across my clit would have me coming.

"I asked you a question, *Dulzura*."

Huh? Oh, right.

"I can imagine it was hard, Sir."

Ben gives a mocking chuckle. "I don't think you can imagine how *hard* it was." He grinds his erect cock into my back, and my pulse picks up speed.

I *can* imagine, actually. The number of times I've had to avert my gaze from this god-like man so I wouldn't soak my panties is actually embarrassing. The urge to touch him, kneel at his feet and beg for him to touch *me* was so strong, I almost gave in.

He didn't ask me a direct question, so I don't respond. He releases my breasts to slide his hands down my belly and slips one finger between my legs, teasing my entrance. I arch into his touch, needing more.

"Such a needy little slut for me," he growls. "Tell me the truth, *Dulzura*. Did you play with *my* pussy while we were apart?"

I *tried* to. I laid in bed replaying every delicious memory of our first two times and got so turned on I had to slip my fingers underneath my pajamas. When I couldn't with my fingers, I tried my trusty bullet vibrator. I can usually make myself come pretty fast, so when ten minutes passed and I still hadn't found relief, I gave up and cursed Ben.

I swallow harshly, not wanting to admit to my failed attempt at self-pleasure, but I don't want to lie to him about it either. "I—I tried to, Sir."

Ben removes himself completely from my body, and I let out an embarrassingly needy whimper at the loss. He walks around me, coming to stand right in front of me, tipping my chin up so I'm forced to stare into his coffee-colored eyes.

"What do you mean you *tried*?"

"I didn't successfully... ya know... *finish*, Sir."

"But you touched yourself?"

"Yes, Sir."

Ben tsks and cups the side of my face, his tone deceptively sweet for the words that come out. "Poor *Dulzura* couldn't make herself come. Desperate and needy, writhing around in her bed with no relief. What will I do to punish you for being defiant?"

"I think me not coming on my own is punishment enough, Sir." I know it won't work. He'll never let me off the hook for disobeying.

Ben tips his head back and gives a husky laugh. A real one, loud and guttural. It sounds a bit rusty, like he hasn't laughed in a really long time, and it sends goosebumps skittering across my body.

"Oh, honey. Nice try. You didn't follow the rules, so now I get to punish you. On the bed. Prop yourself up against the headboard."

I scurry over to the bed, earning a spank on the ass from Ben as I pass him. I get into position and watch as he slowly strips down to just his black boxer briefs. I allow my eyes to greedily take in everything I haven't been able to see at work. The dark hair on his chest, the thickness of his thighs, the hard planes of his chiseled stomach.

He really is a god among men.

Ben walks over to a cabinet and retrieves some things I can't see, then comes and stands at the end of the bed.

"Since you were so impatient you broke my rule, I want you to spread your legs and show me how you touched yourself."

When I don't immediately follow his command, he sighs. "I'm giving you permission to touch yourself, *Dulzura*. So be a good girl, spread your legs, and show me your pussy. Show me how you rode your fingers."

"I—" I clamp my mouth shut since I wasn't asked a question.

"You... what?" he prompts.

"I didn't use my fingers, Sir." Embarrassment makes my whole body heat up. How pathetic is it that I couldn't even get off on a *toy?*

Ben shakes his head. "You mean to tell me you used a toy, and you couldn't get yourself off? Were you so desperate for my cock your pathetic little toy didn't do the job?"

"Yes, Sir."

"Well, there's no toy here tonight. If you're a good girl and show me what a desperate slut you are, maybe I'll give you my cock. But you have to earn it. Now, spread them."

I gulp but slowly spread my legs. I've never touched myself in front of someone before. Sometimes the religious guilt still creeps in when I'm masturbating and ruins the mood, which is why I usually seek out partners.

Touching myself in front of Ben feels too intimate, too embarrassing. But I guess that's why this is a punishment. I already know I won't get myself to an orgasm, even though I'm so pent up. I want his hands. His mouth. His cock. I want *him* to bring me pleasure.

Another reason this is a punishment. He's depriving me of his touch because I broke the rules.

Bringing my hand down to my clit, I start rubbing in harsh circles, wanting to orgasm before he tells me to stop.

I don't get very far before he barks, "Stop."

Chapter 20

Ben

Emma's fingers stop, and she pouts but doesn't protest.

God, I'm filled with so many warring emotions. I thought she wasn't going to show tonight. I sat here, anxiety and rage swirling around me like a dark cloud, trying to figure out how I was supposed to go on at work like nothing was happening if she decided she was already done with our deal.

I was... *disappointed* when she was late. Her reasoning made sense, traffic is unpredictable, but then she mentioned *Jordan,* and I was irritated. Jordan, who I picture as a handsome man. Jordan, who probably wants to fuck Emma as badly as I do. Jordan, her roommate, who probably knows all the intimate details of Emma's life.

Details I'll never learn because she's made it clear this is temporary.

I want it to be temporary.

Right. Sure. Keep telling yourself that.

I want to put her over my knee and spank her ass until it hurts to sit for a week. I want to mark her skin so *Jordan* knows she's claimed, at least for the time being.

Shit, am I jealous?

No, I'm just... horny. Pent up from not being able to fuck for two weeks. That's all this is. Pent up sexual frustration.

Emma still sits spread open, showing me just how wet she is while she waits for my next instructions.

"Is that how you touch yourself when you're alone, *Dulzura?*"

"N-no, Sir."

"Hmm. I didn't think so. Are you just trying to get yourself to come fast so your punishment is over?"

Her shoulders slump at being caught. "Yes, Sir."

"That's not what good girls do, *Dulzura.* Don't you want to be a good girl for me?"

Her eyelids droop. "Yes, Sir, I want to be your good girl."

Music to my fucking ears.

"Then show me how you play with yourself."

She bites her lips and closes her eyes. She looks... nervous. Which isn't an emotion I'm used to seeing from her. I crawl onto the bed and sit cross-legged in front of her without touching her.

"Do you want me to tell you what to do?"

"Please, Sir."

"Start with teasing around your clit, honey. Take your pointer finger and tease yourself."

Emma hesitantly follows my command, bringing a perfectly manicured finger down to tease around her clit.

"Good girl, now use two fingers and slowly push them inside your tight hole. Get them nice and wet. Let me hear how sloppy your greedy little cunt gets for me."

She furrows her brows but does as she's told, gasping as she puts her pointer and middle finger inside herself.

I give my cock a squeeze through my underwear. I want to sink myself into her so damn badly, but I have to wait. "Mmm. Such a wet, needy pussy. Desperate to be filled. Now that your fingers are wet, pull them out and bring them to your clit."

She whimpers as she pulls her fingers out and touches them to her clit, moaning as she applies pressure.

"Does that feel good, *Dulzura*?"

"Yes, Sir," she moans, slowly increasing the speed.

"Use your other hand, middle and ring finger, and slip them inside your pussy, but keep teasing your clit."

God, I love how well she listens. How responsive she is.

"Pump those fingers, honey. Pretend they're mine fucking you."

She whimpers again, and I know she's wishing they really were mine. She bucks her hips when she picks up speed, and it takes every ounce of willpower in me not to bat her hands out of the way and take over.

When her breathing speeds up and her pussy clenches around her fingers, I tell her to stop.

If looks could kill, I'd be a dead man.

"Start again, slowly. You're not allowed to come until I say so."

I bring her to the edge and make her stop two more times. On the fourth time, I wait until she starts again before I shuffle off the bed so I can grab the paddle off the floor.

Emma's eyes widen when she sees the red oak paddle in my hand, and I check for any fear or anxiety, but I only find hesitant excitement. Curiosity.

This room doesn't have a spanking bench, but the bed is the perfect height to bend Emma over and deliver the remainder of her punishment.

"Remove your fingers." She listens immediately. "Good girl, come here."

She scoots to the edge of the bed and plants her feet on the floor before coming to stand directly in front of me. Her eyes keep trailing to the paddle in my hand, interest igniting in her eyes.

"Now, it's time for the remainder of your punishment. I'm going to spank you a total of twenty times. Ten for being late and ten for touching yourself without permission. I'll give you the first ten with my hand, then the last with the paddle."

I instruct her to bend over the bed so her ass is in the air, but she can still grip the sheets if she needs to. When she gets into position and I step back, I groan at the sight of her glorious backside and glistening pussy bared to me.

"Count them out loud for me, honey."

I rub her ass to warm her up and spank her right cheek with no warning, emitting a gasp from her as she counts.

The sight of my handprint on her makes me fucking feral. It looks too good, my hand marking her body.

I pick up my pace on the next four, increasing the pressure each time so when I use the paddle, she's not as shocked. Emma grows increasingly wet with each spank, and on the eighth spank, I angle my hand so it hits the bottom of her ass and her pussy.

She lets out a loud yelp before she counts the number.

By the time I get to ten, I'm tempted to end the punishment here so I can fuck her.

Until I hear her hiccup and take in a shuddering breath.

When I see her face, there are tears streaming down her cheeks.

"Emma? What's your color, *Dulzura*?" I ask quietly. I've had subs cry during impact play before. Usually, it's a cathartic release. They have a safe place to cry, and they know I won't judge them. For some of them, it's even been their goal. Other times, it's been a sign we need to pause the scene.

But Emma's tears gut me. If she had tears running down her face while choking on my cock, that's one thing, but I *never* want to bring her pain to the point of tears. Only pleasure.

"G-green, Sir. I-I'm sorry. I don't know why I'm crying."

I rub a hand down her back to soothe her. "No need to apologize, honey. Are you sure your color is green? We can stop any time."

Emma takes in a shuddering breath. "I'm sure, Sir. I want to continue."

"Okay. Feel whatever you need to feel, *Dulzura*. The paddle will feel different than my hand, so tell me if you need to stop."

She simply nods, so I pick up the paddle and place a hand on her hip to brace her. With a loud *thwack* the paddle meets the flesh of her ass, and she gasps as she picks up where she left off counting.

Chapter 21

Emma

I don't understand why I'm crying.

But I admit it feels kind of... good. Cleansing. It's not like I don't cry—I cry a lot. But this feels like it's coming from a place buried deep inside me. Somewhere I couldn't reach on my own. It feels safe.

Which is *crazy* because the last person I thought I'd ever feel comfortable crying in front of would be grumpy, emotionless Ben Rossi.

Every hit of the paddle makes me feel a bit lighter now that I've let myself feel everything and stopped trying to keep myself from crying.

Ben soothes each hit of the paddle with his big hands, and I'm getting more turned on. This isn't supposed to be something I enjoy, but I do.

Shame tries to creep its way into my brain, but I push it away. I remind myself of all the research I've done. There's nothing shameful about liking a little pain with my pleasure.

Ben lands the last strike so it hits both cheeks, I hear the paddle hit the floor, and then Ben scoops me into his arms and has me straddle his lap while he strokes my hair and my back, whispering praises of how well I did into my ear.

"I'm so proud of you, *Dulzura.* You're so strong. So brave for letting me spank you with the paddle. You took it like such a good girl. So perfect."

Ben smells like clean laundry, peppermint, and something that's only him. It makes me want to snuggle into him and fall asleep.

But that's not what this is.

I feel how hard he is between my thighs, and I experimentally rock against him. I don't want our night to end with me crying. I want to feel him inside me.

"Emma," he warns, tightening his grip on my hips. "What are you doing?"

"I want to feel you, Sir. Please."

"You just had a very emotional experience with the paddling, I'm not sure—"

"*Please,*" I beg, rolling my hips again. "I promise, Sir, I'm good. I want—no—I *need* to feel you." I need the connection with him.

Ben lets out a mixture of a growl and a groan. "Since you interrupted me, *Dulzura,* you'll have to do all the work. Get off for a minute."

I climb off of him so he can take off his underwear, which has a wet patch from me on his lap. *Oops.* He settles back onto the bed with his legs spread as he fists his cock and strokes it slowly twice.

"Come ride me, *Dulzura.* Show me just how eager you are to have your pussy filled."

I jump on the bed and straddle his strong thighs, notching the fat head of his cock at my entrance. I thought he was big last time, but he seems larger now, if it's even possible.

While Ben's hands grip my hips, I slowly sink onto him until our laps are flush together.

"God*damn,* that's it honey. Take all of me," Ben groans.

I sit back up on my knees, which leaves only the head in before I slam back down onto him.

"Fuck yes, let me see these tits bounce. Ride me, Emma. Make us both come," Ben demands before taking my nipple into his mouth.

I don't think too much about him calling me Emma and not "honey" or "*Dulzura*". If I think too much about it, my heart will get involved.

Bracing myself on his strong shoulders, I bounce up and down rapidly while he sucks and nips my nipples and breasts. He bites hard enough I'm sure there'll be a mark tomorrow.

I can't wait.

My ass stings when I sit down fully, and my thighs are starting to burn, but I don't want to disappoint him, so I push through it.

Ben must sense my stamina waning because in an instant, he flips us so he's hovering above me, his face mere millimeters from mine.

I have the strongest urge to grab his face and crash our lips together, but I push the thought away.

"Are you close, *Dulzura?*"

"Yes, Sir. Please, can I come?"

Ben brings one of my legs over his shoulder. "Come for me. Come before I fill your pussy with my cum."

As soon as the words leave his mouth, he starts a brutal pace. The angle makes it feel like he's hitting spots that have never been touched before and within seconds, I'm coming. This release feels like taking a big breath of air after holding your breath. My head feels fuzzy and my limbs numb as the pleasure overtakes me.

When I think my orgasm is about to subside, he pinches my clit and sets me off again, one orgasm rolling into another. My climax must push him over the edge because soon after, his hot cum fills me to the brim.

Ben stills but stays inside me for another minute while we catch our breath. I open my eyes to find he's already staring at me, something unreadable in his gaze. I wish I could read whatever's happening in his head.

"Stay right here. I'm going to get something to clean you up."

I nearly whimper again when he pulls out of me, and to my horror, I feel another few tears roll down my cheek.

I quickly wipe them away so Ben doesn't think I'm over-emotional and overly sensitive. The last thing I need is him deciding he doesn't want to be around me because I'm too much—too needy.

He comes back with a bottle of water and a snack. He quickly cleans me up before ordering me to drink and eat. If he notices my tears, he doesn't say anything as he wraps me in a soft blanket and cuddles me from behind while he strokes my hair.

I know aftercare is important, especially after the way I reacted to the paddle, but this feels too intimate. It's

making me think he cares about me more than he probably does.

After a few minutes of silence, he quietly asks, "Do
you know why you were crying during the paddling?"

"I guess part of me was embarrassed I liked it. But
another part of me felt... safe to cry. Like the paddling
shook loose some emotions I've been holding in."

"I've heard that can happen, and I've had a few subs
cry during impact play. You have nothing to be embarrassed about."

Something akin to jealousy pinches in my stomach,
but I brush it off. I know he's had other subs. He'll have
others after me, so I have no reason to feel possessive over
him.

This is temporary.

"Logically, I know that, but sometimes I forget. I
grew up very religious. Sex before marriage is considered
the second worst sin to murder, and masturbation follows close behind. Sometimes the purity culture bullshit
creeps its way into my psyche and overwhelms me with
guilt."

"That's... a lot to deal with."

I snort. "Yeah, it is."

It's not even the worst thing I was taught, but I don't
need to get into that right now.

"I don't think every other Saturday is working for
me," Ben says after a few minutes of silence.

My heart sinks. He's already done with me. I roll away
and sit up so he can't see my disappointment, covering
myself with the blanket.

"Okay."

I feel him sit up too. "I think we should meet once a week."

I turn around to face him, my pulse kicking up speed. "Are you sure?" I can admit I like the idea while also knowing it's a bad one. More time together outside of work means more time my heart has to get attached.

His face doesn't give way to his emotions. Of course it doesn't. "I'm positive. It was a long two weeks, and I think it'd be good to have more lessons so we can… explore your kinks more."

"Well, we can't next Saturday because we have the Allridge party."

Ben frowns. "Then we can leave the party together and come here."

"I suppose that could work. Jordan can't make it, so I was just going to take an Uber or something."

His jaw tightens like it usually does when I bring Jordan up, which is odd, but whatever. "Okay. We'll meet there and then come here after."

I can't help but feel like this breaks some of the rules of our agreement, but I don't dare bring it up.

CHAPTER 22

Ben

I hate parties. I hate that I'm expected to interact with people I don't want to talk to and make small talk about their dogs, their kids, or their wives.

All while sipping expensive champagne and eating bland hors d'oeuvres.

My ex, Janessa, used to make me come with her to these events all the time because she was a reporter and needed to make connections. It caused more than a few fights between us. I can't pretend to be nice to people I don't know and don't care about. More often than not, she'd be bustling around talking to everyone while I stood in the corner alone, counting down the minutes until we could leave.

She was upset I didn't try harder to be personable and make connections, I was upset she left me to fend for myself in a room full of strangers.

It's been five years since we broke up, and I haven't gone to a single party like this until now.

My father gets asked to come to these events quite often, but I never accept his invitation to join him. He loves showing off Mamà and making new friends.

Mamà loves supporting her husband and getting to dress up.

I don't know how I'm the product of them because I'd rather be at home watching *How It's Made.*

The only reason I agreed to come tonight was because of the promise of what's to come afterwards with Emma.

Emma's running late, but she hasn't texted me to tell me why.

If we were at the club, I could punish her—

No, not the time.

She doesn't need to tell me why she's late. I'm not her boyfriend or even her date. We're just fucking. All that matters is she'll be here in time for us to go to the club together.

Still, it'd be *polite* to give a heads up.

"You look like you're ready to get the hell out of here already," Drew drawls from next to me.

"I am."

"So why stick around? You haven't bothered to come to these things before."

I knew there'd be questions about why I'm suddenly making an appearance, so I have a valid answer at the ready. "I've never been invited to an event by Derek Allridge. I didn't want to offend him by not showing up."

Drew chuckles. "Since when do you care about offending anyone?"

"Since he finally offered a big job to Rossi. We need to present a united front."

Drew nods in agreement. "Makes sense. Personally, I can't wait until it's socially acceptable for me to leave. I finally got my membership request approved at The Temptation Lounge."

One day at work a few months ago, Drew vented to me about how tough dating has been for him. He asked me what my dating life was like and how I was meeting people. I don't know what compelled me to tell him about the club. I don't share my personal life, and I sure as hell don't tell people about the kink club I go to.

I've never regretted it more than I do right now.

My glass of champagne freezes halfway to my mouth. "Oh?" I hope my voice comes out more calm than I feel. "You headed there tonight?"

"As soon as I can."

Fuck.

I can't take Emma to the club if Drew is going to be there. That would put us at risk of being caught, and I'm not ready for this thing to end yet.

I wonder if she would be willing to come to my place...

Before I fully finish forming a plan, the doors to the ballroom open, and I immediately know it's her because it feels like all the oxygen is sucked out of my lungs. Time stands still as Emma enters the room looking like a fucking wet dream—*my* wet dream.

She's wearing a floor length black dress with lace cap sleeves and a slit going almost all the way up to the top of her thigh, giving a peek at that damn garter tattoo that makes me feral. That's not even the worst part. The front of the dress dips down nearly to her navel, her ample breasts barely contained by the fabric hugging them. It's cinched at the waist, and the skirt flows over the curves of her hips like liquid. Her heels are gold and wrap around her ankles, making her muscular calves look divine. Her hair is styled in soft waves again, flowing behind her like a cape. She's got sharp wings of eyeliner accentuating her blue eyes, and her lips are painted a bold red.

My cock stirs at the thought of how good the color would look smeared all over my skin.

Drew whistles. "Damn. Emma looks amazing."

I scowl. "That's our coworker."

Hypocrite.

Drew shrugs. "I'm just stating a fact. Everyone with eyes can see how good she looks. Besides, Derek's already got her occupied with a guy from his team, I wouldn't stand a chance anyway."

I whip my head to where Drew is looking, and my blood simmers with something close to jealousy as Derek introduces Emma to whomever he's with. Emma gives him a megawatt smile and shakes his hand, but I watch douchebro's hand linger a little *too* long on Emma's.

I can't tell what they're talking about, but Emma laughs at whatever he says, then nods enthusiastically before pulling out her phone and handing it to him.

You don't own her. She can talk to anyone she wants. She can call this thing off at any time.

Why do I hate the thought so much?

Before I do something stupid like go over there and try to stake my claim, Mamà and Papà come over to greet me and Drew.

"Mrs. Rossi, you look dazzling as always," Drew says as Mamà wraps him in a hug.

"*¡Basta!* Drew, you charmer." Mamà swats at his arm with a smile.

"The boy is right, *vita mia,* you are more dazzling than all the stars in the sky." Papà places a gentle kiss on Mamà's cheek, causing her to blush.

"*Gracias, mi amor.*" She returns his kiss, then turns her attention to me. "*Mi hijo,* you look so handsome. Did you bring a date tonight?"

"*Gracias, Mamà.* You look as beautiful as always." I place a gentle kiss on her cheek, careful of her meticulously applied makeup. "No date for me." *Unless you count the appointment I have to fuck my coworker.*

Mamà tsks and pushes her lips out in a disapproving pout. Camila Rossi's only wish for her children is to have a great love like she has with my dad, but so far, only my younger sister, Cecelia, has found her happily ever after, leaving my younger brother, Mateo, and I open for my mother's scheming.

More than once, Mateo and I have gone over expecting a nice family dinner, only to be set up on a blind date with someone Mamà deemed the "right match."

Papà leans in and whispers something in her ear, and Mamà's face breaks out into a sly grin. A grin I know means she has something up her sleeve. Her brown eyes twinkle with mischief before she schools her expression.

"Ah, well, that's okay. You are a busy man. Love will come along before you know it." She pats me on the arm and gazes around the room.

My eyes immediately trail to Emma, and my heart does a weird kick.

Papà clears his throat. "Oh, look, *vita mia,* there's Emma. Ben, will you introduce your *Mamà* to Emma? I must use the restroom."

I don't get a chance to respond before Mamà loops her arm through mine and tugs me in the direction Papà pointed, chattering away about how excited she is to finally meet the new project manager. How she's heard such wonderful things about her.

Emma is in the middle of a conversation with an older couple I don't recognize. When she sees us approaching, she politely ends the conversation and walks in our direction.

Mamà, disregarding the rules of society, immediately wraps Emma in her strong embrace. In her heels, Emma is about the same height as my mother, and I expect her to pull away or look uncomfortable, but to my surprise, she matches Mamà's energy, wrapping her arms around her waist.

"Emma! It's so nice to finally meet you. My husband has told me so much about you. But he and Benjamin failed to tell me how outrageously gorgeous you are," Mamà gushes, brazenly looking Emma up and down before shooting me a knowing look.

Emma blushes but gives her a warm, genuine smile. *"Hola, Señora Rossi.* The pleasure is all mine. The picture in Enzo's office doesn't do your beauty justice. And thank you."

"Thank you, *bella.* Call me Camila, please. And please excuse my son and his lack of manners." She leans in and stage-whispers, "Sometimes pretty women make him a little tongue tied."

Emma's blue eyes, alight with humor, meet mine as she replies, "That explains why he has such a hard time with words around me."

I roll my eyes. The two of them meeting is already on my list of top five things I wish never happened, but there's no stopping it now.

Mamá cackles, then abandons me to loop her arm with Emma, leaving me to my own devices.

Without anything else to do, I trail behind them like a lost puppy, trying not to stare at Emma's ass and the way her hips sway as she walks.

CHAPTER 23

Emma

Mrs. Rossi—*Camila*—and I walk around the room as she introduces me to people she knows. Ben, who seems even grumpier than usual, follows us and gives a curt nod when he's introduced.

Enzo joins us soon after, and Camila switches from my arm to his, giving him a peck on the cheek in greeting.

"So, Emma, I see you've finally met the love of my life, Camila Rossi?"

"I have, and she is a delight. You're a lucky man."

"Don't I know it." Enzo gazes at Camila with so much love it makes my heart clench.

I used to want a great love like that. Someone who would look at me like I'm the only person in the room, even surrounded by a hundred people. Someone who, after so many years together, still thinks I'm the best thing that's ever happened to them.

I'll never admit out loud that part of me—a big part, unfortunately—is still a hopeless romantic who wishes to be swept off her feet like a heroine in a romance novel. But life isn't a romance novel. There's no prince or princess charming who's going to magically show up and save me from myself.

I'm not going to meet a random stranger in a bar who'll end up being my soulmate.

I'll never have someone who looks at me like I've hung the moon and the stars.

That's okay, though. Because falling in love means risking my heart, and I don't have the strength for that.

Enzo and Camila ask me questions about my love life, and I swear I feel the tension radiating from Ben when I answer.

Apparently, they saw me speaking with Derek and Jason—the development director for the job I'll be working on. We exchanged numbers since I'll be working closely with him, but I could tell Jason's interest wasn't purely professional.

"Jason's a good man. Hard worker, smart. He'd be a great match for you," Enzo says, and I catch Ben's scowl deepen.

"And he's so handsome. You two would make lovely babies," Camila interjects.

Jason is classically good-looking with his lean figure, perfectly styled light brown hair, and blue eyes. I'm sure our kids would be blue-eyed bundles of joy, not that I've thought much about having kids. I'm not even sure I want them.

I give her an indulgent smile. "While he is good-looking, I don't feel any attraction to him. Besides, I don't want to mix business and pleasure. This job is too important to risk getting feelings involved."

"That is true." She hums, tapping her chin. "Mateo doesn't work for the company." Camila nudges her husband, and he gives a thoughtful nod.

"Very true, *vita mia,* very true."

Before I can ask who Mateo is, a microphone gives an overwhelming screech as Derek stands in front of the room on a little stage to give a speech.

While everyone's distracted listening to Derek talk about how much his company means to him, Ben leans in and murmurs, "We have a problem with tonight."

I turn to him and raise an eyebrow, motioning for him to continue.

"Drew will be at the club."

Fuckity fucking fucks. I didn't know he was a member! That would have been nice information to know in the beginning. I never would have agreed to see Ben at the club if I knew our coworker was a patron.

"Guess we'll have to reschedule," I whisper.

Ben clenches his jaw and very subtly shakes his head. "Not happening. Let's make our excuses and go, I have a plan."

"I can't leave now," I hiss. "It would be rude."

Ben steps closer to me, and I'm assaulted by what is quickly becoming my favorite smell. "My patience is wearing thin, *Dulzura.* If you don't make an excuse to leave within the next twenty minutes, there will be consequences."

My cheeks flame with a mix of arousal and indignation. "We're not at the club right now, so you can't boss me around."

He gives a low chuckle. "I think you want to be my good girl, so you'll listen anyway. You're cute when you try to be defiant, though."

Ugh. I love when he calls me that. And I hate that he's right.

Derek finishes his speech with a toast to his wife for supporting his endeavors, and everyone raises their glasses, then the band he's hired takes the stage, and the dancing portion of the evening begins.

I didn't even notice Jason getting closer to me, but as soon as the music starts, he asks me if I want to dance. I glance at Ben before answering—not that I need his permission. It's a *dance*. His jaw is clenched so tight it's a wonder he doesn't crack a tooth, and his arms are folded over his chest. He taps his wrist in warning, which only makes me want to push his buttons more.

I give Jason a saccharine smile. "I'd love to dance, Jason."

Chapter 24

Ben

I can't believe she's not listening to me.

Well, that's not entirely true.

I *can* believe it.

She's shown time and time again that even if she's a sweet, perfect little sub in a scene, out in the real world? She doesn't take orders from me.

I hate that I kind of enjoy it. Enjoy seeing the fire of indignation in her eyes and the way she holds her head up high when she's standing her ground.

I watch as *Jason* leads her to the dance floor with a hand on her lower back, too close to her delectable ass for my comfort.

I don't recognize the song playing, but it's a slow love ballad. Why this was chosen as the first song, I'll never know.

I don't get why they have a dance floor at all, to be honest. We're not at a fucking prom.

Even if I feel like a high schooler watching the girl I have a crush on dancing with someone else.

No, not a crush. Just fucking.

The song ends, and Emma steps away from Jason and starts walking in my direction. His eyes linger on her ass before our gazes lock. Whatever expression I'm wearing must be intimidating because his cheeks flush in embarrassment before he turns and scurries away to the opposite side of the room.

Good. She's not for him.

Emma doesn't acknowledge me as she walks by, just lightly bumps my shoulder as she passes.

I don't know why her little act of indignation makes me want to smile. Maybe it's because I know I can punish her for it later. I think maybe a little orgasm denial is in store for tonight...

I track Emma as she says something to Derek and his wife, then to my parents, before leaving the room. I say goodbye to my parents before I leave as well.

It only occurs to me halfway out the door that it may look suspicious I left the same time as Emma. I'll come up with a cover story if anyone asks questions.

I find Emma sitting on a bench in the front of the hotel next to the valet, tapping away on her phone.

I hand my ticket to the valet and join her on the bench to wait for my car. I glance over at her phone and see she's typing in her information for an Uber.

"What are you doing?" I bark.

Emma barely glances up from her phone. "Ordering a ride."

"I'm driving you."

She scoffs. "No, you're not. I'm going home."

"The hell you are. We had a plan for tonight." I hope my voice hides the sting of rejection I feel.

"We did, but that plan has been compromised since Drew is going to be at the club. We'll have to reschedule."

I gently pull her phone from her grasp before she can finish ordering a car. "You're coming to my place."

"The hell I am!" A group of people walk out of the hotel, distracting me enough for her to snatch her phone back. She continues in a harsh whisper, "That blurs the lines, Ben. Our deal is to meet at the club. Going to your house feels too... intimate."

I see where she's coming from, but also, "Me being balls deep in your pussy *isn't* intimate?"

Emma rolls her eyes. "That's different, and you know it. If I start going to your house, what's next? You want me to come over after work instead of waiting until Saturday? We start having sleepovers? We have quickies in the truck on the way to jobsites? The rules are there for a reason, Ben."

Mierda. Why do I like the idea of her coming over after work, cooking her dinner, then blowing her back out? Why do I like the idea of waking up with her and being able to sink into her lush body? Why does the thought of fingering her or having her lips wrapped around my cock in my work truck make me so hot?

It's got to be because it's a forbidden fantasy. None of those things are options. Emma's made it clear she's not looking for a relationship, and it's not something I want either...

Right?

"I propose an amendment to the rules since the club is now compromised. Same rules apply in all other aspects, just a different location."

Emma chews her bottom lip as she contemplates her options.

After what feels like hours, she sighs. "Fine."

I suppress a triumphant smile.

The valet arrives with my gray Giulia Quadrifoglio and tosses me the keys. It may be a few years old—a 2016 model—but I love the sleek design, and it makes me feel connected to my Italian roots. Like a gentleman, I open the door for Emma and help her get settled in, then I round the car and settle into the driver's side, keeping an eye out for anyone we might know. Luckily, it seems everyone is still inside enjoying the party.

Emma runs her hands over the leather seats. "Nice ride."

"Thanks."

I don't usually listen to music, so we sit in silence until we merge onto the freeway when Emma lets out a quiet but sharp gasp, her eyes glued to her phone.

"What? What's wrong?" I ask.

"N-nothing. Just some family stuff." She doesn't even look up.

"Everything okay?"

"Fine."

Clearly, everything is *not* fine. I *should* let it go. It's not what we do, and she clearly doesn't want to talk to me about it. We don't ask about personal lives. We don't share intimate details about families or friends or schedules.

But right now, I don't give a fuck.

I'm just about to ask her to tell me more when her phone rings, and she groans before answering.

"Hi, Mom. Yes, I got your text. Is he—"

"No, I don't—but I can—" She throws her head back on a silent groan as she listens to her mom talk.

Emma looks over and gives me an apologetic smile.

I have the overwhelming urge to place my hand on her thigh and give her a reassuring squeeze to show I'm here for her, but I think it would make it worse.

"I was going to ask Jordan—I know, I *know*. We'd stay at a hotel or with Hannah." She pauses, and I can't hear what her mom is saying on the other end. "Can I at least FaceTime him? I didn't get to say goodbye to—" Her voice gets cut off again. "I *know*. I understand. Please keep me updated. Okay. Bye."

Jesus. Does her mom ever let her finish a sentence?

Emma hangs up and presses her fingers to the corners of her eyes and takes three deep breaths before she whispers. "I'm sorry, but I need you to take me home."

I don't like how small and fragile her voice sounds. She doesn't sound like the boisterous, take charge, sunshiney woman I work with every day. She sounds... sad. Defeated.

"I can do that, but I don't know if I want you to be alone right now."

"That's not for you to decide. And I won't be alone. Jordan's home."

Fucking Jordan. Jordan probably knows what's wrong. Jordan probably knows so many things about her, things she keeps hidden from me.

"Will you tell me what the call was about?"

"Why does it matter, Ben? This isn't what we are to each other."

But maybe I want to be.

The thought takes me by surprise but doesn't freak me out the way it should.

I don't have time to examine that right now.

"Because I…" What? Care about her? She'd run for the fucking hills if I were to say that. "Because this puts a damper on our plans, and I know we were both looking forward to tonight. And I'm not heartless despite what you may believe."

After a heavy sigh, she explains, "My mom texted me to tell me my grandpa is in the hospital. He's had issues with his knees his whole life and refused to take care of himself properly. I guess his knee replacement eroded, and now there's an infection? I'm not entirely sure other than it's really, really bad. Somehow, he broke his leg in the hospital today, and they're saying there's nothing they can do other than make him comfortable while they wait for him to—"

Her voice breaks, but she clears her throat and continues, "I told my mom I was going to come to Utah so I could say goodbye, but she doesn't want me to travel alone, but she also doesn't want Jordan to stay at her house because it's a whole thing. She told me there's no reason for me to come anyway when I'll probably just have to come for the funeral later on. I guess I don't have to listen to her, but it's not like I can afford to make two trips, let alone ask someone else to make both."

The traffic lights reflect off of the shiny tears streaming down her face, and my heart cracks at the sight.

"She won't even let me FaceTime him to say goodbye when she knows how much it hurts that I never got to say goodbye to my other grandparents or... other people I've lost."

I give in to the urge to place my hand on her thigh this time, giving her what I hope is a reassuring squeeze.

"I'm sorry, *Dulzura.*"

Emma stiffens at the use of the nickname and squares her shoulders. "It's fine. I'm fine. I'll be fine. Death happens every day, and people move on. Talking to my mom just always rattles me. I'm fine. But I don't know if I'm in the headspace for a scene tonight."

The amount of times she said "fine" indicates she's absolutely *not fine,* but I don't know how best to comfort her. I don't even know if she'd want me to. I don't know how to handle sad Emma.

Angry, fiery, happy, submissive—yes.

But not sad.

I hate it. Not because she's showing her emotions, but because she obviously feels like she can't show them around me, and I have no fucking idea how to help her. But like she pointed out, this isn't what we are to each other.

"That's okay. Plug in your address, and I'll take you home. You said your roommate is home?"

"Yes. They should be back by now." *They?* I thought she only had one roommate. She takes my phone and enters her address, which luckily isn't far off from where we were headed.

The rest of the drive is silent, save for a few residual sniffles from Emma. The silence gives me time to think back on my realization earlier. The one where I realized I might want more from Emma than just a scene partner.

My question is, why doesn't *she* want more? She's obviously an amazing woman anyone would be lucky to have, but from what I've gathered, she hasn't been in a serious relationship in quite some time.

There's got to be a reason, but I don't think she'd tell me if I asked out of the blue. There would need to be a level of trust between us we don't have.

Yet.

Except I don't even know where to begin with earning her trust outside of our scenes. I've dug quite a hole for myself at work, one I'll need a fleet of dump trucks to fill in.

We pull up in front of a row of quaint little one-story townhomes, which look like they were built in the early 2000s. There's a wreath with fall leaves and sunflowers on a pink door matching the number of Emma's address, and I recognize her little blue Honda Civic in the driveway.

"Thanks for the ride, and sorry for ruining our night," Emma says quietly as she opens the door.

I grab her wrist gently before she can get out. "No apologies necessary. Let me know if you need anything. I mean it, Emma. If you need a distraction or someone to yell at, call me."

Emma's lips thin as she gives me a perfunctory nod, then she closes the car door and walks up the driveway to her house.

I wait until she's inside before pulling away.

I spend the rest of the drive home trying to figure out how to make things more than just casual sex with my coworker. Wanting more is going to cause complications I don't know how to handle, and I don't know if she'd even be open to it.

By the time I get home, all I know for certain is I want Emma in any way I can have her, but ideally, I want all of her.

If all she wants is sex, then I'll give it to her, but I'll be blurring the lines of our agreement just a smidge.

This is definitely not how I saw tonight going.

CHAPTER 25

Emma

I cried myself to sleep last night after debriefing Jordy on what was going on with my grandpa. They told me they'd try to make sure they were available to go to Utah with me for the funeral, but I assured them I'd be fine if they couldn't.

I fucking hate funerals. I hate death. I've experienced far too much of it in my twenty-seven years, and I just want a fucking break.

Growing up, the Mormon church taught me that when a person dies, their spirit leaves their body and depending on how "righteous" they are in their mortal existence, the spirit is sent to spirit prison or spirit paradise. The people in paradise get to teach the "prisoners" and "bring them to the gospel."

I was assured I would see my cousin again when he died of cancer when I was nine.

I was assured I'd see Grandma Price again when she passed when I was thirteen.

I was assured I'd see Grandpa Price when he died when I was eighteen.

I was assured I'd see my brother Andy again when he died two years later.

I had already started deconstructing when Andy died, so I spiraled a bit, not knowing if I'd see him again.

Now, Grandpa Monson is going to pass away, and I won't get to say goodbye.

I'll have to suffer through another Mormon funeral. *Gag.*

If I go, the family will whisper about how far off the path I've strayed, and everyone will pry into my personal life. But if I don't go, my mom will yell at me, calling me a disappointment.

What else is new?

Checking the time and seeing it's almost eleven, I roll out of bed and make my way to the kitchen for some food, even though my stomach feels like it's going to reject anything I give it.

Jordy is in the living room reading when I sulk past them; they offer me a sad smile.

I'm just about to open the fridge when the doorbell rings, so I change direction and make my way to the front door.

Looking through the peephole, I'm met with a large bouquet of flowers.

"What the hell?" I murmur as I open the door.

"I'm looking for an... Emma?" the man holding the flowers says, looking at his clipboard.

"Um, that's me."

"Sign here, please."

I take the clipboard and sign, then he hands me the flowers as he takes the clipboard.

"Have a good day, ma'am."

"You, too."

Perplexed, I walk back into the kitchen and examine the bouquet. It's a beautiful mix of purple carnations, pale pink roses, and white daisies filled in with baby's breath. It's something I would pick out for myself if I ever bought flowers. There's a note sticking out in a plastic card holder.

I recognize the neat handwriting immediately because I see it almost every day.

> **Hope these brighten your day.**
> **Missed you last night.**
> **-B**

"Well those are pretty. Secret admirer?" Jordan asks, rounding the counter to read the note in my hand. "B? As in *Ben?* Your coworker and fuck buddy? I thought it was only casual." Their tone holds no judgment, only curious surprise.

Same, though. Why is he sending me flowers?

"It *is* casual. Less than casual. Literally only sex."

Jordan hums. "Flowers don't seem casual to me, Em."

I feel like stomping my foot and throwing a tantrum. "I knowwwww," I whine. "Why isn't he following the rules? He wanted me to go to his *house* last night, Jordy. He tried to comfort me when my mom told me about Grandpa. That's not what we *do*."

Jordan crosses their arms and furrows their impeccably plucked eyebrows. "Why are you so scared of more?"

I point a finger at them. "Don't go all therapist on me, Jordan. I don't need you to psychoanalyze me and my commitment issues. You know why I don't do relationships."

"Actually, I don't know why. I know when I got back from Japan, you and Trinity had broken up, and you told me you were taking a break from serious relationships. I supported it, thinking you needed a short break, and you'd find a serious partner within a few months, but it's been over four years, Em. I find it hard to believe you haven't met a single person you could see being more than a one-night stand. I've given you space, hoping you'd come to me, but I know you're hurting. I just want to know why."

I don't want to have this conversation right now.

I take out two frozen chocolate chip waffles and toss them in the toaster, buying myself time.

Jordan, with their uncanny ability to see right through me, sighs. "I'm going to guess this has something to do with your mother and shitty family on some level because those bitches have shot your self-esteem to hell for as long as we've been friends. But I also think you probably left out a lot of what *actually* went down with Trinity. I didn't push then because I wanted to give you time, but I'm genuinely worried about you."

Tears well in my eyes. This is what I *didn't* want to happen. I didn't want Jordan to be concerned about me when they have so many clients and other people to worry about. I don't tell them that though, because I don't want them to feel like it's their fault. It's not—it's all me.

"Trinity told me what everyone else in my life has told me—aside from you; I'm too emotional. Too needy. *Too much.* But in the same breath she told me I wasn't serious enough about our relationship because I hadn't wanted to discuss having kids or getting married after six months. I also think she was a little jealous of our friendship, but I don't know for sure."

My whole life, Jordan's watched me fall for someone, then get let down when things didn't work out. I'd ignore red flags or misunderstand signals and throw myself into someone who I thought was "the one" just for it to fizzle out or end within a month or two. All my life I've wanted to be loved the way I see it portrayed in movies and books, but I've never experienced that. All I've experienced is a list of heartbreaks longer than Taylor Swift's.

I take a deep breath, sniffling back tears again. "You know how many times I've had my heart broken. You've been there to help me pick up the pieces. I can't keep going through it—getting my hopes up only for them to crash and burn. One night of pleasure isn't enough time to fall in love. If I don't fall in love, I can't get hurt."

Jordan's face morphs into one of concern and... hurt. "Emma, you let *Trinity,* of all people, make you feel like you weren't lovable? When she was pushing *your* boundaries and making you uncomfortable? It's not needy or emotional to take things slow. But four years? It's no way for you to live, Mimi."

A tear slips down my cheek. "How many pieces of myself can I give away before I'm left with nothing?"

Jordan frowns but wraps me in a hug. "I'm so sorry, Emma. I'm sorry I never asked before now. I should have, then maybe you'd see just how loveable you are. You're my person. I love you like a sister, my platonic soulmate. I'm sorry you got your heart broken so many times. But just because your heart has been broken, doesn't mean you aren't worthy of love."

"It's not your fault, JoJo."

"But I didn't realize it sooner. I didn't realize you closed yourself off from finding love entirely. I should have—"

"No," I cut them off. "This isn't your fault. I wasn't honest with you about why I made my sex-only vow. That's not on you."

Jordan pulls back, their hazel eyes locking on mine intensely as they cup my face. "You are an amazing woman, Mimi. Anyone would be lucky as hell to have you as their partner. If anyone deserves the all consuming, once-in-a-lifetime love, it's you. Promise me you'll reconsider your stance and open yourself up to love?"

I look away because I can't promise that. "I will think about it."

"Maybe Ben—"

"Jordy, no."

"Okay." They hold their hands up in surrender. "I can tell you don't want to talk about this anymore, so I'll let you eat your waffles. I love you, and if you want to talk about anything else, I'm here."

"Thank you. I love you, too."

I spend the rest of the day alternating between staring at the flowers and overthinking what they mean.

No one besides my parents and Jordy have given me flowers. While a part of me is wary of what the gesture means and so fucking confused, another part—a part I've tried to keep buried—is squealing and kicking her feet.

That same part of me has already written "Mrs. Emma Rossi" all over her notebook and is planning our tropical island honeymoon.

Even though I want to, I don't text Ben and demand to know why he sent me flowers. Instead, I opt for something simple.

Emma: Thank you for the flowers.

Ben: My pleasure. Glad you liked them.

I ignore the way butterflies take flight in my stomach at his reply.

I'm not looking forward to work tomorrow.

CHAPTER 26

Ben

Emma hasn't been her usual bubbly self this week. I can't tell if it's because of the flowers, the stuff with her grandpa, or something else, and it's driving me crazy. She won't talk to me about it, and she insists everything's fine when I've dared ask.

She's putting on her happy mask with everyone, but her eyes are missing their spark, and when she thinks no one's watching, her shoulders sag. More than once, I've seen her dab her eyes with a tissue. She's barely spoken to me, only when she needs something work related. She's declined my invitations to join me on job sites, saying she needs to get paperwork done, which is a lie. She gets all of her paperwork done on Tuesdays and Thursdays.

Other than the thank you text, she hasn't brought up the flowers. I should have known they were too much, but I'm not good at this. The wooing or whatever. It's been a long time since I've had to do anything romantic, and I was never good at it in the first place. You'd think at thirty-two, I would know how to impress a woman.

Janessa and I were in each other's orbit, sharing the same friend group and living in the same dorm, I don't think I ever even asked her on a proper date. One day, I kissed her, and we never stopped. When our leases were up, it made sense to move in together. The only official thing I did was propose, and even that wasn't some grand gesture. I took her to a nice dinner and got down on one knee with a ring I picked out just a few days before.

I cringe thinking about it. No wonder our relationship never worked out. I definitely didn't have my priorities in order then, but I won't make the same mistakes with Emma.

My dad approaches Emma's office, and she fixes her face into a smile that doesn't quite reach her eyes.

"*Ciao, bella!* Camila wanted me to extend an invitation to come over for lunch tomorrow. We would love a chance to get to know you a little better."

Weird. They never invite just a single person, it's usually a company thing.

"Oh, that's so kind, Enzo. I just—"

"Before you say no, just think about it. Good food, good company! Camila has been talking about you non-stop since Saturday. I will deny my wife nothing, and it would mean so much to her if you would join us."

I can't see Emma, but I'm sure she's biting her lip while she thinks. Obligation and her people-pleasing tendencies are going to make her agree.

"What time should I be there, and what can I bring?" she indulges, and Papà claps his hands in delight.

"Nothing, *bella*. Nothing. Just yourself." There's a brief pause, then he says, "Mateo is eager to meet you."

I don't hear what Emma says after that because of the ringing in my ears.

Oh, hell no.

This is a setup. Mamà's got her matchmaking hat on, and she's trying to set up Mateo and Emma.

Over my dead body.

I don't hear the rest of their conversation over the roar of my blood pounding in my ears, but when Papà walks towards my office I start aimlessly typing so it looks like I'm busy.

He closes the door, which means this isn't a conversation he wants overheard, and takes a seat in the chair across from me.

"I would like you to pick Emma up for lunch tomorrow."

I can't help my disbelieving scoff. "If you're trying to set her up with Mateo, why would I pick her up?"

"Because she knows *you* not Mateo. Yet. I want her to enjoy the day without worrying about driving home." He gives me a mischievous grin. "Mateo can take her home after."

"She'll never go for it," I argue, knowing she'd rather walk than ride with me.

"She already agreed."

So that's what I missed when I was simmering with possessive rage. Papà must read my shock because he chuckles. "I told her you will pick her up at eleven. Be nice, *Beniamino*. She may be your future sister-in-law."

Like hell she will.

With that, he gets up and leaves my office, whistling in delight as he meanders back down the hall.

I pinch the bridge of my nose and take a few deep, steadying breaths, trying to get a handle on myself. Then, I pull out my phone and text Mateo to meet me for a drink tonight. He quickly texts back, agreeing to meet me at a bar I've never heard of close to his work. He's probably oblivious to the fact our parents are trying to set him up tomorrow, so I think it's best I give him a heads up.

It's my brotherly duty after all.

"What?" I bark, not bothering to look up when I hear a knock on my door.

"Sorry," Emma replies, her voice sheepish, which immediately makes me feel like an asshole. "I just wanted to say you don't have to pick me up. I can drive, or Jordan can bring me. I also wanted to know what your mom's favorite flowers are?"

I finally look up, but she refuses to meet my gaze.

"It's not a problem. *Papà* wants you to enjoy the day—meaning he wants to supply you with alcohol. I don't mind picking you up. *Mamà* likes peonies."

"Okay. Thank you. I'll uh, see you tomorrow then, I guess."

"Tomorrow."

STRUCTION // UNDER CONSTRUCTION // UNDER CON

The first thing I notice when I walk up to the bar is the Pride flag next to the half-broken neon McGrath's sign. Mateo is straight as an arrow—as far as I know, so it's curious this is the place he chose—maybe he just likes their drinks. I have nothing against the LGBTQ+ community, but I also don't know many people who are part of it. My mind flashes back to Emma's green ribbon around her wrist. Is she bisexual?

Mateo is waiting for me at the bar, chatting with the blue-haired bartender. He sticks out like a sore thumb in his business casual khakis and blue polo, but Mateo doesn't care much about what people think.

I slide into the empty stool next to him, giving him a clap on the back to let him know I'm here.

"Ah, perfect timing. A prickly pear cider for my brother please, Kit," Mateo says to the bartender.

"Uh, actually, just soda water with lime, if you don't mind. How did you find this place, Teo?"

Kit nods, setting a glass down and filling it with ice, sparkling water, and a lime wedge before moving down the bar to the other patrons.

"I heard they have good cocktails. I didn't realize it was a LGBTQ+ bar when I chose it, but I can't say I hate the vibes. What's stuck up your ass today?" Mateo asks, sipping a shimmery, bright pink cocktail.

"Mom and Dad are trying to set you up with my coworker." I don't want to beat around the bush, just give him the information and go on my way.

Mateo gives me a smirk. "I know. *Mamà* hasn't stopped gushing about her all week."

My jaw ticks. "You're okay with them playing matchmaker?"

Mateo shrugs. "Why not? The dating apps haven't gone well. Maybe *Mamà* actually does know best, and she's my future wife."

My knuckles turn white from how hard I'm gripping the glass. I'm worried it'll shatter into a million pieces.

Before I can respond, the bell above the door jingles, and my gaze darts to Kiera's familiar face and bright pink hair walking through the door with three other people I don't recognize and a head of blonde hair I do.

The din of the bar fades away as Emma walks in, arm in arm with a person with cropped brown hair. I can't tell if they're a man or a woman, but I don't like the familiar way they're touching Emma.

She's changed since work; instead of the jeans and Rossi T-shirt she had on earlier, she's wearing a white dress with an oversized flannel shirt that looks like it belongs to a man.

I sure as hell hope it doesn't.

"Earth to Ben!" Mateo snaps his fingers in my face.

"What?" I bite back, reluctantly taking my eyes off Emma.

Mateo follows where my line of sight was, whistling as he sees who caught my eye. "The blonde babe got your attention? I thought you only liked brunettes, but I guess people change. You should go ask for her number. Maybe she'll be able to fuck the grump out of you."

"That's Emma," I mumble.

"What?" He holds a hand up to his ear.

"That's Emma," I hiss, a bit louder.

Mateo's eyes widen in surprise, his mouth popping open into an "o." Then, his grin turns conniving. "Well, well, well. Since that's my potential future wife, I should go say hello."

He goes to stand up, but I clamp his arm to keep him in place. "Don't."

"Why not? It's the polite thing to do."

"Leave her alone. She's had a rough week. You'll meet her tomorrow."

"But we're both here *right now*. It's as if fate tossed her into my lap." His eyebrows pump suggestively.

Unbidden, an image of Emma sitting in Mateo's lap, snuggling into him and nuzzling against him crosses my mind. His hand in her hair, resting on her hip. Her hand cradling his jaw as she gazes at him adoringly.

My grip on him tightens.

Mateo glances down at where my hand is strangling his arm, then up at me, before his face splits into a wide, knowing grin. "It truly is fate because here she comes," he whispers, and Emma appears on his other side seconds later.

Kit comes towards us but stops in front of Emma as she places her order.

While Kit is making her drinks, Mateo clears his throat.

Emma turns toward Mateo and gives him a brief, kind smile before facing forward again.

Good. Show him you're not available.

Undeterred, Mateo starts talking to her. "Emma? I'm Mateo. Enzo Rossi's son."

Emma's head whips towards my brother, her eyes wide with shock, then she registers I'm sitting next to him, and her eyes dart between the two of us as she taps her nails rapidly on the bar top.

"Hi, uh, we're supposed to meet tomorrow at lunch, I think. Hi, Ben," she adds the last part almost as an afterthought, and I don't like it. I don't want to be an *afterthought.*

"Emma." I take a sip of my drink.

"Well, the fates have aligned so we can meet without an audience. Well, other than my brother. And I must say, I'm grateful for that. *Mamà* was right, you are *stunning.*"

Emma blushes. I can't even appreciate it because she's not blushing for me, she's blushing for my Casanova of a brother.

I didn't know fratricide was on the agenda tonight.

"Thank you," Emma replies with a tight-lipped smile that doesn't quite reach her eyes.

Her body language is screaming uninterested, which Mateo either doesn't notice or doesn't care.

Kit brings a tray of drinks to Emma, but before she can pay for them, Mateo is telling Kit to add it to his tab. Emma protests, but Mateo insists, so she concedes with a furrowed brow and pursed lips. She thanks Mateo again before taking the tray to her table, waving goodbye to us with promises of seeing us tomorrow. Mateo and I both watch her the entire time she walks away.

"Damn," Mateo curses as he turns his back on them. "I thought for sure she'd invite me to her table or continue our conversation. Hopefully tomorrow will go better."

I chug the rest of my soda water, relishing the way the bubbles burn on the way down.

"I don't think she's interested, Teo."

He waves his hand in front of him dismissively. "She was just caught off guard. I can charm her tomorrow when she's not with her friends."

"I think you should leave her alone," I snap.

Mateo studies me for a second, nodding before he barks out a laugh. "You're into her."

"I didn't say that."

"You didn't have to. It's obvious. The look on your face when she walked in, the protective way you talk about her. Why else would you feel the need to warn me beforehand about a set up?"

"Things could get awkward if you date a Rossi employee and it doesn't work out."

"Is that why *you* haven't made a move? You didn't warn me when they tried to set me up with your HR rep." He shudders as he remembers the disaster that was his date with Katrina.

"Drop it, Mateo. I just don't think it's a good idea."

"I think it's a great idea. Even if we don't date, no harm in having a night of passion with her."

I clamp my mouth shut before I rail into him about her not being that type of girl. He's baiting me. I know he is, and it's working.

But more than that, I'm mad because she *is* the type of girl who wants one night. She told me that herself.

We haven't even discussed if we're meeting tomorrow night because she's avoiding me, and I hate it.

Good thing I have time tomorrow before lunch to talk to her.

CHAPTER 27

Emma

Last night, Mateo caught me off guard, and I couldn't put my sunshine mask on quickly enough to appear excited to meet him.

Then, seeing Ben with him threw me even more because we've barely spoken this week—*oops*—and seeing him in a place that's supposed to be a safe space rocked me.

I'm more prepared today.

I left McGrath's early last night to have a good cry and repair my sunshiney armor so I can present as my bubbly self today, even if I don't feel it on the inside.

I don't know how to dress because I don't know if we'll be inside or outside, so I opt for a mustard-colored corduroy mini skirt and a plain black bodysuit I can wear a cardigan over if we're outside.

I'm just adding my jewelry when the doorbell rings, and Jordan calls out, "I've got it!"

I can't make out what they're saying, but I hear the deep timbre of Ben's voice through my closed door, and the sound alone sends a shiver down my spine.

It's like my body knows tonight is supposed to be one of our sessions, and I'm pent up as fuck after not having a release last week.

Despite avoiding him and not knowing where we stand, I've been following his rule about not touching myself. It's been torture, but I don't want to disappoint him.

If he still wants me, that is.

Maybe he's in on setting me up with Mateo, and this is his way of telling me he's done with our arrangement. As much as I want to pretend it wouldn't hurt, even the idea of it makes me want to sob.

I shake my head and clear away those thoughts. They won't help me right now.

After zipping up my boots and grabbing a cardigan, I take a deep breath before opening my bedroom door quietly. The carpet muffles my footsteps, and I find Ben and Jordan in the kitchen talking quietly, a steely look on Ben's face.

I hope he's not being an ass to my best friend, because I'll smack him if he is.

Jordan notices me first, and their face twists into a smug smirk, which has me on alert. Jordan is as sweet as a kitten, but I know that look means they're scheming, and if they're scheming, it can't be good for me, especially after how they tried to get me to agree to open up my heart for Ben.

Ben turns, and my breath catches at his slow perusal of my body. He's looking at me like he's a lion and I'm his prey, and he's calculating how fast he'll need to run to catch me. His gaze is appreciative and overwhelming, and I hate that I want to ask him if he likes my outfit.

His opinion on what I wear doesn't matter.

"What were you two talking about?" I ask, straightening my spine.

Ben and Jordan share a look I don't like. How could they have bonded already in the five minutes it took for me to finish getting ready?

"Just introducing myself. Ben didn't know I was nonbinary or that we've been best friends for over two decades," Jordan answers with a smile. That helps my nerves, it means Ben wasn't being a dick about their gender identity.

"Surely I've mentioned it at work," I say to Ben.

He shrugs. "I know you referred to your roommate as 'they,' but I thought it meant you had more than one. It never occurred to me Jordan was nonbinary."

"Is it a problem for you?" I ask, ready to defend if necessary. I won't tolerate an ignorant asshole.

"Not at all. I'm just happy to have finally met them." Ben gives Jordan a small but rare smile, and they beam back at him.

I don't like this... *camaraderie* they seem to have.

"Okay... Well, we better get going. I don't want to be late and make a bad impression." I grab the bouquet of peonies I picked up this morning from the counter and march to the door.

"It was great to meet you, Jordan. I'll be in touch," Ben says with a nod to Jordan.

"Nice to meet you, too, Ben! Looking forward to it. Have fun, Mimi! Love you!"

"Love you, too. Hate that you two are apparently friends now," I reply, which just makes Jordan grin and Ben chuckle.

Ben follows me out the front door and leads me to his car. He opens the door for me, holding the flowers while I get in, then handing them back before shutting the door and rounding the car to get in the driver's side.

"What did you mean you'll be in touch with them?" I ask as Ben pulls out of the driveway.

"They're helping me with something."

"Oh, good. You're finally going to therapy?"

Ben scowls at me. "I don't need therapy."

I snort. "Right. I forgot. They'd have to surgically remove the stick from your ass first."

"Where was this side of you yesterday at the bar, *Dulzura*?"

Fuck, I forgot how sweet that nickname sounds.

My body responds like we're in a scene. My needy vagina chanting *fuck me, fuck me, fuck me* while my brain tells her to calm the fuck down.

"I was caught off guard last night," I reluctantly admit.

"What about the rest of the week? Hmm? You've been avoiding me."

"I've been busy. My life doesn't revolve around you. Sounds like you need to get your ego checked out along with that stick."

I sure as fuck hope he can't see through my bullshit answer. I've been avoiding him because of the flowers. They flipped the attachment switch in my brain and made me start to wonder what it would be like to spend Saturday nights at the club and Sunday mornings eating breakfast in bed. They made me start to wonder if he'd make room for my clothes in his closet, what our toothbrushes would look like together, and if the scent of my shampoo would mix well with his.

Things I have no business wondering because this thing is *just sex*. That's all it can be. I can't risk my job, and I can't risk my heart.

Ben pulls into a parking lot for a city park, and I look around at all the families scattered about, but I don't see the Rossis.

"Is this where we're having... lunch?" I trail off when I turn and see the intense way Ben's staring at me.

"No, *Dulzura*. I needed to ask some questions."

"Why?"

"Because I don't want you going into this unprepared."

I sigh. "Fine. Ask away."

"Are you aware they're trying to set you up with Mateo?"

I roll my eyes. "Yes. I gathered that when your dad said, 'Mateo is excited to meet you.'"

"And you still agreed to come? Why?"

"I didn't know until after I agreed! What was I supposed to say? 'Sorry, Enzo, I can't date your son because I'm actually fucking your other son.' It would have been rude to go back on my word."

Ben seems to mull over my answer for a minute before he hesitantly asks, "Do you want to date Mateo?"

No. I want you to take me to your place and help me turn my brain off for the rest of the day. I want to date you *and maybe eventually steal your last name.*

I don't say that, though. Because I can't let him think I'm getting attached.

Instead, I shrug. "Why not? I've already tried one Rossi brother, might as well try out the other one. Do a side-by-side comparison. Ooo, maybe we could have a threesome. I do love a good 'why choose' romance. There's something hot about it being two brothers."

I could be imagining it, but I swear Ben growls. "I don't share, honey. Especially not with my brother."

I push my bottom lip out. "Bummer."

In a flash, Ben has his hand wrapped around my throat in a possessive—yet surprisingly gentle—grip, and he's leaned over the center console, pulling me forward so our noses are an inch apart.

"I think I need to make something clear, so listen carefully. You're going to be polite to Mateo, but you're not going to give him any indication you're interested. You're mine, *Dulzura*."

I swallow thickly. "I'm not yours," I whisper weakly.

Ben chuckles darkly, like he knows I'm full of shit, then brings our faces closer so the tips of our noses touch. His hot breath fans against my mouth, and I've never wanted to break my "no kissing" rule more than I do right now.

"Tell me you won't leave with him. Tell me I get to have you tonight." It's not a request, but a demand.

"Drew?" is all I can respond with.

"You already agreed to come to my place."

"Ben, I—"

"*Please.*"

I don't think I've ever heard him beg, and I'm helpless to deny his plea. Especially when I want it just as badly.

"Yes, Sir."

"Good girl." His hand releases my throat, and I nearly whine at the loss.

He sits back and pulls out of the parking lot, acting like our conversation never even happened.

I have more questions now than I did before, and I feel I'm not prepared for any of the answers.

CHAPTER 28

Ben

Emma fits in with my family like she's meant to be here.

Mamà pulled her into a hug and gushed gratefully about the beautiful peonies she brought. Emma and Cici hit it off immediately. She saw Cici reading on her Kindle when we walked in, and they've been talking about books for half an hour. Even Cici's fiancé, Adam, has engaged in a conversation with her, and he's very shy.

She gave Mateo a polite greeting when we first got here but has otherwise been ignoring him in favor of Cici.

She's also ignoring me, but at least I know she's coming home with me.

Mateo looked a little dejected when she brushed him off, but Mamà told him to keep trying, and I had to bite back a possessive protest. If I know Mamà, she's already planned to sit them next to each other at the table.

I may have suggested she'd be more comfortable if I was seated at her other side since she knows me, and Mamà agreed easily, which put me at ease.

Once the antipasto platter is ready, Mamà calls for all of us to sit at the large dining room table. I sit on Emma's right, Mateo on her left, with Papà at the head of the table, and Mamà, Cici, and Adam opposite us.

We sip on wine and eat the various meats, vegetables, fruits, nuts, and cheeses on the platter while everyone—mostly Mamà—asks Emma a million questions, and I relish the way her cheeks stay a lovely shade of pink at all of the attention.

"Did you grow up in California?"

"No, I grew up in Utah. My best friend's parents moved us out here shortly after I turned twenty."

"Oh, I hear Utah is lovely, but I've never been. Do you have any siblings?"

"I'm the youngest of ten kids, actually."

I nearly spit out my wine. "Ten?" I clarify. Everyone else at the table gasps.

Emma pats me gently on the back, chuckling lightly. "Yes. I have a blended family. My mom was married before and had four kids, my dad has five from his previous marriage, and then they got married and had me."

"Ah, so you're the glue that holds them together," Papà teases.

Emma flinches slightly and forces out a laugh. "I guess so."

"Are you close with your siblings?" Cici asks.

"Not particularly. I see some of them maybe once a year when I visit."

"You see your parents more than once a year though, right?" Mamà looks offended. I find it hard to understand, too. I can't imagine not seeing Cici, Mateo, or my parents weekly—daily in Papà's case.

Emma takes a sip of wine, drumming her nails on her thigh. She's nervous. I hate that I can't ease her nerves. I want to take her hand and run my thumb along her knuckles. Let her know I'm here for her, that I've got her.

"Not usually," is her vague answer, and Mamà gasps.

"*¿Por qué no?* Your parents must miss you greatly."

Emma's lips try to stay tipped in a pleasant smile, but sadness swirls in the depths of her blue eyes. I get the feeling this is a tough subject for her, dulling her brightness.

"*Mamà*, I think this might be a personal thing Emma doesn't want to talk about," I interject, a little more bite in my tone than necessary.

Emma gives me a small, grateful smile, and Mamà studies me curiously but nods.

"I'm sorry, Emma. I didn't mean to pry or make you uncomfortable."

"It's okay. I wish I had a family as close as yours. Circumstances have just made it virtually impossible for that to happen."

I want to know the circumstances so badly. I want to know why she's closer to her childhood friend than any of the people she's related to. I want to know how they hurt her and how to make it better. I can tell Mamà is itching to know, too, but she keeps her questions to herself.

Conversation shifts to Emma's schooling, and what made her want to work in construction, and her answers make me feel even worse about the way I treated her when she started at Rossi.

She has a genuine passion for the work we're doing, and she's very knowledgeable. It's no wonder Derek chose to work with her. Papà was right in giving her a chance.

Once we've had our fill of the antipasto, Mamà brings out the main course.

Our family meals are a good blend of mostly Italian and Puerto Rican dishes, and today is no exception. Mamà has prepared *Bistec Encebollado*—a marinated slab of beef topped with onions—with a side of white rice, beans, and a mixed green side salad.

Earlier, I saw the flan she made for dessert in the fridge. It will pair perfectly with our afternoon espressos, and I'm eager to see if Emma likes the creamy dessert. Perhaps if she does, she'll let me feed it to her. I'd get to watch her plush lips wrap around the spoon and—

Not the time.

Once our food is dished up, I watch with rapt attention as Emma takes her first bite of the tender meat. She lets out an appreciative groan as the flavors hit her taste buds, and Mateo snickers from her other side.

Emma shoots him a glare. "What are you laughing at?"

Mateo bites his lip to keep from chuckling again. "I'm just glad to see you enjoying the food."

"I grew up in a household where pepper was considered spicy. Sue me for appreciating food with actual flavor." She uses a perfectly manicured nail to poke him in the arm, which makes him grin even wider in return.

It seems my *Dulzura* has forgotten she needs to be making it clear she's *not* interested in my brother.

"Camila, your food is impeccable. You may never get rid of me," Emma teases, and Mamà beams.

"You're welcome here any time, *bella*. Anyone who appreciates my cooking can be part of our family."

We clear our plates while Cici updates us on wedding planning, and Emma hangs on her every word, asking about every tiny detail from the colors to the flowers, and then begs to see her dress. Cici pulls up a picture and hands the phone to her, and Emma gushes about how perfect she looks in it.

I can tell Cici likes having another woman to talk about wedding prep with. She and Mamà are close, but Cici's only other female confidant is her college best friend. Cici's been on me and Mateo about getting married so she can have a sister. She and Janessa never got along well, so I'm sure Cici is hopeful Emma will become a permanent part of our family.

I zone out of the conversation as a future with Emma flashes before my eyes. Emma in a white dress, walking towards me with a bouquet of flowers on our wedding day.

Emma and I going to work together, being able to kiss her and hold her hand openly whenever I want.

Emma, her belly round with our child. Or, if she doesn't want kids, a dog, maybe. I don't care.

All these thoughts should terrify me and send me running, but they don't. They feel like goals to reach instead of fantasies to dream of. It solidifies the thoughts floating around about making her mine in more than the bedroom.

A zap of pain to my shin makes me turn to look at the little sprite next to me.

"Your mom was asking you a question," Emma murmurs out of the side of her mouth.

Sure enough, I look up to find Mamà's curious gaze on me, a sparkle of mischief in her brown eyes. I know that look. It's the look she gets when she thinks she knows something she doesn't fully understand.

I clear my throat, "*Lo siento, Mamà.* I was distracted by the wonderful meal. What did you ask?"

She hums like she doesn't fully believe me. "*Está bien, hijo mío.* I was just asking if you are seeing anyone new?"

My eyes dart quickly to Emma, who appears relaxed save for the way her nails are drumming on her thigh again.

"I am," I answer, and Emma's head whips towards me.

"Oh, that is wonderful! How did you meet her? How long has it been? Is it serious?"

I should have said no. I don't know why I said I am; this just causes more problems. "It's new. Just in the last month. We met at a... club. It's not serious. Not yet anyway."

"You haven't had a serious relationship since Janessa, so this girl must be special. What's she like?" Cici asks.

"She's... pure sunshine," I say honestly. "She's insanely gorgeous, easily the most beautiful woman I've ever had the pleasure of meeting. But it's not just about her looks. She knows how to connect with people on a level I've never been able to. She knows how to make people smile and feel comfortable with her, even if they only just met. She's meticulous with her planning and asks insightful questions. She thinks outside the box. She's passionate about her job and is fiercely loyal to the people she cares about. I've never met anyone like her." A small smile pulls at my lips.

"Oh my God," Cici whispers, hand over her heart. "You're so gone for her! You *never* talked about Janessa like that."

"This girl seems special, *Beniamino*. But you say things are not serious?" Papà asks.

"No. She's a little skittish. I think she's been hurt before and is worried about being hurt again, so I'm taking my time. Trying to win her over."

Mateo clears his throat, so I look over at him. My eyes automatically dart to Emma, who's gripping her fork so tightly I swear she's going to bend the metal. She refuses to meet my gaze, and her cheeks are as red as a tomato.

"Is she worth all the effort?" Mateo asks.

I don't hesitate to answer, "Absolutely."

CHAPTER 29

Emma

"Absolutely," Ben answered, but he wasn't looking at Mateo. He was looking at *me*.

At first, when he said he was seeing someone, my heart rate increased, and rage bubbled in my stomach, souring the delicious meal because I am *not* going to be a willing accomplice to cheating.

Then he said he met her at a club, and I realized he was talking about *me*.

But the things he was saying... how he described the woman... He couldn't have been describing me, right? He doesn't *like* me. Sure, he likes our scenes, and he likes fucking me—otherwise he wouldn't keep doing it—but he doesn't like me as a person.

Right?

The conversation shifted after that, even though I could tell everyone had more questions for Ben.

I have more questions for Ben. Who's Janessa? Was he truly talking about me? On the very off chance he wasn't talking about me, why the fuck is he still fucking me when he has someone he's clearly so smitten with?

Dread washes over me in a harsh wave. Maybe that's why he wanted me to come to his house tonight. He wants to get in one last session before he ends things to go be with whatever sunshine woman has captured his heart.

Camila brings out a delectable looking flan topped with a berry medley. I've never had flan before, and I'm sure it tastes divine just like the rest of Camila's cooking, but I can't taste anything over the bitterness of rejection sitting on my tongue.

I *knew* this would happen. I knew I would get attached to him and he would smash my heart into a million tiny pieces. I tried so hard not to, and yet, I still did.

Stupid, Emma.

I offer to help Camila clean up after we're finished, but she shoos me away, insisting guests don't help.

"Mateo, why don't you take Emma on a tour of the house?" Camila suggests, obviously still set on her match-making scheme.

Mateo looks from his mom to Ben to me then shrugs. "Come on, Emma. I'll show you my childhood room." His dark eyebrows bounce twice with innuendo as he holds his arm out for me to take, and I can't help but giggle.

I like Mateo in a brotherly way. Sure, he's handsome and charming. Funny and obviously a serial flirt but I don't feel the tingles in my lower belly like I do with his brother. I don't wonder what his hands would feel like caressing my body. I don't have the urge to kiss him.

Ben's jaw is clenched when I glance at him as I take his brother's arm. I'm sure I'll get an earful about it later. Maybe even a few spankings, but he doesn't get to be upset when I'm only trying to be a polite house guest. Or when there's the tiniest possibility he's seeing someone else.

Could this all be fixed with a simple conversation? Sure. But I'm scared of what the conversation will entail, and I'd rather put it off as long as possible.

Ignorance is bliss, after all.

Mateo shows me around the first floor, bypassing the kitchen and dining room, and walks me down a hallway which leads to the primary bedroom and an office. Then, he takes us upstairs, letting me stop to inspect the family pictures hanging on the walls.

Ben isn't smiling in most of the pictures, instead wearing a scowl like the camera has personally offended him. I stop at one where Cici is a baby, Mateo looks to be about two, and Ben around four or five. Ben's eyeing Cici warily, like he's not sure he likes her.

"So, he's always been grumpy, then?" I ask Mateo, gesturing to the picture.

Mateo laughs. "Yeah. He's been serious for as long as I can remember. But I think it's just a façade. I don't know why; it's not like our parents were super strict or something super traumatic happened to him. At least, not that I know of. Maybe it's an oldest sibling trait."

"Maybe," I reply noncommittally.

"Are your older siblings not grumpy?"

I think about my dad's oldest, Henry. He's twenty years older than me, so we've never been close. He's a bit of a douche, but I don't think I'd say he's grumpy.

My mom's oldest, Michael, is super chill. He hates drama and likes to be left alone. He's always cracking jokes and trying to lighten the mood.

"I honestly couldn't tell you much about my oldest brother. I didn't really know him until I was eight, and he was already almost thirty. He's kind of just an asshole."

Mateo frowns. "I can't imagine not knowing my siblings. But I only have two, so our situations are different."

I snort. "Yeah. I guess you could say that."

I can tell he wants to ask more questions, but I motion for him to continue up the stairs. He leads me to a closed door, and when he opens it, I immediately know it's Cici's old room. The pink walls and floral bed sheets are soft and feminine, matching her perfectly.

Mateo confirms it's hers then leads me to the next door.

"Now, don't feel bad, but you're not the first girl I've had in my room." He winks as he opens the door.

I feign offense. "How *dare* you! I'm supposed to be the *only* girl you have in your room."

"Don't worry, you can be the most memorable." He pumps his eyebrows again, and I smack him on the arm. "Ooo, I like 'em feisty."

"Oh, stop it." I giggle, taking in the room. I imagine there were plenty of posters or memorabilia covering the pale blue walls when he lived here. The queen bed is topped with a navy-blue comforter, but the room is warm and inviting just like Mateo.

Mateo grins. "The color of the walls match your eyes. It's almost like *fate.* Has anyone told you how pretty your eyes are?"

I roll my eyes. "You are quite the charmer, Mateo Rossi. Has anyone ever told you that?"

"All the time. But I like hearing it from you most," he drawls as he steps closer to me so our chests are almost brushing. His voice is low when he asks, "You're the girl my brother was talking about, aren't you?"

I swallow, looking anywhere but at him. "I don't know," I answer honestly.

Mateo uses two fingers to tip my chin up so I'm forced to look at him. He and Ben look related, but not the same. His eyes are brown, like Ben's, but they're lighter, softer. Closer to a golden brown than Ben's deep coffee-colored ones. There's a glimmer of humor there, and the laugh lines around his eyes crinkle when he smiles at me.

"I think you are. And I think he's going to burst into this room any second and rip me a new one for touching you. Ben has always been a possessive man," he teases. "As his little brother, I like pushing his buttons."

I'm about to argue that he's being ridiculous. Ben would never do something so dramatic. But not ten seconds later, the door clangs open, and Ben stands in the doorway, arms folded across his heaving chest. "Get your hands off of her."

From this angle, I'm sure it looks like Mateo and I were about to kiss. Mateo winks at me again before he removes his fingers from my chin and steps back. "I was just showing Emma my room, nothing nefarious."

"You need to be standing an inch away and touching her face to show her your room?" Ben snaps.

Mateo shrugs. "Wanted her to have the full experience."

"*Mamà* wants your help in the kitchen."

"Does she? I thought she'd be done with—"

"Now."

I watch Mateo bite back a smug, confident grin before he leaves with a wave and a wink to me. He whispers something to Ben that makes him grind his jaw before he's out the door.

"Let's go see my old room," Ben demands, and I follow, rolling my eyes at his alpha-hole attitude.

Ben leads me across the hall, opening the door to his childhood bedroom. I expected a navy-blue room, or even black, to match his grumpy personality. But instead, the walls are a calming sage green. The bedspread is dark gray with matching green embroidery.

I don't get to see much else because Ben's large body is pressing mine up against the now closed door.

"Why was he touching what's mine, *Dulzura?*"

I want to fight him. I want to tell him I'm not his. But for some reason, all I can do is tell him the truth. "He told me he thinks I'm the girl you were talking about at lunch, and that at any second you were going to burst through the door and get mad at him for touching me." I smile. "I guess he was right."

"Fucking Mateo," Ben grumbles, but he doesn't confirm nor deny he was talking about me at the table. I try not to let it affect me.

"I wasn't fucking him, actually," I tease, trying to hide my anxiety with humor.

"And you never will." Ben nods resolutely. "We're leaving now. So let's say goodbye."

"What? Why?"

His jaw works back and forth. "Because if I have to watch you flirt with Mateo any longer, I might kill my own brother."

I huff. "You're being *so* dramatic right now. I wasn't flirting with your brother. We were literally just talking."

"He touched you, Emma. I'd say that was more than talking."

I'm partially irritated at his protectiveness but mostly swooning. No one's ever been possessive of me like this. "Whatever. Let me thank your parents for lunch, and we can go."

He doesn't say anything, just nods and walks out the door.

Chapter 30

Ben

I t took us twenty minutes to leave my parents' house because Mamà wanted to send Emma home with leftovers, then Cici wanted to exchange numbers so they could go talk more about book recommendations and plan a shopping trip sometime.

Finally, after Mateo gave her a hug—that was a little too long for my liking—we're on the road to my place.

As soon as we drove away, Emma's shoulders slumped like a weight was lifted from them. She's been quiet ever since, intermittently tapping away on her phone when she receives a text. I wonder who she's texting. Is she texting Cici? Or Jordan to tell them about lunch? Is she telling them she didn't have a good time and trying to come up with an excuse to leave?

When I glance at her again, her face is pulled down into a frown. Is her mom texting her again? Did something happen with her grandpa?

It's truly none of my business, but since I was there when she got the news, I feel like it's polite to ask, "How's your grandpa doing?"

She sighs then tips her head back against the headrest and closes her eyes. "They transferred him back to his house because there's nothing else they can do for him. He's incoherent and out of it most of the time. I asked my mom again if I could come out and say goodbye, but she said no—and I know I'm an adult and can make my own choices, but not following my mom's directions is a recipe for disaster. I found out my two oldest sisters—my dad's kids, who don't even *know* him—are there. My cousin texted me to ask if I was coming too because apparently everyone else gets to say goodbye to him, but I can't based on some made up rule my mom's made. Probably because I'm the family disappointment, and she doesn't want me to taint his last few days with my sins."

Her mom sounds like a bit of an asshole. I don't even know how to help her right now, but I want to more than anything.

"Do you want me to take you home? We don't have to go through with tonight if it'll be too much for you."

"No, I want..." she trails off.

"What do you want, Emma?"

"I want you to help me turn my brain off for the night. I don't want to think anymore," she whispers, like she's ashamed of it.

"I can do that. I'll help you clear your pretty head for a while."

"Thank you."

"My pleasure."

Emma is quiet as I give her a quick tour of my house. It's nothing spectacular, just a three-bedroom, two-bathroom, rambler style home. It was a foreclosure, and I spent the better part of a year fixing it up and making it livable.

I try to see it through her eyes. The kitchen isn't grand like my parents', but it's a decent size with butcher block countertops and bluish gray cabinets with gold handles—Cici's doing. I would have kept them the ugly beige color they were originally, but Cici told me I needed to make it look homey. I don't know if Emma cooks, but I can picture her sitting on the counter while I make dinner. She'd chatter on about whatever new hyperfixation she has, and I'd listen because as much as I grumble about how much she talks, I love it.

My house is always so quiet, I know she'd breathe life into the still space.

"Nice place," Emma says distractedly, glancing around the living room. Her gaze snags on an old family photo, and she walks closer to inspect it.

"Thank you. *Mamà* and Cici helped a lot with the decorations and furniture so it didn't look like a 'bachelor pad,' and while I put up a fight initially, I'm grateful because I didn't have any idea where to start." I don't add that I picked out the furniture for my bedroom, the office, and the guest room, which is only ever used for a specific type of "guest."

"I was wondering if it was them or Janessa."

I eye her, trying to read her tone. She doesn't seem upset I've never talked about my ex-fiancée, maybe just a little confused.

"I bought this place after we broke up."

"How long ago was that?"

"Almost five years ago, and I bought this place a year after."

"How long were you two together?"

"We started dating just after college, so almost five years. We were... we were engaged. For two of those years."

Emma's mouth pops open into a little "o," and she nods. "That must have been hard. Ending an engagement."

"It was hard to separate our lives after spending so long together. But it was the right thing to do. Janessa didn't want to settle in one place. She's a reporter and was always looking for the next story to follow, the next big lead. She wanted to travel and try living in different places. I'm content with my life in San Diego and at Rossi, and when I told her I didn't want to quit my job to follow her around, we decided we weren't going to work."

Emma nods. "That still sucks. Thinking you have a future with someone and then it all just... crumbles."

I step closer to her. "Sometimes, the things we think we want aren't the things we need, and sometimes what we need are things we never considered. Sometimes, people are only here for a moment, and others are here forever."

Emma swallows harshly but doesn't say anything in response.

"Let me show you my favorite room in the house." I hold my hand out to her, and she nods and takes it. Something inside me settles being able to touch her again. Something warm and gooey seeps through the cracks in my hardened heart—cracks caused by the woman next to me—and fills me with warmth. Something more than lust, cementing my desire to make her mine for more than one night at a time.

I lead her down the hallway to the spare bedroom and open the door. At first glance, it looks like any other guest room in any other house. But the bed frame is custom-made with hidden hooks and slats for restraints. The dresser in the closet has a lock on it because it's where I keep all of my supplies. This room hasn't been used in any capacity in almost a year.

Emma looks around then spins to face me. "Didn't you say your room looked like the one at the club? This sure as hell doesn't."

She's right, it doesn't look like the club's room. Instead, the room is a nice navy blue with gray accents. I changed the sheets and put on the waterproof mattress protector before tonight in anticipation of Emma agreeing to come home with me.

"I said my room was *similar*. I think my family would have found it suspicious if I'd painted it black with red under lighting."

"Fair. That would have been an awkward conversation."

Fuck, I like seeing her here. Too much.

I step into her personal space so she has to tip her head back to look me in the eyes. "Are you ready to play, *Dulzura*? Are you ready to be my good girl and let me take away all the thoughts in your pretty head?" I stroke down her cheek gently, relishing in the heat that colors them pink. Her eyes hood as she bites her lip.

"Yes, Sir." And just like that, she slips into her role.

My cock hardens instantly. I've missed this. Our dynamic. Having her close.

I've missed *her*.

"I'm going to change out of my clothes. While I'm gone, I want you to strip completely, fold your clothes, and place them on the dresser, then lay on your back on the bed."

"Yes, Sir."

"I'll be back in a minute. There's a bathroom just across the hall if you want to freshen up." I lean in, intending to kiss her on the lips, then remember her rule, diverting my mouth to the top of her shoulder. I kiss her there, then turn and walk out, shutting the door behind me.

I walk into my own bedroom, which reflects my personality a bit more than the rest of the house. The walls are a dark gray, and the only furniture in here is my bed and side tables. I go into the mostly empty walk-in closet, and images of Emma's colorful wardrobe mingling with my clothes almost makes me crack a smile.

I bet she's as organized with her clothes as she is with her notes. She probably has some intricate organization system she uses.

I strip, leaving only my black boxer briefs on. I'm already tenting them in anticipation of what's to come, but I squeeze myself through the fabric in an effort to calm down. It isn't about me tonight.

Emma needs to get out of her head right now, to not have to think about her grandpa or work or anything else plaguing her. It's my job to take care of her tonight, to make sure she doesn't have to feel anything other than pleasure. A job I take seriously. We haven't explored overstimulation yet, and I think tonight is the perfect time to do so.

I want her to be boneless and so out of her mind with pleasure she can't think of anything else.

I stand at my bedroom door and listen for a minute to see if she's moving around the bathroom in the hall, and when I hear nothing, I open the door and walk to the kitchen. I pop the bottle I need in the microwave so it's nice and warm, then I make my way to the guest room door.

"I'm coming in, honey," I call out before I slowly open the door.

I'm pleased to find Emma followed my directions. Her clothes are neatly folded on the dresser, and she's laying in the middle of the bed with her eyes closed. Her chest heaves with every deep inhale, her perfect breasts tempting me to take a bite. I want to cover them in my marks, leave her with reminders of our time together for days to come.

I pad across the room to the closet, opening the drawer that holds the brand-new toys I bought specifically for Emma. I pull out a vibrator, nipple clamps, and the fuzzy pink handcuffs that I couldn't resist. They reminded me so much of her vibrant personality I had to get them.

I take everything over to the bed, and Emma's eyes open, sparkling with interest when she sees what I'm holding.

I hold up the nipple clamps. "Do you know what these are?"

"Nipple clamps, Sir."

I hum. "Yes. Have you ever used them before?"

"No, Sir."

A slow grin makes its way onto my face. I like that this is another first of hers I'll get to have.

I hold up the handcuffs. "Hands above your head, *Dulzura.*"

She complies, putting her wrists together above her head. I climb up so I'm straddling her waist and situate the cuffs over her wrists. These look more like leather wrist cuffs than handcuffs, lined with a fuzzy pink material so they aren't as harsh on her delicate skin. They have a snap button that's easy to undo in case she needs me to release her quickly.

I open the discreet compartment on the headboard that holds a lead with a clip that will trap her hands above her head.

Once she's clipped, she gives an experimental tug.

"Are you comfortable?" I whisper, leaning close to her ear.

"Yes, Sir."

Satisfied with her answer, I grab the bottle of honey from where I set it on the floor by the bed. I hold her gaze as I pop the cap and drizzle the warm, thick substance on her collarbone, over her chest, and down her stomach.

She gasps as the honey hits her skin, and I tear my gaze away to watch the golden liquid slowly slide down her ivory skin.

I replace the cap on the bottle and toss it to the floor before leaning over to lick up the honey settling on her collarbone.

I groan when the flavor of Emma mixed with the sweetness of the honey hits my tongue.

"Fuck, Emma. Honey doesn't even compare to your sweetness, but damn does it taste good on your skin."

I lick the trail of honey down to the top of her tits, laving away the amber liquid and making her squirm. When I get right above her nipple, I suck hard enough to mark her skin, and she whimpers and moans at the sensation, squeezing her thighs together, seeking relief.

Knowing she'll be wearing my mark around our coworkers, even under her clothes, fills me with pride. I want to leave one on her neck where they can see, but I know I can't. Not yet.

I move my mouth to cover her nipple, swirling my tongue around the drops of honey on the hard little bud. Once it's clean, I keep licking and sucking. I need to get it as hard as possible so I can use the clamps. Once her nipple is ready, I grab one end of the clamp and close it around the pink tip.

"Oh," she gasps, arching into my touch.

I give the same treatment to the other nipple, making sure it's stiff enough for the clamp to secure around it.

Once both clamps are in place, I give the chain connecting them a gentle tug. "How does that feel, honey?"

"So good, Sir," she moans.

"Look at how lovely your breasts look, *Dulzura*. I think they'd look particularly stunning with jewels pierced here." I tug on the chain again. "Or maybe some beads with my initials, hm? So everyone knows who they belong to. Every time you'd see yourself naked, you'd be reminded of who owns your pleasure."

God, that thought is hot.

I flick each nipple again with my tongue, then make my descent down her body, licking up the remaining honey and tracing every valley, curve, and swirl of ink with my tongue and lips. When I get down to her mound, I gently nip at it, causing her to squirm. I spread her pussy lips apart, growling when I find she's already wet and her clit hard and ready for me.

"There she is. Such a needy little thing. Do you need me to kiss it better, honey?"

"Please, Sir."

I give the nipple clamps another tug as I lick between her lips and swirl my tongue around her hard clit. She bows off the bed with a yelp at the sensations, and I groan as I finally get a taste of her again.

So fucking sweet.

I usually like to play a little, build her orgasm slowly, but since she's looking to turn her brain off, I plan on giving her as many orgasms as she can handle, so I won't be taking my time tonight.

I let go of the nipple clamp chain and insert two fingers into her as I circle my lips around her clit and suck. I pump my fingers quickly against that spot inside of her, and her answering moans are like sweet, sweet music. The chain on the hand cuffs rattles as she tugs on them, trying to move her arms. I grin against her cunt at the frustrated whimper she makes.

I pop off long enough to say, "Come for me, *Dulzura.* Make a mess of my sheets."

Then I dive back in.

As soon as I give her permission and give the nipple clamps another tug, she detonates.

My fingers slow but don't stop as I reach up and tug off each nipple clamp.

The blood rushing back into her nipples should make them tingle, adding to the stimulation I'm giving her pussy.

"How are your arms, *Dulzura?*"

She blinks, glancing up to where her wrists are still attached to the headboard.

"They're fine, Sir." She wiggles her fingers to prove her point.

"If you need me to take them off, you let me know." It's a command, not a question. She responds with an affirming nod.

I pick up the bullet vibrator and turn it on. My fingers—which are still inside her—start to move quickly again. Her body jolts as the vibrations hit her clit, and she tries to close her legs, but I keep them open with my shoulders.

I thought since she's already had one orgasm, I'd have to work harder for another one, but I was wrong. After just a few minutes, her pussy pulses on my fingers, and her moans pick up. I press another finger into her and work them harder on her sweet spot.

"Oh, *fuck.* Sir, please, can I come again?" she whines.

"So good for me, asking so politely. Go ahead and come for me, honey."

I up the vibrator's intensity, and she comes with a harsh cry, "Ben!"

Not "Sir."

Ben. I should punish her for forgetting to use the honorific, but I can't find it in myself to be upset she said my name.

"Fuck, yes. That's so beautiful, honey. Look at how wet you've made the sheets. Such a slutty little pussy, taking three of my fingers," I murmur as her pussy pulses through her orgasm.

When she subsides, I pull my fingers and the vibrator from her, turning off the device and tossing it on the bed somewhere.

Her pussy is glistening with her cum, and I can't stop myself from leaning in and licking it up.

"God, you taste so good. I don't think I'll ever get enough of you."

I flick her clit again with my tongue, and she gasps, "I can't, Sir."

"You can't what, *Dulzura?*"

"I can't come again, Sir."

I look up at her from between her thighs and give her a sinister smile. "Oh, honey. We're just getting started."

CHAPTER 31

Emma

Ben wasn't lying.

I don't even know how many orgasms I've had tonight, or how long we've been going. It could be an hour or twelve—I have no clue.

Ben released my wrists around the fourth orgasm, taking care to rub the feeling back into them before he promptly flipped me over so I could straddle his face.

My pussy is sore and overstimulated, my thighs are beard burned, and my body is sticky with sweat and honey residue. But for the first time in maybe ever, I don't have a single thought in my brain other than Ben and the overwhelming pleasure he's bringing me. I feel a little dizzy, and my limbs are relaxed.

When my arms can no longer hold me up, he lays me down on my back and uses the vibrator on me again.

"What's your color, *Dulzura*?" he asks as my umpteenth orgasm subsides.

"G-green, Sir," I croak.

"Are you sure? We can stop whenever you want."

"I want your cock, Sir."

Ben smiles. "Such a greedy little slut. Do you think you've earned it, *Dulzura?*"

"Yes, Sir."

Ben hums, then crawls up my body. "I'll give you my cock, *Dulzura,* if you promise to come on it. Give me another one. Show me how much you love getting fucked by me."

"I prom—" My sentence breaks off with a moan as Ben thrusts into me in one swift move.

"Fuck, honey. Needed this pussy. Been missing it so much. Never want to go that long without it again," he mumbles as he pulls out and slams back in.

I can't even appreciate his words because his pubic hair chafes against my abused clit as his cock punishes my pussy. The sensation is overwhelming and delicious at the same time.

"I wish you could see yourself right now, Emma. Looking so thoroughly fucked. So wrung out. You look so fucking beautiful. You're taking everything so well. Such a perfect little slut for me."

My pussy clenches around his cock at his praise. I'm sure I look well fucked. My makeup is probably ruined and my hair a frizzy mess, but Ben thinks I look beautiful.

Ben pulls out and flips me over so I'm facing the foot of the bed and he's kneeling behind me.

"Look at how good we look together," Ben rasps, gripping my hair in his hand and using it to turn my head towards the arched mirror in the corner.

I gasp as I take in the scene.

Ben looks like a god with his golden skin and chiseled jaw. My pale skin, marked with ink, is a lovely contrast. He was right about me looking thoroughly fucked, but I'm also glowing. My hair looks like spun gold in his grip, and my eyes are glassy, making the blue look electric.

He thrusts into me from behind, and I want to close my eyes at the sensation, but I force them to stay open so I can watch the muscles in his arms flex as he thrusts.

The new angle means he's hitting me even deeper, the meaty head of his cock hitting my G-spot with every thrust. I didn't think it was possible to orgasm this many times, but still, I feel another building.

"I feel you clenching, *Dulzura*. Come again for me."

"I can't," I protest, and Ben spanks my ass.

"You *can*. You *will*." He spanks me again, then his thumb presses against my back hole.

"Someday, I'm going to put my cock in this tempting little hole."

I tense.

"Not tonight. I'll need to take some time stretching you to take me here. But I'm sure you'll enjoy it."

I want to deny I will, but I've played with myself there and have enjoyed it. Still, having Ben's massive cock inside me *there* is as daunting as it is enticing.

Ben doesn't stick his thumb inside me, but he does apply pressure which only increases the pleasure of my impending orgasm as he picks up his pace.

"Yeah, you'll like it. I'll make you my good little anal slut in no time. You'll be begging to have me fill this sweet ass every fucking day before you know it."

Fuck, I forgot how dirty his mouth can be.

My release is *right there,* but I need something more to get me over the edge.

"Please, Sir," I whimper.

"What do you need, honey?"

"I-I don't know, Sir. Just... *more.*"

Ben pulls my head up so our bodies are almost flush and reaches around to pinch one of my nipples—still sticky from the honey--while he sinks his teeth into the top of my shoulder.

The angle change and the added pain send me over the edge, and I think I scream as my orgasm overtakes me. My vision goes dark as my release crashes through me with the strength of a freight train.

"That's it, *Dulzura.* I knew you had one more in you. Such a good girl for me. Squeezing me so tight. I'm going to fill this pussy, watch me drip out of you."

He grunts, then hot ropes of his cum paint my pussy. As soon as he releases his hold from around my chest, I flop onto the bed, completely boneless. My brain is swimmy and floaty, and all I want to do is sleep for ten years.

I'm vaguely aware of Ben pulling out of me and walking around the room before returning with a damp cloth to clean between my thighs.

I try to keep my eyes open because I need to get my bearings so I can go home, but they keep closing involuntarily.

Ben picks me up and cradles me to his broad chest, and I hear the crinkle of a water bottle in one of his hands.

"What are you—"

Ben shushes me before I can finish my question. "Relax, honey. I'm taking you to the shower. I can't have you all sticky in my bed, and you've made a mess of these sheets."

I begin to protest that a shower feels too intimate, but now that I'm no longer high off of orgasms, my skin is starting to stick to itself, and a shower sounds nice.

I also know arguing with him about aftercare would get me nowhere, so I don't put up a fight as he sets me in the glass encased shower. I really don't want to wash my hair without my special curly products, but I'm sure there's honey stuck in the strands.

I just hope he has separate shampoo and conditioner and not a ten-in-one.

His bathroom is black and white with touches of dark green in the décor. There's no bathtub like the bathroom by the guest room, just a large shower stall.

Ben turns the water on to the right temperature and silently lathers a clean washcloth with his body wash before gently rubbing down my skin, paying extra attention to the parts where he drizzled honey on me.

I wash my hair with his shampoo while he washes my body. His scent permeates the shower, and I already know I'll have a hard time wanting to shower it off me when I get home.

When that's done, he directs me under the spray to rinse off. I gently comb some conditioner through my hair before he hands over face wash to scrub away the makeup I was wearing.

I feel exposed. Raw. Vulnerable.

This feels too much like a serious relationship—I'm just glad he didn't demand to wash my hair for me. That would have been *too* intimate.

I'm too tired to deal with it today. I can panic about it tomorrow.

Once Ben has deemed us clean, he helps me out and pats me dry with a fluffy towel before leading me into his bedroom. My eyes are already partially closed when he sits me on the bed and directs me to drink the rest of the water in the water bottle.

Once it's gone, he lays me down and covers me with a soft blanket, before rounding the bed and settling in next to me.

"Rest now, *Dulzura,*" he whispers.

My body is intent to obey his commands because I fall asleep within minutes, even though I know this is blurring the lines.

CHAPTER 32

Ben

When I wake up the next morning, my bed is empty, and the spot where Emma was sleeping is cold. I throw on a pair of sweatpants and check the guest room, but she's not there either. Her clothes aren't on the dresser, so I can only assume she woke up sometime last night and hightailed it out of here.

I check the kitchen and living room for a note or something to give me an indication she's okay. That *we're* okay. But I find nothing.

There's a cocktail of emotions stirring in my gut.

I'm angry that she probably got into a stranger's car in the middle of the night so she could go home—away from *me.*

I'm worried she didn't make it home and something bad happened to her.

I'm angry at myself for not being clear about her sleeping over. I'm angry at myself for breaking another one of her rules because she said she never spends the night. How could I let her go home when she was half asleep when already in the shower?

But mostly, I'm just... hurt. I'm hurt she didn't leave a note. That she thought leaving in the middle of the fucking night was a better option than sleeping in my bed and waking up in my arms.

She told you what this was. It's not her fault you didn't listen.

I walk back into the bedroom when my phone buzzes on my nightstand. I check it and see a text from Josh.

Josh: Hey bro, want to grab dinner at River's End tonight and catch up?

Ben: Sure. 6?

Josh: Sounds good. See you then!

Then, I notice I still have an unread message. I click out of Josh's thread and find a message from Emma.

Emma: Sorry for bailing in the middle of the night. I didn't want to wake you up. Kiera picked me up on her way home from the club. No need to worry about me!

I guess it's good to know it wasn't a stranger who picked her up, and she did leave me a note. But it still hurts to know she'd rather sneak out than sleep next to me.

I already learned Emma has her read receipts off, so I don't know if she reads it immediately. Still, I sit and wait for the text bubble to pop up.

It never does.

After ten more minutes of aimlessly scrolling a news website while waiting for her to text me back, I decide I've been pathetic enough. She's not going to text me, and I have shit to do before dinner.

STRUCTION // UNDER CONSTRUCTION // UNDER CON

Josh is waiting for me in the waiting area of River's End and greets me with a hug and a slap on the back.

"It's been a while, my man! How've you been?"

"Pretty good. What about you?"

"Business is steady, so I can't complain," he says with a big grin.

Josh reminds me of a puppy. He's very... *energetic.* Not to mention he's charming as hell. He's got a Disney prince vibe to him that just makes people trust him, I guess.

I still don't know how he convinced me to be his friend. It probably has something to do with the fact he likes to talk, and I like to listen. He was unrelenting with his friendship in high school, and then we got partnered for doubles in tennis, and we've been best friends ever since.

We shared a dorm in college for the first two years, then shared an apartment with his brother during our junior and senior years. When Janessa and I moved in together after graduation, we rarely saw each other because she took up my free time.

He was there for our engagement party with a smile on his face, and then he was there with beers when Janessa and I ended things. I don't deserve him as a friend, but I'm glad he's here anyway.

We make small talk about our respective businesses and families while we wait for our table, then we're led to our table by the hostess.

Josh and I sit in silence as we peruse the menus, then our waitress comes and takes our drink and food orders.

As soon as she walks away, Josh turns to me with an expectant smile on his face.

"So, how's Emma doing?"

"Why the fuck would I know that?" Did she tell him something? How does he know about us?

Josh's brow furrows. "Because you work with her?"

Right.

I try my best to be nonchalant with my answer. "I thought you meant in general. You know I don't get personal with my coworkers. She's doing good. She picked up on things pretty quickly and even landed a job with Derek Allridge."

"Daaaaaaamn. Way to go Emma. I knew she'd be a good fit for Rossi. I'm glad your dad took a chance on her."

"Yeah, I guess," I grumble.

"You two don't get along, do you, Mr. Grumpy?" Josh teases.

"We're fine. We're coworkers. Nothing more." The words taste bitter on my tongue, and I take a sip of my drink to try and wash it away.

Josh gives me an unamused look. "Really? That's it? You're telling me Emma—with her bubbly personality and ability to connect with everyone—hasn't charmed you *at all*?"

She's charmed the pants right off me.

I can't stop thinking about her.

I'm pretty sure I'm in love with her.

I shrug. "What can I say? She knows I'm a lost cause."

Josh snorts. "I doubt she thinks that. She's determined to make everyone feel comfortable with her—like they can trust her. She's probably just waiting for the right time to strike. She's very observant. I wouldn't be surprised if she started showing up with your favorite coffee in tow just so she can break down your defenses and make you her friend."

"Why would she want to break down my defenses?"

"Emma's gone through a lot of shit in her life. I don't know if you know anything about her family, but they made her feel like she's only worth what she can do for other people. She wants everyone to like her because she thinks it's the only way she's valuable to someone. Don't get me wrong, she's one of the most genuine people you'll ever meet, but she also doesn't always know when to rest."

I don't tell him I know some of what her family is like. I know all about how she has nine fucking siblings, and not one of them seems to care about her. I don't tell him her mother won't let her say goodbye to her own grandpa.

Instead, I tell him, "Well, she's already on Ralph's good side, so it's only a matter of time before she worms her way onto mine."

Josh laughs in return and shakes his head. "Ah, good ol' Ralph. When is he retiring?"

We spend the rest of our dinner talking about work related things, family, and Josh's dating life while I stealthily avoid talking about mine. I know Josh views Emma as a little sister, and I don't need him giving me a speech about breaking her heart.

Later that night, when I'm laying in bed, I think about Emma and how I'm even more determined to crumble whatever walls she's built so I can make her mine.

CHAPTER 33

Emma

I knew falling asleep in Ben's bed was an omen or some shit that something bad was going to happen.

I spent all of yesterday worrying because for once I hadn't had the urge to sneak out in the middle of the night. For once, I wanted to bask in the heat of another person's body and wake up next to them.

But my heart is already too attached, and waking up to his deep morning voice, watching him go through his morning routine, knowing how he takes his coffee, and eating breakfast together like a couple would completely break me.

So I texted Kiera and asked her to pick me up. It was pure luck she was working the closing shift at the club last night and getting off at the same time I reached out, or I would've taken a rideshare, and I didn't really want to do that alone at one in the morning.

Everything seemed to be fine yesterday. I thought I was just overreacting.

Until my mom called me at six this morning while I was getting ready for work to deliver the news I was anticipating but still wasn't prepared for.

Grandpa Walter passed away in his sleep last night, the funeral will most likely be Friday. It was in his funeral plans to have the grandkids sing *Nearer, My God, to Thee* at the funeral, so I better come prepared to perform. Guess my six years of school choir will finally be put to use.

"And please, Emma," Mom sighs. *"Try to remember you'll be in the presence of family. Of children."*

In other words: *"Please cover your tattoos and take out your nose ring so no one knows you're such a heathen."*

Now, I'm running late to work because I couldn't stop crying long enough to get my makeup done.

Jordan was there to comfort me, and when I asked them if they would come with me to Utah, they cursed and apologized profusely because they have a conference in San Francisco this week they can't get out of since they're a key-note speaker. I felt like an asshole for forgetting that.

I assured them I'd be fine. It's not their fault this happened. I've made the drive alone before, and I've faced my family my whole life. I'll be fine.

Now, pulling into work, I take a deep breath and plaster on my mask as best I can. I'll need to talk to Enzo about taking the rest of the week off, but I'm sure he'll understand.

I just have to get through today and pretend like nothing's wrong, then I can fall apart.

CHAPTER 34

Ben

Something's wrong.

Emma always gets here at 8:45 a.m. on the dot. She puts her lunch in the kitchen downstairs, then comes upstairs and says good morning to the team. Once she's in her office, she opens her blinds before sitting down at her computer and making a list of the things she needs to get done for the day.

Today, she didn't get here until 9:05 a.m. I'm assuming she didn't bring lunch because she didn't stop in the kitchen before coming up. It wouldn't be odd if she had a lunch meeting, but I checked her calendar this morning, and her schedule is wide open. She didn't say anything to anyone this morning, either. Just kept her head down and scurried to her office.

When I'm positive she's engrossed in her morning planning, I assess how she looks. Her curly hair is pulled back into a braid, which isn't unusual, but the puffiness of her eyes, lack of makeup, and tinge of redness to her nose is.

She's been crying. A lot, from what I can tell.

Was she crying over me?

Before I can get up to say something, Papà walks into her office and closes the door. They don't turn the glass opaque, so I watch them talk, but I can't hear what they're saying. I've never wished to be a fly on the wall, but I find myself wishing for it right now.

Get a hold of yourself.

I pretend to type while I watch out of the corner of my eye. Emma keeps wiping away tears as they fall, but I can tell she's trying to keep a bright smile on her face. Papà leans over and takes her hands in his while he talks. She nods at whatever he's saying, then they both stand, and Papà wraps her in a big hug.

I shouldn't be jealous my father is comforting the woman I'm falling in love with, but I am.

I want Emma to come to *me* for comfort. To trust *me* with the things that bother her.

But I'm glad Papà is there for her, even if Emma doesn't want me to be.

When Papà leaves her office, he shuts the door behind him and walks across the hall to my office and closes my door. Just as he sits down, I see Emma pack up her bag, shut off her light, and leave the office without saying a word to anyone.

"Where is she going?" I ask, my tone more frantic than I want it to be.

"She's taking the rest of the week off. She has a family emergency and needs to be in Utah by Friday."

Fuck. Her grandpa probably passed away.

Why didn't I think about that? I knew her grandpa wasn't doing well. That should have been my first thought when I saw her crying.

"She's driving to Utah alone?"

Papà shrugs. "I assume so. When I asked if she had someone to go with her, she said her roommate isn't available."

I shake my head. "I don't think that's a good idea."

"Well, *Beniamino,* I don't think so either, but I'm not in a position to tell her what to do. I'm only her boss, not her father. I gave her the week off—paid, of course. She told me she could finish out today, but I told her to go home and take some time for herself before she makes the drive."

I already know what I need to do, but I don't know how to go about this without exposing my feelings for her to Papà. It's not that I don't trust him, but I haven't even told Emma how I feel. I should probably tell her first.

"You've barely used any of your paid time off this year. Take the week off and go with her." Papà demands, crossing his arms.

"Why would I go with her?"

I don't think I've ever seen Papà roll his eyes, but he does as he mutters in Italian before giving me a look like I've insulated him. "You think *Mamà* and I didn't see you two on Saturday? You don't think we know you well enough to know when you're romantically interested in someone? Sure, you haven't dated anyone since Janessa, but you never looked at her the way you look at Emma. I don't know Emma as well as I know you, but I can tell there were no sparks between her and Mateo. But you two? You could have set the house on fire with the sparks flying between you.”

“I don’t—”

“Ah, ah, ah. Don’t try to deny it, *Beniamino*. As your boss and your *papà* I’m telling you to take the week off. We can handle whatever might come up. She needs you more than we do right now.”

I don’t give my parents enough credit. I thought I kept my feelings secret, but I guess I was wrong. I don’t know how to tell Papà this is just sex. Emma doesn’t want more.

“Fine. I’m... falling for her. But she wouldn’t want me to come with her. Whatever is between us doesn’t seem to be enough to make her want me for more than one night at a time.”

“Oh, *figliolo*. Even though she tries to hide it, I can see the hurt in that girl’s eyes. For all her sunshine, she’s still scared of getting burned. She needs to know you’re not going to give up on her. I think going with her to Utah is a good start. Besides, it’s clear her family isn’t going to be a shoulder for her to lean on. She needs someone in her corner if she’s going to face them.”

If Jordan can’t go with her, then yeah, she’s going to need someone to lean on. I don’t like the idea of her driving to Utah alone, then facing her family alone and heartbroken.

“Did she tell you when she’s leaving?”

“Tomorrow morning. But since I gave her the day off, she might leave tonight. You better go now so you don’t miss her.”

I save the document I was working on and lock my computer, then grab my work bag and stand to leave. Papà follows me out of my office.

I turn to him and give him a hug. *"Grazie, Papà."* *Thank you, Father.*

"Prego, figliolo." You're welcome, son. "I'm excited to have a new daughter-in-law soon." Papà smirks.

"Don't get ahead of yourself."

But I know he already has. I'm sure Mamà has already planned our wedding, and she and Cici are already planning on Emma coming around for Christmas in a little over two months.

Visions of Emma sitting on my lap while my family gathers around the tree and opens presents assault me as I make it to my truck.

I want that.

I want her to wear the silly matching pajamas Mamà still buys for us. Emma would probably be thrilled to see me in the printed monstrosities. She'd probably help Mamà and Cici pick them out.

I shake my head when I get in the driver's seat. I have a few hurdles to jump over before I can get into matching pajama territory.

The first one is getting her to agree to let me come with her to Utah.

I send a text to Jordan.

Jordan: About two hours. Please tell me you're going to make a grand gesture and go with her? I can't go with her because of a conference, and I don't want her to go alone. I know our plan was for you to take it slow, but she needs you right now.

Ben: I don't know if this is a grand gesture, but I'm not letting her go alone. Plans change, but my feelings haven't.

Jordan: It is a grand gesture. Don't let her push you away now. She needs someone else on her side.

Ben: I'll be by her side as long as she lets me.

Forever, if I have it my way.

Chapter 35

Emma

I appreciate Enzo telling me to take the day off, but without the distraction of work, I don't know how to stop the sadness from consuming me.

I haven't stopped crying since I left work, and if I can't stop, I don't know how I'm supposed to make the eleven-hour drive. When Jordan comes with me, we split the driving so we're able to make it all in one day, but with how I'm feeling, I don't think I should try it by myself.

If I leave tonight, I could stop in Vegas and break it up into two days instead of driving straight through... That would be easier than trying to do it all in one day.

I wish Jordan could come with me. Hannah already texted to tell me I was welcome to stay with her if I didn't want to stay with my parents, which would upset my mom. I don't know if I can handle four days of my mother's belittling on top of the grief and dealing with the rest of my family. I told Hannah I'd just get a hotel.

Her babies are almost ten months old, and I don't want to add to her plate.

Times like these, I wish I had a significant other to come with me as a buffer. To have someone to lean on instead of having to stand strong all alone.

I hate being around my family. I hate funerals. Being able to hold someone's hand and lean on them when I'm forced into these situations would make them more bearable.

But I made the choice to not be serious with someone—to not let anyone in. I have to live with the decision. It's not someone else's responsibility to help me carry my emotions. It's mine alone.

I'm in the middle of packing when there's a knock on the door. Must be a package for Jordan. They're in sessions today, so I'll just let the delivery person leave the package on the porch.

A minute later, there's another knock, and my phone buzzes with a text.

Ben: Open up, honey. I know you're here because your car is in the driveway.

Why the hell is Ben here?

I pad out of my room and open the front door. Sure enough, the bane of my existence and object of all my fantasies is standing in front of me wearing a Rossi Construction polo and jeans that hug his thighs.

Why does he have to be so handsome?

Ben's brows are furrowed as he takes in my appearance. I've changed into comfy hot pink leggings and an oversized threadbare T-shirt with a logo of a band I've never heard of. I never put on makeup today. My eyes are puffy, and my nose is red from crying.

"What are you doing here?" I ask, my voice smaller than I want it to be.

"I'm here to take you to Utah."

"How did you—*Enzo*." I pinch my nose. "I don't need you to take me to Utah. I'm a big girl. I can go alone and handle myself just fine."

Ben steps toward me, and I step back. We follow this pattern until he's inside the house. He shuts the front door with his foot and stands chest to chest with me, a determined expression on his face.

"This isn't about you not being able to handle yourself. It's about you not *needing* to do it alone. I'm sorry about your grandpa, Emma. I can't imagine what you must be feeling, but I can't just sit here while you suffer eight hours away. I won't let you go through this by yourself."

"Eleven," I murmur, blinking back tears.

"What?"

"It's eleven hours away. Not eight."

Ben gives me a half smile. "Then I'm for sure not letting you drive eleven hours alone."

I don't want to lean on Ben because when our agreement ends, I'll have to deal with it alone. When another tragedy inevitably happens in my life, I won't have him to rely on to help keep me steady.

Besides, having him meet my family sounds *serious*. I haven't brought anyone I've dated back to meet my family because they're so judgmental and rude. Their opinion on who I'm dating doesn't matter to me, so why would I subject them or myself to unnecessary ridicule.

Ben taps my forehead gently. "I can feel you thinking. Tell me why you don't want me to come."

"Because we aren't together. Because my family is... a lot, and I don't want to field questions about who you are. Because you have to work, and you shouldn't be burdened with taxiing me around and dealing with me because I cry a lot when I'm sad."

Ben frowns. "Okay, one thing at a time. First, we can *say* we're dating even if we aren't."

I scoff, "We can't do that. Hannah already used the fake dating trope."

Ben's frown deepens. "I don't know what that means."

Of course he wouldn't know what it means.

I wave him off. "Never mind. I haven't brought someone to 'meet the parents' since high school, so they'd already be suspicious. Especially since I never told my mom I was dating someone in the first place."

He shrugs. "Just tell her it was casual, so you didn't want to say anything. But now we're serious, and you needed me to come hold your hand through this."

"I can't tell her that either. She can't know how much I'm hurting right now."

"Why the hell not? Your grandpa passed away, *Dulzura*. That's something to be sad over."

I don't know how to explain this to someone who hasn't left the church, but I guess I have to try.

"I left my lifelong religion when I was eighteen. Growing up, I was taught if I left the church, I'd never truly be happy, and that's what my family believes. I can't let on if I'm miserable because they'll use it against me to prove I made the wrong choice. So happy is all I can be. If she finds out I'm distraught over Grandpa dying, she'll say I need to come back to church so I can see him again in the afterlife. She did it when my brother died. She used his death to manipulate me."

I don't think I've ever seen Ben speechless, but he's staring at me like what I'm saying is preposterous.

It is *preposterous.*

"How—*why* would a parent treat their child that way?" he mumbles more to himself than to me, but I still hear it.

I shrug. "I don't know. I learned at a young age any negative feelings I had would be attributed to not being faithful enough. When in reality, I've been severely depressed my whole life. I saw a therapist when I left the church, and she told me I've had clinical depression and anxiety—along with my neurodivergence—my whole life. I've gotten really good at pretending it doesn't exist, and medication helps, but sometimes it's not as easy to put on the mask."

"Your parents never helped? They never saw the signs?"

"They did, but they thought it could all be fixed if I were more righteous." I want to move on from this depressing topic, so I continue, "Anyway, what's second?"

Ben blinks, then scrubs a hand over his face like he's trying to keep the words in his mouth. "My dad already gave me the week off. He didn't feel comfortable with you going alone either."

"Oh."

"Yeah, *oh*. And the third thing. The one about me being 'burdened' by you." He uses air quotes around burdened. "It's not a burden to help you carry the weight of your emotions, Emma. Whoever told you that in the past clearly wasn't strong enough to do it—but I am. It's also not a burden to spend time with you. In fact, I think this could be fun. I can help you take your mind off of the sadness, even if it's only for a little while."

"But why would you want to?" I blurt out.

Ben steps closer again and cups my face. "Because you deserve it. Because I want to spend more time with you. I want to be here for you, Emma. Please let me."

His espresso eyes look so sincere. He sounds so genuine, I don't have a choice. "Okay. But we're sleeping in separate hotel rooms."

He chuckles condescendingly. "Not a chance, *Dulzura*. You snuck out on me once already; I'm not going to let you do it again."

I roll my eyes. "I can't sneak out if you're my ride."

He raises an eyebrow.

Oh, right. I already did that.

"We'll share a room because it's cost effective," he declares. "I won't force you to share a bed—since it seems to make you uncomfortable—but if a single bed is the only one available, I don't have any control over that."

I want to tell him I'm not uncomfortable sharing a bed with him. I'm *too eager* to share a bed. I think sharing a bed with him for a whole night would probably tip me over the edge, and I'd fall completely in love with him.

You're already halfway there.

Actually, now that I think about it, this road trip will be the thing that tips me over the edge. I'm going to have to come back and end our arrangement because by the time we're back in San Diego, I'll be so in love with Ben Rossi I'll need another week off of work to recover from the heartbreak.

"Let me finish packing, and then we can go pack your stuff," I say, trying to stop the spiral of thoughts.

"I already packed. I didn't want to give you any reason to tell me no."

Of course he did.

"I planned on stopping in Vegas tonight so I wouldn't have to drive straight through."

Ben nods. "Works for me. I know just where we can stay."

"I can help drive if you get tired—"

"No. You get to sit pretty in my passenger seat. I'll do the driving."

I don't have it in me to fight him. "Fine."

Chapter 36

Ben

While Emma finishes packing, I make myself comfortable on the desk chair in her room.

Her room is... not what I expected. Her office at work is so organized and neat, but her room is the complete opposite.

There's a pile of clothes laying on the end of her queen-sized bed. Her sheets are hot pink with matching pillowcases, but instead of a matching comforter, she's got some type of homemade quilt that looks like it's made out of old T-shirts.

Maybe it's because she's been packing, but instead of putting her clothes back in the closet if she doesn't want to take them, she tosses them on the end of the bed.

She has a wall full of random pictures in mismatched frames above her baby pink desk, which is covered in an array of office supplies and random pieces of mail. There's a full-body mirror standing next to her clos-et—which is bursting with shoes and clothes. I can barely see inside the attached bathroom, but what I can see is makeup and skin care stuff strewn across the counter.

Is it possible for someone to be so organized in one aspect in their life, but not another?

It seems like Emma is.

Instead of it being off-putting, I find it makes me like her more. I want to know all the messy and disorganized parts of her. See what she hides beneath the mask.

For the last twenty minutes she's been flitting between the bathroom and the bedroom, rolling clothes—I've counted eight outfits, not including pajamas—and gathering her toiletries.

"Do you need eight outfits for a not-even-five day trip?" I ask, watching intently as she rifles through what I assume is her underwear drawer. I want to know if she's bringing any more of those pretty, lacy sets.

"I like to be prepared. I don't always know if I'm going to want to wear the outfit I have planned. I know it's silly, but I want to have options." Her voice is quiet, and she won't look at me as she says it. I think I've hurt her feelings.

"That makes sense. I usually wear the same thing every day, so I have no trouble packing. Will they all fit in your duffle, or do you need another bag?"

She finally looks at me. "Uh, they should all fit. Thank you."

"For what?"

"For not making fun of me for being an over-packer."

Something pokes at my heart. Has someone done that in the past? Have they made fun of her for wanting to be prepared? I may not understand why she does it, but I'm not going to make fun of her for it.

"You shouldn't have to thank me for that, but you're welcome. What else do you need to pack?"

Emma closes the drawer and drops the bundle of underwear in her bag before I can see it.

"I think just my phone charger and my Kindle." She grabs the items and zips her bag.

Then, she grabs the pillow off of her bed and shoves it between the two smaller handles on the duffle bag before slinging it over her shoulder.

"You know hotels have pillows, right?"

"Yes. But *my* pillow is the perfect firmness and has already been broken in. Hotel pillows are usually too lumpy or too fluffy, and then I won't be able to sleep."

I guess that makes sense.

"Okay then. Last chance to grab something before we hit the road." I glance at the time on my phone. "We should be able to make it to Vegas by eight with a few pit stops."

Emma glances around her room again, then double checks the bathroom before she deems herself ready.

When she goes to reach for the duffle bag, I swoop in and grab it before she can.

"I can carry my own bag," she huffs.

"I know. So can I. Let's go, honey."

Emma follows behind me as we walk out her front door. She locks it, then we walk to my car where I deposit the bag into the back seat, then open Emma's door for her.

She picks up the plastic bag in her way. "What's this?"

"Road trip snacks." I give her shoulder a little shove to get her to sit down so I can close the door, then round the car to settle into the driver's side.

Emma's rifling through the bag with her brows furrowed when I close my door.

"How did you know these are my favorites?"

I shrug. "I pay attention. You and I have spent a lot of time in the car together."

"I didn't know you paid attention to those kinds of things."

I start the car, then look her dead in the eye when I say, "I pay attention to everything about you, *Dulzura.*"

I watch Emma's throat work on a swallow. "Well, thank you. It was very thoughtful of you."

"I take care of what's mine."

Whatever reply she had is cut off by my phone connecting to the Bluetooth, and the voices of the podcasters coming over the speakers.

When I get it turned off, Emma gives me an unamused look. "Are you seriously listening to a podcast about *construction*?"

"It's our field!"

"You're not supposed to make it your whole life! Listen to a true crime podcast or an audiobook for crying out loud."

"Got any recommendations?"

"Actually, yes. There's a great new audiobook out now about a vanilla businessman who gets snowed in with two loggers who are *really* into primal play and—"

"*Che cazzo?* What the hell kind of books do you read?"

Emma smirks. "That's tame compared to the other one I just read about a mafia boss who breaks into this girl's apartment and watches her sleep and then stalks her until she falls in love with him. Ooo or I could tell you about the one where her two step-brothers—"

"Nope." I turn the construction podcast back on as I pull out onto the road. Emma shakes her head, but I see a small smile tugging at her lips.

This girl keeps managing to surprise me.

CHAPTER 37

Emma

B en refused to listen to any of my smutty audio-
books while we drove, claiming he didn't need any
help in that department.

I have to agree. Book boyfriends don't hold a candle to
Benjamin Rossi.

Even though I love my dark romance, after some of
the things I've been through, a real life stalker isn't hot.
It's scary.

I managed to get him to agree to a true crime podcast,
but he made me turn it off after two episodes because he
was so aghast these things actually happened, and that
people talk about it so casually.

After I turned it off, he let me pick the music. I settled
on my sad girl playlist because as much fun as I've had so
far, I'm still extremely heartbroken about Grandpa.

I'm also wildly anxious to see my parents. I haven't
been back to Utah since last May when I came to cele-

brate Andy's fortieth and went to Wes's concert with my cousins.

The concert was the only good part of the trip.

The rest of the time was spent trying to avoid upsetting my narcissistic sister Hailey because my mere existence pisses her off and dodging all the "life advice" from the rest of my siblings who don't know a single fucking thing about me but feel like they get an input in my life.

Halfway to Vegas, I turn the music down. "I should probably warn you about my family."

"I think I've been sufficiently warned. What else could there possibly be?"

I blow out a breath. "You have no idea. I won't bore you with the details, but I feel like you should be adequately prepared in case they say something out of pocket—which they will."

"Alright. Hit me."

I explain again how both of my parents have kids from previous marriages and because of their ten-year age gap, it means I have siblings who are closer to my mom's age than my own. That until I was thirteen, I had only seen two of my oldest siblings a handful of times. How my dad's two youngest lived in Illinois with their mom, and when I was around five their mom stopped letting them visit for the summers.

I explain that I grew up with my mom's kids, and my sister Hailey is the one I've lived with longest, but she hates me simply because I was born.

I tell him how my whole life I was told I was the glue meant to bring the families together, and I was burdened with the responsibility of bringing my siblings back to the church.

"Something... happened to me in high school, and my family didn't handle it well. That's when I started to realize my family didn't really care all that much about me. They did things out of obligation, but they didn't like *me*," I say, not sure how deep into it I should go with him.

"You don't have to tell me what happened, but just know whatever you say, I won't judge you for it."

The sun is setting as we get closer to Vegas, so it's easier to bare my soul in the dimming light of the setting sun.

"The longish short story is when I was sixteen, I met a guy on a dating app. He was twenty, so I didn't think much of the age difference since it was only four years. He was a member of the church, too, so I thought it automatically made him a good guy—I was wrong. He started getting really aggressive and possessive. He would get upset if I didn't text him back immediately, even when I was in school, and he made me feel guilty for just being a regular high school student. He would get upset when I would go to dances with my friends, demanding all of my free time. I tried to end it multiple times, but he would manipulate me into coming back to him. I was with him for a year before I finally told my parents because I was so scared.

"Hailey's husband is a cop, and I guess legally he had to report it, even though my parents wanted to just brush it under the rug. We had recently moved, but my brother was still living in the old house with his family. They needed to know about the guy because he knew my old address."

Tears spring to my eyes. I hate talking about this. It's hard not to feel ashamed for the danger my family could've been in.

"I don't know exactly what my parents told my brother Neil, but he asked me 'Did you screw him?' I never willingly gave myself to the man. He manipulated me. Everything I did was out of survival. Then, my family started referring to it as the 'mistake' I made. It was labeled statutory because of our age difference, and in the eyes of the court, I was an active and willing participant, even though I was manipulated.

"About a year later, before I moved out, Hailey and I got into an argument about God knows what, and she told me it was my fault I was raped. She said I made everyone else's life miserable because I was stupid. Then, one of my other sisters told me I was ruining his life by taking him to court. That I was being dramatic because I regretted sleeping with him."

Ben's hands tighten on the steering wheel, and he shakes his head. "That's fucked up, Emma."

"I know. I should have known better—"

"No," he barks. "It's fucked up that your sisters—your *family*—would blame you for that. You were a kid. You needed support, not blame."

"You don't even know the whole story," I argue weakly.

I saw a trauma therapist after I graduated high school, and she helped me realize what happened wasn't my fault, but it took a long time. Sometimes, when I have to tell people the story, doubts creep in, and I start thinking maybe it *was* my fault. That if I had been smarter or less trusting, none of it would have happened.

"I don't need to know the longer version. I know your family was in the wrong for how they treated you. I'm sure there's more, so we can circle back later if you want to tell me the whole story, but just know I don't think any part of what happened was your fault."

"I—okay." I take a deep breath. "After, things were... not great, but tolerable when I moved in with Jordan's family after graduation. I didn't see my family much. I had a boyfriend, a job, I was taking online classes, and Jordan's parents were talking about moving to California. I was considering moving in with my boyfriend.

"Then, four days after New Year's, my mom called me at six in the morning while I was getting ready for work. She told me Andy was missing, and I needed to come home to be with the family so they could search for him. Apparently, he had been missing for a few days." My tone turns bitter every time I say it because no one even thought to tell me he was missing until it was too late.

"The police wouldn't do anything since he was a grown man in his thirties. He lived with my brother Alex and his family at the time, and they were worried. They tracked him to a casino in Nevada, but one of Hailey's high school friends saw him, and he left. So when I got to my brothers' house, my parents and brothers went out to search. A few of them split off and decided to search an area Andy liked to go to four-wheeling."

I hate the next part the most.

"While we were waiting to hear how the search was going, Alex's wife checked the mail and found an envelope full of cash and a note from Andy apologizing he couldn't give them more to help with rent. At the same time she was reading the note, Hailey's husband called and told her they found..." My voice breaks as tears start to stream down my cheeks. "They found his truck, still smoldering, with him inside."

Ben curses under his breath as one large hand makes its way to my thigh. Not even caring about our rules right now, I place my hand on top of his.

"We were all distraught, but I had to hold it together and get us over to my parents' house. I can still vividly hear my mom's cry of pain when we pulled in the driveway. I had to get my niece from daycare because her parents weren't in any state to do it. I was brushed aside with funeral planning. They made me feel like because I was only his half-sister, I wasn't allowed to grieve him the same way they did."

Ben squeezes my thigh. "That's fucking awful. I can't—I don't even have words to express how fucking sorry I am. You deserve better. Was your boyfriend at the time at least a good support system?"

I bark out a laugh. "Not at all. He was upset I didn't want to have a nerf gun fight with his siblings the night of Andy's funeral."

"He sounds like an asshole."

"Yeah," I sigh. He was an asshole. I broke up with him two months later because he was upset I was still sad about Andy's death. I leave that part out, though.

"Did you ever find another note, or anything to help give your family closure?" Ben asks quietly.

I shake my head. "No. We can speculate the reasons—*have* speculated. All of us have struggled with some sort of mental illness, but Andy was never diagnosed, so we don't know for sure. We don't even know exactly how he died—or when—because of the damage the fire did to him and his truck."

"I'm so sorry you had to go through all of that, Emma."

I give him an appreciative smile. "Thank you."

CHAPTER 38

Ben

"Sorry for dumping all of that on you in the middle of the desert with nowhere for you to run," Emma murmurs, her fingers gently running over my knuckles. I don't think she realizes she's still touching me.

I like the casual touch way more than I thought I would. I was never overly affectionate with Janessa. We didn't hold hands in the car. She never laid her feet on me while we lounged around on the couch. We didn't hold hands while grocery shopping or sitting at the dinner table.

But I want all the casual touches with Emma.

I want everything with her.

I want to *be* everything to her.

I'm honored she trusts me enough to share things that are so personal, so raw. But I wish we weren't in the car so I could comfort her better.

I *hate* that I can't take away the pain from her past. I hate that her family treated her so poorly she's scared to let anyone in.

Maybe I shouldn't go to the funeral with her. If I see any of her siblings or her parents, I can't promise I'm going to be able to keep my cool. They don't deserve any of Emma's time or tears.

I flip my palm over and lace our fingers together, giving her a reassuring squeeze. "Don't apologize, honey. I'm honored you trust me enough to tell me. I just wish I could do more to help you."

Emma gives me a sad smile and squeezes my hand back. "I appreciate it, but I don't need help. I've handled it on my own for this long, and I'll handle it when our arrangement is over."

Ouch. Her words feel like a fucking CAT 825 soil compacter rolling over my heart.

Oblivious to my internal wounds, she continues, "I just wanted to give you some insight into my relationship with them in case they say something. I need you to be prepared to just... brush it off and pretend it didn't happen."

Pretend it didn't happen? "Why the fuck would I do that?"

"They don't do confrontation well. It's easier to just keep the peace and cry about it later."

"I don't like it, but I'll do it for you." I'd do anything for her, but I don't tell her that yet. She still thinks this is temporary.

"Thank you, Ben." She gives my hand another squeeze, then turns the music on, effectively ending the conversation.

That's okay. We're only about an hour from the hotel, and I still need to process the information Emma's given me. I need to form a plan to show her I'm not like her family. I won't abandon her in her lows, and I won't give up on her when things are hard.

This road trip is the perfect first step.

UNDER CONSTRUCTION // UNDER CONSTRUCTION // UNDER CON

An hour later, I pull into the loop in front of the Cosmopolitan and—against her protests—make Emma stay in the car while I get us checked in.

The woman at the front desk asks if I want a room with one bed or two, and I begrudgingly ask for two, even though I'm going to try my darndest to get Emma to stay in my bed.

"Is there any way I could get a room with a balcony overlooking the strip?" I ask while she looks at her availability.

"Yes. The Corner Tower suites offer a strip view with a balcony. Unfortunately, those rooms only have one bed."

"That's fine. I'll take it." I wonder how pissed Emma will be when I tell her. Hopefully, she'll forgive me after she finds out what I have planned.

The lady takes my information and credit card and gives me the keys to our room on the forty-second floor, then I go back out to the car where Emma is talking on the phone.

"...told you Jordan couldn't come. I'm just going to stay at a hotel with Ben so he doesn't feel like I've abandoned him." She pauses while the other person talks, pinching the bridge of her nose. "I'm not going to make a scene, Mom. Ben just didn't want me to come alone." Another pause. "Yes. I'll see you Wednesday. Bye."

When she hangs up, she lets out a long breath.

"What did your mom want?" I ask as I pull out of the front area and make my way to the parking garage.

"To make sure Jordan wasn't staying at her house. When I told her I was bringing you instead, she wanted to make sure you weren't staying at her house. Then, she threw a fit when I told her *I* wasn't staying at her house. As if I'd just abandon you." She shakes her head.

"I won't feel abandoned if you want to stay with your parents," I offer.

"No. That's the last thing I want. I want to stay with you. I mean—you know what I mean." I can't see in the dim lighting of the garage, but I'm sure her cheeks are tinged pink.

"I know, honey. C'mon. I'm hungry. Let's go order some room service, and you can take a nice relaxing bath in the big tub."

"Room service? Big bathtub? What's the occasion?"

I don't answer her right away. I get out of the car, grab our bags and sling mine over my shoulder while Emma grabs her pillow.

Before we walk away from the car, I use my free hand to tip her chin so she's forced to meet my eyes. "The occasion, *Dulzura,* is I get you all to myself for the night, and you can't run away. There's no one to distract or interrupt us. I want to spoil you and hopefully cheer you up at least a little. Let me do that, okay?"

Emma licks her lips. "Yes, Sir."

"I'm not expecting anything from you other than a full belly and a good night's rest," I warn. "You've had a long day."

"I know. But… I think I'd sleep better after a few orgasms."

I search her face for some kind of sign she's only saying this because she thinks I want her to, but I don't find anything other than earnestness.

"If you're a good girl and do what I say, we can play. I have something special I wanted to try tonight, but I wasn't sure if you'd be up for it. Are you up for it?"

Emma nods eagerly, and I chuckle at her enthusiasm.

"Let's go then." I grab her hand and lead her to the doors into the hotel.

CHAPTER 39

Emma

I've never stayed at The Cosmopolitan in Vegas before. I usually stay at The Hilton or a Best Western. I've even stayed in Circus Circus once, but the room Jordan and I were in looked like it hadn't been updated since the eighties, and it felt a lot like the beginning of a horror movie.

The Cosmopolitan is far fancier than I would have chosen for one night, but Ben didn't let me have much of a say. We walk around the outside of the casino floor before we find the elevators that will take us up to our room.

The elevator is quiet as we ascend, but it's charged with anticipatory energy. I'm emotionally spent from finding out about Grandpa and then trauma dumping on Ben, but I'm also antsy with nervous energy and restlessness from sitting in the car for five hours.

I'm glad we decided to stop for the night instead of driving straight through, but I'm also nervous to sleep in the same room as Ben.

Ben finds our room and uses the keycard to unlock the door, letting me enter first. The bathroom is immediately to my right, and I see the aforementioned big bathtub and a glass-encased shower that looks like it could fit five people.

I step further into the room and am greeted with the sight of the bright lights of the strip through the sliding door leading to the balcony.

Then I see the *one* bed.

I twist to scowl at Ben. "What happened to *two* beds, Benjamin?"

Ben sets the suitcases down and shrugs. "I couldn't get two beds *and* a balcony over the strip."

I narrow my eyes at him, even as my heart flutters at the idea of sleeping next to him. "What's so important about a balcony?"

Ben gives me a rakish smirk. "You'll see if you're a good girl and let me spoil you. Now, tell me what you want to eat."

Ben lets me scroll through the menu on his phone, and I eventually end up ordering mushroom ravioli. I don't know what Ben orders, but he instructs me to get in the bath while we wait for the food to arrive since it'll probably be an hour.

I go into the bathroom—thank *God* the tub doesn't look crusty and dirty—and turn the faucet to hot so the tub can fill while I gather my things.

Ben is sitting on the end of the bed on his phone when I walk back into the room.

I open my suitcase and remove a set of pajamas, toiletry case, and my dirty clothes bag. Then, feeling bold, I strip off my T-shirt, bra, leggings, and underwear before shoving them into the dirty clothes bag.

When I turn around, Ben is looking at my body like he's seeing it for the first time. His gaze is hungry, predatory. But it's also... soft. Admiring. It makes me want to hide under a blanket just as much as it makes me want to preen.

"Let me know when the food gets here," I chirp as I walk past him.

I hear his feet shuffle along the carpet, following me to the bathroom. I don't bother closing the door as I set my toiletry case on the counter and pull out a claw clip. My hair is still in a braid from earlier, but since it's so long, I need to clip it up to make sure the ends don't get wet.

Once it's clipped up, I turn and put a hand in the half-full tub, checking the temperature. It's hot but not scalding. Perfect.

I step over the edge, then slowly sink beneath the hot water, hissing as my body adjusts to the temperature.

When I'm fully settled, I close my eyes and let out a sigh of relief as my muscles start to release some of the tension from the day.

"Does that feel nice, *Dulzura?*" Ben rasps—presumably from the doorway.

I don't open my eyes when I respond, "Mmm. I love baths. The bathtub at my house is too small for me to sit in comfortably because my thighs and hips get squished, so I don't get to take them as often as I'd like."

"That's a shame," Ben hums.

I pop one eye open and see his broad frame leaning against the doorframe. "Are you just going to stand there and watch me the whole time?"

"Does me watching make you uncomfortable?"

"No, I just feel like I should be giving you a show or something."

Ben chuckles and steps further into the bathroom, kneeling by the tub where my head's resting. "I don't need you to do anything other than relax." He pushes a button I didn't see before, and the water begins to swirl and bubble while the jets hit me from all sides.

Ohhh, that feels nice.

Ben hands me my phone next. "Put on one of your spicy romance books or some relaxing music. I'll be back when the food gets here."

Then, he leans in like he's going to kiss my forehead before he realizes what he's doing and stops halfway and pulls back.

I shouldn't be disappointed——I'm the one who made the rule. But I am.

I made the rule so I wouldn't get attached. So things would be just sex—just physical. No attachments. No feelings.

But I'm already fucking attached. I already fucking *feel* things.

Whatever is happening between us, the lines are getting blurred—who am I kidding? They've been blurred for a while. At this point, the line is dust, just waiting to get blown away by the next breeze. Holding hands in the car was so simple, but it had me picturing Sunday drives and holding hands in his work truck. My heart is demanding we ignore the lines I've drawn, pouting because it wants to give itself over to Ben completely.

I squeeze my eyes shut to stop from crying again, since this is a stupid thing to cry over. I did it to myself. I got myself into this, and I can't be upset he's a good guy and respects my boundaries, even if I want him to break them right now.

We're adults. I could have an adult conversation with him and tell him I want to make an amendment to my limits, but I feel like it's a recipe for disaster—especially since we'll be sharing not only a room but a *bed*.

He turned us into the goddamn one bed trope. That asshole.

At least we've already had sex. There's no unresolved sexual tension to make sharing the bed unbearable. We won't be staying awake, wondering who will break and make the first move.

I guess now, it's a matter of who falls first.

Spoiler alert: it'll be me.

It *is* me.

I could be reading into every gesture, finding any reason to open my heart to the emotions I've kept locked away for so long.

Maybe the hand holding, the road trip, the tender way he's been looking at me is just him taking care of his coworker because of his dad's orders. Maybe he sees this as an opportunity for one last week of wild sex before he calls off our arrangement and I go back to the club to find another Dom. I hate that idea. I trust Ben with my body and my pleasure. I don't want to start over with someone else.

I must've lost track of time because Ben knocks softly and opens the bathroom door with a tray of food.

I start to stand. "Let me just dry off and—"

"No, stay in the tub," Ben commands, setting the tray on the bathroom counter.

"I can't eat in the bathtub."

"I'm going to feed you."

"*Feed me?* I'm perfectly capable of feeding myself."

Ben levels me with a stern look. "Do as you're told, *Dulzura*. Let me feed you your dinner, then we can have dessert. I need you to be energized for what I have planned."

"Yes, Sir." My pussy clenches at the command in his tone. "But... how will you feed me and eat at the same time?"

Ben holds up a plate with some sort of wrap on it. "I can eat this one-handed. Don't worry about me."

I bite my lip and nod.

I can't wait to see what he has planned.

CHAPTER 40

Ben

I never realized feeding someone could be so... erotic. But every time Emma's pink lips wrap around the tines of the fork and pull off another bite of saucy ravioli, my dick twitches.

She's been patient as I've fed her bites of her dinner while I eat my own. The only sound is the soft classical music playing from her phone and the soft clink of the fork on the ceramic plate.

The places her skin isn't touched by ink are tinged pink from the hot water, and she's got a beautiful flush to her cheeks.

I swipe the last bite of her ravioli through the sauce and bring it to her lips, then discard the plate on the counter next to my empty one.

When I turn back to Emma, she's swirling the water around with her finger while looking anywhere but at me. I don't understand why she'd be nervous right now, but I'm not going to go any further until I know she's okay.

I sit on the edge of the tub again and stick my fingers in the water. Finding it closer to chilly than warm, I grab one of the fluffy hotel towels and hold it out.

"Let's get you out of the water."

Emma nods, then stands, and I watch a droplet of water fall from her shoulders, down over her collar bone, down her chest, until it finally drips off of her perky nipple.

I follow another drop down her side, over the curve of her hip, until it falls into the crease where her thigh meets her pelvis.

I stand, gripping her hand to help her out of the tub so she doesn't slip, then pat the towel over every inch of her.

She reaches up and unclips the claw clip from her hair and sets it on the counter, then goes to undo the braid in her hair.

I still her hands with my own. "Leave it in."

"Yes, Sir."

"Emma." She turns towards me but doesn't look at me. "Look at me, please."

When she tips her chin up, there's a heavy emotion in her eyes I can't place.

"I know it's been a long day for you. Are you up for playing tonight, or do you want to just go to sleep? And don't say what you think I want to hear."

"I want to play. I want to know why you decided to pick a room with a balcony over a room with two beds."

I bring one hand up and run it slowly down her arm, goosebumps follow in its wake. "I think you're going to like it, *Dulzura*." I turn her around so she's facing the mirror, and I trace the intricate details of her sleeve as I whisper in her ear, "Look how lovely you are. How beautiful your body is, covered in artwork. I especially love this one." I run my finger over the delicate depiction of a hummingbird nestled between two daylilies. It's my favorite part of her sleeve. "Do you know how many people stop and stare at you?"

She shakes her head, her braid brushing against the fabric of my shirt.

"A lot, *Dulzura*. I have to keep myself in check when we go to job sites because all of the men stop to admire you. They all want you so badly."

"H-how do you know, Sir?" she asks as I stroke one of her nipples with my finger.

"Because I know exactly how they feel. I know what it's like to want you. Every day is a challenge to keep my hands to myself, when all I really want to do is pin you to the glass in your office and show everyone you're *mine*."

Emma's breath hitches at my words, and I chuckle. "Oh, you like that idea, don't you? What a deviant little slut. Wanting our coworkers to watch me wring pleasure from your body."

I move my hand down to cup her pussy, finding her clit swollen and ready for me. I give it a little pinch, and she moans, throwing her head back and arching her hips forward.

"I'm not fucking you in the bathroom, honey. I have other plans. Go sit on the edge of the bed while I get undressed."

"Okay, Sir." As she turns to walk out of the bathroom, I give her voluptuous ass a swat, which makes her yelp and scurry faster.

Once she's completely out of the bathroom, I take a deep breath and slowly undress myself.

I almost kissed Emma on the forehead today when I left her in the bath. I've never done something like that; something so tender. But it feels like second nature with her. I want to kiss her pouty lips. I want to give her forehead kisses when she's sad. I want to hold her hand as we walk around the grocery store.

I'm wondering if I'm projecting the disappointment I thought I saw. I probably am.

If Emma wanted me to kiss her, she would tell me. Right?

I shake my head to get myself to focus on the scene instead of my twitterpated feelings for the sunshine girl waiting for me.

I bundle my clothes together and walk out, my half hard cock twitching when I see Emma sitting with her legs spread on the edge of the bed. She's so short her feet dangle almost comically over the edge, not even close to the floor. I toss my clothes in my bag and kneel on the floor in front of her.

Right now, even though I'm technically the dominant one, she's my goddess, and I'm ready to worship her.

"Time for dessert," I murmur right before I lick languidly between her pussy lips. She's not dripping wet, but she's wet enough that I groan when her flavor hits my tongue.

I know I had her less than seventy-two hours ago, but it's been too long. How have I been going a whole week without having my mouth on her pussy?

I pull back just long enough to tell her, "I want you to come fast so I can show you why I wanted the balcony. Come when you want, *Dulzura*. I need you dripping and ready to take my cock."

Then, not wanting to waste any time, I suck her clit into my mouth. Emma falls back and arches into me, and I see her fists clench the sheets out of the corner of my eye. She moans as I alternate between sucking her clit, thrusting my tongue into her, and nibbling her pussy lips.

I know her better than every MEP Plan and Shop Drawing I'm in charge of, so I slide two fingers into her wet heat and find the sensitive spot inside her, hooking them up over and over while flicking my tongue on her clit.

"Oh, *fuck*," Emma squeals, and I feel her pussy clamp down on me. I pick up the pace, and in less than a minute she moans loudly as she comes.

I pull back, peppering her with praise as she slowly comes down from her high. Then I stand up and look at her.

Some of her hair has come out of her braid and is framing her face, and her body is flushed.

She looks absolutely stunning.

"Do you want to taste yourself, *Dulzura?*" I purr, running my fingers through her wetness.

"Yes, Sir. Please," she rasps.

I go to put my fingers in her mouth, and she shakes her head. "I want... I want your mouth."

I freeze. *Surely she doesn't mean...*

"Kiss me, Sir. *Please*," she begs, sitting up onto her elbows and pursing her lips.

God, I want to. So badly. But not like this.

I shake my head. "Our first kiss isn't going to be in the middle of a scene, honey. I need to know it's not just the orgasm talking."

Emma pushes her bottom lip out into a pout, her blue eyes glassy and full of desire—and maybe a little bit of hurt at my rejection.

I want to give in, but I can't. I can't in good conscience do it without a serious conversation, even if every part of me is screaming to crash my lips against hers. Claim her in a way no one has in four years.

"Don't pout at me, *Dulzura*. I'm barely holding on here," I grit out.

Emma sighs but nods, flopping back down onto the bed. I lean over her and cup her face with my hand.

"Hey, it's not because I don't want to. It's all I've wanted to do since the moment I saw you across the room at the club. But I can't—I can't go past your limits without a conversation."

"Okay," she whispers, giving me a sad smile.

"Tell me your color, Emma. If you want to call 'red' and go to sleep, we can. Do whatever feels right for you."

"Green, Sir. I want to know about the balcony."

I grin, grabbing her wrists gently to help her stand. "Then come here, honey. Let me show you why I chose this room."

Chapter 41

Emma

I can't believe I begged him to kiss me like a lovesick puppy.

So stupid, Emma.

Of course he wasn't going to do it, but I hoped...

I don't know what I was hoping for.

"Our first kiss isn't going to be in the middle of a scene, honey."

Ben was gentle with his rejection, and I'm still holding onto the fact he wants to kiss me.

It's naive, really. How I thought not kissing would keep me from falling for him. Maybe I've been wrong all along about kissing leading to feelings because I fell for him anyway.

Ben leads me out of the sliding glass door and onto the balcony; the cool air hitting my heated skin makes me shiver. The sounds of the strip float up to us. Horns honk, lights flash, and music pulses from somewhere nearby. From up here, the people look like little ants. I'm too far away to make out any features, but I can see them walking.

Couples hold hands, there are groups of friends or family laughing and chatting, holding those big cups of alcoholic slushies. I can see the performers with their big feather headdresses and a few street performers with various musical instruments.

I've never actually spent time on the strip, even though I've been to Vegas quite a few times. It would be easy to get lost in the sea of people.

Ben steps in behind me and cages me against the glass balcony—and I'm suddenly aware I'm bare-ass naked forty-two stories above an entire crowd of people.

I try to back up, but Ben stops me. "They can't see you all the way up here, *Dulzura*. But what if they could?" He runs his hands up my sides and around my front to cup my breasts while he grinds his hard cock into my back.

"What if they looked up here and saw the way my cock fills your tight pussy? What if they stopped to admire what an obedient little slut you are for me? How needy you are. I bet they'd be so jealous. They'd wish they were me."

He pinches and tugs my nipples as he talks lowly into my ear. The picture he's painting makes me squirm but not from embarrassment.

I *want* people to see me—to see *us*. I want them to see how Ben pleasures me. I want them to see how hot we are together. I want them to see that big girls are just as desirable as thin girls and that Benjamin Rossi goes feral for my plus size body.

I moan as his fingers trail lower and slowly rub my clit. "Yeah, you like that idea. When we get back, I'm going to take you to the club's exhibition room. I'm going to tie you to the bed and let people see how greedy your pussy gets for me. Show everyone what a good little submissive you are for me. How delicious you are when you come."

Ben strums my clit and alternates pinching my nipples. I shouldn't like the thought of people watching us so much, but I do. I want Ben to show me off. Be proud of me.

I want him to claim me as his.

"Wh-what about Drew, Sir?" I whimper.

Ben pulls back and gives me a harsh slap on my ass before he growls, "Don't *ever* mention another man—another *person*—when I'm about to be balls deep in your pussy. You will think only of *me* when I'm about to fuck you. As for Drew, he can watch for all I care. Then he can spend every day at work knowing what you look like when you come, but knowing he'll *never* be the one who brings you such pleasure."

He punctuates his declaration with another harsh slap then kicks my legs apart with his feet. "Spread your legs, *Dulzura*. Grip the railing because this is going to be hard and fast. I want you to scream. Let all of Las Vegas know who you belong to."

Even though I'm skeptical of the position, I follow his command, spreading my legs and gripping the railing. Ben still has to squat to get his cock nudged at my entrance because I'm so short, but it doesn't deter him.

He thrusts into me harshly, making me cry out at the delicious intrusion.

"That's it, honey. Let me hear it."

His grip on my hips will surely leave behind bruises, but I don't care. All I care about is the overwhelming pleasure he's bringing me. Every thrust rubs the thick head of his cock along the sensitive spot inside me, coiling my orgasm tighter and tighter. The thought of someone seeing us heightens the ecstasy until I'm right on the precipice.

I'm almost at my peak when Ben pulls out of me and spins me around, lifting one leg up over his arm and thrusting into me as his other hand grabs my ass in a bruising grip. I have to stretch up on my tiptoes to keep from being lifted off the ground completely.

It's a good thing the railing comes up to my chest because I'd be hanging over it dangerously if I were any taller.

"I need to see your face when you come," he growls as he continues his relentless thrusting.

I don't have much to grab onto, so I plant my palms on his shoulders, digging my nails in when he hits a particularly sweet spot.

"God, Emma. You always grip me so well. You were meant to be mine. I'll never get enough of you."

"You make me feel amazing, Sir," I whimper, and Ben groans.

Ben snakes his hand between us to strum my clit as he continues to pound into me. "Need you to come. Squeeze my cock, honey. Make it nice and sloppy."

Three more brutal thrusts and the coil inside me snaps; I come for him, screaming just like he wanted.

"That's it, *Dulzura.* So beautiful when you break for me. Everyone down there wishes they were the ones making you scream, but they're not, are they? Who makes you feel this good?"

"You do, Sir."

"That's." *Thrust.* "Fucking." *Thrust.* "Right." Ben moans loudly as his hips stutter, and his warm cum fills me to the brim.

Both of our releases drip down my thighs as he pulls out of me and gently lowers my leg to the ground.

"Come on. Let's get you cleaned up." Instead of letting me walk, he scoops me up bridal style and carries me into the bathroom.

He sets me on the edge of the tub while he starts the shower.

"Do you want to wash your hair?" he asks, and I shake my head.

He walks over to where I left my claw clip earlier and grabs it and a hotel shower cap before twisting my braid up, clipping it and gently placing the shower cap over my head.

Wordlessly, he directs me under the spray of the shower while he gathers my toiletry bag before he joins me.

I get déjà vu as Ben squirts some face wash onto his fingers before gently rubbing it into my skin. He directs me under the spray to wash it off. Then he lathers a different washcloth with my body wash and gently cleans every inch of my body.

Just like showering at his house, this feels more intimate than fucking. I feel stripped completely bare for him, especially after all I dumped on him in the car.

I wait for the panic to sink in, but it doesn't. I feel like crying from gratitude, and the urge to run from him—from the feelings bubbling under the surface—is nowhere to be seen.

The adrenaline from the scene is wearing off, and the emotions from today are starting to catch up to me, making my eyes heavy with exhaustion.

Ben quickly washes himself then hops out of the shower and dries himself while I stay under the warm water. Then, when he's dried off and in a pair of underwear, he turns off the shower and pats my body dry before wrapping me in the towel and sitting me once again on the edge of the tub.

He takes the shower cap off before he finds my body lotion and lathers the cream into my legs and arms.

"I don't know in what order to do your skincare," he whispers, holding up my Vitamin C serum and chlorophyll discoloration serum.

"I can do it." I lean forward to grab the bottles, but he moves them just out of reach.

"No, just tell me what to do. I feel bad I didn't get to do it on Saturday. Let me take care of you."

"There's a rosewater spray in there. That's first, then before it dries, you do the green bottle—just two drops will be enough. Then the dark blue under eye cream and finally the purple moisturizer."

Ben finds all the products and lines them up in order, applying them gently to my skin in the order I told him. His calloused fingers are rough against my skin in a way that makes me melt.

I don't know how he knows my skincare routine is important to me, but my heart feels like it's about to burst. Ben's all grumpy and growly at times, but when we're alone, I get to see a tender side of him I'm greedy to see more of.

Once he's applied the moisturizer, he wets my toothbrush and instructs me to brush while he does the same.

Once we're done, he unclips the claw from my hair and undoes my braid before running my wide-tooth comb through the frizzy waves. He finds a satin scrunchie and holds it up with his eyebrows raised in question.

I nod, holding my hand out to take it from him, but he bats it away again. Then he gathers my hair into one fist before gently wrapping the scrunchie around to create a loose ponytail on top of my head.

"How do you know how to do this?" I whisper, reluctant to break the calm silence.

"At one point you told Katrina braids aren't healthy to sleep in, especially for curly hair. You told her it was best to sleep with a satin scrunchie tied loosely on top of your head. Ideally, a satin bonnet, but you get overstimulated by them so you don't have one."

That conversation was almost a month ago. I didn't even know Ben was paying attention when he came into the breakroom because he was on his phone.

My mind swirls with so many questions I feel a little dizzy. I want to ask him what else he's overheard. I want to know *why* he's retained the information. What it means that he remembers something so inconsequential.

The hopeless romantic in me is trying to convince me he cares on a deeper level than just sex or friendship. But I can't let myself get my hopes up.

"We have a long drive ahead of us tomorrow, *Dulzura*. Let's get to bed." I take Ben's outstretched hand, and he leads me out of the bathroom. He helps me slip on my sleep shorts and cropped tank top before exchanging the hotel pillow for my own and tucking me under the covers.

My eyes are already closing by the time Ben rounds the bed to turn off the lamp and slips under the sheets.

"Goodnight, Ben," I whisper.

"Goodnight. Sweet dreams, *Dulzura*."

CHAPTER 42

Ben

When I wake up, I'm expecting to be cuddled to death by Emma, but she's barely moved throughout the night.

She's facing me, her brows pinched in a scowl and lips in a downward tilt, like she's having a bad dream.

I check the time and see it's almost eight o'clock in the morning—time to get on the road soon.

I use my thumb to smooth out the furrow between her eyebrows, gently tracing the curve of her lip and her perfect cupid's bow.

I'm immediately brought back to last night when she begged me to kiss her. I can't believe I had the strength to deny her. But we have to talk first. I have to be sure it wasn't only a lust-induced haze that made her want it.

And if she *does* want it, I'm not just going to kiss her immediately. Her first kiss after four years needs to be at the right moment. *Our* first kiss together is the step towards forever I've been wanting.

At least, I hope it will be.

As I continue to lightly trace the face of the angel who's stolen my heart, her blonde lashes flutter open, and she blinks her baby blue eyes at me. A soft smile graces her face before she quickly sits up.

"*Shit.* What time is it?" She turns to grab her phone and checks the time, then her shoulder slump in relief. "Oh good. I thought it was much later."

"We have time for breakfast before we hit the road. Then we should probably get gas. I don't know how many gas stations are between here and Utah."

"We'd be fine, but gas is probably a good idea. I was going to ask you yesterday, but would it be possible to make a pitstop when we cross into Utah?"

I shrug. "Sure. Where?"

"A little town called Gunlock. I try to make a point to stop and visit my grandparents' graves when I come. It's been a minute since I've visited."

Jesus. How many people has this girl lost?

"Of course. Just tell me where to go."

"Thank you, Ben. I really appreciate it."

"No thanks needed. I'm happy to do it."

ISTRUCTION // UNDER CONSTRUCTION // UNDER CON

After breakfast and getting gas, Emma puts on another playlist, and we've had a pretty quiet car ride. I think she's back in her head about seeing her family and attending her grandpa's funeral. I wish I could do something more to take her mind off of it.

When we pass over the border and get closer to St. George, my breath is taken away by all the red rock.

"Wow, Utah is stunning."

"Yeah." Emma sighs. "Too bad the state is run by a corrupt religion."

"What do you mean?"

"Utah houses the headquarters of the Mormon Church, which has a lot of influence over the government. Alcohol laws are super strict, and there's no gambling. There are church buildings and temples everywhere. You can't really escape it here."

"Is that why you moved to California?"

Emma tilts her head side to side while she thinks about her answer. "Yes, and no. Jordan's parents wanted to move to a place that was more protective about transgender rights. I wanted to be in a place where I wouldn't be scared to be my true self. Jordan's an only child, so their parents kind of adopted me as their own after I truly fell out with my family. They helped me apply to college and get financial aid, they've met most of my previous partners, and they've celebrated my wins. It was a no-brainer to move with them when they asked."

"I'm glad you had them. They seem really great."

"They are. They're the best pseudo-parents I could've asked for."

I don't know what to say to that. I want to ask her to meet them, because it seems like they're an important part of her life, but I know I still need to tread carefully.

"Can I ask you something personal?" I muse.

"My word vomit isn't enough for you?" she teases. I give her a flat look. "Ask away. I'm an open book."

"I noticed you had a green ribbon on at the club, and you don't say 'boyfriends' you use the term 'partners.'" I don't know how to ask outright, but I don't have to.

Emma chuckles. "You've seen the pink, purple, and blue flag in my office, yes?" I nod. "I'm bisexual."

"I wondered, but I didn't want to assume."

"I'm open about it. I'm not ashamed of it. You can ask me anything you'd like."

"Good. I never want you to be ashamed of the things that make you you."

Emma gives me a smile in return, and the topic of conversation changes.

Emma directs me away from the St. George traffic, through a formation of red and white rocks that looks vaguely familiar, and through some hills that look like volcanoes. When I point them out, Emma laughs and tells me they *are* volcanoes, but they're inactive.

We pull into a small town with two gas stations, a small strip of businesses, and a church all on the main road. We turn down a side street, and I follow a bumpy road to the Gunlock cemetery.

It's small, barely half an acre with a run-down park across the gravel road and a structure that looks like sketchy bathrooms.

"Do you want me to come with you?" I question when Emma doesn't immediately get out of the car.

"Only if you don't find it weird that I talk to them still."

Talk to them?

I shrug, "As long as you're not performing a séance."

Emma gets out of the car, and I follow her as she opens a white wrought iron gate in need of a bit of WD-40. I follow her down the cracked sidewalk and over the dried grass—avoiding stepping on the other graves—until we come to a gray upright headstone.

Emma plops herself in the crunchy grass, and I follow suit next to her, reading the inscriptions.

Their last name, Price, is carved on a banner above a mountain range with an elk on one side and a pine tree on the other, then there are two names and their birth and death dates.

Blythe June Prior
21 Feb 1925
18 Jan 2010

Rupert Lance
27 Jan 1923
24 May 2015

"Hi, Grandma and Grandpa," Emma says, like she's just talking to someone in their living room. "I brought a visitor with me. His name is Ben. He's my... coworker?"

I nudge her arm with mine. "I'm more than just her coworker."

Emma cups her hand over her face like she's trying to tell me a secret. "I can't exactly tell them you're my Dom, can I? They'd probably keel over if they found that out."

I roll my eyes at her but cup my own hand over my face and reply, "I think they can probably hear you even if you do this, so you just told them anyway."

"Fuck. *Shit.* Sorry, Grandma and Grandpa. But, to be fair, you guys weren't exactly saints with the language. You probably think I didn't hear you, but I did."

Emma proceeds to tell them all about graduating college, how she finally landed her dream job at Rossi. She tells them about the plans for Derek's project and how excited she is to be part of something so big.

Then she tells them how sad she is that her other grandpa is gone. She recounts how Grandpa Walter and Grandma Eileen came down when Grandma Blythe passed away to show their support and how she hopes they're catching up with each other in the afterlife.

The wind, which was blowing softly when we arrived, has stopped completely, and I hear some cattle mooing in the distance. Emma speaks to them so freely, without a care that, to someone else, it might look strange to be talking to a headstone.

"Sorry I didn't bring flowers; I didn't plan on stopping by. But I'm glad I did. I miss you both like crazy. I hope you're proud of me, even if I'm not living exactly the way you guys probably wanted when I was younger. I'm sure you thought I'd be married and have a gaggle of kids by now."

Before she can say anything else, her phone rings. "Oh, this is my cousin, Hannah. I'm going to take this and be right back. That okay?"

"Go ahead, honey."

"Hey, Hannah…" Emma stands and walks to the other end of the cemetery.

I clear my throat, feeling a little silly wanting to talk to a headstone. But if Emma can do it, so can I.

"So, you already know Emma and I are… coworkers. But I'm actually falling—*have* fallen—pretty hard for your granddaughter. I haven't told her how I feel, though. She's kind of skittish. I don't blame her, not after everything she's been through."

I look over my shoulder to see Emma with her back turned, still talking on the phone, so I continue. "I haven't felt this way about someone...ever. And I was engaged. I promise I'll take good care of her. I just want her to know how worthy of love she is. I want her to let me love her."

I hear the crunch of the grass as Emma comes back. "Okay, we can go." She holds out her hand to help me stand up, and even though she's so much shorter than I am, I let her help me up.

I interlace our fingers so she can't walk away.

"Bye, Grandma and Grandpa. Love you." She leads me to the car, our fingers still intertwined.

CHAPTER 43

Emma

Hannah's call made me feel a flutter of excitement about being in Utah, instead of the dread I was feeling before.

Apparently, some of our other cousins who have left the church are coming to the funeral, and I'm excited to see them. Hannah invited all of us over for dinner on Thursday so we can catch up.

Hannah invited our cousin Talmage, too. He's a firefighter, and I saw him a couple of times when he came out to California to help with the summer wildfires.

At first, I was nervous to hang out with him because I walked away from the church, and he's one of the family's golden boys. He never treated me like I was someone to be afraid or ashamed of. He never asked me about why I left—we never really talked about the church at all, honestly. I don't know where he's working now, but I know he moved back to Utah last August for good. Last I heard, his engagement ended.

Talmage, Elli, and Hannah are the only family members I truly feel comfortable around and trust.

Elli's sister, Izzy, is supposed to be there as well. I don't know her as well because she wasn't even a teenager when I moved away, but I'm eager to get to know her now that she's an adult.

"Everything okay?" Ben asks as we pull back onto I-15.

"Yeah, my cousin Hannah invited me over for dinner Thursday night. Some of my other cousins will be there too…" I told Hannah I'm traveling with a friend, and she said he's more than welcome to join us, but doesn't that feel… *serious?*

Ben clears his throat. "Do you want to go by yourself? I'm fine staying at the hotel alone."

"No, I don't want to go alone. I just don't know how to explain what we are. I mean, Hannah and Elli are chill, but I don't know how kinky their sex lives are. Talmage would probably be uncomfortable because as far as I know, he's still in the church, and sex isn't discussed freely. I don't know how to say 'we're coworkers, but on the weekends I get on my knees and obey his commands' without it being weird."

Ben doesn't respond right away, so I look over and study his face. I can't see his eyes because of his sunglasses, but his jaw is tight like he's holding back, and his hands are gripping the wheel tightly.

"It would just be simpler to say we're dating," he says evenly.

"I told Elli and Hannah last year I don't do relationships," I argue, even if it is half-heartedly.

Logically, I know people can change. It has been over a year since I said it, and I *have* changed.

I want to be in a serious relationship with Ben, but I don't know if he wants the same, and I don't know how to be in one when I'm still scared of giving my heart to someone only for it to be given back to me torn to shreds.

But Ben... he seems different. I want to believe he's different. I want to believe he wouldn't break my heart. What if we don't work out? What if right *now* he finds the fact that I sit in front of a slab of stone and talk to my deceased grandparents charming, but in a year or two, he finds it exhausting? What if he really wants kids, and when he finds out I'm not sure I do, he decides I'm not worth it?

People can change their minds.

"People can change their minds," Ben echoes my thoughts. "What reason did you give them for not wanting to be in a relationship?"

"I honestly don't even remember anymore. Probably something about my ex wanting to move too fast and then dumping me. Typical heartbreak-turned-me-into-a-jaded-relationship-phobe stuff."

I vividly remember Morgan—Hannah's husband—telling me someone was going to come along and change my mind. I laughed it off but secretly hoped he was right.

I guess maybe in a way he was—it just took longer than I expected.

"Is that why you swore off relationships? Because of your ex?"

Why is Ben's car trauma-dump central?

"Yes, and no. My ex, Trinity, and I were in vastly different places in life. She wanted to get married and start a family, and I was still trying to figure out what I wanted to do with my life. She told me I wasn't taking our relationship seriously, but in the same breath told me I was too emotional, too needy. *Too much.*" I don't mention I was tired of people having to pick up the pieces after a breakup. How I felt like a burden to Jordan because I got too in over my head.

"And after how your family treated you growing up, you felt like it would be easier to not let anyone else in?" Ben guesses.

I blink because *yeah.*

"Something like that," I mumble, suddenly finding my nails *very* interesting.

Ben nods slowly like he wants to say more but isn't sure *what* to say.

Same. I still don't fully understand why Trinity thought that.

We sit in silence as we drive through the hills of southern Utah. I'm glad Grandpa didn't pass when it's snowy, because this area can get nasty during a snowstorm, and the hills can be extremely dangerous.

I'm lost in my thoughts as I watch the hills pass. Occasionally, there are black dots of cattle grazing in a field or a random sign for one of the national parks scattered around Utah, but it's nothing I haven't seen a thousand times before.

I know the drive from Gunlock to Cottonwood Heights like the back of my hand from the many trips we made to see my grandparents before they passed.

My mind wanders to what a real relationship with Ben would look like.

Usually, when you start a romantic relationship, you don't see the other person for forty hours a week. You get date nights and weekend sleepovers, but you're not around them constantly, right?

Would one of us have to quit Rossi? It would have to be me, since it's his dad's company. But I don't know if I'd be able to get another job in the field since it's so male-dominated. And I like it at Rossi. It feels like the perfect fit for me.

If we both stayed at Rossi, would there be rules against touching at work? Obviously, we wouldn't be fucking in the breakroom, but would he kiss me goodbye before he left the office to check out jobsites? Would he hold my hand in the safety briefings and foreman meetings? Or would he keep his distance?

Would we drive to work together or separately if we spent the night together? It would make sense to drive together, but I don't know if Ben would want to be around me *so much*.

And why would he want to be in a relationship with me anyway, when he's already getting the benefit of regular sex without having to do the boyfriend stuff like grocery shopping or listening to me explain the monster smut I'm reading in-depth?

"What are you thinking about so hard over there?" Ben breaks through my thoughts, and I blink over at him.

"Monster smut," I answer.

Ben's eyebrows shoot above the rim of his sunglasses. "Pardon?"

"I read a book about a gargoyle who would turn to stone if he didn't find a mate by his thousandth birthday. But he *did* find his mate, and she got to experience the pleasure of his vibrating tail. Then there was the part-man, part-gator one. I'm still trying to picture how big his gator dick is supposed to be and *how* it fit inside a human."

Ben looks mortified. "What the hell kind of books are you reading?"

I roll my eyes. "Don't be a prude, Benjamin. There's a whole community out there that loves monster smut. They even make monster-dick shaped toys. I've always wondered what it would feel like to be knotted and—"

"*Knotted?* Like... how dogs mate?"

I snap my fingers and point at him. "Exactly. They make cock rings that feel like knots, or they make dildos with knots on them. I feel like it would hurt, but I've never tried it, so I don't know."

Ben's still got his eyes on the road, but his jaw is slack, and he keeps rubbing his chin.

"How the hell did you go from talking about your past relationships to thinking about monster dicks?"

I sigh, not wanting to get into it with him while we're driving. "I wish I knew."

CHAPTER 44

Ben

Despite how badly I want to have a conversation about our relationship in the car, I need to be able to look her in the eye and hold her hands while we do. So Emma puts on a playlist with more artists I've never heard of, and we've been alternating between comfortable silence and her asking me questions about myself.

I didn't realize until she asked me about my childhood how much I've—unintentionally—kept from her. *I* know a lot about her because she talks a lot, and I like to listen to her, but *she* doesn't know much about me because I usually don't open up to coworkers or people I'm having sex with.

But if I want Emma to see me as more than a fuck buddy, I know I need to open up to her. I've been inside of her, but she doesn't even know what I went to school for.

I tell her how my childhood was as good as it could have been. We weren't always well off. Papà and my Nonno worked long hours for most of my childhood so they could get Rossi off the ground. I tell her how Sundays were always my father's one day off so he could spend time with us. In the warmest months, he'd take Mateo and me surfing while Mamà and Cici would build sandcastles on the shore. Other times, we'd take a drive through San Diego, and Papà would point out all of the places he was helping build.

I tell her I started helping out with the business when I was fourteen. I wanted to be part of something special. I wanted to help build things like my dad. Even when I was just laying pipes or digging trenches. Even sweating and covered in dirt, I knew it was what I was supposed to be doing.

Papà ran the business out of a small mobile office for years, slowly saving and expanding our reach until ten years ago when we were able to build the building we're in now.

I tell her my Nonna lived with us after my Nonno passed away when I was thirteen. She only lived with us for four years before she passed as well. I never knew Mamà's parents because they passed away before I was born.

I tell her Mamà and Papà are both only children, so I don't have any cousins I'm close to. Only Mateo and Cici.

I tell her I went to San Diego State University so I could still be close to home and help out when I needed to. I got my bachelor's in Construction Management with a minor in Accounting. Papà tried to sway me away from being part of the business because he didn't want me to work there out of obligation. But when I thought about doing anything else, it never felt right.

"When I graduated from college, *Papà* made me do a full-fledged interview in order to get the job. I had to give him a mock plan for a new build and convince him why I would be a vital asset to Rossi." I chuckle, and Emma giggles.

"*I* didn't even have to do a full on interview."

"I *know.* I think it's part of the reason I was so upset he hired you. He wouldn't even hire his own son without an interview, but he hired some random girl based on my best friend's recommendation and a phone call. Now, I think he just wanted to make sure this job was what I really wanted."

Emma bites her lip. "Are you still frustrated he hired me?"

"No. You're a natural at what you do, honey. If I'm frustrated, it's because I have to look at you all day every day and pretend I don't know what your lips feel like wrapped around my cock."

"Ben!" she scolds with a half-hearted scowl.

I shrug. I'm not lying. I've sat in my office and stared at her through the glass, picturing her plump lips wrapped around my cock more than once.

They're very distracting. Especially when they're covered in gloss or smiling or pursed in concentration. Basically all the time.

Even now, when I should be soaking up the beautiful sights of the mountains covered in reds and oranges and a light dusting of snow at the very tippy top, my mind is on the woman next to me.

That's when it hits me.

"You have this mountain range on a stamp on your left arm, right?"

Emma nods. "Yeah. Snow Canyon. I also have the Wasatch Mountains and the opening to Big Cottonwood Canyon on stamps." She points to all three scattered on her left arm. "Even though my family is shitty, the state holds a lot of fond memories and importance. I wanted to be able to take a piece of it with me wherever I go."

"That's beautiful. I don't think I've ever asked what your tattoos mean. I assume the arrow and mountains on your shoulder with the dates is for Andy?"

Emma smiles. "Yeah. It was my first tattoo, along with his signature in white ink. I had an artist go over it in black a few years ago." She holds her arm out and shows me a signature nestled between a pinecone and a snake. "I don't have a lot of tattoos that *mean* something. I just like having art on my body. Some pieces have a special meaning—like the stamps—but most don't."

"Which other ones mean something to you?"

"The hummingbird in my sleeve is for my grandparents. They had a bunch of feeders on their porch, and we'd spend hours watching them through the window. The butterfly above my knee is colored in the bisexual flag colors—and for me—represents a transformation. It was one of the first tattoos I got after I moved out of Utah and felt like I could truly be my authentic self."

"That's beautiful. Should I start calling you *mariposa?*" I tease.

Emma scrunches her nose. "Please don't. Morgan calls Hannah 'Butterfly,' and I think it would be weird to have the same nickname."

"All right. *Dulzura* it is."

"You've never told me what it means."

"It means 'sweetness.' I knew from the moment we met you'd be the sweetest submissive I've ever been with, and I was right." I give her a wink and even though she rolls her eyes, her cheeks get a little pink.

Conversation dies off as we inch closer to her hometown, and the anxiety rolls off of her in waves. I hate seeing her like this. Coming back to the place she grew up should be joyful and exciting, not something that makes her nervous.

I wish I were better with words so I could comfort her better, but I'm not, so I do the only thing I can think of.

I reach across the console and gently grip her hand, intertwining our fingers together before bringing her hand up to my mouth to kiss the back of it. She doesn't pull away, so I keep her hand in my lap.

I follow the map to the hotel, and when we get there, I begrudgingly let her hand go so I can go check in.

This time, I *do* get a room with two beds—even if I really don't want to.

CHAPTER 45

Emma

The next morning, after a fitful night of sleep I'm claiming is due to anxiety from having to see my mother—*not* because Ben and I didn't share a bed—I'm getting ready to take Ben to one of my favorite coffee shops when my phone rings.

I groan seeing my mom's name flash across my phone. *Speak of the devil, and she will appear.*

"Hi, Mom."

"Your cousins are meeting today at two to go over the musical number for the funeral on Friday."

I roll my eyes. *Yeah, I got here safely. No, I only planned to show Ben around today, so I can for sure make it. Thanks for letting me know in advance.*

"Okay. At Grandpa's church?"

"Yes. Are you sure you remember where it is? It's been a long time since you stepped foot in there."

"Unless they moved it in the last seven years, I remember." I barely hold in the sigh that wants to escape.

"Good. Then after, you and your... *friend* can meet us for dinner. We're thinking Hughes. They just opened a location in Cottonwood Heights."

Fantastic.

"I don't know if Ben will be comfortable with that."

I don't know if I will be comfortable with it.

Mom gives me a disappointed sigh then tsks. "Emma, your father and I want to meet the first man you've brought home since you moved to California. We want to be introduced to him before family dinner on Friday—which we expect you and your *friend* to attend. It's only fair we meet a stranger before he's invited into our home."

I flinch at her calling Utah "home." It hasn't been home in a long time.

"Fine. What time?"

"Four-thirty. Just remember this isn't California. You can't dress like you would there."

"Got it. See you then. Bye, Mom." I hang up before she can say anything else.

The *one* time my parents came to visit me in California was a surprise visit. It was nine in the morning on a Saturday, and I was wearing a crop top and pajama shorts when they rang the doorbell. My mom was so mad about what I was wearing when I answered the door, she ranted about it for ten minutes.

Now, every time I'm in Utah, she reminds me I can't wear a crop top because I will make people "uncomfortable."

It's *October*, though. It's not like I'm going to be sporting booty shorts and a tube top when the weather is chilly.

"I take it we have a change of plans for today?" Ben asks from his bed.

"Yeah. Apparently, I have to go practice the musical number for the funeral with my cousins at two, then we're going to dinner with my parents. We're having a family dinner at my parents' on Friday after the funeral, too."

"Sounds good to me. I could do with a homemade meal instead of takeout."

I can't help the snort that escapes me. My mom's a good cook by Mormon white lady standards, but compared to Camila's food, she doesn't hold a candle.

Ben's brows furrow. "Why are you laughing?"

"I can't *wait* to see how you feel about my mom's cooking. Remember what I said about pepper being spicy in my house growing up?"

Ben groans. "I forgot about that. I guess I understand why *Mamà's* cooking made you moan the way you did."

"Oh, Benjamin. You are in for a *treat.*"

Luckily for us, the drive from Cottonwood Heights to my grandparents' church building in Bluffdale isn't too long.

When I park, I only see two other cars in the parking lot. As Ben and I get out, Talmage's sisters, Lauren and Lacey, get out of their own car, and Lacey rushes to me with a bright expression on her face.

"Emma! Hi! How are you? You look so pretty." She looks so similar to Talmage with her dirty blonde hair and big blue eyes.

"Hey, Lacey. Thank you, so do you." To my surprise, she wraps me in a hug, and I let out a surprised *oof.*

"Lacey," Lauren hisses at her sister. "You didn't even ask."

Lacey steps back and looks at me sheepishly. "Sorry, Emma."

I give her a reassuring smile. "It's okay. This is my... boyfriend, Ben." I motion to him, and he holds out his hand. "Ben, these are two of my cousins, Lacey and Lauren."

"Nice to meet you both," Ben says with a strained smile. I hope he's okay because he has a long week ahead of him; he has *a lot* of people to meet.

Lacey's cheeks flush red as she delicately shakes his hand, tucking her hair behind her ear.

Yeah, girl, I get it. He's super hot.

Lauren gives him one firm shake and spins around to walk into the building.

We all follow suit.

I haven't been inside a church building since the summer after I graduated high school, and my skin prickles with anxiety the closer I get.

Do I think God is going to smite me down as soon as I step inside?

No.

But it's still extremely uncomfortable.

Growing up in the church, I was taught the only places I could truly feel close to God and Jesus were in the temple, at church on Sundays, or in a "Christ-centered home."

I always wondered why God or Jesus would want to join his followers in a place that feels so... boring. Before the 2000s, churches had more unique layouts and designs, but now, all the newer buildings look nearly identical. From the brick on the outside, to the carpet on the floors—and walls. From the paintings to the couches, everything looks like a carbon copy of the church down the street.

Temples are much the same, if the new ones I saw along the freeway are any indication. They're just massive, gaudy buildings that scream, "We have too much money on our hands, so we're building this structure to get attention."

It's hard to believe the same Jesus who trashed the temples in the Bible because people were using it as a market would be okay with the church spending their money on garish places of "worship."

But what do I know?

When we get to the chapel, my other cousins are already sitting in the choir seats chatting quietly. Lauren climbs the stand, sits down at the piano, and starts arranging the music while Lacey greets our other cousins.

"You can go wait in the car. You don't have to sit here," I whisper to Ben.

He grabs my hand and gives it a gentle squeeze. "I'll be fine, honey. Sing pretty for me." He gives me a wink before gently pressing his lips to the back of my hand, then releases me to go sit down on the first bench on the right-hand side.

Katelynn, Lacey, and Rachel's eyes are darting from me to Ben rapidly, and I can tell they have questions. Lacey, unlike Rachel and Katelynn, doesn't look disgusted. She looks like every other sixteen-year-old who's crazy about love.

I would know, I was like her once.

Lauren clears her throat. "Grandpa wanted this arrangement of *Nearer, My God, to Thee*. Emma, do you know the lyrics?"

I nearly roll my eyes. People act like because I'm not a member anymore means I've forgotten *everything* drilled into me growing up.

Music has always been a big part of my life. I learn lyrics faster than I learn math equations, and when you're singing at least six songs every Sunday, you learn them pretty dang fast. I turned to a lot of the songs I learned for comfort during anxiety attacks and sleepless nights. I'm a little offended she assumes I've forgotten them.

"Yes. I know the lyrics."

"Great. Let's run through it and—"

Talmage half jogs, half walks the length of the chapel, doing a double take when he sees Ben.

"Sorry I'm late. I had to finish up some paperwork. Emma! Good to see you." He wraps me in a hug, then whispers only loudly enough for me to hear, "I'm assuming the scowly man on the bench is yours?"

I nod against him.

"Nice. Well, let's get started. Kyle, you're taking bass?"

Kyle nods once.

"Emma and I will be singing soprano then." Katelynn sighs like it pains her to sing the same part as me.

"And Rachel and I will take alto," Lacey confirms.

After we all have our sheet music, we gather around the piano and run through it part by part.

We all were—or in Lacey's case, are—in some sort of choir or music-related extracurricular in high school, which is why we're the ones tasked with performing at the funeral.

Even though the only singing I tend to do is in the shower now, it's easy to let the music take over. As soon as we run through it once, muscle memory kicks in, and we've got it down in twenty minutes.

I would say no one expects this to be a professional level performance, but Grandpa had a doctorate in music and headed the music department at one of the universities for years, so they kind of do.

We agree to run through the number one more time the day of the funeral, just to be safe, and then everyone packs up and leaves.

Rachel and Katelynn eye Ben warily again, making a point to go out the opposite side of where he's sitting. I'm sure between the two of them, the whole family will know by the end of the day the black sheep brought a companion to the funeral.

Chapter 46

Ben

Emma sings like an angel.

I never knew she had a voice like that. I've seen her mouth the words to songs in the car, heard her hum along once or twice. But I've never heard her sing. Is it because she's shy? I have a hard time believing that.

I will admit the song was a little... *culty,* I guess is the word. A little ominous and a little strange, but hearing it come from her...

It gave me chills. I want to hear more of her voice.

It almost distracted me from the feeling of undiluted judgment coming from some of the people in the room. I can't tell if it's judgment because I look grumpy, their religious biases, or the fact I'm here with Emma, and they think she's unworthy to be in this chapel.

Emma walks down the few steps with the dude who came in late, and I stand when they make it to the bench I was sitting on.

He looks like the girls we met when we got here. They all have blonde hair like Emma's, but his is a dark golden blonde where the girls' hair is a bit lighter. He's got a neatly trimmed mustache the same color as his hair.

"Ben, this is my cousin Talmage. Talmage, this is my boyfriend, Ben."

Goddamn, I like hearing her call me her boyfriend. She said it in the parking lot too, but this time is less tentative, more *definitive.* Like she's certain in her choice. It makes my heart flutter so bad I wonder if I need to see a doctor.

What would happen if she called me her fiancé? Husband?

I know she thinks this is a temporary label we're giving her family while we're here, but I'm determined to make it stick—make it *real.* Then I can eventually upgrade my label to husband.

Slow down, Ben.

Talmage gives me a bright, genuine smile and holds out his hand. "Nice to meet you, man."

I shake his hand, impressed by his firm handshake. "You, too." I nod toward the logo on his T-shirt. "You a fireman?"

Talmage glances at the logo and beams with pride. "Sure am. Captain of Station 2 in Springville."

I don't know much about rankings regarding the fire department, but the title of Captain sounds impressive, so I nod and offer my congratulations.

"Thanks, man. I've got to run, but I'll see you two at Hannah's tomorrow?"

Emma confirms, and we follow him outside and get into our respective cars.

Emma's shoulders slump as soon as her butt hits the seat. After I start the car and pull out of the parking lot, I reach over and give her thigh a squeeze. "You sounded great up there, honey. I had no idea you can sing."

Emma sighs and rolls her head to look at me. "Thank you. I was in choir and musical theatre all throughout junior high and high school. I took voice lessons for years and even spent a week at vocal performance camps a few summers before I graduated. I guess it wasn't all for nothing."

"You never wanted to pursue music as a career?"

She shrugs, her fingers absently tracing over my own. "I told my mom when I was nine I wanted to go to Juilliard for college, and she told me I'd never make it. I knew it would only ever be a hobby. I was never the lead or chosen for any solos, so I figured she was probably right."

"She never tried to support your dream at all?"

"Nah. She wanted me to be a nurse like my sister dreamed of, but I can't stand the sight of blood or bodily fluids. It took me forever to pick a major and decide on Construction Management because I never knew what I wanted to do."

"I'm so sorry, honey." I flip my hand over and interlace our fingers, giving her another reassuring squeeze.

She squeezes back.

"It's not your fault. There's no point in trying to change the past."

No, I guess not.

"Anyway," Emma continues, "are you ready to meet the parents?"

As ready as I'll ever be.

Emma's parents are... not great.

They didn't even try to hug her when we got to the restaurant.

I mean, I figured things were tense between them after everything she'd told me before, but *Jesus.* They're bad.

Her mom, Jane, looked like she would rather lick the dirty floor than shake my hand when we were introduced, and her dad, Dirk, tried to make a joke the minute he met me.

"About time my daughter brought home a man. She needs someone to tame her wild ways."

I didn't laugh, and neither did Emma. Instead, her shoulders slumped, and she shrunk in on herself.

I could tell it made him feel awkward when I didn't play along, but I don't give a fuck.

As we're seated, I study the two people in front of me. Emma doesn't look much like her parents.

Dirk's hair is completely white, and his bushy eyebrows are almost the same color. His eyes are a pale green hidden behind bifocal glasses. Sunspots litter his skin like he's prone to being outside in the summers, and there's a tuft of white chest hair sticking out of his flannel shirt. When we were walking to the table, I noticed he walks slightly hunched over, and I make a mental note to ask Emma how old her dad is.

Jane looks much younger than her husband. Her short bob is dyed blonde, but it looks like at one point it may have been a similar color to Emma's. Her eyes are a darker blue than Emma's, and they don't hold the same warmth as my *Dulzura's*.

To my dismay, there are no alcoholic beverages on the menu. I think Emma and I could both use a little to get through what's undoubtedly going to be an awkward dinner. Instead, I order a Coke, and Emma orders a strawberry lemonade.

Dirk asks Emma how she's liking her job, she tells him she's loving it, but then he doesn't ask any follow up questions.

Instead, he goes on and on about the latest updates to the new private school they're building. I can tell Emma doesn't really care, but since she's in the world of construction, she asks insightful questions and keeps him talking. He speaks to her like she's an unintelligent child and not a knowledgeable woman, and I hate it, but I keep my mouth shut.

"So," Jane starts after we order, "how did you two meet?"

Emma and I share a look, and I motion for her to tell the story.

"Ben's dad is the owner of Rossi Construction. He's a PM there as well."

Jane sighs and shakes her head. "Oh, Emma."

"Is that how you got the job?" her dad asks, narrowing his eyes at me. "Did you give her the job so you could get with her?"

"No, sir. My father offered her the job after her old boss, one of my friends, put in a good word for her. I had nothing to do with the process."

Jane ignores my comment. "What happens when you two break up? Your boss isn't going to fire his own son. You're ruining your career before it's even started."

"All due respect, Mrs. Price, but I'd rather lose my own job than ever put Emma's career in jeopardy. If for some reason our relationship doesn't work out, I would step down."

"You would?" Emma whispers from next to me.

"Of course I would."

"Well, as sweet as the sentiment is, you can't work together and be in a relationship. What does your father think about this?" Jane accuses.

Just as I'm about to explain, the waitress comes back with our food and sets our respective dishes in front of us.

"I hope you don't plan on eating all of that, Emma." Jane points her fork at Emma's burger and fries.

Emma shrinks in on herself again, but she doesn't respond.

I've never wanted to punch a woman before, but I want to right now.

I lean over and place a kiss on Emma's shoulder. "You eat as much as you want. Just save room for dessert later."

Emma's cheeks turn a lovely shade of pink as she nods.

Jane glares at me. "She should be watching her weight if she expects to keep a man happy."

"I'm more than happy with her just as she is. She doesn't need to starve herself to keep me."

Emma squeezes my thigh under the table.

"Well, at least you've brought a man home." Jane sighs. "Your cousin Ava divorced her husband of six years to move in with her *friend*. She told your aunt they're 'in love.' Ava and her husband have two kids! What kind of example is she setting for them?" Jane puts air quotes around "in love."

"Didn't Ava and Shea get divorced over two years ago? When did she move in with her girlfriend?"

"Six months ago."

"Okaaaaay... so Ava divorced him before she moved in. And as for the example she's setting for their kids? She's showing them that love is love. There's nothing wrong with two women being together."

"It's inappropriate to shove it in the kids' faces! She's probably trying to make her daughter gay. Marriage is between a man and a woman. That's it," Jane states with an icy glare towards Emma.

Jesus.

We're saved from further conversation by the server asking how our meals are tasting. That seems to be the unspoken end of the discussion about her cousin.

We sit in uncomfortable silence while we eat, and I don't get it. They don't see their daughter very often, but they don't ask her for updates on anything other than work.

I get why they're avoiding talking to me since they don't think I'll stick around, and they're clearly racist, but I don't understand why they won't talk to *her*.

"Emma, I hope you've packed something appropriate for the funeral," Jane clips out of nowhere.

"I did," Emma says.

"Well, I'm having trouble finding anything that covers my knees. All the dresses are just so short nowadays. I wish they made the bigger women's clothes in normal sizes. They always have the cutest things."

What the fuck?

CHAPTER 47

Emma

I fucking hate talking about clothes with my mom. I hate shopping with her even more, so I avoid it at all costs.

When I was here last year, she roped me into going shopping with her and when we walked through the plus-size section of Target, she clicked her tongue and said, "These are *huge*. There's no way any of them will ever fit me."

The clothes she was holding were my size.

It was a blow to my self-esteem. It doesn't help that every time I see her, she's "concerned" about my health and tries to fat-shame me into going on a diet.

I've worked really hard to learn to accept my body for what it is. I don't love my body every day, but it's gotten me through a lot, and it deserves to be cared for.

I've told her time and time again how she should refer to it as the plus-size section instead of the "bigger lady" section or the "full-figure" section, but she doesn't listen, nor does she care.

Luckily, I ask if they have any upcoming trips planned with her twin, Janet, which forces her to change the subject. Apparently, they're planning a cruise to Hawaii for the spring.

When the check comes, my dad insists on paying, even though Ben offers. I used to think it was because my dad is a generous man, but now I realize it's how he asserts his dominance and shows off his wealth.

They don't hug me goodbye, just confirm Ben and I will be at the funeral on Friday and dinner afterwards.

When we get back into Ben's car, my eyes well with the tears I've been holding back all night.

"I'm so sorry they're so awful."

"Emma, I promise you have nothing to apologize for. I just don't understand how two people so awful were able to produce you."

I don't know what to say, so I just shrug.

We don't talk as we make our way back to the hotel. It's a welcome change from the strained conversation at dinner.

I hate having dinner with my parents. They never talk, which I find odd. Why even ask me to come if you're not going to talk to me?

But I know it's all for show. They're hoping they'll run into a ward member or one of my dad's coworkers and get to flaunt me around.

Even if they hate everything about me.

They hate my tattoos. They hate my nose piercing. They hate my decision to leave the church. They hate that I'm bisexual. They hate that I moved away from Utah—away from *them*—and found happiness and haven't asked them for anything.

Sometimes, I think they just hate *me*.

My tears have dried by the time we enter the hotel room, and even though it's only seven o'clock, I'm exhausted.

"What would you like to do for the rest of the night?" Ben asks, leaning against the wall by the door.

"I think I'd just like to read and relax, if it's okay?"

Ben smiles softly at me. "Of course it's okay. Do you want to shower first?"

I nod and gather my clothes, heading into the bathroom to take a quick shower.

When I come out, Ben gathers his stuff and takes it to the bathroom.

I grab my Kindle and settle on my bed, opening it up to where I left off in the book I'm reading.

"Please," Cami whimpers as I tease the fat head of my cock at her entrance. She's so wet, I could slip inside with no resistance at all.

"Patience, Pet. You've been teasing me all day with this damn pencil skirt. How am I supposed to get anything done when all I want to do is bend you over my desk?"

I have her bent over said desk with her hands bound behind her back with the tie I've been wearing all day. I didn't plan on fucking my assistant today, but when I heard her telling a coworker about a date she was going on tonight, I knew I had to make my move.

She needs to know she won't be dating anyone else because she's mine.

I asked her to stay late to help me recover a file I "accidentally" deleted. I stayed put in my chair while she stood in front of my computer, and I ogled the way that damn pencil skirt hugged her ass. I couldn't resist running my hands up her strong thighs, slipping under the skirt to feel the soft skin beneath.

Her breath hitched, but she didn't stop me as she continued clicking around for a file that never existed in the first place.

I stood from my chair and pressed my front against her back, running my hands up her sides.

"S-sir. This is wrong."

"Is it?" I mumbled against the soft skin of her neck, inhaling the sweet, vanilla scent of her.

"Yes. You're my superior. I could lose my job."

"I'm the owner. I would never let that happen, Pet. Let me make you feel good. Please, Cami."

After a half-hearted argument, she let me taste her decadent pussy.

Now I'm about to fuck the object of my obsession for the last year.

"I'm going to make your pussy cream all over this cock, Cami. But you can't come until I say." I don't let her respond as I thrust my hips to the hilt, groaning as the tight heat of her envelops my length.

She—

"What are you reading?" Ben's voice makes me snap my head up.

"Uh, a romance book about a boss and his assistant."

Ben prowls towards the bed slowly, like a panther assessing its prey. "Tell me what's happening in the story, *Dulzura*. What's got your cheeks flushed and thighs clenching?"

"He, uh." I lick my lips, and Ben's gaze tracks the movement. "He has her… bent over his desk. With her hands tied behind her back. He just thrust inside her for the first time after eating her out."

Ben hums as he reaches the end of my bed, crossing his arms as his eyes rake over my body.

I'm in a cropped tank top and loose sleep shorts, but you'd think I was in the world's finest lingerie by the look in Ben's eyes.

The tank top is white, so when my nipples pebble under his stare, he smirks and licks his lips.

"Why did he tie her hands behind her back?"

"T-to punish her for teasing him all day in her outfit."

Ben hums again and mumbles, "I can relate."

He glances around the room and turns back to me with a wicked smirk after he notices the small desk in the corner of the room.

"Would you like to reenact the scene, *Dulzura?* Can I bend you over this hotel desk and fuck you with your hands tied?"

God, yes.

"Yes, Sir."

Ben grabs my ankles and pulls me to the end of the bed, my Kindle tossed somewhere as I yelp.

He cups my pussy with his hand, no doubt feeling the heat radiating off of it. I'm not wet yet, but I will be soon.

"These little shorts are a tease, honey. Did you wear them just to punish me?" He teases the hem, slipping his warm fingers underneath the fabric and rubbing small circles into my thigh.

"No, Sir. They're just comfortable to sleep in."

Ben hums as he removes his hands and traces them slowly up my sides. "What about this thing you call a shirt? Hm? Your nipples are practically begging for my tongue. Did you wear this just to get my attention?"

He pinches one of my nipples to punctuate his question, and I let out a loud moan.

"N-no, Sir."

"I don't believe you, *Dulzura*. I think you wore this just for me. But let me tell you a secret." He leans over and puts his mouth next to my ear, causing goosebumps to erupt all over my body. "You *always* have my attention."

I let out an embarrassing whimper when Ben moves off me, and he chuckles. He walks over to his duffle bag on the floor and rifles around until he finds what he's looking for—an emerald green necktie.

"This is the only tie I brought with me for this trip, *Dulzura*. I think it'll work for what I have planned, though. Then every time I wear it, I'll think of you, bent over and at my mercy." He tosses it on the bed before standing between my legs again.

He hooks his fingers into the waistband of my shorts and pulls them off my legs slowly, groaning when he finds I'm not wearing panties.

"No panties, *Dulzura?* That's naughty."

"It's to let my pussy breathe at night, Sir."

"Are you saying you haven't been wearing panties any of the times we've shared a room?"

"Yes, Sir."

"*Fuck*." He runs a hand down his face, glaring at my pussy like it's offended him somehow. He shakes his head and holds out his hands.

I take them, and he helps me stand. He lifts the hem of my tank top over my head and tosses it on the bed, my nipples get even harder in the cool air of the room.

"Stunning," Ben whispers, thumbing one nipple and then the other. "On the desk, honey."

I awkwardly maneuver myself until I'm sitting on the desk, and Ben steps between my legs. I look up at him and find myself once again wanting to beg him for a kiss. But the sting of rejection from the last time is still there, and we haven't talked about it again.

I think he might be thinking the same thing as he brings his thumb up to my mouth and presses it between my lips. "Suck. Make it wet."

I close my lips around his thumb, swirling my tongue around the tip, mimicking the way I would suck his cock.

He pulls out of my mouth with a wet pop, slips his thumb down to my aching clit, and rubs gentle, teasing circles on my sensitive bud.

My head falls back between my shoulders, but Ben's hand grips the hair at the nape of my neck and pulls until my face is tipped up towards him.

"I want your eyes when I make you come on my fingers, *Dulzura*." He slips two fingers into my pussy. "I want to watch them roll back when you coat them in your sweetness."

He thrusts his fingers and swirls his thumb around my clit with the efficiency of someone who knows my body better than I do. It feels like hardly any time passes before my orgasm crests and sends me careening over the edge with a loud moan.

Ben's gaze never leaves mine, even as my eyes roll back from the pleasure.

"That's it, honey. You look so pretty when you come for me. *Fuck.*"

He pulls his fingers from me and presses them to my mouth. "Clean my fingers."

CHAPTER 48

Emma eagerly sucks her own release off my fingers, and I almost come on the spot just watching her tongue.

"So eager, *Dulzura*. You're always so good for me. I love watching your mouth on my fingers almost as much as I like it on my cock."

Emma's lashes flutter at my praise, and she smiles around my fingers. I pull them from her mouth and yank her off the desk to flip her over so her chest is against the wood. Her toes barely reach the floor, but she doesn't complain.

I grab the tie from the bed and pull her arms behind her back, knotting it loosely. The green against the ivory skin of her wrists is tantalizing.

"Stay just like that, honey." I quickly shuck off my clothes and toss them on the bed.

When I step back behind her, I grip the base of my cock and tap it on her clit. She arches back to gain more friction, but I stop her with a grip on her hips.

"I'm going to fuck you hard and fast as punishment for the way you've teased me." I spank her ass, and she moans. "I need you to come for me again, *Dulzura.*" I notch the head of my cock at her opening and slowly push in until I'm fully seated inside her.

"Fuck. Like a damn glove. Every single time." I'll never get tired of the way her pussy grips my cock. I'll never get tired of watching her ass jiggle as it bounces off my thighs. I'll never get tired of the way she pulses when I hit a particularly sensitive spot.

I grip her tied wrists as I set a brutal pace, and the desk slams into the wall with every thrust, but I can't find it in myself to give a shit about it right now. I'll pay whatever damage fees need to be paid.

She cries out when I hit her hard and deep, and her legs shake as her orgasm overtakes her. I feel her gush of arousal coating my cock. *Fuck.*

"That's fucking right, *Dulzura.* Come for me. I love the way your pussy pulses. Feels so damn good. Love it when you mark me with your cum."

She moans again, and I continue my pace. I need to feel her come again. I pull the tie, making her back arch more to hit at a different angle. She moans my name, her pussy clamps me so hard it makes me see stars.

I spill my release deep inside her right before she comes, groaning her name as my thrusts slow down.

I untie her wrists while I'm still inside of her, then I pull out and rush to the bathroom to find a washcloth. When I turn around to exit the bathroom, Emma's standing in the doorway with her clothes in hand, a trail of cum running down her leg.

"What are you doing, honey? I was coming to clean you up."

Emma bites her lip. "I have to pee anyway. I can do it."

I furrow my brows, confused about this sudden need to do it herself. I hand over the washcloth and step out of the bathroom so she can take care of her business in private, even though everything in me is screaming not to leave her alone.

I dress myself, then sit on the edge of the bed while I wait for her to come out of the bathroom.

When she finally does, her hair is up in her usual bedtime ponytail, and she's got her pajamas back on. All traces of what we just did are gone save for the blush on her cheeks when she sees me.

My senses are telling me something's wrong, so as she walks by, I grab her wrist gently. "Are you okay? Was that okay? I didn't hurt you, did I?"

Emma gives me a small smile. "It was perfect. I'm not hurt, just... in my head a little, I guess."

"I guess I didn't fuck you hard enough, then," I tease, but she only gives me a half-hearted chuckle in return. "You can talk to me, Emma."

She sighs. "I know. Dinner tonight was a lot, and I know family dinner on Friday will be worse. I feel bad subjecting you to all of this. This isn't what you signed up for."

I stand and cup her face, making her look me in the eyes. "I'm exactly where I want to be, Emma. I don't want you to feel bad when I'm choosing to be here. I've got you, okay?"

She nods, and her eyes flick to my lips like they did earlier. We haven't broached the topic of kissing again; I would now if I thought she'd be open to the discussion.

But it's just one more thing to put on her plate, and I don't want her to feel pressured.

"Let's go to bed. I think we're both in need of some rest."

She nods in agreement, and I reluctantly let her go so she can get in her own bed.

Soon, she won't feel the need to distance herself from me.

I hope.

STRUCTION // UNDER CONSTRUCTION // UNDER CON

The next day, Emma takes me up Big Cottonwood Canyon to see the fall leaves.

The peak time for the fall colors is the first weekend in October, so we're a little late, but it's still stunning.

We stopped at a little lodge and restaurant for lunch and spent the day getting to know more about each other outside of the bedroom.

It felt like a first date, and it was perfect.

I've never seen her so at peace. It's like, as soon as we got into the crisp mountain air, the weight of all her problems blew away on the light breeze.

I want to be the one to put the easy smile on her face. I want to be her peace.

Now, we're back at the hotel to freshen up before we go to dinner at her cousin's house.

Since we've been here, Emma's outfits have been more on the conservative side, covering a majority of her tattoos. I attributed it to the colder weather, since it's the most logical reason.

But as she walks out of the bathroom, I'm beginning to wonder if it's to make the people around her more comfortable.

She's wearing a maroon skirt, which looks like it's made of suede, and a black mesh long sleeve shirt over a black tank top doing nothing to hide the ink all over her arms. The skirt is short enough the bottom of her garter tattoos peek out underneath the material.

"You look incredible," I rasp, greedily taking her in.

Emma gives me a beaming smile. "Thank you."

She slips on her black ankle boots and grabs her purse. "Ready to meet my cousins? I promise they're nothing like my parents."

"I'll admit I'm a little nervous, but I'm ready."

She gives an overexaggerated gasp. "Benjamin Rossi gets nervous?"

I scowl at her teasing tone, but I don't respond.

I wasn't nervous to meet her parents because I knew she wasn't looking for their approval. She's not close enough to them for their opinion to matter.

But the same can't be said about her cousins.

I'm nervous they won't like me, and it will be the thing to end our situation once and for all.

I don't want this to end.

I don't tell Emma any of that, though.

CHAPTER 49

Emma

Hannah and Morgan's house is like something out of a suburban dream—complete with the white picket fence.

As we pull into the driveway, Ben whistles as he takes it in. "This is a nice area. What did you say they do for work?"

"Morgan owns a flower shop, and Hannah works at the library. But Morgan used to play for the Denver Mustangs."

"Wow. Not intimidating at all," Ben grumbles as we walk up the driveway.

"Morgan is one of the best guys I've ever met. No need to be intimidated."

We ring the doorbell and hear little feet shuffling before Hannah opens the door with a baby on her hip. A blonde girl pokes her head out from behind her.

"Emma! I'm so glad you're here." Hannah gives me a one-armed hug while the baby immediately grabs onto my hair and pulls it towards her mouth.

"Me too! This is Ben." I motion to the man next to me as I wince.

"Poppy, don't be rude." Hannah chuckles, helping to untangle my hair from Poppy's tiny fist. "Nice to meet you, Ben. I'm Hannah."

"Nice to meet you, too. Thanks for the invite."

"Of course!" Hannah gives me a sheepish smile. "Sorry about the grabby welcome."

"It's all good. Babies love to pull my hair. Hi, Poppy," I coo to the chubby-cheeked girl. I peek around Hannah and give the older girl a smile. "Hi, kiddo. You must be Aly. I'm Emma, and this is my friend Ben."

"Hi. I like your tattoos," she says shyly.

"Thank you."

Hannah ushers us inside when she hears a crash and a squeal.

Ben and I take off our shoes at the entryway, and he bends to whisper in my ear, "You sure seem to like it when *I* pull your hair."

I gently smack his chest as my cheeks heat.

I really do.

We follow the sound of voices to the kitchen and find Morgan kneeling on the floor wiping up some sort of sauce while Hannah holds both babies.

"Can I take one of them from you?" I ask Hannah.

"Sure! That would be great. Morgan's parents are coming to take the girls for the night, but they're running a bit behind, and this one wanted to help Dada cook." She shifts to hand over Violet, and I take the chunky baby.

"No worries. I don't mind hanging out with you cuties. You must be Violet. Hello, sweet girl." Violet looks from me to her mom, like she's not sure what to do in this situation.

Then, her big green eyes lock on Ben over my shoulder, and she just stares.

I hear Ben chuckle from behind me. "Hi, pretty girl." Violet gives him a big gummy grin.

Morgan's head whips up at the sound of Ben's voice, and he gives me a knowing smirk. I roll my eyes at him. I'm sure he's remembering last year when he told me someone was going to come along and change my mind about dating.

Jokes on him, though, since Ben and I aren't dating.

He stands and tosses the paper towels in the trash, washes his hands, then extends one to Ben.

"Hey, man, I'm Morgan."

"Ben. Nice to meet you."

Morgan turns to me and wraps me in a familiar hug, even though I've only met him once over a year ago. "Good to see you, Emma."

"Same to you, Flower Daddy."

Morgan chuckles and shakes his head at my joke as he walks back around the counter to resume whatever he was doing before we came in.

Ben steps up behind me and practically growls, "I'm the only man you should be calling 'Daddy,' *Dulzura*."

My thighs automatically squeeze together. Now is *not* the time to explore a daddy kink.

The doorbell rings, and I hand Ben the baby without a second thought when Hannah hands off Poppy to me and goes to answer the door.

I'm expecting Elli and her fiancé, Wes, but Hannah walks in with an older couple who must be Morgan's parents. His dad is tall as hell and looks intimidating at first, but his eyes soften as soon as Aly catapults herself into his arms, and the twins immediately start jabbering and squirming when they see their grandparents.

"There are my girls!" Morgan's mom gushes. She does a double take when she sees Ben holding Violet. "Hello, I'm Iris. This is Axel. We're Morgan's parents. You must be Hannah's cousin?"

"I am. I'm Emma, this is Ben."

Poppy squirms to be let down, so I put her on the floor, and she crawls to her grandma.

"Oh, look how fast you are, Poppy girl. You're going to be walking in no time, and then we'll really be in trouble." Iris bends to pick up Poppy, who starts babbling like she's catching her up on everything that's happened today.

I go to take Violet from Ben, but he waves me off. He looks... comfortable with her. He's swaying slightly while she plays with the button of his flannel shirt and chews on her fist.

My ovaries explode, and suddenly I wonder what a child who's half Ben and half me would look like. Would they have his tanned skin and my blue eyes? Or would they have my hair texture and his hair color? Would they be stoic and quiet like him or sassy and boisterous like me?

I haven't decided if I want kids or not. There's so many factors that play into that decision, and it's not one I take lightly. Does Ben even want kids? We haven't talked much about it.

Woah, Emma. Slow the fuck down. You aren't even really dating.

When I tune back in to the conversation, Ben and Axel are talking about something construction related, and Hannah is gone—probably to grab the girls' things for their sleepover. Morgan is briefing his mom on the girls' schedule, and Iris is listening intently.

The doorbell rings. "I'll get it!" I say, since I'm not in the middle of a conversation.

Elli, Wes, Izzy and a guy I don't recognize are standing outside when I open the door, and Elli immediately wraps me in a hug.

"Emma! I'm so happy to see you."

"You, too, Elli. Hi, Wes."

"Emma! This is my boyfriend, Luke." Izzy pulls the curly haired boy to the front, and he gives me a big grin and an enthusiastic wave.

"Nice to meet you, Luke."

Luke bows, and I chuckle.

They follow me inside and take off their shoes before meeting the rest of us in the kitchen. We do more introductions with Iris, Axel, and Ben.

My cousins all do a double-take when they see Ben, and Elli waggles her eyebrows at me, mouthing, *"He's hot."*

"I know," I mouth back.

Wes playfully grabs Elli by the hips and tries to shove her away from him while covering her eyes.

She rolls her eyes and goes up on her tiptoes to give him a chaste kiss on the cheek, then says something only he can hear while pointing to her engagement ring.

"Oh my God! I totally forgot to congratulate you two! Let me see it!" I grab Elli's left hand and inspect the ring. It's an oval shaped diamond on a simple gold band, but it fits Elli's personality perfectly. "It's beautiful. Good job, Wes." I nudge him with my elbow.

Wes's fair cheeks turn a little pink. "Thank you. It was my mom's, actually."

My heart lurches. Wes's mom passed away when he was a teenager, so I know it must mean a lot to have his girl wearing his mom's ring. "Oh, that's lovely. Have you guys set a date yet?"

Elli shakes her head. "No. There's talk of another tour, and Wes has an album to record, so we're waiting until things die down a bit."

"Well, I'm happy for you. I'm glad you have time to plan so you can have the wedding of your dreams."

"Thanks, Emma."

Hannah comes down the stairs with three bags and drops them at the bottom before giving Elli and Izzy hugs and greeting Wes and Luke.

Hannah and Morgan take the girls out to the car to say goodbye while Izzy chatters on about college and how difficult the commute is from where they live in San Marcos. They're thinking of renting a place of their own in San Antonio.

When Hannah and Morgan return, they start pulling out salads, garlic bread, and what looks like homemade lasagna.

Talmage arrives right as we're about to dish up, apologizing for being late. He got caught up at work then got stuck in traffic.

He looks like he hasn't slept at all since yesterday. There are dark bags under his eyes, and it doesn't look like he's had time to shave, but he still gives us his golden boy smile like nothing's wrong.

Maybe I can see through it because I'm used to wearing my own smile as a mask, even when I'm feeling down.

We dish up the food buffet style and sit down at the large farmhouse table in the dining area attached to the kitchen before we dig in.

Chapter 50

Emma

After dinner, where everyone took turns giving updates on their lives, my cousins and I clean up the kitchen while the guys run to grab ice cream for dessert.

I know they're giving us privacy so us girls and Talmage can catch up with each other, but I can't help the way my heart twinges when Ben walks out the door.

I also can't help the bitter sting of jealousy watching Wes kiss Elli, Luke give Izzy a kiss on the cheek, and Morgan give Hannah a forehead kiss before they leave. Ben gave my arm a quick squeeze, and I could tell my cousins have questions about it.

Sure enough, as soon we see the headlights retreat from the driveway, Elli whips around and says, "Spill it, Emma."

I sigh from where I'm putting dirty dishes in the dishwasher.

I avoided talking about how Ben and I met and our rocky history at dinner because I'm embarrassed. Not of Ben and not of our kinky sex life but of how cautious—let's be real, scared—I am. How I'm lying to people by saying he's my boyfriend when I don't even know what we are.

"Yeah, what's the deal with you two?" Izzy asks.

"We're not actually dating. We're just coworkers... having fun?" I know Izzy is almost nineteen, but the last time I saw her she wasn't even a teenager, so I don't know how explicit I can be.

Izzy rolls her eyes. "Please don't think you have to spare the details because of me. I lost my virginity as soon as I got to Texas."

"Isabelle!" Elli scolds, but Hannah and I chuckle.

"Oh *puh-lease,* Els. You think I can't hear you and Wes through the walls of our shared apartment?" Izzy drops her voice to mimic Wes's. "*So good for me, baby. You like it when I spank this—*"

Elli smacks her palm over Izzy's mouth, her face red as a tomato while Hannah and I crack up laughing.

"We don't need a reenactment of my sex life, Iz."

Izzy must lick Elli's palm because she pulls back with a gag and wipes her hand on Izzy's arm while Izzy grins deviously.

My heart lurches. I envy their relationship. I'm not close with any of my sisters.

"I'm just saying, Emma doesn't need to be so vague. It's clear there's sexual tension between them. I'd be shocked if they *hadn't* fucked—sorry for the language, Talmage."

Talmage's face is a little pink, but he just waves her off. "All good. Tonight, I'm one of the gals—uh, you know what I mean."

"Fine, we're just friends with benefits," I finally admit.

Hannah snorts. "Right. All friends with benefits make a twelve-hour drive to a different state for a funeral of a person they didn't know. Emma, that man does not want to be your friend. He wants you to take his last name."

"We agreed this is only sex. There's no way he sees me as more. He knows—and you all know—I don't do relationships. As soon as we're sick of each other, we'll end it. No harm, no foul." I don't even believe myself at this point.

"And then what? You'll just see each other every day at work and pretend nothing happened?" Elli asks.

I truly haven't thought that far ahead. I haven't wanted to. I haven't wanted to think about this ending because I know it's going to hurt like a bitch. It's going to wreck me, and I'll have to go on like nothing ever happened.

I swallow a sip of the hard cider I never finished at dinner. "Yeah. Probably."

"Emma, you're being dumb," Izzy deadpans.

I scoff. "Okay, *rude.* I'm not being dumb."

"Then at the very least you have blinders on because I agree with Hannah," Elli chimes in. "You didn't see the way he was looking at you at dinner."

"H-how was he looking at me?"

"The same way Wes looks at Elli. The same way Morgan looks at Hannah. But not the same way Luke looks at Izzy only because I think comparing him to a nineteen-year-old is a little weird. No offense," Talmage says the last part to Izzy, and she just waves off his apology.

That can't be true. Can it?

Wes looks at Elli like every love song in existence was written specifically for her. Morgan looks at Hannah like she hung the moon. Both men are completely obsessed with their partners.

"We haven't even kissed," I blurt out, and all four jaws drop.

"What do you *mean* you haven't even kissed? How are you fucking if you aren't kissing?" Izzy shrieks. It's still weird to hear her curse.

"You don't have to kiss to have sex. We just... skip that part and get straight to the good stuff. I haven't kissed anyone in four years, and it works just fine."

"Four *years?*" they all say in unison.

"It's not that big of a deal!" I state.

"Making out is the best part of foreplay! When the kisses turn messy and harsh, all lips and teeth and tongue. When touches get greedy and desperate..." Elli trails off, her eyes taking on a glassy look.

Talmage's face is turning redder by the second, and I'm wondering if he regrets staying now.

"I have to agree. Kissing is severely underrated. And I've only kissed two people in my entire life," Hannah adds.

"Why are you so afraid of kissing? Or relationships?" Izzy asks.

Damn, they're hitting me with the hard questions. I explain my thinking. How kissing leads to feelings, and feelings lead to heartbreak.

"It's just safer."

Hannah, Elli, and Izzy are looking at me with matching pitying expressions, and I can't stand it. They don't understand. They all have amazing partners who practically fell into their laps.

Sure, Hannah's ex-husband was an absolute piece of shit, and Elli doesn't have a stellar dating past, but both of their experiences lead them to the men they're with. Izzy was lucky enough to find "the one" in *high school*. That's *so* rare.

I know Talmage was engaged a year or so ago, but I don't know if he's dated anyone since. I wonder if he feels like me.

"I know you've been burned in the past, but take it from two people who didn't want to see what was right in front of them." Elli motions to herself and Hannah. "The best thing we ever did was take a chance on our guys."

Hannah nods her agreement. "Ben's a good guy, Emma. I don't think you have to worry about him breaking your heart."

"Take a chance on love. And for God's sake, put that man out of his misery and let him kiss you!" Izzy adds.

"I have to agree with them, Emma. You'll regret it if you let him go. Don't wake up years from now wondering 'what if?'" Talmage sounds like he's speaking from experience.

"We're circling back to that in a minute," Izzy whispers to Talmage.

Maybe they're right. Maybe it's time to finally let someone in. Ben's already shown up for me more than anyone else I've seriously dated.

"I don't know how to let him in," I admit quietly.

All four of them wrap me up in a group hug as tears rim my lash line.

"Talk to him. Tell him how you're feeling. A relationship is built on trust, so trust he'll see the darkest parts of you and still want you."

I hope they're right. He's already seen more of me than I've shown anyone in a long time, and he hasn't run. That's got to mean something.

"Okay, fine. I'll take a chance. Can we move on and talk about Talmage now?" I joke, and Talmage shakes his head.

"No, thanks. My love life is non-existent. Just work, work, work." He laughs awkwardly.

"Nope. You're clearly trying to work through something, so spit it out, dude." Izzy pats his shoulder reassuringly.

Talmage's shoulders slump. "I'm just... tired of the dating thing, I guess. When my engagement ended, I was relieved because we weren't very compatible, but I was dreading the idea of dating again. My parents are on my case about getting married. I hate that I'm still in the Young Single Adult ward because so many of the women are a good six years younger than me—some are a whole decade younger. I don't want to date someone younger than twenty-five. And..." he trails off and rubs his hand over his mouth.

"And..." I prompt.

"You guys are happy? Even though you're not in the church?" He looks at each one of us like he's looking for validation.

All four of us know what it's like to want to leave but worry our lives will get worse if we do. We all know it takes a lot of strength to finally free ourselves from the dead weight of the church.

Talmage doesn't seem like he's asking because he wants to judge us. He sounds like he's looking for answers he hasn't been able to find.

"My life's never been fuller or happier," Hannah answers, and we all nod in agreement.

"Sure, our lives aren't perfect, but they wouldn't be perfect in the church either," I add.

"But don't you guys miss your families? Don't you miss the community or—or the sense of safety in the church?"

"I mean, not if my family's love comes with conditions," Elli says. "I found a family—a community—with Wes's friends. It's much healthier and more reliable than the one I grew up in. And I think I speak for all of us when I say the church wasn't a safe place for us."

Talmage's eyebrows shoot to his hairline, and his mouth drops open. "What do you mean it wasn't a safe place for you?"

The four of us each had different experiences in the church, but the result is the same: the church hates women.

"I was blamed for having multiple miscarriages. They said it was because I wasn't worthy," Hannah explains.

"I was told if I lost weight, I'd have a better chance of getting a husband," Elli adds, and Hannah and I murmur our agreement.

"I had to have meetings with the bishop every month between when Elli left and I moved out because everyone was worried Elli would 'steer me down the wrong path,'" Izzy admits.

Talmage looks at me, and I debate keeping this to myself, but I think he deserves to know. "I was told it was my fault I was raped. My rapist and I went through the repentance process at the same time, and he was able to obtain a temple recommend in less than two months, but I wasn't even allowed to take the sacrament until three months later. I was labelled as a risk and wasn't able to serve a mission."

Izzy and Talmage both gasp. They're the only ones who didn't already know. I'm sure there were whispers around the family, but no one knows the full story because no one really cares enough to ask.

"Are you serious?" Talmage whispers.

"Unfortunately. I'm going to be blunt with you, cousin. The church is only a safe place for white men. Specifically, *wealthy, straight,* white men. But it's not a safe place for women or people of color. Not even children. The church protects itself and its assets before protecting the members."

Talmage looks like he's just been served raw chicken with a side of moldy bread and an uncooked potato.

"I knew it sucked, women not having the opportunity for priesthood, but... I didn't realize..."

Izzy pats him on the back almost condescendingly. "The system doesn't seem broken to those who benefit from it. Sounds like you've got some research to do."

Talmage just nods. "Yeah. I guess I do."

Chapter 51

Ben

I like Emma's cousins' partners—her cousins, too. Morgan's hilarious and super chill. Wes is quiet, but he's kind and teases Luke relentlessly in a way that reminds me of my relationship with Mateo. Luke is still a kid, but I can tell he's a good one. They all treat their girls like they're the best thing to ever happen to them. They look at them like they're the sun, moon, and all the stars.

I probably look at Emma the same way.

I thought it would be awkward to tag along with them and not have Emma's familiarity to keep me company. While I miss her, I'm not uncomfortable.

"So, Ben, you must be a great guy to lock down Emma. She was pretty adamant about not being in a serious relationship last year," Morgan says from the driver's seat.

I huff out a laugh. I don't know if I can open up to them without hurting Emma, but I could really use some advice. I can't ask Mateo or Papà like I usually would.

The urge to ask virtual strangers for advice about a woman I'm not even dating feels strange, but their significant others are related to her, so maybe they have more insight than I do. And I could use all the help I can get.

"If I tell you something, can you promise it stays between us?" I ask the group.

All three of them say "no" at the same time, and we all laugh.

"Sorry, but I won't keep things from Elli. Whatever you say will be shared with her, but I can promise it won't be repeated further if you don't want it to be," Wes says, the other two murmuring their agreement.

I can respect the fact they don't keep things from their girls. It's clear they all love them infinitely and would do anything for them. Even Luke, who's not even twenty, has a healthier relationship than I've ever had.

I sigh. "We're not *actually* dating. It's just sex. Emma hasn't been in a relationship in over four years, and she's..."

"Skittish?" Morgan finishes.

"Yeah. I don't want to push her too hard and risk losing her. I've already fallen head over heels, but I doubt she feels the same way."

"Take it from someone who almost let the girl of his dreams go because I didn't think she felt the same way," Wes says, "you'll regret not telling her how you feel. Even if it might scare her away, you'll never know if you don't try."

"I agree. My situation is different, obviously. I waited until Hannah was ready, but she's the one who ended up making the move to take us from fake to real. She was still dealing with the aftermath of her divorce at the time. I think if you wait for Emma to make a move, you'll be waiting a long time."

I sigh. "That's what I'm afraid of. You all think I should just... buck up and confess my feelings?"

All three of them say "yes" at the same time.

"But I suggest waiting until after tomorrow. You probably know how... *delightful* a lot of the Monson extended family can be. I'd wait until the emotional toll of tomorrow is over,." Morgan says "delightful" like it's an insult, and I almost laugh.

I learned over dinner that Emma's parents aren't the only shitty ones. Elli and Izzy's parents haven't talked to Elli in well over a year, and they stopped talking to Izzy after she moved out in August.

Hannah's mom hasn't even met her grandkids because she treated Hannah so horribly.

Talmage's parents seem *decent,* but he didn't talk about them much.

I hate that they all have terrible or non-existent relationships with their parents, but I'm glad they at least have each other.

When we get back to the house, we walk in to find the girls and Talmage on the U-shaped sofa in the living room, laughing about something.

Luke settles in front of Izzy's legs, and Wes leans over Elli to give her a quick kiss, both of them handing the girls' ice cream to them. Morgan kisses Hannah's forehead, and I try not to let my jealousy show.

I hand Talmage his ice cream, then sit by Emma, desperately wishing I could give her a kiss, too.

She gives me a soft smile and murmurs, "Thanks," as I hand over her cookie dough and brownie shake.

"What's got you all laughing so hard?" Morgan asks as he settles next to his wife.

Talmage groans and shakes his head. "I don't want to repeat it."

"Me either!" Emma says around a mouthful of shake.

"Well, now I need to know. I don't know *any* embarrassing stories about Emma," I say with a playful nudge.

She scowls at me.

"We were just reminiscing about the time we had a family reunion at Bear Lake. Talmage and Emma were seven and six, and Talmage gave Emma a big ol' kiss on the lips and asked her to marry him," Elli says with a wicked grin.

"Emma agreed, and then everyone had to explain it wasn't okay to marry your cousin. Emma and Talmage were *devastated*," Hannah adds.

"My mom told me I would go to *jail* if I married him. I was terrified!" Emma shrieks through a fit of giggles.

"Wow, I didn't know I needed to be wary of your own cousin, honey," I tease, and Talmage holds up his hands.

"Don't worry, man, I'm no longer interested. I have someone else in mind."

"Ooo," all the girls say.

"Do tell, Tal," Izzy demands.

Talmage's cheeks immediately turn pink, and he shakes his head. "It—She—*ugh*." He scrubs a hand down his face. "It's complicated."

"Isn't it always?" Emma asks, and everyone gets quiet and exchanges glances.

"Tell me another embarrassing story about Emma," I say to combat the awkward tension sticking to everything in the room.

"When we were around ten or twelve, we went on a family camping trip. Emma, Elli, and I shared a tent, and we were having a screaming contest to see who could scream the loudest. Emma has a set of lungs on her and won, but we all got in trouble for it. Emma's also the wildest sleeper I've ever had to share a bed with. We're talking *all over* the bed," Hannah shares.

"Okay, but *you* were the one who ended up on *my* pillow and forced me to sleep on the hard ground for the rest of the night!" Emma accuses.

"Remember the home video we made with the giant mushroom? Hannah pretended to be some type of singer who got stuck in the woods, and a wizard made us hunt for a giant mushroom to get you back home," Elli says.

"Oooh, yes! Remember the video the family made the year Elli was born about the 'cereal' killer?" Emma cackles as she explains the strange plot of a movie about someone "killing" a bunch of cereal because everyone thought the kids ate too much of it.

Wes, Morgan, Luke, and I share bemused expressions. This family is strange.

"It sucks they stopped doing those family campouts by the time I was old enough to go. It sounds like you guys had fun," Izzy pouts.

"I think the camping trip with the mushroom was the first one in about a decade at that point. Then, they just stopped doing them for some reason. At least you got to experience Grandma and Grandpa's Lagoon days," Elli says with a sympathetic smile before explaining. "They used to take the whole family to the amusement park and buy us ice cream after we rode on Rattlesnake Rapids. It was the best day of the year."

"That's true. But they stopped doing those when I was like eight. Grandpa's knees got bad, and he couldn't ride anything anymore."

The room gets eerily quiet for a few moments after that. Elli and Hannah lean in closer to their partners seeking comfort, and Luke starts lightly rubbing Izzy's legs in a soothing gesture.

Emma shifts her weight and starts plucking at the hem of her skirt like she's trying to find a loose string.

"Tomorrow's going to suck, isn't it?" she finally says, breaking the silence.

"Yeah. But I'm glad we were able to hang out before. It's comforting to know no matter what the rest of the family thinks, we still have our little group of black sheep to turn to. Sorry, Talmage, you're the white sheep who keeps getting drawn back to our little outcast flock," Hannah says.

Talmage waves her off. "I'd rather be accepted by the black sheep than have the herd accept me only if I live up to their standards."

CHAPTER 52

I fucking hate funerals.

I think it's morbid having the embalmed body of a loved one sitting at the front of the chapel while people talk about their life.

Mormon funerals inevitably end up being a lesson about the gospel. It's never truly centered around the person we're here to celebrate and mourn and more about what the gospel says will happen in the afterlife.

Elli's dad uses his speech to call all of the family members who have strayed to come back to church because if we don't, we'll never see Grandpa again. He talks about how Grandpa never wavered in his faith and never strayed from the path, and his only wish was for his posterity to do the same.

Elli and I lock eyes when he says that, and even though she subtly rolls her eyes, I know it hurts her because it hurts *me*, and it's not my dad saying it.

It hurts that, while we're grieving a man who was so important in our lives, we have to be poked and prodded about our choices. They use our grief to try to guilt us into coming back to a church we no longer believe in. A church that—in mine and my cousins' cases—has done more harm than good.

I tried to convince Ben to stay at the hotel. I told him I'd be fine alone for the funeral.

But as I realize again that my family will offer no comfort, I'm glad he's here to subtly brush against my thigh letting me know he's here for me.

When it's time to sing with my cousins, I try not to let my eyes stray to Ben. But he becomes my anchor when the emotions of the music wash over me.

When I sit back down, he pulls a travel size pack of tissues out of his suit jacket and hands it over before gently squeezing my thigh and letting his hand linger. He leans in and whispers, "You sounded great up there."

His words only make the tears flow harder.

I'm sure my mother will have something negative to say about my performance. She can never just tell me I did a good job. She always has to pick apart every aspect of everything I do and tell me exactly what I did wrong.

But not Ben.

After my chat with my cousins last night, I know I need to tell Ben how I feel and see how he feels about me, but the conversation feels too heavy right now with the funeral.

Plus, he may not want to be around me anymore after he meets the rest of my family.

I wouldn't blame him.

My mom's reasoning for having a family dinner only a few hours after the funeral luncheon is beyond me.

Ben and I opted for skipping the luncheon because I needed some time away from the sad, judgmental gazes of my extended family before being tossed into the lion's den of my immediate family.

I also need to get out of these tights before I lose my mind.

I hate tights. But they cover the tattoos my dress doesn't cover, so I opted for being uncomfortably squeezed into scratchy fabric that feels like sausage casings over everyone being "offended" over the artwork on my legs.

As soon as we step through the hotel room door, I kick off my shoes and literally rip the tights off my legs. I pull off the long-sleeve, black skater dress—one I haven't worn in forever but keep for occasions like today—to find Ben looking at me with a smirk.

"You could've asked me for help, *Dulzura*."

My cheeks flush at the image of Ben ripping the tights off of my body.

"Sorry, I was overstimulated. I felt like they were squeezing me to death."

"You don't have to apologize. If I had to wear those things, I wouldn't last ten seconds let alone the four hours you've been enduring them. Are you going to wear the dress to dinner at your parents?"

I shake my head. "Absolutely not. I'll end up punching someone if I have to be uncomfortable for another minute." I pull out some loose, denim-colored cargo pants and a long sleeve rib knit shirt and hold it up for Ben. "I still have to hide my tattoos, but at least I'll be comfortable."

Ben shakes his head as he pulls his tie loose and unbuttons his shirt. "I still don't understand why you have to cover up your tattoos. Or why you had to switch your nose ring for a stud."

I sigh as I redress. "Because my mom is offended by my body art. She scoffs and warbles about how much money I've wasted, how tattoos are for criminals, and tells me I look like a bull with my nose ring—even though it's not a septum piercing. She's repeatedly asked why I would subject myself to the pain of the needle, but she doesn't actually care to understand the answer."

Ben's changed in the time it takes me to spill my guts, so he sits next to me on the bed and quietly asks, "What's the answer?"

His espresso colored eyes are so soft and gentle when they lock with mine.

"I used to... harm myself when I was younger. Nothing as extreme as cutting, but I would scratch myself or bang my head on a wall or a table. I didn't realize until I got my first tattoo I was trying to feel something other than the anxiety of simply being alive. The buzz of the needle hurts, obviously, but it helps me focus on the sting of pain in that area instead of the pain of... everything else happening in my brain."

Ben frowns. "I don't understand how your parents never noticed anything was going on with you."

"They did notice—well, my mom did. I would have fits of anxiety over small things and then swing into depression, telling my mom I didn't want to be alive anymore. She would get mad and threaten to take me to a mental hospital but never actually followed through even though I probably would have benefited from it. I've been in and out of therapy since I was four years old. The only time it seemed to *actually* help was when I didn't go to a church approved therapist after high school."

"*Jesus*. What kind of mom gets mad at their child about that?"

I could tell him how all throughout junior high and high school, whenever I told my mom I was feeling down, she'd tell me it was because I didn't read my scriptures or pray enough. She would tell me I wasn't faithful, and only the faithful are happy. She would tell me to go reflect on what The Lord wanted me to do because if I wasn't doing it, I was probably just feeling guilty.

I could tell him how my mom was a big advocate for mental health in the ward. She even went as far as getting my therapist at the time—who was an old high school friend of hers—to come to the relief society activities.

But as much as she put on a show for the ward, when it came to her own daughter, my mental health issues became a nuisance. A bother. It worked to her advantage when she wanted to play the victim of the mentally ill daughter but at home? I was *too* emotional.

I was *too* needy.

I was *too* unreasonable.

I was *too much*.

But I don't tell him any of it because we're about to go to their house, and I don't need to give Ben more of a reason to want to fight them. I'm sure there will be reason enough without me bringing my childhood trauma into the mix.

Instead, I simply say, "The kind who doesn't want people to judge her."

I check the time on my phone, groaning when I see it's time to leave.

"Ready to dive into the lion's den?" I ask as I slip on my shoes.

"Let's do this." Ben holds his hand out, and I take it, immediately feeling like I can handle what's to come with Ben at my side.

Chapter 53

Ben

I was not ready. Not even close.

The moment Emma and I walked in hand-in-hand, the entire house grew quiet, and everyone stared at us like we were complete strangers. I guess I am, but Emma's not.

Emma's mom and dad met us at the door, and Emma's mom gave her a critical onceover that I could tell made Emma uncomfortable.

They studiously avoided looking at me until I broke the silence.

"Good to see you again, Mr. and Mrs. Price."

They didn't return my greeting.

That's fine, I don't need to be fed fake niceties.

They walked away while Emma and I took off our shoes, and I heard Jane parrot the same sentiment as at dinner: "At least he's a man."

After that, Emma took me around the room and introduced me to probably thirty people I vaguely remember seeing at the funeral. It would be difficult to remember everyone's names if I bothered to learn them.

But I remember Hailey's. Because she's a bitch.

Hailey immediately asked me—after looking at me like I was shit on her shoe—what Emma did to lure me into a relationship.

Emma snapped at her to shut up.

Hailey told her to stop being so sensitive, then walked away.

Emma's niece, Georgia, pulled her into a conversation and has been talking non-stop for fifteen minutes about her junior high school. I've been sitting silently next to her while the tween talks so fast I can't keep up.

Emma, seemingly unconsciously, rests her hand on top of mine on my thigh while she listens intently to Georgia and asks her insightful questions. I can tell Georgia misses her aunt, and it hurts to know Emma's missing out on a closer relationship with her.

Dirk interrupts the chatter around the room to announce it's time for a prayer before we eat, and as he says it, I notice only a few people in the room bow their heads and close their eyes. Instead, they keep sneaking glances over at me or just making faces at their kids.

It makes me wonder if Emma isn't as much of a black sheep as she thinks she is, or if she's just held to a higher standard because she was raised to be a certain person and she hasn't lived up to the standards placed on her.

After the prayer, everyone lines up and makes their way around the expansive kitchen island covered in food. Tonight's menu is rice with some type of chicken gravy and a slew of toppings. There's shredded cheese, carrots, lettuce, crispy chow mein noodle pieces, green onions, tomatoes, and… pineapple?

"What is this?" I whisper in Emma's ear as we wait in line.

"Hawaiian haystacks. You put everything on top of the rice. You can mix it in, too, but it's supposed to look like a haystack."

"There's no way this is actually Hawaiian."

Emma shakes her head, and her eyes shine with amusement. "No. The pineapple makes it Hawaiian."

"The—*What?* You can't be serious."

Emma bites her lip to suppress the grin at my outrage. "I wish I weren't. It's got to be some type of cultural appropriation for sure. I know it's a strange combo, so if you don't want to eat anything, we can get something after."

I sigh. "I'll try anything once. Even if it is cultural appropriation."

Emma dishes up her plate first, and I notice she only puts the chicken gravy, cheese, carrots, and crispy noodles on her rice. From what I've gathered about the woman I'm probably in love with, she has an aversion to vegetables. She also probably doesn't like the texture of the things mixed together, which I can't blame her for.

I put a little bit of everything on mine. Might as well go big.

Once we've dished up, we pick a spot at one of the picnic tables set up in the large living room just off the kitchen. It's currently empty, but I'm sure it'll fill up soon. I just hope Hailey doesn't try to sit here. I'd probably have to kick her in the shin.

Emma watches me as I scoop up a bit of everything onto the spoon and take my first bite.

Oh God, what the fuck?

I will give Jane credit where credit is due because the chicken is soft, and the rice isn't crunchy, but *holy shit* is it bland. Emma really wasn't kidding about pepper being considered spicy.

All the toppings mixed together shouldn't work, but I guess they kind of do. It gives it some texture rather than it just being *mush*. The flavors get drowned out by the blandest brown gravy I've ever had.

Emma must understand my reaction because she covers her mouth and fake coughs to cover the laugh trying to break free.

"Now you see why I adore Camila's cooking so much," she mumbles as she pats me on the back.

I've never been more grateful for Mamà's cooking. I swear here and now to never take it for granted ever again.

CHAPTER 54

Emma

Growing up, family dinners always ended with a game of Uno or Imagine If. Many of my siblings are competitive, and it meant feelings got hurt sometimes, but overall, I think everyone had a good time.

Now, after dinner and dessert is done, everyone just wants to *talk*.

I hate it.

I don't need to hear about my oldest brother's latest "business venture," I don't want to hear about Hailey's latest fad diet and "miracle" drink.

I don't want to answer any more questions about my job. I don't want to subject Ben to the interrogation either, but I don't have much of a choice because I'd get berated if we left early.

My whole life, my family split up into cliques of my mom's kids or my dad's kids, and I was awkwardly left bouncing around from one to the other, trying to fit it in. When I was younger, I had my nephews to play with since some of them are my age, but as an adult, I don't have a place in either group.

Nothing has changed.

Ben is sitting on one end of a large U-shaped sofa with me next to him. My parents are on the opposite end, and my sisters Shannon and Amanda—along with my sister-in-law Kate—fill in the middle, having a conversation I'm not really following.

The kids have all gone downstairs to play, and the rest of my siblings are in their own conversations across the living room.

"So how did you two meet?" Kate asks me, apparently done with the conversation with Shannon and Amanda.

I like Kate. I think she's one of the kindest, most genuine people I've ever met. She's funny, smart, and a great mom.

I also think she's way too good for my brother, who treats her and their kids like they're beneath him.

But I've never said anything because it's not my place.

I wasn't prepared for this question, because the *real* way we met would make my mother pass away from scandal, and the rest of the room would clutch their pearls and call for repentance.

Not that my family is dramatic or anything.

Ben—who hasn't stopped touching me in some small way the entire time we've been here—squeezes my knee reassuringly.

"Ben and I met at the construction company we both work for. His dad is the owner, and Ben is also a project manager."

Kate awes while everyone else's eyebrows shoot to their hairlines, and my mom shakes her head and lets out a disappointed sigh. I don't know why she's acting like she didn't already know.

Amanda gasps. "Why would you do that to your career?"

"What is that supposed to mean? I'm not doing anything wrong by dating Ben." I can already tell this conversation is going to be bad.

"Well, fraternizing with people in the company is already bad enough, but the owner's *son*? What if you two break up? They're not going to keep you around."

Ben clears his throat. "I can assure you, Emma's position at the company isn't compromised by our relationship. My father hired her with only a phone interview, so I think it's safe to say he'd rather keep her than me." Ben tries to laugh it off, and I appreciate him trying to defuse the situation, but he doesn't know my siblings.

Amanda's head whips to me with narrowed eyes, but it's Hailey who pipes up first from across the room, bringing everyone's attention to our conversation.

"You always did like to spread your legs and then play the victim. Is that how you got the job? You slept with his dad, and now you're trying to keep your job by sleeping with his son?" Hailey smirks at her harsh blow, knowing she's hit a spot that's tender and easily bruised.

I feel Ben tense beside me, and a tingle starts in my nose before making its way to the back of my eyes. I've always been a crier. It doesn't matter how strong I try to be. Any big emotions and, inevitably, tears will overflow.

My mom half-heartedly scolds Hailey. My entire life, I've been waiting for my mom to stand up for me and shield me from the venom that drips out of Hailey's mouth, but she never has.

Instead, it's always me trying to protect myself, but still getting burned anyway. No matter how many harsh words she spits at me, it's always me who ends up in trouble for trying to stand up for myself.

This time is no different. I don't understand how a parent can choose to protect the bully over the one being bullied.

Hailey shrugs. "What? It makes sense, right? Why else would he be dating her? She's just damaged goods." Hailey's eyes rake over me with clear disgust.

Maybe—and yeah, I'm being bitchy—she can't understand a genuine connection with someone because her husband is a cheating piece of shit who looks like a thumb.

Amanda, who I think has always hated me too, nods along with Hailey. "Just remember he has a career too, Emma. You can't cry rape just because he hurts your feelings or breaks up with you."

My lower lip wobbles, and I bite down on it to make it stop, but I can't stave off the flow of tears now that the dam has broken.

I can't look at Ben, terrified of what he must be thinking. He must think I'm so weak. Just sitting here letting myself be berated by the people who share my DNA, not saying anything.

There's no way he's going to want to continue our... whatever the hell we are after this. I don't blame him.

"Is he even a U.S. citizen? Are you even here legally?" Ian, Hailey's husband, asks from the other side of the living room.

I angrily swipe away my tears and glare at him. "He's half Italian and half Puerto Rican, dumbass. Don't start spewing racist bullshit. "

Amanda's sixteen-year-old son, Dallin, who's just been scrolling on his phone replies before Ian can. "Puerto Rico is a part of the U.S. If he was born there, he's a U.S. citizen. They teach that in geography class."

Ian grumbles something and storms out of the room.

I'm too anxious to even appreciate the blow to his ego.

"Emma, you better watch your mouth in my house. I will not tolerate that type of language," my dad snaps, pointing a finger at me.

Ben stands and holds out his hand to me before I can answer. "It's time to go, *Dulzura.*"

I stand and grab his hand; I'd do anything he tells me right now. "I'm so—"

"Shh. It's not you who needs to apologize." He looks around the room at the people who are supposed to be my biggest supporters, but none of them will meet his gaze.

"You should be ashamed of yourselves. Ashamed of how you've treated her. She has every right to cut every one of you out of her life and not look back. If I were in her position, I'd have done it a long time ago. She's given you more grace than you deserve, and she's done it all on her own."

He looks at me, his eyes bright with an emotion I can't place. "But she's not alone now. She has me. And I'll be damned if any of you hurts her again."

Ben looks at my parents. "Not that any of you deserve to know, but I would quit my job before I ever risked Emma's career. She's extremely talented. She's kind. She's smart. She's the most incredible woman, despite the toxicity she was raised in. I'm lucky she took a chance on me. I won't lie and say it was nice to meet you. But I will say, thank you for letting me into your home and for dinner."

Then he drags me to the door and slips on his shoes before helping me slip on mine. Without another word, we get in the car, and he pulls away from my childhood home. Away from the toxicity of my family.

Tonight caused a shift in our relationship. The walls I was trying—and failing—to keep erected have cracks splintering through the bricks, and my heart is begging me to let Ben in.

The air in the car is charged even though we haven't said anything.

I don't even know *what* to say.

No one's ever stood up for me like that. I'm sure Jordan probably would have, but I never let them. The possibility of my parents lashing out at Jordan and it tarnishing their view of me was too much of a deterrent.

God, I can't believe Hailey and Amanda said those things. And Ian? Another wave of embarrassment slithers up my spine, and my nose burns with the threat of oncoming tears.

"I'm sorry," Ben rasps from the driver's side, shaking his head. "I'm so sorry, honey."

"For what? It's *me* who should be apologizing for them."

The hotel is only a few minutes from my parents' house, so he pulls into a parking spot and shuts the car off.

He rounds the car, opens my car door, and helps me out, but before I can step away, he cages me against the car. The cool metal of the vehicle is a stark contrast to the heat of Ben's body as he cups my face with one hand, forcing me to meet his eyes.

"I'm sorry if I overstepped back there. I just... couldn't listen to them anymore. I felt the hurt radiating from you, and I couldn't stand it."

I lick my lips, and Ben tracks the quick path my tongue takes. "You didn't overstep. I'm the one who should be apologizing. I've never had anyone stand up for me before. I'm not upset at you for standing up for me. It was..." *Everything*.

If my heart wasn't attached before, it sure is now.

It's signed the papers, and Ben owns it now, even if he doesn't want it.

"It wasn't even a second thought for me, Emma. You shine even through all the hurt you've experienced, but... I want to see how much brighter you can shine when you're loved the way you deserve."

What is he saying?

"I don't think I know how to let myself be loved like that," I whisper.

His eyes dart down to my lips and back up. "Let me help you learn. Let me be the one to help you shine brighter."

Ben leans in agonizingly slow, never breaking eye contact. His lips are mere millimeters from mine, and I feel the words as they leave his breath. "Color?"

"Green," I breathe.

With more tenderness than I've ever experienced, Ben's lips meet mine, and I have my first kiss in over four years.

Ben's lips capture my bottom one, and our mouths mold together like they're the last two pieces of a puzzle. My heart soars and sighs with relief at how good, how *right* it feels. It's slow and achingly sweet and full of unspoken words. The dichotomy of emotions rolling through me makes tears pool in my eyes.

One tracks down my face, and I taste it as it falls between our lips. He must taste it too, because he pulls back to look at me. I chase his lips with my own. I don't want to stop now that I've started.

"Was that okay?" Ben whispers. His breath fans across my lips, and I shiver. He must think I'm cold because he grabs my hand and leads me towards the door of the hotel. "Let's get you inside."

CHAPTER 55

Ben

I knew kissing Emma would be life-changing. I just didn't know it would cause a cataclysmic reaction in my soul.

Our kiss wasn't what I was expecting.

It wasn't all lips and teeth and tongue. It was a gentle breeze blowing the remaining shreds of my sanity away and revealing the last parts of Emma she kept hidden from me.

I don't want to stop kissing her, but I refrain from mauling her in the elevator, and I don't shove her against the door when we get into our room like I desperately want to.

I know the most important thing right now is for us to talk, but now that she's let me taste her sassy mouth, I can't get enough. I want—no, *need*—more.

Emma turns around once the door is shut and bites her lip—the lip I had the pleasure of tasting not five minutes ago.

"We should probably talk," she rasps as she takes off her coat.

"We should," I agree as I toe off my shoes.

"We need to figure out where to go from here."

"I know where I want to go, *Dulzura*."

"Where is that?" She fiddles with the sleeve of her shirt.

"Home. I want you in my house. I want you in my bed. In my life—everywhere." I cross the few feet of space between us and cup her face, feeling the heat from her cheeks as they blush. "I want to take you to the club on Saturdays and show you off, then spend Sunday mornings making breakfast together. I want to show up at work together and go home together at the end of the day. I want to meet your friends. I want to plan surprises with Jordan. I want you to color-code our schedules and help me grocery shop.

"But mostly, I want to be your peace. I want to be your comfort. I want to hear every thought that crosses your brain, even the dark ones you don't want anyone else to know. I want to hold your heart in the palm of my hand and have you trust me to treat it with the utmost care."

Emma's cerulean eyes dart between mine like she's waiting for me to say, *"just kidding."* Like she's trying to figure out if this is all a joke. None of that is coming. She should know I'm a serious guy. I don't do jokes.

"This was supposed to only be sex." She shakes her head. "You aren't supposed to want more."

I tilt my head as I absorb her words. *I* wasn't supposed to want more. Does it mean she does? Does it mean she's been hiding her true feelings this whole time?

If that's the case, she did a fantastic job because I had no idea.

"But I do. My life was dull and gray for years. Boring. Until you opened the curtains and showered me with your sunshine and bright colors. I know this is probably a lot, and it probably feels sudden, but it's not sudden for me."

Emma blinks at me. "What if you... get tired of me? What if I become needy and overwhelming and you think I'm too much? What if—"

I cut her off with a peck on her lips. She'll work herself into a tizzy if she keeps going, and I don't want her to get carried away.

"If I could go back and sucker punch every person who's made you feel like you weren't worth staying for, I would. And I'd start with your shitty family, then move on to every ex who made you feel like a burden. There will be times when you're emotional. I already know this. There will be times when you'll need my undivided attention, but honey, you've had it this whole time. My whole world revolves around you already—you're my sun. I'm not scared off easily. I'll be right here to reassure you every time you have doubts."

Emma's lower lip wobbles as tears line the bottom of her eyes. She's cried so much today—this whole week, really. Every wave of tears feels like a wrecking ball to my chest.

"I wasn't supposed to get attached. You weren't supposed to be sweet to me. You were supposed to be the grumpy coworker who knows how to fuck my brains out but then doesn't want anything to do with me after."

"Yeah, well you were supposed to be a stress reliever. You weren't supposed to be my dream girl. Guess we were both blindsided."

I can tell there's more she wants to say, but she's had a long day with the funeral and the confrontation with her family. There are a million more things I want to say, and at the top of the list are three little words which will surely be too much for her right now.

"We can talk more about this in the morning. You've had a long day, and we both need our rest for the drive tomorrow." I place a tender kiss on her forehead, and her lashes flutter closed.

We decided we would leave early tomorrow morning so we can drive straight through the day instead of stopping in Vegas again.

Maybe we should stop anyway and get married, so she knows how serious I am about her.

Well, Ben, sei impazzito. *You're crazy.*

I shake off the bizarre thought. "Would you like to go to bed now, or would you like me to take care of you?"

"I want you to take care of me, but—"

I cut her off with a kiss.

God, I love that I can do that now.

"I know there are probably a million thoughts and worst-case scenarios swirling around in that beautiful head of yours. I promise—tomorrow while we drive—you can ask me all the questions you need to. Tonight, let me help you clear your head for a while. Let me worship you the way you deserve."

"Okay."

I strip her of her clothes and have her lay on the bed while I unbutton my flannel shirt.

Emma's eyes track my fingers as they undo the buttons and expose my skin, and when I finally get my shirt off, she licks her lips as her eyes roam over my torso. It's a heady thing, having her full attention.

It's a heady thing having *her*.

I hope I can keep her forever.

After I've removed my clothing, I crawl over her on the bed, nestle my hips between her thighs, and lower my face to hers.

The kiss starts out gentle and exploratory as my tongue parts her lips and caresses hers. She makes a mewling sound that goes straight to my dick and makes me lose my damn mind. I've been robbed of the sweetest sounds by her no kissing rule, and I plan on spending a long time making up for it.

The kiss turns frantic and needy as I suck on the tip of her tongue, and she threads her fingers through the hair at the nape of my neck, tugging gently. I kiss her harder, trying to permanently ink my kiss onto her lips so she never forgets what it feels like. I want her craving my lips as badly as I've craved hers.

I circle her gorgeous throat with my hand to hold her in place so I can devour her mouth the way I need, greedily swallowing every sound coming out of her mouth.

I pull back enough to mumble, "I feel like I've been dying of thirst for years, and you've finally quenched it and brought me back to life."

It hits me, then. I can finally, *finally* kiss her neck and mark it the way I want to, now that we've blown her rule to smithereens.

I give her one last lingering kiss on her lips then kiss both of her cheeks, her nose, her chin, then trail wet, sloppy kisses down her jawline and neck. She gasps when my teeth scrape along her sensitive skin before I bite down and suck.

I pull off of her and admire the bloom of red which will turn purple soon. A mark not easily covered unless she wears a turtleneck.

A mark that says she's *mine*.

Mine. Mine. Mine.

I'm greedy. I want to mark every part of her pale skin not covered with ink. I don't want anyone to doubt who she belongs to—especially her.

Emma keeps raising her hips, looking for friction she won't get from the position we're in, so I trail one hand down her sternum and over her plush belly before I cup her pussy and feel her practically dripping for me.

"Oh, honey. You need something in here, don't you?"

"Yes," she moans.

"What do you need, hm? Tell me. Let me take care of you."

"Need your cock, Daddy. Please!"

We both freeze and stare at each other. I can tell she didn't mean to say that, and she's freaking out.

I watch her throat bob with a swallow, and she shakes her head.

"I-I'm sorry. I don't know why—"

"Say it again," I growl.

I didn't think I had a daddy kink. Age play isn't my thing, and past partners always sounded whiny to me when they tried using the moniker.

But with Emma?

It feels like she's giving up the last bit of herself she was holding back. It feels like she's trusting me implicitly to take care of her and know what she needs.

"I need you to take care of me... *Daddy.*"

I capture her lips again as I thrust into her agonizingly slowly, swallowing her answering moan.

This isn't going to be rough like our other times. No, this is slow, sweet. This isn't a means to an end to find release. This is...

This is making love.

"That's right, sweetheart. I'm your Daddy now." *Thrust.* "You come to me when you need something." *Thrust.* "I take care of you." *Thrust.*

Her pussy clamps on me with every declaration, and the effect is dizzying.

"Yeah, you love it, don't you? You love that you can trust me to take care of you." Another slow thrust. "You love that you can let go with me, be your true self. Give me every part of you, Emma, even the ones you want to hide."

Emma blinks up at me, her eyes glassy. Then her lip wobbles, and a tear runs down her cheek.

"I'm sorry." She sniffles. "This so isn't sexy."

I stay seated inside her while I move down to my elbows so I can hover right over her face.

"Don't apologize. Do you want to stop?"

Emma shakes her head adamantly. "No... I just... I'm feeling... a *lot.*"

I stroke her cheek and give her a chaste kiss. "Tell me what you're feeling."

She shakes her head again.

I start thrusting slowly again, whispering against her mouth. "Let me tell you what I'm feeling, *Dulzura*. I'm feeling like you're perfect for me. Like you were made specifically for me. That you were always meant to be mine."

Emma's eyes roll back as I hit a particularly tender spot, and her pussy pulses. I snake one hand between us to rub gentle circles on her clit, and she bows off the bed at the contact.

"Open your eyes for me, honey. This next part is the most important."

She opens them up, and I'm almost bowled over by how full of... *love* they are. How vulnerable and open. Her oceanic gaze is swirling with the same emotion I feel, and I can tell it's on the tip of her tongue, but she doesn't want to say it first.

I continue thrusting into her and strumming her clit as I admit what I've known for weeks now.

"I feel like I'm in love with you, Emma."

That seems to be the thing that tips her over the edge, and her pussy squeezes the ever-loving shit out of my cock.

"Ben!" she moans.

"That's it, *Dulzura*. Squeeze the cock of the man who's fucking crazy for you. You own me, body and soul, so *take it.* Are you ready to take my cum?"

"*Please.*"

I pick up the pace of my thrusts until my balls draw up, and I explode inside of her as stars explode behind my eyes.

Emma won't meet my eyes while we clean up and get ready for bed, but she doesn't fight me when I ask her to sleep in my bed.

She may not fully believe me right now, but I'm going to have all day tomorrow to show her how serious I am.

She may not be ready to say it back, but I know she feels it, too.

CHAPTER 56

Emma

I'm still reeling from last night.

From Ben telling me he's in love with me to the gentle way he... *made love* to me.

I can't believe I called him "Daddy."

I already knew the church gave me daddy issues, but I didn't realize it would manifest by me using it in the heat of the moment.

But it didn't feel weird. It felt... comforting.

It didn't have anything to do with my dad, just a feeling of safety. Ben knows how to take care of me, and more importantly, that I can *let* him take care of me.

I don't really understand it, but it pleased Ben, and I always want to please him.

Even if I'm fucking terrified after his declaration.

What does *I feel like I'm in love with you, Emma* even mean?

Does he just feel like he *could* love me? Or is he *actually* in love with me?

Does being *in* love mean the same thing to him as it does to me?

Isn't it too soon? I mean, it's barely been two months. We hadn't even kissed until last night!

God, that kiss.

My lips are still tingling from the possessive way he kissed me.

"I feel like I've been dying of thirst for years, and you've finally quenched it and brought me back to life."

Jesus. I didn't even know how to respond to that. That's the kind of declaration made in romance novels and movies, not in real life to your fuck buddy.

I've barely slept. Mostly because my brain won't shut the hell up and stop running around in circles trying to figure out what Ben means, then trying to figure out if I want to tell him how *I* feel. Then trying to decide if I want to just... run away from my feelings again.

I almost blurted it out when he asked how I was feeling last night. But I couldn't bring myself to say the words and risk rejection. I didn't want him to think it was in the heat of the moment.

Like I'm wondering if his declaration was in the heat of the moment.

Part of me worries it was, but another part of me really wants to believe he means it. The little girl who was never loved how she deserves wants the kind of love he talked about—the kind of love she's dreamt of all her life. An all-consuming love, but one that feels safe.

Can Ben really be that for me?

I mean, he kind of already is. The man has heard more of my trauma in the last week than anyone else—other than Jordan—and didn't run for the hills. He met my family for Christ's sake!

I snuck out of bed while he was sleeping so I could get ready and get a handle on all of my emotions before I'm stuck in the car with the man I'm in love with—who says he's in love with me, too—for over ten hours.

Ben knocks on the bathroom door, and I let him in so he can get ready. I try to sneak past him out the door before he can grab me, but he snakes his arm around my waist and pulls me in for a tight hug, placing a gentle kiss on my forehead. The tender press of his lips makes me want to cry all over again.

"Good morning, *Dulzura*. I should be ready to go in ten."

I nod against his bare chest, feeling his heartbeat under my cheek like I did last night when I was laying on him. It's steady and calm and helps soothe some of my frayed nerves.

Ten minutes later, both of our bags are packed, and we're making one last sweep of the hotel room before heading to the car.

"Can we make one last stop before we go?" I've been avoiding visiting Andy's grave. It always feels like re-opening a barely healed wound whenever I see his name engraved on the stone, but I don't know when I'll be back in Utah to visit.

"Andy?" Ben asks, and I gape at him.

"Uh, yeah. How did you know?"

"You haven't asked, but I figured it would be important for you to visit him. I was going to ask if he was buried in the Cottonwood Heights cemetery so I could take you to see him before we left."

It feels like my voice is filled with gravel as I confirm that's where he's buried. Ben plugs the address into his phone, and we drive there in silence. Ben holds my hand, and I try not to let it shake.

He thought about it—about me, about Andy.

About how important it would be for me to visit him.

What am I supposed to do with this man?

Marry him. The love starved girl in my head screams, and I have to ignore her.

He was supposed to be a grumpy asshole who only wanted to fuck, but he's turned into a fucking love-struck, gooey sweetie pie who does things like hold my hand, kiss my forehead, and take me to visit my deceased brother.

We walk through the neatly trimmed grass of the cemetery towards a familiar pine tree in front of Andy's grave. His headstone is framed with fallen pine cones, which means some of my nieces and nephews have been here recently.

His headstone is engraved with his name, his birth and death dates, the Denver Mustangs logo, and a depiction of snowy mountains and a pine tree.

I plop down in the cold, dead grass, and Ben sits next to me.

"Hey, big bro. Grandpa Monson died, and his funeral was yesterday. If there actually is an afterlife, I'm sure he's already wrapped you into one of his death grips of a hug. Um," I motion to the man next to me, "this is Ben. We're—"

"Dating. I'm her boyfriend," Ben interrupts and shoots me a wink.

I roll my eyes, even as my heart flutters.

Ben, to my utter shock, continues to talk to Andy like we're in a bar talking to a real person and not the cold cemetery talking to a slab of marble.

"Heard a lot about you, man. But Emma didn't mention you were a Mustangs fan. Did you know your cousin married a former player for the team? Morgan Fowler. Emma probably told you already."

"I told him last year when I met Morgan the first time. Andy's such a big fan he even had cans of promotional beer. My parents found some in his golf clubs last year."

Ben laughs and shakes his head. "That's awesome. Did you drink it?"

I shake my head. "It expired like two months before he died. I don't know what alcohol does when it expires, but I wasn't going to try it."

"I don't blame you." He turns back to face Andy. "Now, no one in your family asked me what my intentions with Emma are, so I'm just going to tell you. Andy, I'm head over heels in love with your sister. I'm going to marry her someday—if she lets me. I'm going to get her pregnant—if it's what she wants. And I'm going to spend the rest of forever proving to her how much she deserves love. I'm going to spend the rest of my life watching her shine."

My mouth drops open, and my cheeks heat. "That's a bold declaration to a dead man you don't even know."

Ben shrugs. "It seems like he was the only family member who ever treated you well, so he's the only one who gets to know my intentions. I'll keep making declarations until it sticks in that gorgeous brain that I'm serious."

"And you are? Serious?"

With no hesitation he answers, "Yes. But if you don't want to say it yet, that's okay. I can wait."

He says it so surely. Like he just *knows* I'm already completely gone for him. Like it's not even a question of *if* I'll say those three little words but *when*.

He's right, of course. I do want to say them. But not in front of my brother's grave.

"Thank you. For being patient with me," I finally say.

He leans over and places a gentle kiss on my cheek. "Anything for you, sweetheart. Now, is there anything else you want to say to Andy? I can leave you alone for a bit if you need."

I look down at Andy's name etched into stone which will hopefully last forever, even if I'd rather him be here. There are so many words I wish I could say to Andy in person. I wish I could tell him how much I love him. How sorry I am for how hard I pushed him to come back to church when I was younger, even though I was just following my mom's directions. I wish I could ask him more about his thoughts before he passed away. I wish he were still here. I wish I knew why things ended the way they did. I wish I had answers.

But I don't say anything like that—to Ben or my brother.

"No, I think we should get on the road. Love you, Andy."

I pick up a stray pine cone sitting by me and leave it on his headstone, then Ben helps me up and holds my hand all the way to the car.

"How are you feeling?" he asks as we pull away from the cemetery.

"Ready to be home and go back to normal," I admit, even though I don't know what *normal* will look like after Ben's declarations of love.

Ben was patient with me as I peppered him with questions in between bouts of complete silence while we drove.

"What brought on this sudden change of heart?"

"It wasn't sudden. It's been building for weeks now."

"Are you in love with me or are you in lust?"

"If we never had sex again, I'd be happy to spend the rest of my days simply holding your hand. Sex is just a bonus."

"What if your dad thinks one of us should quit because it's a conflict of interest?"

"Then I would look for another job."

On and on, I voiced every question and doubt I had, and he never once sighed at me or looked at me like I was exasperating. He never told me I was being ridiculous or dramatic.

The bricks I thought were firmly cemented around my heart crumbled to dust with every surety he gave me, and now I know without a shadow of a doubt I can trust him with my heart.

I just don't know how to tell him.

We're approaching Vegas when my phone rings, and my mom's name flashes on the screen.

I really, *really* don't want to answer, but I know she'll just blow up my phone if I don't.

"Put it on speaker," Ben commands, and I do, even though I think this will end terribly.

"Hi, Mom."

"I hope you plan on stopping to say goodbye before you leave."

"Ben and I left this morning. We're driving straight through and wanted to get an early start."

"Well, that's rude of him to take you away before you said goodbye to your family. Do you even know the trouble he's caused? Hailey's demanding I cut you off for how he spoke to us."

Ben rolls his eyes.

"She's one to talk. Hailey's more dramatic than my junior high production of *Seussical*," I grumble.

"Your little friend was *rude*. I don't know why you're even with him. You can't possibly be okay being with a man that... *aggressive*."

"I'm with him because he's an incredible man. And he wasn't aggressive. He was standing up for me. Something no one else has done for me my whole life."

"You don't need standing up for! If you weren't so sensitive or so—so—*dramatic* you wouldn't find yourself in these situations. You can't be the victim every time, Emma."

"When it comes to Hailey's poisonous tongue, I've always been the victim. You've never *once* protected me from her. Even when I was a child. The things she and Amanda were saying were so cruel, Mom. And you didn't do anything. Not to mention Ian's racist comments."

Ben pulls off of the freeway and into a gas station.

My mom sniffs. "Well, were they wrong? You got yourself into that situation in high school. If you weren't so careless, if you stayed true to the gospel, it wouldn't have happened. If you hadn't been so *dumb* to throw yourself at—"

Ben snatches the phone from my hand.

"Mrs. Price, I will not tolerate you talking to the love of my life like that. Until you're ready to apologize, you will not contact her again." He stares directly into my eyes as he says, "I'm her family now—me and Jordan and her friends. The ones who love her unconditionally and want to see her succeed. I'll protect her at all costs." Then, he presses the red button to end the call and places my phone in the cupholder between us.

The silence in the car is only broken up by the sound of my breathing and the sounds trickling in from outside.

A car honks. People walk by, and their conversations carry on the wind. The gas station attendant's tinny voice echoes over the speakers.

"I'm sorry if I overstepped," Ben finally says, then steps out of the car, leaving me speechless.

I unbuckle myself to follow him, but he rounds the car and yanks open my door, leaning down until we're face to face.

"Actually, I'm not sorry. Fuck your mom. Fuck your entire immediate family. You should have cut them off much sooner, Emma. But I know you want to keep the peace, and I'm sure cutting them off would have been hard to do all on your own, but you're not alone now. You have me. You have Jordan and Kiera and your other friends. You have my family, and you have your cousins."

"Thank you for standing up for me twice in twenty-four hours."

"Emma, it's not a hardship to protect you, to *love* you. *Please* get it through your head. I'd do anything for you."

I push him back slightly so I can get out of the car. I reach up to clasp his face in my hands, and his stubble tickles my palms.

"I love you."

Ben's eyes widen, and the biggest smile I've ever seen breaks out on his face. "Say it again, *Dulzura*. Please."

"I love you, Benjamin Rossi. I don't know how I got so lucky, but I'll forever be grateful you're the one who decided to stick around—to try. I didn't want to do this in a gas station parking lot but—"

Ben wraps his arms around my waist and smashes his mouth against mine, cutting me off before I finish my sentence.

He's done it a few times since our first kiss. I can't say I mind.

We get lost in our kiss. Me wrapping my arms around his neck and him gripping my hips and pressing his growing erection into my belly.

"Get a room, lovebirds!" someone yells, and Ben and I break apart to see a gruff old man hobbling by with a cane shaking his head.

Ben waves to the older gentleman and turns back to me with a big smile, tucking a stray lock of hair behind my ear.

"In case it wasn't glaringly obvious, *Dulzura*, I love you, too."

"Does this mean you're officially my boyfriend?" The label feels juvenile. Too inconsequential.

"You can call me whatever you want, as long as you call me yours."

CHAPTER 57

Ben

I'm on cloud nine walking into the office on Monday. Emma didn't agree to spend the night with me last night, since she wanted to unpack and catch up with Jordan about the trip and Jordan's conference.

It was the worst night's sleep I've had all week.

But even though I'm running on two hours of fitful sleep and four shots of espresso, I still feel *fantastic.*

Emma and I are going to talk to Papà today so she can have the peace of mind that she's not going to lose her job, and I'll finally be able to show her off. If I know Papà, he'll just be happy that I'm happy. He would never jeopardize either of our careers.

I came in early today to catch up on emails, and apparently Emma had the same idea.

I hear the click of her heels before I see her, and the sound brings a smile to my face. I stand from my desk and lean against the doorway of my office, taking her in before she sees me.

She's wearing a black bodycon dress that hugs the dip of her waist and the flare of her hips and falls just above her knees. Over it, she's got a burnt orange cardigan, and on her feet are heeled black boots, which hug her calves and reach up to her knees.

I know it's been less than twenty-four hours, but I spent nearly every second of last week with her, so spending one night without her was agonizing.

"Good morning, gorgeous."

Her head whips up from her phone, and she glances around at the empty offices before scurrying over to me and throwing her arms around my neck. I kiss her, probably a little more sensually than I should at our place of employment, but I don't care.

I missed her.

"Hi. I missed you," she mumbles against my lips.

"God, I missed you too, honey. Promise me you'll spend the night with me soon."

"Well, well, well, what do we have here?" Papà's voice comes from down the hall before she can answer. Luckily, he sounds amused and not upset, but Emma probably can't tell the difference.

Emma tries to step away from me like we've been caught doing something bad, but I keep an arm around her waist and give her a tug so she's standing at my side. We're in this together.

"Good morning, Mr. Rossi." She gives him a wobbly smile.

"Emma, no need to be so formal. It's good to have you back. I take it things went... *well* in Utah?" Papà's eyes dart to my hand on her hip.

Emma nods as her cheeks turn pink. "Yes, thank you. It's good to be home, though."

I clear my throat. "Can we talk to you in your office, *Papà*?

He nods once. "Yes, of course. Come on, you two."

Emma looks up at me while she shakily inhales and exhales, anxiety swirling in her eyes. I give her hip a reassuring squeeze. I'm positive there's nothing for us to worry about.

We follow Papà to his office and sit in the two chairs on the opposite side of his desk.

He leans back and steeples his fingers, looking between Emma and me with a scrutinizing expression.

"*Papà*, Emma and I are together." No point in beating around the bush. This conversation needs to happen.

"Is this true, Emma?" Papà asks, and Emma nods her head.

"Yes, Mr. Rossi."

"*Sono innamorato di lei.*" *I'm in love with her.* I declare in Italian.

His thick eyebrows raise to his hairline. I didn't think he'd be so surprised, but I probably should have. I mean, I haven't had a serious girlfriend since Janessa, so for me to show up with the coworker I was adamant about not hiring and declare we're not only in a relationship, but I'm in love with her is probably a total surprise. Even if he's the one who sent me with her to Utah in the first place.

"*Lei si sente allo stesso modo?*" *She feels the same way?*

I look over at the girl of my dreams, the one who declared her love for me in a gas station parking lot. "*Sì.*" *Yes.*

Papà beams, glancing between the two of us with something akin to pride in his eyes. "This is excellent news! Let me get Katrina to draw up some paperwork for you to sign just to make it above board. As long as you're not neglecting your duties because of your relationship or being inappropriate in the office, I see no issue with this."

Emma's shoulders slump with relief. "Thank you, Mr. Rossi. I promise this won't affect our work."

Papà waves his hand. "*Bella,* for the last time, call me Enzo. Or better yet, call me *Papà*! We're family now. And I'm not worried about you at all. You work much harder than any of the boys. *Beniamino,* however..." he trails off and shakes his head.

Emma's answering giggle is so sweet it makes my teeth ache in the best way.

"Perhaps you should trade offices with Alex, so Ben can't spend all day staring at you."

"Absolutely not. She stays right where she is. If my performance starts lacking, then we can talk about it, but I promise I won't spend all day staring at her." Just... some of the day.

Papà clearly doesn't believe me, and he's enjoying messing with me. "I'm in the process of getting Emma her own truck—"

I shake my head. "I can take her where she needs to go."

"Ben," Emma chides. "Our jobs aren't always going to align. I can't keep relying on you to take me to job sites. What happens if we have emergencies at two different sites?"

I don't think I've ever pouted in my life, but *boy* do I want to right now. "Fine. But once you move in, your work truck stays here, and I'll bring you to work and take you home."

Papà laughs, and Emma looks at me incredulously.

"We aren't moving in together anytime soon," she argues, but it's weak.

"We'll see, *Dulzura*. We'll see."

ISTRUCTION // UNDER CONSTRUCTION // UNDER CON

By the end of the next week, everyone is over the shock of our relationship, and everything is back to normal.

Well, a *new* normal.

A new normal where Emma and I eat lunch together in one of our offices. A new normal where I get to kiss her when she comes into the office. A new normal where on Friday mornings, I pick her up for work, and she brings a bag to sleep at my house *all weekend.*

Emma didn't want to move too fast, so she refuses to spend the night during the week. I know she's still worried about me getting sick of her, but she doesn't need to be. I want more time with her, not less.

I'd pack her stuff and move her in immediately if I thought she'd agree to it.

I can't get enough of her.

But I know this relationship is new, and she's still wary, so I'll be patient and take whatever she's willing to offer. I'll earn her trust one day at a time and prove I'm not going anywhere.

Once we're off work today, I took her back to my place so she could change. We're going to dinner with her friends tonight, and I can tell my girl is nervous.

I have just the thing to take the edge off.

She's currently in the bathroom, fixing her makeup, and I'm sitting on the bed waiting for her to come out so I can give her the things I've picked out.

The click of the door opening draws my attention, and I nearly swallow my tongue as I see Emma walk out of the bathroom in a pale pink lingerie set.

"*Santa cielio, Dulzura.* Are you trying to get me to cancel dinner?" I rasp.

"Is it working?" she asks with a seductive smile but an undertone of anxiety.

I stand and cradle her face in my hands. "What are you worried about?"

"That they'll think we're moving too fast. That they'll tell me I'm crazy because we work together. Or they'll think I only got the job because we slept together. Or they're just waiting for our relationship to fail like all of my previous ones have. Or—"

I place my finger over her lips so she stops talking, and she scowls. "I think those are all anxieties your family has put in your head. I've met Jordan, and I've met Kiera. I don't think either of them are going to think any of those things."

"You're right. Jordan has been supportive the whole time. They would have told me if they thought this was a bad idea."

"Good. They're very wise, you should listen to them more. Now that we've got that covered, I have something I think will help take your mind off the anxiety."

I grab the small black box off of the bed and hold it out for her.

Emma's eyes light up as she takes it. I've noticed she likes presents, even if it's just a simple bag of chips from the gas station.

I already have a list a mile long of things I plan on buying her, just to see her reaction.

She opens the box and gasps as she sees what's nestled inside. She takes the plug out of the box, holding it up and examining the hot pink heart shaped jewel on the back and testing the weight of it in her hand.

"Turn around, honey. Hands on the bed. Let me see that beautiful ass."

Like the good girl she is, she turns and braces herself on the bed.

I grab a bottle of lube from the bedside table before coming back and pulling her panties down until they're hooked around her ankles.

As I kneel behind her, I see the plump lips of her pussy begging to be tasted, so I lean in and lick from her clit to her asshole, circling my tongue around her tight hole. Emma gasps, rocking her hips back into my mouth as I probe it with my tongue.

"Someone's eager to have her asshole fucked, isn't she? Does it feel good, *Dulzura?*"

"Yes, Daddy. So good."

I drizzle some lube over her asshole, rubbing it with my pointer finger, and she tenses. "I'm going to stick my finger in now, take a deep breath for me."

She does as she's told, and on the exhale, I gently press in to the first knuckle. She tenses again, so I use my other hand to find her clit and rub gentle circles, helping her relax as I slide my finger in further.

Once she starts rocking back into my touch, moaning and whimpering with each thrust, I add a little more lube and a second finger, stretching her so she can comfortably take the plug.

"I wish you could see how beautiful you look stretched around my fingers, honey. I can't wait to feel this tight hole stretched around my cock." I can't resist taking a bite of the meat of her ass as I continue working my fingers inside her.

Her whimpers grow, but I don't want her to come, so I pull my fingers out and spank her when she protests. "Patience, *Dulzura*."

I pick up the plug and drizzle some lube on the end before pressing it against her hole. It's bigger than my fingers, so I instruct her to take another deep breath while I work her clit again, pushing the plug past the ring of resistance until it's fully inside her.

I twist the jewel on the end, and Emma moans.

"How does that feel, honey?"

"S-so full. *Fuck.*"

"Not as full as my cock's going to make you feel. But we don't have time for that now." I pull my fingers away from her and pull her panties up her legs. "We have to go. Get dressed." I punctuate my command with another gentle swat to her ass before I go to the bathroom and wash my hands.

"You're not going to let me come?" she pouts.

"No. And unless you want me to keep you on edge *all weekend* you'll go get dressed right now so we aren't late." This weekend we're testing out her limits with free use. Any and all of her holes are mine to use however and whenever I please until she goes home Sunday night.

"Okay, Daddy," she acquiesces before pulling on a hot pink, long sleeved jumpsuit that hugs her curves.

"Let's get this over with," she grumbles as we head out the door.

Tonight is going to be fun.

CHAPTER 58

Emma

Tonight was the last piece of the puzzle I needed to fit into place to finally be able to feel... secure.

I didn't lose my job.

Ben didn't lose his job.

Jordan is happy for me.

The rest of my friends are happy for me.

I'm happy for me.

Ben took their interrogation like a champ, and Jaime texted me on the way home telling me I didn't do the man justice with my description. They all seem to love Ben, and I'm happy everyone important in my life gets along.

It was hard to focus at dinner with the weight of the plug shifting every time I moved. I'm sure my face was flushed the entire time, and I'm hoping my friends thought it's just the single gin and tonic I drank.

But they probably knew better.

Ben kept lightly caressing my thighs or squeezing my hip. Every touch sent a spark of desire straight to my vagina, and every time I clenched my thighs together I felt the plug and my arousal heightened even more.

By the time we're pulling into Ben's driveway, I'm ready to fuck him in the front seat of his car, but he's acting like we're coming home from a normal night out. He's not mentioned the plug once nor given me any clue as to what he's planning. We walk into the house and Ben goes to the kitchen to get a glass of water, telling me about something Jaime said about... something. I can't focus long enough to understand what he's saying.

"Emma, are you even listening to me?" He's suddenly right in front of me, and I blink up at him, which must be answer enough because he chuckles. "Poor *Dulzura*. Are you distracted by the shiny plug in your ass?"

I nod.

Ben walks over to the couch and sits down, spreading his legs and pointing to the ground in front of him. "Take off your jumpsuit and kneel."

I rush to obey, shucking my clothes and kneeling between his legs, eyeing the bulge in his pants. I want it.

"You're so quick to listen tonight, honey. Are you eager to have my cock in your ass?"

"Yes, Daddy. I want it so bad."

Ben leans back against the couch. "Take my cock out."

I lean over and unbuckle his belt and unzip his fly. He lifts his hips so I can help him pull his pants and briefs down around his thighs, his cock springing free.

"Good, now kiss it—only kiss it. Show me how badly you want it."

I take the base of him in my hand and place wet kisses along his length, starting at the base and working my way up to the tip. I pull his foreskin back and kiss the head, making him hiss.

"I love the way your lips feel on me, honey. Now spit on it. Get it nice and sloppy for me."

I gather the saliva in my mouth before letting it fall from my lips and over the tip of his cock, I bring my hand up to work the wetness down his shaft, using it to stroke him.

"God, that feels so good. Put me in your mouth, *Dulzura*. Earn your reward."

He gathers my hair in a ponytail and helps guide his hard cock into my mouth, I trace the veins on his shaft with my tongue, cupping his balls in my hand. I pull back and take a deep breath before taking him as far as I can, gagging a little when he hits the back of my throat but recovering quickly.

His groans of pleasure spur me on, and I start bobbing my head in a steady rhythm. I don't *want* him to come down my throat, I want him to come inside me. But if it's what gets me the prize I'm desperate for, I'd swallow it like the good girl I am.

Suddenly, Ben pulls my hair, and I pop off of him, spit and drool dribbling down my chin.

"Alright, honey, I'm not coming in your mouth today. You've earned your reward. Go to the guest room, take off these pretty underthings, and get on the bed on all fours."

I scramble to my feet and rush to the guest room, taking off my bra and panties as I go. When I get on the bed on all fours, I hear Ben behind me, clicking the door shut and kneeling behind me on the bed.

He tugs the jeweled end of the plug—something I wasn't expecting—pulling a moan from my throat.

He chuckles as I rock back into his touch. I should be embarrassed about how needy I am for him, but I'm not. Ben loves when I become a whimpering, needy mess for him.

"Are you ready for me, *Dulzura?*" he whispers.

"Yes, Daddy. Please. I need it. Need to feel you."

"Mmm. I love it when you beg." He pulls the plug out of me, and I immediately feel empty. The desire to beg again is strong, but I wait. I hear the click of the lube bottle and feel the cool liquid land between my cheeks.

Then, the head of his cock is there, pressing into me slowly. Even though the plug stretched me out, it's still a tight fit, and I tense when it starts to burn slightly.

"*Fuck.* You've got to breathe for me, honey. Let me in. Play with your clit and relax."

I snake my hand down to my clit, feeling how wet I am as I draw tight circles and try to relax my muscles. Ben pushes in farther, the stretch seems impossible. How the hell is my body capable of this?

But then the slight bit of pain subsides, and Ben is fully seated inside me. His hips are flush with my ass and—

"God, I feel so full," I whimper.

"You feel so good, honey. So fucking tight. A perfect fit. I'm not going to last long, but I promise to take care of you."

I know he will. He always does.

Ben pulls out, leaving just the tip in before he thrusts back in, then he does it again and again. Setting a steady pace that has my eyes rolling into the back of my head.

My fingers on my clit falter, but I try my best to keep up the rhythm, wanting to go over the edge at the same time as him. A few more thrusts, and he stills. Feeling him pulse inside me sends me over edge with a sharp cry of his name.

We collapse on the bed, and Ben pulls out of me and cuddles me from behind whispering praises of how good I did for him, how proud he is of me for trying something new.

We shower together, and he washes my body like he usually does after a scene, and this time when we fall asleep, it's with my head on his chest and his arm around my waist.

CHAPTER 59

Emma

Six Months Later...

The past six months have been a whirlwind of work, holidays, date nights, and sex.

Around Christmas, I started spending some weeknights with Ben. Now, half of my clothes are at his place, along with another set of toiletries so I don't have to keep toting them to and from work. I know he's waiting for the right time to ask me to move in, and I know Jordan is probably itching to ask Moss to move in with them. They're still denying their feelings, but I see the sparks between them.

On days I don't sleep at Ben's house, he picks me up and takes me to work, and on the weekends, we spend our time playing. We go to the club at least twice a month because Ben likes to show me off, but I much prefer our free use weekends where Ben likes to fuck me when I'm in the middle of cooking or doing laundry. We even had a risky encounter in a grocery store where he dragged me into the family bathroom and fucked my face until he came down my throat.

The first time we ran into Drew at the club, things were awkward at work for a bit, but we've all seemed to come to an agreement that we don't talk about the club or what we do there.

Things at work have picked up with the start of Derek's project, so Ben and I don't get as much time together as we did before.

I love my job. I love watching the progress and knowing it's my knowledge helping the project get built. I love that the foremen come to me to ask questions about materials or plans. I'm starting to learn Spanish so I can better communicate with members of our crew, but it's slow going.

My parents have been calling every month to try to guilt me into breaking up with Ben for the "issues" he's caused. They've claimed he's brainwashed me into cutting off my family and convinced me they're a problem when really *he's* the problem. They still think he's just using me or I'm using him to get my job.

They don't understand he's far from a problem. He's finally helped me realize I don't deserve to be treated the way they've treated me. He's shown me how I *should* be loved. I still break down in tears after every call, but Ben's always there to reassure me he's not going anywhere. That he loves me and I don't have to go through this alone.

Tonight, Ben and I are going to another gala, this time for a big retail developer Rossi built a strip mall for in the past.

Ben grumbled when I told him about it, but agreed to go after I told him he could pick out my dress.

It's a win for both of us because I don't have to make decisions, and he takes pride in knowing he got a say in dressing me up.

He's picked out a lovely mauve floral print dress with long balloon sleeves and a top that resembles a corset. The skirt drapes from my hips in flowy chiffon with a slit up the side, which shows a peek of my garter tattoos when I walk—something I've learned he loves to see.

I walk out of the bedroom in search of my favorite gold heels when I find Ben in his black-on-black suit sitting on the couch with three boxes of varying sizes next to him and my heels in his hand.

God, he looks delicious. But my focus is on the boxes. Did he get me presents?

"You look incredible, *Dulzura*. Come sit, and I'll put your shoes on for you."

I follow his order, sitting on the couch and watching as he kneels before me and delicately slips the heels on, buckling the clasp around my ankle.

"I have some gifts for you," he says, picking up the smallest box.

I open it to find a gold key on a pink heart keychain.

"Move in with me."

"I-I can't leave Jordan without a roommate," I protest half-heartedly.

"Jordan already has a roommate lined up. You're already half moved in, honey. I want you here all the time. You can change anything you want to make this place feel like home to you, but I don't want to spend any more nights apart. I need to see you every minute of every day."

Tears well in my eyes, but I blink them away. "Okay. I'll move in with you."

Ben's smile is radiant. He's been smiling a lot more lately, and he's even started asking our crew members more personal questions. I can see how hard it is for him to open up, but I love that he's trying for me.

He hands me the largest box, and I nearly drop it when I open it.

"Is this—"

"A collar? Yes." Ben pulls out the hot pink leather necklace with two gold chains attached. I've seen one similar to this online. The chain is on a pulley system so it can be pulled tight across the throat.

"B-but isn't it too soon?" I whisper in disbelief.

Ben shakes his head. "I've been waiting years for you, Emma. There's no one else I'd want to wear my collar. This one is only for at home or if we're going to the club. This one..." He grabs the third box and opens it to reveal a delicate gold chain with a "B" engraved on the tiny heart pendant. "This one is for every day."

"It's—they're beautiful, Ben. But are you really sure?"

"I've only ever been more sure of one other thing, honey. Can I put this collar on you? Please?"

I want to ask what he means, but I'm at a loss for words. I nod, and a single tear falls over my lash line.

"I need your words, Emma."

"Yes, I'd be honored to wear your collar, Ben. Thank you."

Ben clasps the gold chain around my neck, nestling the pendant right between my collar bones.

"Stunning," he whispers, wiping away another tear and placing a gentle kiss on my lips. "Now, about the only thing I've been more sure of." He kneels back down—this time on only one knee—and my heart stutters in my chest.

Is he...

He pulls something out of his pocket, and it takes me a minute to register what I'm seeing. A bright pink marquise shaped stone surrounded by tiny white diamond details. It's the most beautiful ring I've ever seen.

"Emma Lucille Price, I love you more than I've ever loved anyone else my entire life. I was living in darkness until you brought your sunshine in and showed me what I never knew was missing. We may have had a rocky start, but I'll forever be grateful our paths crossed. You've already agreed to wear my collar, but will you agree to wear my ring and take my last name? Will you marry me, Emma?"

"Yes." I nod frantically. "Yes, yes yes."

Ben blows out a breath of relief as he slides the ring on my finger, scoops me up, and sits down on the couch with me on his lap. He presses a frantic kiss to my mouth, holding me close to him.

"I was so worried this wouldn't be grand enough for you. I was going to do it at the gala, or take you back to Utah, but I—"

I cut him off with a kiss. "This was perfect. I don't need a big grand proposal. I just need you."

"I'm sorry for ruining your makeup," he whispers, gently wiping away some smudged mascara.

"It's okay. Do I have time to fix it?"

"Yes. We can be fashionably late. Or we can skip it all together and stay here and celebrate," he murmurs, nipping at my throat.

"We can't skip it! I need to show off my favorite new accessories. Your parents are probably dying to know how your proposal went."

"They... didn't know I was planning on proposing." Ben winces.

"Oh, they're going to be so mad. Camila is going to curse you out for not telling her."

"I know, I know. Fine, we'll go. But prepare for *Mamà* to ask you a bazillion questions about the wedding even though we don't have any set plans."

"I can't wait."

STRUCTION // UNDER CONSTRUCTION // UNDER CON

Camila screamed when I showed her the ring, then promptly swatted Ben behind the head and started speaking rapidly in Spanish to him. His face flushed with embarrassment at whatever she was saying, looking at Enzo for backup, but Enzo just held up his hands like "what can I do?"

As Ben predicted, Camila spent the majority of the dinner portion asking me questions about color schemes, flower arrangements, catering, and decorations. She's already planning a day for us, Cici, and Jordan, to go shopping for wedding dresses.

I know I'm going to have to tell my parents I'm getting married, and while a part of me hopes they'll set aside their biases to come support me, I won't let them ruin my special day with their racist ideologies and conservative views.

I'd rather have a happy day with the family I've found than a day stressing that my parents aren't going to approve.

By the end of the gala, my social battery is so drained I nearly fall asleep on the way home.

Home.

That's what Ben's place is now. I don't need to change anything about it—okay, maybe it needs a few more splashes of color, and his kitchen definitely needs to be reorganized—to make it feel like home. We could be living in a studio apartment or a mansion.

All I need to feel at home is Benjamin Lorenzo Rossi.

EPILOGUE

Ben

Five Years Later…

Today's the day we've been preparing for since Papà announced his plan to retire two years ago.

He brought Emma and me into his office to tell us he wanted to retire before he turned sixty-seven, and he wanted us to take over the company.

I was hesitant at first. I still don't like doing the schmoozing or making the personal connections that have made Rossi Construction what it is today, but Papà explained it's why he wants us to do it together.

Emma's going to take over the interpersonal connections and hiring while still overseeing a few projects a year, and I'll handle the day-to-day operations and logistics of the business.

My wife and I make an excellent team.

Emma and I had a conversation right after we got engaged about what we wanted our future to look like. Emma expressed her fear that she wouldn't be a good mom because of how she was raised, and she didn't want to have to give up her career if we were to have a baby.

I assured her if she wanted kids, we'd figure out a way for her to have a career and be a mom.

Right after Papà told us he wanted us to take over, we revisited the conversation and decided kids weren't in the cards for us. We're both eager to expand Rossi and help it thrive. Perhaps in a few years, we'll revisit it again, but for now, Emma and I are happy with it being just us.

Emma cried and told me when growing up Mormon, she was told her future children are waiting in Heaven for her to get pregnant so they can come to earth, and she feels like she might be letting her non-existent kids down by choosing not to have any. She had a long talk with Elli—who's also chosen to be childfree—and felt a lot less guilty about her decision. My family was understanding and supportive. Cici and Adam have two kids of their own, so we get our fill of my nieces and get to go home and sleep alone. Mateo's wife already had two kids when they met and are expecting their third, so my parents have more than enough grandkids, and Emma and I get to be the cool aunt and uncle who spoil them.

Instead of human kids, we rescued two pit bulls—Rollo and Jewel—from the local shelter, and Emma treats them as if they're our children. They get matching pajamas and a full stack of presents on Christmas, Emma goes all out for their birthdays, and they even get to come to the office with her on Thursdays.

They're here today for Papà's retirement party, dressed in custom-made Rossi Construction bandanas.

Emma and I are in his old office, and she's making me practice the speech she's written for me. I hate speaking in front of a crowd, but I know it's important this speech comes from me and not from my more eloquent wife.

Cici knocks on the door and pokes her head in. "We're ready for you."

"We'll be right there," Emma says, and when Cici's gone, she comes over and gives me a slow kiss. "I know you're nervous, but you've got this. I'll be right next to you. I'm so proud of you, Ben."

"Thank you, honey. I'm glad you're my partner in all of this."

"Me too." She grins. "Come on, boss. You've got a speech to give."

Emma takes my hand and leads me to the shop where our employees, vendors, and business connections are gathered eating snacks and chatting. Emma stops us in the middle of the room, and Drew whistles loud enough to grab everyone's attention.

"Thank you all for coming," I start. "My dad has put his blood, sweat, and tears into making this company the success it is today. He's spent long days and nights working hard to keep it afloat. It started as a two-man team, and now, we employ over one hundred people. I'm honored he's trusted me and my lovely wife, Emma, to take over the company which has built so much in San Diego. I promise to uphold his legacy and to live up to the Rossi name. Thank you, *Papà*, for teaching me how to be a hard worker and what it takes to be the best man I can be. Thank you for trusting me—us—to take over your legacy. *Ti amo.*" *I love you.*

Papà and Mamà wipe away tears before wrapping Emma and me in bear hugs.

"Sono così orgoglioso di te, figlio mio." I'm so proud of you, my son, Papà whispers in my ear as he hugs me. *"Farai grandi cose." You're going to do great things.*

"Grazie, Papà." Thank you, Father.

The rest of the party passes by in a blur of handshakes and business advice, congratulations, and wishing I could steal Emma away for myself.

By the time we get everything cleaned up and get home, it's nearing ten o'clock.

Emma puts the dogs to sleep in their crates and joins me for a shower where we trade passionate touches and make love slowly. I love these slow and gentle times just as much I love the high intensity and passion of a scene.

As we lay in bed and talk about the day, Emma tells me all about the exciting new things she wants to implement at Rossi like the Christmas Savings program—a program where our employees allot a certain amount of money to be taken out of each paycheck, and in November, they receive the saved funds—and the free English and Spanish classes so everyone on our crew has a way to communicate with each other.

As nervous as I am to try and live up to the legacy Papà has created, having Emma by my side makes it feel so much easier.

I'll forever be grateful I couldn't resist the temptation that is Emma Lucille Rossi.

THE END

ACKNOWLEDGEMENTS

First of all, I want to, of course, thank my husband. Who listened to me yap and plan and cry about this book over and over, but never once got tired of me. He encouraged me when I felt like throwing in the towel, held me when I broke down and didn't feel good enough, and cheers me on every second.

I want to thank Brit and Jen at The Author Experience for believing in me and hyping me up. I wouldn't be ready for this book to be out there if it weren't for them.

To Krisit and Nikki, thank you for hyping up Ben and loving this story.

To my readers, THANK YOU. Your support means the world to me, and you're the reason I keep doing this.

To my real life version of Hailey: I hope one day you find peace with the hand life's dealt you, and you heal from the hurt you've dealt with. Stop making other people miserable just because you are.

To my parents: You'll never read this, but I want to say I'm doing something I'm proud of, even if you're not. Thanks for the trauma, I guess.

To my real life Andy: I miss you more than words can say. I hope if there's an afterlife, you're proud of me.

To my own late grandpa: I know this isn't the kind of writing you wanted me to do, but you said one day I'll change the world with my words. Here's hoping you were right.

About the Author

Daisy Wren lives in the Utah Valley with her husband and three kids. When she's not writing her next book (or working her corporate job), she's reading, cooking, and spending time with her family. Daisy's love of writing has been prominent since childhood, and she's always felt a call to share her stories. A hopeless romantic since she first saw *The Phantom of the Opera* at age eight, she's been writing her own love stories ever since. Daisy is a former member of a high demand religion and hopes to bring light to the issues of the church she was raised in, while also telling beautiful stories about life after leaving. Please visit her at www.DasiyWren.com, or on social media for updates about upcoming releases and for bonus content!

Tiktok: @daisywrenauthor

Instagram: @daisywrenauthor

Threads: @daisywrenauthor

ALSO BY DAISY WREN

Loving the Sinner
Living for Truth